THE MAGIC SCALES

BOOK 1 OF THE DENTHAN SERIES

To Geraldine

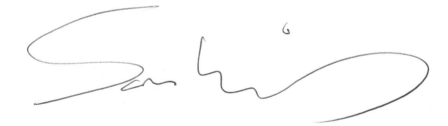

SAM WILDING

Published by Olida Publishing
www.olidapublishing.com

First printing: April, 2008

Printed in the United Kingdom

Cover Design: Jeremy Robinson – www.jeremyrobinsononline.com

ISBN: 978-0-9558789-0-9

Visit Sam Wilding on the World Wide Web at: www.samwilding.com

For help and advice in dealing with asthma, please visit
www.asthma.org.uk

ACKNOWLEDGEMENTS
For their input at the early stages: John and Greg. To Allyson and
her two boys, David and Andrew, for being my guinea pigs. To
Sara, at the end, who gave it the final once over. To Raine, Mela-
nie, Katie and David Young. Nancy at the SOA and my mum and
dad, Jessie and Stewart. My brother, Stewart, and sister, Angie. **To
my family** ~ for their undying patience and tolerance when I had
my face stuck in a laptop or buired in a pile of papers; especially
Katrina, my constant reality check.

The Magic Scales was written in the wee small hours for my eldest boy – Ryan, but it was also inspired by, and is dedicated to, his brothers and sisters: Emma, Ruth and Joe…
LOVE YOU ALL

CHAPTER ONE

A STRANGER CALLS

High on Bruce Moor, James moved over the rough ground towards the ancient circle of stones. He smiled to himself and stopped for a moment to take in the view. Known to the locals as the Jesus Rocks, this random collection of standing stones cast an eery imprint on an otherwise flawless blue sky. The base of each stone was pitted and covered in damp green moss that glistened in the sunlight, but the tips looked as though they'd been dusted by a sprinkling of orange icing sugar, the cold granite a mosaic of day-glow lichens and algae.

Moving closer, he noticed the familiar white graffiti etched on the tallest stone. The letters had begun to fade and for some reason this added to his feelings of dejection and sadness. He plumped himself down on a springy tussock of heather and gazed out over the loch below. Although the sky was as clear as a bell and the weather warm, the loch's dark waters still managed to fill him with a sense of foreboding.

He couldn't understand why his dad had decided to leave home without saying goodbye. There'd been no explanation, not even a note or an apologetic mumble on the answering machine. All of his dad's clothes were still folded in his cupboard and the books he'd collected and cherished over the years remained undisturbed on their dusty shelves.

Quickly wiping away the tear that rolled down his cheek with his sleeve, James tried to imagine what his dad might have said if he'd actually taken the time to say goodbye -

"It's like this, Son - I've really enjoyed knowing you for the last ten years, but I have to go away for a while. I'll be back to go for walks and bike rides, and

maybe to bake some of those terrible cakes that nobody can eat; I'm just not sure when."

His dad's deep, reassuring voice still rattled round in James's head, and he wondered, sadly, how long it would take before he forgot how it sounded.

It upset him when his mum refused to talk about his dad's disappearance. She couldn't even say his name without throwing something or shouting. So James gave up. He didn't need the hassle. He just wouldn't mention it any more. Not to her.

It was still all very weird ... his dad had vanished, yet nobody was doing anything about it. There were no search parties, no 'missing dad' posters, nothing on the T.V. - Just embarrassing gossip in the local rag that said things like - 'local Scout leader, Mr David Peck has, in wife's own words - *done a runner.'*

So, he thought, *his mum was happy to talk to the papers about it, just not her own son.*

Everyone in Drumfintley knew what his mum was like. She was fiery, unpredictable, even a little scary. She always said exactly what she thought without a care in the world for the consequences.

His dad, on the other hand, was the complete opposite. David Peck was reliable, safe, normal, even boring, in a nice sort of way. James knew that *'doing a runner'* just wasn't his dad's kind of thing.

Frustrated, James picked up a smooth, rust-colored pebble and threw it as hard as he could against the largest of the stones. He was going to show them all. His dad hadn't run off. James knew, in his heart, that something bad had happened. That's why he'd climbed all the way up to Bruce Moor. This was the last place his dad had been seen alive, and James was determined to find some kind of clue that would prove everyone wrong.

After a puff of his inhaler and another stretched-out sigh, he blinked and refocused. There, beside the small, half-buried stone he thrown a moment before, a little animal lay dead.

Crushed flat, its eyes bulged out of its furry brown head like two tiny, black marbles. The poor wee thing's delicate legs were splayed and pressed deep into the soft peat.

Curiously, its tongue lay several inches away from its flattened head. Caught in the gory trap of its own needle-sharp teeth, it glistened like a twisted worm at James's feet. "Yuck."

Stretching forward to grab a clump of heather, he stood up and moved a little closer. It looked as though the creature had been killed, mid-pounce. It had literally been stopped dead in its tracks.

Squinting down at the flattened pelt, James took a moment to try and work out if the dead animal was a stoat or a weasel. One had, he was sure, a long, bushy tail, while the other only possessed a small stump. It was then, as he was trying to recall which of the two animals had the bigger tail, that he noticed the footprint.

The cause of the little creature's demise was now clear. It had been squashed flat; stamped on, ruthlessly trampled to death. *But by what?* he wondered. *What kind of creature could move fast enough to do such a cruel thing?* Stranger still, judging by the mark on the ground, the lunatic, or whatever beast had made the print, had been barefoot. James could still see the indentations made by its long, skinny toes. He counted them under his breath. "One, two, three… Three?"

He placed his own foot beside the imprint for comparison.

It was huge, at least four times longer than his, not counting the three spindly toes.

Moving further into the Jesus Rocks, James scanned the ground for any other matching prints or marks.

While there were signs that the beast had moved away from the stones, a few of its prints eventually merging into the heather, he saw no trace of the beast inside the circle.

Ruling out a prank of some kind, James ran a hand through his short, mousy brown hair and considered the possibilities. He remembered, apart from his dad's disappearance, that the local paper had recently run a series of stories about "big cats", which James had read with great interest. It turned out that some very stupid people, who'd once kept panthers and lions as pets, had let them go into the wild because the government had decided to make them pay extra taxes.

The paper had gone on to say that only recently Mrs. Galdinie, an eccentric Italian lady who owned the sweetshop, had seen a tiger prowling amongst the bins at the back of her shop. The paper had also said that Mr. Mullet, the shepherd from Glenhead Farm, was convinced that some kind of large predator was responsible for his missing sheep.

Unnerved by the thought of a huge cat prowling the moor, James cursed his own stupidity for climbing up to such a lonely spot in the first place, and then wondered if a big cat might actually attack a ten-year-old boy. *Of course it would,* he thought. *Ten-year-old boys are probably its favourite kind of food, next to bin spillings and raw sheep.*

Looking round, he wondered if the creature might still be on the moor. *Is it crouching down in the heather watching me now?* he wondered. There were plenty of gorse bushes and rocks it could be hiding behind, poised to attack, waiting for him to come within striking distance.

His paranoia growing by the second, he edged back into the stone circle. Strangely, the further he moved away from the trampled animal, the more uneasy he became. Alone amongst the crooked stones and far above the safety of the village below, he slowly became aware of a change on the moor.

The curlew's trilling song faded. One by one, the skylarks fluttered down from the sky, silent, as if they'd been shot by some unseen hunter. Soon, the only thing he could hear was the rustle of the heather at his feet, but then that stopped too.

Now, there was nothing at all but complete and utter silence.

In some kind of terrified response, he'd held his breath. But unable to keep this up for long, he took gulp of air and coughed. All he could hear now was his own laboured breathing. Growing louder and louder by the second, the sound of his breath took on an eerie, unearthly tone that soon became unbearable. Goosebumps sprouted on his bare legs and a cold shiver tickled the base of his spine as he strained, once more, to catch a glimpse of the thing that had squashed the tiny animal flat into the dirt.

There was nothing at first, but before long, he had the uncomfortable feeling that someone or something was watching him.

"Brilliant" he whispered to himself, "some deranged monster is going to attack, and there's nobody around to save me."

He convinced himself that he would die alone and in agony. He pictured his dad pinned to the ground, helpless and seconds from death. Now *he* was going to disappear, too. He could just see the headline in the Drumfintley Herald: "Giant killer cat slaughters father and then eats son for dessert."

On the verge of panic, James steadied himself against the biggest of the standing stones. When the ground beneath his feet suddenly began to shake, his eyes widened in outright terror.

Screaming, he bolted out of the Jesus Rocks and tore down the hillside.

Without once looking back, he ran as fast as he could, across the moor and then down through the dark woods.

Unseen branches clawed at his hair and whipped his skinny, bare legs. Half running, half stumbling, he skidded over the rocky farm track until, breathless and blinded by sweat, he reached the tarmac steps that lead to the underpass. He stopped inside the corrugated tunnel that would take him back to Drumfintley and steadied himself on the cold, steel wall. Fighting for every lungful of air, he fumbled for his inhaler and eagerly sucked in the snowy white mist. Within seconds, the horrible sensation of drowning that had built in his chest, began to ease.

Coughing out the majority of the mist, and still panting, he staggered on through the tunnel until he could see the familiar, moss-covered rooftops of Drumfintley. He felt the warmth of the sun on his face and cursed himself for his brainless overreaction. Upset about his dad, he'd let a wretched bag of trampled fur freak him out. He'd run off like a maniac and nearly triggered an asthma attack into the bargain. He shuddered at the thought of having an attack, alone out on the moor. *Potentially just as lethal as being mauled to death by a big cat,* he thought, *and a lot more likely.*

He took a shaky breath and felt the blood rush to his cheeks. The familiar noise of cars and lorries roaring along the bypass above his head was strangely reassuring. Even the graffiti and the smell of stale wine and wee that lingered in the tunnel brought him back to a world, free of big cats and moor monsters.

Breathing better, he decided to move out of the tunnel and walk down to the village shop on Main Street. The store kept a good selection of wildlife books and leaflets on hand for the odd tourist who stumbled into the village by mistake. There was a good chance of finding a picture of a weasel or a stoat in there, he decided. He needed something to take his mind off the feeling of dread that had engulfed him on the moor.

Not wanting to attract the attention of the gossipmongers, James sneaked into the shop behind Mrs. Galdinie and hunkered down, out of sight. He rummaged, unseen, amongst a muddle of magazines, books, and a copy of the Drumfintley Herald, before pausing to listen.

He could hear the unmistakable voice of the village drunk, Gauser. He was a stout, scruffy man who held his trousers up with twine and sported a moth-eaten soldier's jacket that stank of stale booze. "No doubt about it," growled Gauser in his Irish lilt, "Cathy Peck has the temperament of a killer, so she has."

"What!" Mrs. Galdinie exclaimed.

On hearing his mum's name, James made a small space between the magazines and peered through. He could see Mrs. Galdinie's appalled expression. He smiled to himself as she bristled to his mum's defense. "There's nothing wrong with Cathy Peck!" she announced.

Gauser placed another pack of sausage on the counter and nodded his head. "No dat's right, nothing that a twenty year stretch in the nick couldn't fix."

He turned his back on Mrs. Galdinie and instead addressed the checkout girl, who looked, James thought, more receptive to the old tramp's blabberings.

"Have you ever seen the Peck woman on one of her rants?" Gauser slurred the word 'rants', and then steadied himself against the till.

The skinny checkout girl giggled and leaned forward. She spoke softly, "Wait until I tell you this one..."

Gauser screwed his face up into toothless grin spun round to face Mrs. Galdinie. "See!" he slurred.

The girl began. "Cathy Peck came in last Christmas for some custard; at least I think it was custard." She drummed her fingers on the till and looked thoughtful for a moment. "Anyway, she had James and that poor husband of hers with her. Well... for reasons best known to herself, Mrs. Peck erupted. Went for her man, there and then, like some deranged tiger."

James twitched at the mention of the word 'tiger'.

The checkout girl gave Gauser a swift nod. "That poor son of hers was *so* embarrassed." She took Gauser's money and handed back his change. But the Irishman wasn't ready to leave. Far from it.

Mrs. Galdinie fidgeted impatiently behind him.

The checkout girl continued with her story, "Cathy Peck actually grabbed her man by the throat, and when her son asked her to calm down, she clattered him right across the ear and then barged out of the shop."

James rubbed his left ear as he recalled the clout.

Gauser moved closer and assumed a pirate-like tone, his voice all husky and gravelly. "The throat, you said?"

The checkout girl looked confused. "Well I think it was..."

"You said the Peck woman grabbed her man by the throat, didn't je?" Gauser persisted.

The checkout assistant nodded, looking unsure of herself.

"Now, dat's where you're off the mark," roared Gauser. The wrinkles on his puce face shifted to form a smug expression. "David Peck wasn't strangled." He moved his puffed up lips close to the girl's ear and in a whisper laced with spit, said, "He was poisoned!"

The 'p' of poison was to blame for the biggest dousing of phlegm.

"Poisoned!" The attendant's startled expression had caused several other shoppers to shop a little closer. She wiped her ear with her cuff.

James watched as Mrs. Galdinie, losing patience, pushed Gauser aside.

While holding her nose, she handed the checkout girl the exact amount for a tub of double cream and shook her head. "Estupido!" she scolded, sounding a bit nasally. "What about di big cat at my bins, eh? And why did di polis arrest old Archie MacNulty then?"

Gauser waved Mrs. Galdinie and her suggestions away with a terse flick of his thick, dirty fingers. "Away with je. Big cats my a…" He paused, pulling on the twine that held up his trousers. "As fir MacNulty, well, he was the last person to see him alive, dat's all. MacNulty's always up on the moor poachin' way his ruddy ferrets."

"You're a rude man, no?" said Mrs. Galdinie, her penciled brows scrunching into a petulant frown.

As she made for the door, six other shoppers looked away, needlessly busying themselves in an effort to avoid her gaze. She was well known for putting a hex on people or, even worse, banning them from her sweet shop. She sold best homemade tablet in the world, and the tastiest ice cream.

Nobody had noticed James as he knelt flicking through the comics and now, trapped behind the wall of crisps and magazines, he didn't dare move. His only thought was how he might escape from the shop before anyone saw him, before people became overcome with embarrassment and apologised, or pretended they were talking about something else altogether other than his mum and dad.

He couldn't believe that people thought his mum was a murderess. It was bad enough when they thought that his dad had deserted them. He felt sick.

The shop door had just swung shut behind Mrs. Galdinie when the bell pinged a second time. Someone else stepped inside. The newcomer's massive frame loomed over the till and everyone stopped their flustering and gossiping.

James, still clutching a small book on Scottish mammals, thought back to the little animal he'd now confirmed as a stoat and looked down at the stranger's feet. There were no spindly toes or anything but the stranger himself was a bit of an oddity. He was unusually tall and carried a large, gnarled stick in his left hand. His clothes were old fashioned, even frumpy, and they were made of a material James had never seen before. Long, black hair fell over his broad shoulders giving him the appearance of an eccentric recluse or perhaps a rock musician.

"Good day." The stranger's voice was deep and sounded well educated. "Could someone point me in the direction of Drumfintley Park?"

Everyone in the shop looked at each other wondering who would be the first to answer but, suspicious of anyone who kept their sunglasses on inside, they hesitated.

James stood up. "I can help."

The whole shop, with the exception of the stranger, gasped at the shock of seeing James Peck emerge from behind the comic rack. But James knew that this was the only way to leave with some sense of purpose and pride. He placed his book back on the shelf. "I can take you there if you like," he offered, trying to sound as nonchalant as possible. He struggled to stifle a building asthmatic cough.

"Thank you, but a few pointers will suffice," said the stranger.

James wasn't sure what 'suffice' meant, being only one week away from his eleventh birthday, but he took his chance and stepped out onto the street with a huge sigh of relief, glad to be free of the shoppers' stares and mutterings.

As the stranger followed him out of the shop, James saw him stop for a moment to sniff in the warm Drumfintley air. He scratched at his temple irritably for a few seconds and then stared down at James.

"It's not far," James reassured, wincing in the bright sunlight. "Do you see the church spire?" He pointed towards St. Donan's.

"Indeed, I do," replied the stranger, moving past him.

"Well," James shouted after him, "when you get as far as the church, turn right and you'll see the park."

"Thank you, and many felicitations to you, my boy," the stranger replied.

Struggling with the word 'felicitations', James raised his hand to wave, but the stranger was already on his way.

James experienced an incredible feeling of dèjá vu and suddenly wondered if this outsider knew anything about his dad's disappearance or even about the footprint on the moor. He didn't look like a detective or an insurance assessor. Both had been sniffing round their house in Willow Terrace over the last few weeks. But he did have the look of someone who might know things that your normal, everyday Drumfintleyite may not.

James decided to follow him.

He wished his best friend Craig were here, just for some support, but if he were to double back for his pal now he might lose track of the stranger. No, he could do this by himself. He would just have to make sure he kept well out of sight. Besides, anything was better than listening to those doom-merchants back in the shop.

As soon as the stranger turned down Park Street, James followed. After a few seconds, however, he had to duck behind a green telephone exchange box. The stranger had skidded to a stop, his long, black hair fanning out as he glanced back up the street in James's direction. James froze and waited until he heard the clicking of the stranger's funny stick against the tarmac before he looked out. Ahead, the tall eccentric moved on towards the rusting, wrought-iron gates that marked the entrance to Drumfintley Park.

The stick, he decided, was not for support since the stranger moved quite briskly. So much so, that James struggled to keep up with him.

Once in the park, James darted off the main path and slipped into the bushes amongst the chip pokes, crisp bags, and lager cans. The park was always a dump after the spring fair.

Deflated, James reasoned that the stranger was probably one of the show people who'd left something behind and had returned to find it. But if that were so, why would he need directions to the park?

A horrible scream interrupted James's train of thought. "Arghh!"

In his efforts to hide himself in the rhododendron bushes, James had lost sight of the stranger, but he was sure that the scream had come from the direction of the old bandstand. He crouched down low and crawled through the dead leaves and rusting lager cans until he could just see the back of the stranger's head.

James tensed as the stranger spoke - "I'm too busy for this nonsense, understand? You've had plenty of time!" The stranger thumped his gnarled stick into something soft and another yelp echoed up through the trees."I have to finish things in Denthan, so, can I rely on you to find him and kill him? I mean, it's not as if he'll be capable of any magic in his present form, is it? All you have to do is step on him and that will be that!"

Unbidden, a pulse flicked in James's neck. He fumbled for his inhaler, but paused to listen as the second voice echoed up from below.

"Listensss ssssire... Upsss there, in the bushessss... Did you hear thatsssss?"

James ducked down praying that his cough would stay trapped in his chest.

"I thought I heard somethssss…"

But before the hissing voice could finish, the gnarled stick found its mark once more.

"Argh! Ssstop hurting. Pleasssss…"

James had never heard a voice quite like this one before. An evil hissing sound overlapped every syllable. He covered his mouth and let his cough hiss free through his fingers.

The stranger's voice masked his spluttering - "It's only your underdeveloped imagination, Sleven. Now, can you kill him or not?"

"Yes, yes, yesssss…" whimpered Sleven.

Watery eyed, James wondered who this Sleven had been instructed to kill. He edged forward, then slowly raised himself up onto his elbows. Lifting his head an inch at a time, he reached a point where he could just see inside the old bandstand. To his alarm, it was now completely deserted.

Where have they gone? James banged his head on a branch and then shuffled back through the bushes the same way he'd come in. Soaked through with sweat and short of breath, he saw the park gates up ahead. Tall and ominous, they loomed high over the flowerbeds and litterstrewn lawns. *Where is the stranger, and his hissing accomplice?* He wondered. Glancing between the park gates and the bushes behind him, he tried to decide whether he should make a run for the gates or walk out slowly, as if nothing terrifying had happened at all. He had just plumped for the slow walk when a voice filled his head.

"About time, too," it said.

James threw himself to the ground behind the nearest black, Council bin. This was a different voice from the ones he'd heard back at the bandstand.

"Quickly now. Get me out of here."

This voice was rich and full of character, but it also sounded slightly indignant. To James's horror, it seemed to be only inches away. He peered over the edge of the bin, only to pull back with a yelp as a wasp flew out of a lemonade can.

"Yes, that's right, I'm in the bin. Look again!" ordered the voice impatiently.

This time, James eased himself up onto his knees and peered down into the bin. There, behind an orange nappy sack and a pile of half eaten chicken-fried-rice, something moved. It flashed gold, then orange and yellow in the sunlight. Still scanning the park for danger, James picked up a twig and prodded the nappy sack to the side. Underneath, he saw a clear plastic bag half filled with water. It contained a little goldfish.

Looking about nervously, he lifted the bag from the rubbish and slumped back down behind the bin. He prodded the bag gently to see if the fish was still alive.

"Stop that!" scolded the voice. "There's no time to waste. You have to get us out of here!"

James blinked and held the goldfish closer to his face. He was definitely losing it. He looked round the side of the bin, but there was no one there. It couldn't be the fish.

"My name is Mendel," the voice continued.

James dropped the plastic bag and pushed himself away from it, kicking backwards across the grass as he balanced on his elbows.

He'd seen its fishy lips move.

"I...I don't think I'm feeling too well," James groaned.

"You look healthy enough to me," remarked the voice. "However, I don't rate your chances of remaining that way if we linger here much longer."

James couldn't believe what he was hearing. The voice in his mind was as clear as any hi-fi, and the only possible source was the goldfish. *How could that be possible?*

Then, to James's horror, the bushes behind him rustled loudly. A branch snapped and a fat wood-pigeon broke cover above his head. He flushed in panic and scrambled back onto the path that led to the gates, but he'd left the goldfish on the grass beside the bin. Without really knowing why, he dashed back and snatched up the little creature before sprinting for the wrought-iron gates.

"Not so fast, please! You're making me feel quite sick." The voice rattled round in James's head as he ran up Park Street, but he was too busy trying to get as far away as he could from whatever had startled the wood-pigeon to pay much attention to what it was saying.

As he turned the corner onto Main Street, he chanced a look behind him. Back in the park, he could have sworn he'd seen a bald, lanky man slip into the rhododendron bushes. The heavy black bin, where he'd found the goldfish, now lay overturned, and its muck and filth were scattered all over the path.

"Sleven will not follow us in daylight." The voice in his head almost caused James to trip.

"Wh…who is this Sleven?" James felt a bit stupid talking down at the little fish.

"Sleven is the least of our worries."

"*Our* worries?" said James, suddenly regretting picking up the goldfish.

"Look, I think it would be best if you just got me back to your house as quickly and as smoothly as possible, James." The voice had adopted a more friendly tone.

"How do you know my name?" James felt his mouth become dry and he was beginning to grow short of breath again.

"Try and remain calm," said the voice, "I will explain everything once we're safe."

As James ran up past the village hall and into Willow Terrace, he tried not to think about his mum's possible reaction on seeing the goldfish. She was very anti-pets.

Growing more frightened with every step, he bounded past the Fyffe's Mondeo car and raced up his garden path. He pushed open the door, dashed inside, and slammed it shut. After slipping the bolt, he placed the bulging plastic bag on the first step of the wooden staircase and looked, blankly, at the tiny goldfish swimming around inside. Staring at the strange creature, James's head reeled with images of the longhaired stranger and with the blood curdling sounds made by the one called Sleven. He just knew that these people were involved in his dad's disappearance. He didn't know how or why, exactly, but he was convinced that they were, and it frightened him.

He pinched his arm just to make sure he wasn't dreaming.

It stung like mad.

CHAPTER TWO
THE BLUE CRYSTAL

"*That* Peck bloke didn't just wander off," said Constable Watt, determined to get a reaction out of the old desk sergeant.

The sergeant's big red face was buried in the pages of the Drumfintley Herald.

"And, in my book," Watt continued, "your man, MacNulty, hasn't got the brains to carry out anything like this." He pinged the front page of the paper that carried the headline: 'The Peck Mystery Continues.'

The sergeant looked up, his eyes narrowing.

Constable Watt knew that the mere mention of MacNulty would get a reaction. "No Sarge, my money's still on the Peck woman."

"Aye, she's got the brains alright," said the old sergeant, "And she put you in your place a few times last week; but a killer? No, I don't think so." The sergeant had a face like a ripe pomegranate and a smoky voice that rattled deep in his chest. "There's something strange about the whole affair," he rasped, "but let's leave it to those so-called experts up in Stendelburgh." The sergeant paused to stir a cup of milky tea with his biro. "Besides, you've got enough on your plate trying to catch the litter louts in the park without testing yourself too much, Watt." The old sergeant sneered and turned to the last page of the Drumfintley Herald.

His expression suddenly darkened and his forefinger began to vibrate over a photograph in the sports section.

Archie MacNulty was holding a trophy of some kind. The line beneath the old scoundrel's toothless grin read: "Archie MacNulty has yet again succeeded in winning first place in the ferret section of the Fintleyshire Pets Gold Cup. Once more, Drumfintley can be proud of its famous church organist and ferret aficionado."

"Ferret aficionado?" the old desk sergeant screeched. "Ferret aficionado! More like, champion poacher!" Sergeant Carr hated Mac-Nulty with a vengeance. For years, MacNulty had pestered him with his numerous after-hours jaunts up on the moor. Just two months before, Sergeant Carr had almost nabbed him, but MacNulty was a sly old devil. He'd denied all knowledge of the nearby hemp sack that had contained the ten dead rabbits.

"It's more than twenty feet away, Sarge," he'd said, "could be anybody's." Then, knowing it would wind up the old Sergeant even more, MacNulty had smiled his usual gummy smile and proceeded to mumble in Gaelic.

The Sergeant screwed up his ruddy face and shook his head. "I mean, how can anyone in their right mind say that keeping ferrets as a bloomin' sport? This rag is definitely getting worse." He scrunched up the paper and tossed it into the wastepaper basket.

"Well good luck to him, I say," said Constable Watt, digging his thumbnail into his forefinger in an effort to suppress a grin.

The Sergeant twitched.

Constable Watt was convinced that the Sergeant would still try to fit up MacNulty for the Peck case, and he was equally sure that no missing persons department up in Stendelburgh would get the better of the old policeman.

Sergeant Carr mumbled down at the crumpled paper in the bin. "I'll show him. Then let him gabber and gloat…"

Watt drew back as the grumpy old sergeant thumped his chubby fist down onto the pitted desk that separated the outside world from the inner sanctum of the station. "Look Watt, you never know what goes through a man's head when he's pushed to the limits. Sometimes, enough is enough, and they snap." Carr sipped his tea and boiled with rage. "It's time for another all-nighter up on the moor, Watt. And this time, you're coming with me. It's time you found out who the real villains are here in Drumfintley."

* * *

James had left the goldfish beside his bed. After rummaging about at the back of their garage, he'd found an old tin bath, a bit bashed and a little rusty, but just right for the job. He lifted it up to his bedroom and filled it with tap water from the bathroom. From time to time, black waves of paranoia rolled over him, making him sweat copiously. Every couple of minutes he peered out the window, half expecting to see the longhaired stranger or perhaps his deranged, hissing accomplice walking up the garden path. He shuddered at the thought of those two ne'er-do-wells somehow being involved in his dad's disappearance, and wondered about going straight to the police. But there was the small matter of the talking fish to consider.

"I could do with some fresh water, please," said the voice.

James turned round to look at the goldfish on his bedside table. "Are you really talking to me?" he asked.

"Yes, I am," said the fish. "And can I also remind you that my name is Mendel?" The fish named Mendel pushed one big, golden, googly eye against his bulging plastic bag. "Needless to say, I've ended up in my present form by ill fate rather than by design."

"You mean you're not normally a goldfish?" asked James.

"That would be correct," said Mendel, his tone sounding slightly reproachful. "Fresh water?" he prompted.

"Oh, yes, of course." James held the bag over the old tin bath and undid the knot that kept Mendel inside his little fairground prison. "There you go!"

Mendel slipped into the water and sighed with relief. "Three weeks in a plastic bag. I thought I was going to die in there. How can your race be so cruel to their fellow creatures?"

"My race?" said James, "you mean you're not from Drumfintley?"

"Not exactly," Mendel answered, sounding excited as he raced round his new home.

"We used to have a goldfish," said James, changing the subject. "But the cat smashed the bowl and…" James thought back to the cat licking its lips after its fishy snack and wished he hadn't begun the story. "Anyway, I'm sure we've got some grit and stuff somewhere." He pulled his chair across the floor and placed it beneath his wardrobe. Then, standing on his tiptoes, he fumbled around amongst the boxed games and piles of magazines. "Ah! Here they are." He lifted a small carrier bag down from his wardrobe and pulled out the various bits and pieces. With a sense of self-satisfaction, he smiled down at Mendel and tipped a heap of blue and orange-coloured gravel into the water. Then, after spreading the little stones round the bath, he dropped in a plastic castle followed by three clumps of fake seaweed.

When he was done, he took one more look out of his bedroom window. "The people in the park were looking for you, weren't they?" said James.

"Indeed they were. But you came along, just as I predicted."

"Predicted?" asked James.

"Chance and science are interlinked, my boy. Quite fascinating if you do the right calculations." Mendel's tone became serious. "Sleven will still try to kill me tonight."

"Why?" James paced his room, nervously twirling his blue inhaler.

"Because he would not dare fail his master." Mendel's tone grew even more ominous as he added, "Unless you help me, he may yet succeed."

James bounced back down onto the bed. "I've already helped you. What am I supposed to do now?" He felt his stomach tighten as he thought of what he'd got himself into. If only he'd stood up earlier and endured the shopper's stares, he wouldn't be in this mess. If only he hadn't followed the stranger, if only his dad had waited home that night instead of traipsing up the hill in an effort to avoid his mum's bad mood.

Becoming more morose by the second, James noticed the two blue and white neckerchiefs dangling from his wall. Pinned there by his dad, the Drumfintley Scouts colours reminded him of the time he'd won the orienteering competition. A little plaque said: "1st prize, James Peck, the fifth Drumfintley Scout group." That was a year ago, when everything had been normal.

"Mendel?" James approached the tin bath intending to ask the one question most important to him, the question that had burned in his mind night and day for three weeks. He cleared his throat. "It's about my dad. Do you know where...?"

"I'm sorry, James. I don't think I can help you with that. Not yet."

"But I haven't finished!" James blazed with an anger inherited from his mum. "I mean, I haven't asked you what I want to ask you!"

Mendel replied calmly, "It's what people don't say that reveals their most inner thoughts. But I really must insist you come a little closer." Mendel's voice had a sleepy ring to it. James knelt down beside the tin bath, seething in silence. He could still see the goldfish down amongst the fake weed, flicking its fins, pulsating.

"I need you to help me," said Mendel, "and to do this properly I need you to touch my scales."

James drew backs little. "What?"

"Just put your hand into the water," whispered Mendel.

As soon as the words came into his mind, James felt an incredible urge to put his hand into the cool water. When his fingers broke the surface tension of the liquid, he flinched. He could feel every molecule brush against his skin. Like a million tiny needles, the water jabbed at him and soothed him at the same time. Slowly, the cuff of his shirt disappeared beneath the surface...

"Aagghh!" James screamed as his forefinger brushed against the golden scales, electricity shooting up his arm and forking down into his heart. An incredible tightness gripped him. He was panting. Trying to catch his breath.

"Don't move," ordered Mendel. "Just remain still for a minute or two. I'm sorry about the pain involved, but if I had explained the whole process, I doubt you would have helped."

The moment his thoughts and memories returned to him, James's eyes flashed open and he kicked himself away from the bath. Every muscle felt stiff and sore. "W...what? You tricked me!"

"I said don't move." Mendel's voice echoed round in his mind. "I'm sorry, James, but you will soon see that by making this connection you have probably saved us both. Now sit up and look at me."

James pulled himself back over to the tub, intent on tipping the whole lot, fish and all, down the toilet when, all of a sudden, the water in the tin bath began to ripple. He felt a tickle in his throat, and then he muttered something that sounded like, "Wwwviswwinpoowwlww." Tears ran down his face, and a persistent knocking sensation thumped inside his head. Despite the pain, he almost laughed out loud at the ridiculous word that'd spilled from his lips. It sounded like someone talking underwater.

He gulped as the water in the tin bath turned blood red, then switched to a deep tropical blue.

"You're a wizard!" James exclaimed, his throat suddenly dry. But there was no reply. Wisps of smoke spun round on the surface of the water, then cleared to reveal a familiar sight. The nine stones pillars that formed the Jesus Rocks were there, as clear as a bell, on the surface of the water. Standing proud of the heather they looked like the fingers of some long-forgotten giant that had been buried under the hill. Even the familiar graffiti marring the biggest stone couldn't stop him from the feeling that he was seeing something differently for the first time.

"You are now looking into a vision pool," explained Mendel.

"I was there this morning," said James, thinking back to the little, squashed stoat, the strange footprint, and the uncontrollable panic that had overwhelmed him.

"I know you were," said Mendel, "but there is something in the stone circle that may help us both." He paused. "You felt something there this morning, didn't you, James?"

"Yes. Well I… Are you really a wizard?" pressed James.

"I prefer the word scientist, if you don't mind," Mendel replied. "Much less mysterious and wishy-washy. Don't you think?"

"I suppose." James gulped. "And my dad?"

"Your father's disappearance *may* be linked to the same dark magic that brought me here."

"It may? I mean, it might?" James replied.

"Yes," said Mendel. "And I may be able to help you if you can help me."

"Help you do what?" asked James, dreading the answer.

The image of the Jesus Rocks in the vision pool became blurred until, with a sound like fat spitting in a hot pan, the water bubbled and then settled again. The picture now centred on the biggest stone.

"I need you to help me get back home," said Mendel.

James stared at the standing stone and wondered what Mendel meant by home. More importantly, he wondered how his dad could possibly be involved in this whole weird scenario.

"James, you need to go back there today. I need you to retrieve a blue crystal that lies at the base of this stone." The vision pool changed perspective, suddenly, spiralling up and away from the main stone.

James felt sick. "But Sleven and the stranger," he began. "Was that Sleven's–"

"…footprint you saw this morning?" finished Mendel.

James hated it when Mendel delved into his thoughts. It felt like he was being robbed.

"Sleven's, I should think," continued Mendel, "but don't worry. I've told you already. He won't brave your sunlight on a day like this."

The vision pool zoomed in on a patch of grass just beyond the body of the crushed stoat.

"James," said Mendel, "the blue crystal buried here is crucial to our survival."

"What do you mean by *our* survival?" whispered James.

The downstairs bell buzzed into life.

Annoyed by the interruption, James pushed himself to his feet. "Why can't you get the crystal yourself? Just do some magic or…"

A familiar voice cut him short. "James!"

It was Craig, his best friend.

James shouted down through his open bedroom door. "How did you get in?"

Craig, however, was already tramping up the stairs. "The front door was wide open, ye numpty!" he bellowed.

James was positive that he'd pulled it shut. "It can't have been."

"No, that's right, I just walked straight through a closed door!" Craig laughed his usual laugh, the one that began with a titter and ended in a guffaw. Tall for eleven, he had blond, spiky hair and a face full of freckles. Craig feigned a Drumfintley accent and said, "Ye cumin oot te play?"

Catching Craig by the arm and leading him back down to the front door, James shook his head. "You know, it's really pathetic when you do the Scottish accent thing. You're from London. Stick to your own weird accent."

James paused on the front steps and looked back up in the direction of his room. Relieved that he had shut his bedroom door behind him, he was just about to suggest they go up onto the moor when Craig said, "Fancy going up to the Jesus Rocks? I mean I know we've not played there for a while because…" Craig wasn't the most diplomatic boy in the world. "You know…? That's where your dad lost the plot and scarpered." His friend gave a big, toothy grin and was about to blurt out some other pearl of wisdom when James pulled him back into the hallway.

A black VW Polo screeched to a halt at the front gate.

"It's mum," said James, in a sharp whisper.

"You mean, the wicked witch of the west?" laughed Craig.

A laugh cut short when a familiar voice said, "Witch? I'll witch ye!" Cathy Peck narrowed her eyes at James, as if he'd said it.

James immediately pointed a finger at Craig. "it was…"

"Get yourselves out-side! A dry day like this, and you two are sat in front of the telly growing fatter by the minute!"

Struggling with five carrier bags and a bunch of keys, she barged past Craig and narrowed her eyes at James.

James tried to explain, "We weren't watching TV, Mum."

"Yeah, right," she snapped. "You're a born liar, just like your dad."

James stared at the floor, burning with embarrassment, annoyed by the way she'd spoken about his dad in front of Craig. "We'll get out of your way, mum," he muttered.

"So you're just going to let me struggle with the rest of the shopping?" She sneered at them both before flicking a strand of long, black hair from her eyes and marching on past them.

"Thanks for dropping me in it, *pal*," whispered Craig.

"What did you expect?" snapped James.

His mum whisked passed and they followed her back out to her car.

James thought that Craig would probably quite enjoy watching his mum struggle with the rest of her shopping bags, so he was quietly relieved when his best friend lifted a huge bottle of diluting juice from the roadside.

"That's right. Get your gormless friends to do all the work. And stop hunching over like that! No wonder you can't breathe!" James knew she hated the way he wheezed and spluttered all the time.

"Why can't you just leave it for once?" James whispered angrily.

Unfortunately his mum had very good hearing and a can of beans whizzed through the air, just missing his head.

"Hey! What was that for?" James protested.

Cathy clenched her fists. "In! You're grounded for the rest of the day!"

"But..." protested James.

"One more word and I'll make it the week," she snapped.

When she'd disappeared into the house, James turned to Craig and pulled him close. "Look, can you go up to the Jesus Rocks by yourself?"

"In!" Cathy Peck's voice resounded from the kitchen as she thumped an assortment of straining bags onto the kitchen table.

James spoke quickly to his friend. "The biggest rock has a blue crystal buried at its base. It will be brilliant in geography class on Monday. How about it Craig, will you go and get it?"

Craig stared at James in complete disbelief. "What are you on about? We don't have geography on Monday, and what blue crystal is this?" He made the mistake of following James into the house.

"Out!" screeched Cathy. She picked up another can of beans.

Craig put his hands up, as if someone had just pulled a gun on him, and backed out the front door.

"In!" This time Cathy stared hard at James and thumped the can down on the kitchen table.

Just before Craig stepped outside, James ran to the front door and grabbed Craig's sleeve, "Just go and get it! I'll explain everything tomorrow. Trust me. I need you to…"

"James!" Cathy Peck had caught hold of James's ear. "Get in now," she threatened, her face red with rage, "or I'll make it a month."

As soon as Cathy turned, Craig mouthed the words - 'wicked witch of the west', and nodded, as if there was nothing more sure.

As James was dragged into the kitchen, he watched his best friend edge down the garden path. He wasn't sure that Craig would go all the way up to Bruce Moor by himself. He was a lazy oaf at the best of times.

Craig, however, surprised James when he winked and gave him the thumbs up just before stepping back onto the hot tarmac pavement.

* * *

Poor sap, thought Craig, no *wonder his dad has done a runner.* He kicked a small stone up Willow Terrace.

"Goal!" he shouted, jumping up and down as the small stone smacked into the hubcap of an old, bottle-green Morris Minor parked outside number fifty-four. A net curtain twitched as a large round face appeared in the window above. Just discernible above a cascade of double chins, Ephie Blake, a portly lady who kept a continuous watch on the street, stared down at him. She spent hours peering from her high perch, determined to catch somebody doing something they shouldn't.

Craig gave her a freckle-faced smile and waved before marching on towards the underpass. Knowing he would soon reach the flaky green façade of Galdinie's Sweet Shop, he fumbled in his pockets for some change. But there was nothing. Not a single, sticky penny. "Brilliant," he muttered.

What on earth was James on about? he wondered as he continued onward. The bit about the geography lesson was a complete load of tosh, which, of course, made Craig curious. Digging around up on the moor for a couple of minutes wouldn't be that tedious. Besides, he wanted to see if James's blue crystal really existed.

Being prone to frivolous temptation, he darted up the side of Galdinie's shop then sauntered back down again, carrying a small, garden trowel. *Might come in handy*, he thought. He punched the air and held the trowel up above his head like some kind of trophy.

After about an hour or so, Craig was standing in front of the biggest standing stone. The large white letters were faded but he could still make out the words, 'Jesus Saves'. The warm summer breeze cut through the heather and ruffled his spiky, blond hair. Something dead had drawn a cloud of flies into the circle and they pestered him as he began digging round the base of the stone.

"What the…!" Craig gripped his throbbing wrist. The handle of the trowel had split in two. Wincing in pain, he scraped the remaining soil away with his good hand until he eventually spied an old piece of cloth. He pulled hard on the material until it slid over something smooth. A glint of deep azure blue made him smile. He lifted the crystal free before sitting down in the heather. About the same size as his TV remote control, it was surprisingly heavy and incredibly beautiful. Craig held it up to the sun. He laughed as a cascade of little white dots to danced over his face.

* * *

Far away in Denthan, the tall stranger tensed. He made a fist with his left hand then relaxed, letting his long, black hair fall down over the back of his ivory throne. He closed his cat-like eyes and delved deep into the thoughts of Craig Harrison.

CHAPTER THREE

WHAT A RACKET

Magical shapes lit up the sky over James's house, but in Willow Terrace nobody noticed a thing, not even nosy Ephie Blake at number fifty-four, who lay snoring and muttering beneath a pile of discarded sweet wrappers.

In their baskets, all the dogs were safely curled up, twitching and snarling at imaginary cats, while all the cats continued prowling the Terrace, oddly oblivious to the cold morning mist that danced over the Peck's house. Sparks flew over the frosted slates and random flares of light traced the windowpanes. First blue and then a piercing yellow, the colours shot up into the morning sky, glowing brightly before forming candescent clouds of mist that danced and shimmered in the early dawn.

For the entire night, James had lain awake on his bed, hoping beyond hope that there would be no sign of Sleven or of the tall stranger, both of whom seemed intent on murder.

Mendel's rich voice had remained silent since the previous afternoon and James wondered whether the little fish had taken umbrage at his failure to retrieve the blue crystal from the Jesus Rocks. It wasn't his fault, he'd been grounded. Well, not technically. At any rate, he now doubted whether Craig would have trailed all the way up the hill on his own.

Suddenly, something flashed yellow outside the window.

"Did you see that?" James sat up, dragging his bedclothes over to the tin bath. "Mendel, wake up!"

The little goldfish didn't move from his hiding place in the fake weed. Just an orange blob amongst the green-feathered plastic, his fins beat rhythmically in the stillness of the cold water.

"There are lights and stuff outside the window," said James. He paused to look up at the ceiling. "And there's something on the roof!" Breaking into a prickly sweat he grabbed the heavy, rubber torch that lay under his bed.

When Mendel did eventually speak, his words struck terror in James's heart. "Oh dear, it looks like Sleven has decided to pay us a visit after all."

This was the last thing James wanted to hear.

Mendel sounded surprisingly calm considering the circumstances. "James, you must go outside now. I need you to face him."

"What!" James wheezed his reply, completely gobsmacked at the idea.

Mendel continued to give his terrifying instructions as though he was merely reading out some vaguely amusing pet story, the kind you get at the end of a nasty news bulletin, slotted in at the last minute in a useless attempt to cheer you up. "Only then will we find out whether my mind-merge has worked. If it has taken, I should still be able to do my magic through you."

James was annoyed by Mendel's blasé tone. "And if it hasn't? What if…"

A large, blue flash shook the room this time, silencing James. A slate fell past the leaded windowpane.

"James, you need to trust me. Just go outside!" Mendel's voice seemed to lead him, to force him onwards.

Outside, James steadied himself on the coalbunker and shone his rubber torch up into the multicoloured mist that had engulfed his house.

"Timetrance," said James in a fishy, bubbly voice. And again, only louder, "Timetrance!"

His face flushed as he tried to mouth the fishy words that actually sounded more like "Twiwimwmwetwrawnwcwe…" It was just like the sound you got when you pinged your lips up and down with your fore-finger while trying to speak at the same time.

The knock-knock-knocking sensation had returned, making James feel like he had cold lumps of ice bumping against each other inside his head.

But the spell, for James guessed that's what it was, changed nothing.

The swirling lights raced even faster over James's roof until the colours rushed together to form a blinding flash of pure white light. Red and yellow dots spun round at the back of James's eyes, but he could see well enough to spot a strange, misshapen creature coming toward him. "Sleven," he whispered to himself.

Sleven had a toad-like head that seemed far too heavy for his skinny neck. But unlike any toad, his mouth contained row upon row of needle-sharp, black teeth that dripped yellow, steaming slime. Sleven was no man, nor any kind of creature James had ever seen before.

Craning his neck to look up at Sleven's evil, slit-like eyes, James felt the torch waver in his hand. This caused a strobe effect that made Sleven look even more horrid.

Spying James, Sleven jerked his oversized head back in a series of grotesque twitches that caused him to temporarily lose his footing.

James gulped when he saw the size of Sleven's feet. Extremely elongated, each one had three skinny toes that wiggled like spider's legs as the creature struggled to keep his balance on the slates. Sleven hissed with annoyance and gripped onto the ridging of the roof.

Watching Sleven as he tried to steady himself, James saw that he had no ears, only two gaping holes that ran from where his ears should have been, down towards his hideously toothed jaw. The drool that dripped from the side of his mouth splashed onto the ice-cold slates, causing small clouds of steam to rise up through sparks that spun and danced round his long, twisted legs. Slowly, Sleven tilted his big head and focused in on James. He hissed a split-laden hiss and said, "Wheresss iss Mendelssss?"

James whimpered, cringing as the monster continued to blink in his direction. He didn't know what to say.

The torch slipped from James's sweating fingers. But instead of fear, he felt an overwhelming anger begin to burn inside him. He looked the beast in the eye, showing courage he never knew he possessed and said, "What have you done with my dad?"

Only briefly distracted by James's question, the huge, toad-like form of Sleven shrugged, shook his big head and then leapt down from the roof towards James. He bounced onto the ground and swung a long skinny arm at James's throat. Three razor-sharp claws sliced through the bitter night air.

James opened his mouth to scream but the word "timetrance" followed rapidly by "snufflight" burst from his lips instead.

Only inches from James's frightened face, Sleven froze, split into a million pieces, and collapsed back in on himself with a blinding blue flash and a pathetic gurgle.

James took a sharp breath and fumbled for his torch. There was no trace of Sleven, only a disgusting eggy, sulphurous, farty stink that made James cough and gag.

"What was that thing?" James wheezed before covering his mouth.

Oddly, Mendel's voice, when it came into James's head, was tinged with sadness. "That poor wretch belonged to a race that once possessed the most ancient of magic powers, but..." he paused, "I fear Sleven was the last of his kind. The Swamp Troll or *Sygentius trolificus*, to be precise, is now no more."

"Well, good riddance to him," James snorted. He immediately sensed Mendel's disapproval, but was too troubled by the stench to really care. "What is that smell?"

"Smell...what smell?" said Mendel.

James began to make his way back towards the front door. "So, you can see what I can see, but you can't smell what I can smell?"

"It would seem that way, wouldn't it?" said Mendel.

"Lucky you!" said James, pinching his nose. He could hear Mendel splashing about and hoped that the fish wasn't spilling bathwater over his newly polished pine floor. Sleven was scary but his mum was a nightmare.

A sudden statement from Mendel cut through his concern. "James, we have a problem with your friend."

"What, Craig?" exclaimed James, stopping at the front door and peering down Willow Terrace.

"He has the crystal," announced Mendel.

"How do you know that?" asked James, waving traces of mist away from his face.

"He has the crystal, and we need to use it before anything else comes through the gateway," said Mendel.

James wondered what Mendel meant by the word gateway. Did he mean that more magical creatures like Sleven were going to come after them. What had Mendel done to deserve this?

Teeth chattering in the cold Drumfintley dawn, James looked up at his mum's bedroom window. "She'll go crazy if she finds me out here."

Mendel's voice sounded tired. "Your mother is completely unaware that you're outs..."

"James!" an irate voice interrupted. "What are you doing out-side? In your pyjamas? With no shoes on? Do you know what time it is?" His mum peered down at him from her window.

"I was getting the milk, mum, and..." James knew it was a pa-thetic lie. He didn't even bother to finish.

"At four in the morning? The milk's not even here! Get inside right this minute, you idiot! You're grrrounded tomorrow, as well!"

She yelled so loud that several lights flicked on in the terrace and a sleeping cat, which had been lying on Mr. Fyffe's wall, fell off into a steel bin. "Bang! Meow! Sssssssss..." Hearing the noise, sev-eral small birds and rodents took cover in the bushes.

James's heart sank. There was no way his mum would calm down now. She'd be like this for at least the next two days. *How does she get the energy to be so angry for so long?*

Cathy Peck pushed her head further out of her window and continued her rant, "Get to your bed! Wash your feet first! You're just like your dad... An idiot!"

As the word 'idiot' echoed off the red brick walls of the houses on the opposite side of the street, a few more lights flicked on.

Whenever his mum yelled at him, there were always four or five commands, questions and/or statements all mixed up in one ve-nomous screech. Never knowing what to do first, he inevitably took too long to pick out the most important piece of information and ended up getting yelled at even more.

"Don't just stand there, gawping! Get inside! And what's..." She pinched her nose. "What's that smell?" She slammed her window shut, muttering something about sewage problems and pathetic Coun-cil spongers.

Across the street, Ephie Blake's curtains twitched.

Before James reached the top of the stairs, he heard his mum slam her bedroom door shut. The timber frame house was still shaking when Mendel spoke again in James's head. "Your mother is feeling down."

"Very down," whispered James. "Very, very down," he whis-pered again, only louder. "We definitely have to find a way of saving your skin, or scales, or whatever it is we're doing, without disturbing my mum again. Can't you put a 'Nice Person Spell' on her? Or a 'Mute Spell' or..."

"I can't do that, James," said Mendel, "Your mother has every right to be angry. I mean, you shouldn't be out at this time of night anyway, should you?"

For the second time in twenty-four hours, James felt like tipping the annoying little fish right down the toilet. "But you're the one who wanted me to go out there in the first place," he spluttered.

Mendel's tone was conciliatory. "Yes, I suppose.   But in your mother's eyes..."

"I'm just a pest," said James, breaking into an asthmatic cough.

"Stop coughing!" his mum's words made him try to hold his breath.

"She doesn't know what's happening," said Mendel, "and I get the impression that she is a little depressed."

"Depressed?" hissed James. He looked down at his mud-encrusted feet. "What about me? I miss my Dad more than she does."

Feeling suddenly weary, James slumped down on his bed and gazed up at the blue and white neckerchiefs that criss-crossed his bedroom wall. "Mendel... If I help you to get back home, do you promise to help me find my dad?" he asked, yawning loudly. His eyelids felt like a pair of lead aprons.

The wizard's voice became fuzzy as sleep swept over James. "I will try... I just hope your friend, Craig, has been very careful with the crystal. Otherwise we are both dead already."

But James had drifted off in a series of sniffs and snores.

CHAPTER FOUR

CUPBOARDS AND SMELLS

James opened one eye and stared at the digital clock. It was one minute past eight. As slowly as he could, he turned his head, opened the other eye, and then looked across his bedroom floor. It was still there. Like an ugly wart, the old, bashed tin bath sat on his nicely polished pine floor, and all the horrors of the night before flooded back into his mind.

The coughing began quietly, but soon grew into the usual early morning crescendo that often resulted in James being physically sick.

The bedroom wall soon reverberated with the sound of his mum's knocking. Three hard thumps on the plasterboard, followed by the usual, "Shut up! I'm trying to sleep!" She'd never been the Florence Nightingale type.

James sat bolt upright as the sensation of drowning increased. Then, as he shook his head in an effort to clear his airways, a bubbly noise that sounded something like, "Wwweezwwungwww," spluttered from his lips.

He gasped, then drew in a lungfull of wonderfully fresh air. As quickly as it had begun, his coughing fit stopped. The drowning sensation had gone. He could actually straighten his back. The sweat and panic drifted away and he felt as though he could run all the way to the Jesus Rocks and back without once stopping to fumble for his little, blue inhaler.

He spun himself round to face the rusty tin bath. "Mendel?" He waited for the wizard's voice.

"Good morning, James."

"You…you made my asthma go away. My cough's gone."

The googly-eyed goldfish came into view. "Feeling better?"

James stood up and stretched his arms above his head. "I feel fantastic! I can breathe without wheezing. Listen!" James stooped over the bath and took a large breath of morning air. "Nothing. No rattle or whine. How…?"

"Did I do it?" Mendel finished.

James screwed up his face in annoyance, but the wizard-goldfish had made his asthma go away and that counted for something.

Mendel swam into view. "What you call asthma is simply an irritation of the bronchiole mucus membrane that results in a reduction in the diameter of the airways, which results in the build up of discharge, which results in a sensation of…"

"Drowning," James finished, remembering the way he felt only seconds before.

Mendel circled his plastic castle. "Quite!"

James hadn't really understood Mendel's explanation. Neither was he sure that the fish wizard had actually answered his question, but no matter what magic Mendel had, or would ever perform, to James, nothing would surpass this.

There was a click, click, clicking sound coming from the tin bath. James peered down to see that Mendel was mouthing bits of grit and stone from the bottom.

"Yuck!" he exclaimed in disgust. "What are you doing?"

"It's a fish-thing," said Mendel, "it helps me think." Mendel's voice sounded irritated and restless now. "Your friend definitely has the crystal. I can sense it."

"You already said that last night. You were also going to say something about my dad, but you never did," said James.

Mendel swam close to the surface, flipping his tail with a splash before zooming down to the bottom of the bath again. "The crystal, if used properly, is a kind of key. It can make the stone circle on Bruce Moor function as a gateway."

"Are you saying that my dad has gone to another place?"

"It's a possibility. Either by accident or…"

"Or what?" James's eyes widened.

"Or he's been taken there on purpose." Mendel moved amongst the fake weeds.

"Why would anyone, or anything, take my dad to another place? What other place?" James half expected to start wheezing any second and, through habit, he lifted his inhaler, just in case.

"I'll explain everything to you once you bring me the crystal, James. There's no time to waste, so for now, you'll just have to do as I say. Before you go, however, please remember these three things…"

Mendel's bulging orange eye appeared above the surface of the water. "Do not unwrap the crystal. Do not touch the crystal with your bare hands and, most importantly, do not expose the crystal to sunlight." Mendel flicked his orange tail three times, as if to emphasize each point, before slipping back down beneath the surface.

Quietly, James felt a building sense of foreboding. "You didn't say any of this yesterday."

Mendel didn't reply.

If Craig had the crystal, James would bet all the gold in China that his friend had broken all three rules already. He had to do something.

Unfortunately, the bits and pieces that made up his real life could not be ignored. It was all very well for Mendel to say, go now and get the crystal, but James had chores, homework and especially his mum to think about. It was a Sunday and he had church, the weekly breakfast trip to his crazy Aunt Bella's and, oh yes, he was 'grrrounded.'

Perhaps if he told his mum what was going on she might let him go. He wondered how he might put it... *Mum, a magic goldfish has just cured my asthma and says that monsters have abducted dad. So I'm just off to Craig's to fetch a magic crystal. Is that okay?*

Yeah, right! She'd ship him off to the nearest mental institution without a second thought. No, he would just have to risk going to Craig's house without permission even though, using every short cut and back road he knew, it would be impossible for him to reach his friend's house without being seen.

"There's no choice, James," Mendel piped up again.

James let out a long sigh. "Can't I even think without you jumping into my head all the time?" He heard the goldfish rearranging the grit in the bath and soon realized that he didn't really have a choice. If he was going to help his dad, he had to at least try.

It was still only eight-ten in the morning and mum would be dozing for at least another twenty minutes. He might be able to pull it off if he left right away.

After slipping on a pair of football shorts and a new white shirt, he opened his bedroom window and stretched down the four feet or so until his feet brushed the coal bunker below. It was still damp, and he slipped on the mossy felt that sloped towards the lawn. With a small scream he bashed off of the coal bunker and squelched onto the soaking wet grass.

Standing up slowly, James looked down at his sodden shorts. It felt like he'd wet himself.

As the cold morning air hit his chest, he braced himself for the inevitable coughing fit, but when nothing happened he smiled and punched the air triumphantly. This was fantastic! *Had his asthma really gone for good?*

Uncomfortably wet, but exhilarated, James waddled towards the back fence as fast as he could. He slipped through a well-worn gap and edged behind Mr. Fyffe's Ford Mondeo. Hauling up his cold, wet shorts, he scanned the street for any signs of life. There was nothing except a few nervous cats and a seagull picking at an abandoned poke of chips. James eased out from behind the car and then belted past Ephie Blake's house towards the Beeches housing estate.

Craig's house was semi-detached, roughcast and rundown. Normally, the only way up to his best friend's bedroom was to scramble up a dodgy, plastic drainpipe at the back of the house, but since James was soaking wet and would probably slip and hurt himself he decided, instead, to pick up a handful of tiny, white stones and lob them at Craig's window. A few hit target, but the rest landed back in James's hair. One or two even slid down his neck and found their way into his soggy shorts.

"Craig!" he whispered as loud as he could. "Crai—Arrghhh." This time his forced whisper turned into a yelp as a big, yellow, furry thing with bad breath pounced on him. For a split second, he imagined another monster had made its way through the stone circle on the moor.

"Bero!" he yelled. "Gerrofff!"

Bero had him pinned to the ground in a Golden Retriever death grip. James couldn't move and the old dog was drooling long strands of slobber onto his nose.

"Get off me, you big brute. Get…" James panted.

"Bero!" Craig's voice called out from above. "In! Now!" Craig peered down and shook his head. "Ye numpty! Look at the state of you! What's happened? Why so early?"

James stared up. Craig was beginning to sound just like his mum. "Let me in," he pleaded.

Craig grinned and came down to meet him.

Amazingly, Craig's mum, Jean, had slept through the whole thing so, accompanied by Bero, they slipped into Craig's poster-papered room, shutting the door behind them as quietly as they could.

James was just about to sit on the bed when Craig grabbed hold of his filthy shirt. "Uh-uh." Craig waved his finger at James and pointed to his dripping wet trousers.

"Fine. Fine!" moaned James. He remained standing. "Did you get the blue crystal?" He took note of the time on Craig's digital clock. It read eight twenty-one.

"You mean that weird prism thing?" said Craig.

James nodded, although he'd never actually seen the crystal himself.

"Yeah, of course I did. It's in the cupboard." Craig opened a squeaky, moulded door.

There, beside what remained of a twisted garden trowel, James saw some kind of bundle. The crystal, if that's what he was staring at, was wrapped in a dirty, blue cloth.

"How do you know it looks like a prism?" asked James, growing worried as Craig bent down and picked it up. "Stop!" he shouted.

But the cloth had already fallen to the floor. "Cool your jets!" hissed Craig. "You'll wake mum."

"For goodness sake, cover it up!" James cried, his anxiety rising.

"You cover it up, ye ungrateful numpty." Craig tossed the crystal towards James. "And after me going all the way up to the moor by myself," he added.

James automatically sidestepped the flying crystal, then stared in horror as it bounced onto the bed. Hesitating for a moment, he snatched it up and looked about the bedroom.

Craig toyed with Bero's floppy, brown ear as James yanked a plastic supermarket bag from under the bed.

James popped the crystal inside the bag. "Okay," he began, "it's not just for the geology project."

"No kidding," said Craig.

James flushed. "I'll tell you more soon, but I need to get back home before my mum wakes up."

Craig picked up the blue cloth and threw it back into his cupboard. "Tell me now."

"I can't," moaned James.

Craig shook his head disdainfully. "You know, it's hardly worth being pals with you at all, is it? Your nut of a mum's got you permanently grounded."

James saw Bero's ears flatten and heard Errol, the paperboy, trying to stuff the Sunday supplement through the letterbox downstairs.

"I'll explain later, Craig. I promise." Without looking back, James edged down the stairs. He waited a few seconds until Errol had moved away and then slipped outside.

"You better!" Craig shouted down after him.

"I promise!" said James, his voice trailing off as he shot up Craig's garden path.

Turning round the corner of Craig's house, James spied the village hall but failed to avoid the little present left earlier by Bero. He slipped on the mess, but just managed to regain his step and keep running.

"Thanks, Bero," he muttered as he ran up the path toward Willow Terrace. To his dismay, he was beginning to wheeze again and the little sharp stones in his wet boxers were jagging his bum. He glanced back at the clock on St Donan's church tower.

Three minutes to go.

As he bolted up his garden path and dashed into the garage, he prayed that his mum was still sleeping. "Where is it?" he mumbled to himself as he fumbled about on a shelf above his head. It was packed with old, clay pots and rusting garden tools. Dust, dirt and an assortment of washers and nails showered over him but, eventually, he found it—the spare backdoor key. It felt cold in his hand.

One minute to go!

He slid into the kitchen, kicked off his poo-encrusted trainers, opened the washing machine, stripped off his filthy shirt, and was just about to chuck his shorts into the wash drum when the kitchen door squeaked open behind him.

"James!" His mum had the look of a beast about to pounce. Her eyes were wide and her teeth were clenched in anger. "What are you doing standing in the kitchen with no clothes on?" she hissed.

James opened his mouth but nothing came out.

"Why is the washing machine on? And...and what's that smell?" she shouted. Her eyes flicked over to the poo-encrusted trainers.

James eased the crystal behind his back.

Cathy Peck's hands curled up into a pair of fists as she yelled, "You're grrrounded!" Not quite satisfied with this, she sucked in a lung-full of rancid air and screamed, at the top of her voice, "AGAIN!"

CHAPTER FIVE

A TRIP TO THE CHURCH

The blue crystal lay next to Mendel's tin bath. Partly concealed by an old pair of swimming trunks and still wrapped in the supermarket carrier bag. James had made sure that the large gem remained well protected from the bright sunlight that filtered through his bedroom window.

Mendel congratulated James. "You did well to bring the crystal here so soon."

"Yes, well now I'm grounded for two days and Craig is totally confused. I have to tell him something." Exhausted, James pulled on his socks and forced his heels into his new, black shoes.

Bang, Bang, Click.

He thumped the floor until the stiff leather finally gave way and foot slipped into position. He hated messing about with laces. "Mendel, I think my asthma is coming back," he said.

"Ah well, you see, that spell was only a quick fix. I would need my own laboratory and a good deal of time to give you permanent freedom from your curse." There was a hint of frustration in Mendel's voice. "And time is one luxury we don't have."

James sprinkled some fish food on the water and watched the strange little wizard make his way to the surface. His thick, fishy lips mouthed "mpah, mpah, mpah" as he bit and nibbled at the blue and red flakes. In between mouthfuls Mendel asked, "Where is the blue cloth that protected the crystal?"

James kicked the crystal further under the rim of bath and wondered how to answer the wizard without making him angry. "It was all a bit rushed in Craig's house so I think it may have been left behind."

Mendel stopped eating. "So you exposed the crystal to the light?"

James knew that the wizard could read his thoughts, so there was no point in lying. "We might have done," he answered tentatively.

"Didn't you remember the three things that I told you? You can't begin to understand what we're dealing with here." This was the first time Mendel had raised his voice in such a way.

"It wasn't a case of remembering anything," said James, "since you didn't tell me about those three rules until it was too late! And no, I have no idea what we're dealing with *here*, because you won't tell me what we're dealing with. You haven't explained about the stones on the moor, the stranger, or my dad!"

Mendel replied with a sigh of resignation. "Place the crystal, wrappings and all, into the bath."

As James lowered the heavy lump of crystal into the water, Mendel tried to explain. "The standing stones on the moor, or the Jesus Rocks, as you call them, are actually the ancient gateway I spoke of yesterday. I was sent through this gate from another world called Denthan."

"Another world?" James was still coming to grips with a talking fish, never mind another world. "Isn't Denthan the place I heard the stranger talking about?"

"Most probably."

"So, who is the stranger?" asked James.

Mendel swam towards the crystal. "I'll come to him soon enough. The dice have been cast, James, which unfortunately means that your world and mine are now in terrible danger." Circling the crystal, Mendel looked up at James with his big, googly eyes. "When pointed in the right direction, and on saying the correct spell, this crystal will take us back to Denthan."

"You mean, I need to come with you?" James stared down into the water, hoping Mendel would say 'no'.

Mendel stopped swimming. His gills opened and closed a few times before he said, "I can't do any magic without you, James. You see, now that we've made the connection, our fates are inextricably intertwined."

James was horror-struck. "I'm not sure what you mean, Mendel. Are you saying, whatever happens to you happens to me?"

"In a way, yes," said Mendel.

James bit his lip. "And my dad, how does he fit into all this?"

"My suspicion is that your father was simply in the wrong place at the wrong time. He is gone, but your heart tells me that he is still alive."

"How can it do that?" James knelt beside the tin bath.

Mendel took a moment to consider this. "Well, now that I'm connected to you, I am able to tell that you are still connected to him, just as you are to your mother. I suspect your father may have been drawn through to my world."

James began coughing. He reached for his inhaler.

Mendel waited for James to take his medicine, then continued. "If you help me now, there's a chance that we may find your father. You see, I was sent here, in this form, as a kind of punishment...punishment for something that I discovered."

James thought back to the hideous Sleven and the mysterious, tall stranger. "Did they send you here, Sleven and the stranger?"

"In a way," said Mendel. "But I need to tell you a story to explain it properly."

"Well, tell it then." James sat himself down next to the tin bath. He waited in anticipation as Mendel swam away from the crystal and circled the plastic castle.

"Where I come from," he began, "we were lucky enough to have a kind and noble King called Athelstone. He was loved and revered by his people and all was well until, one day, he went hunting in a great forest called Eldane. While chasing a black stag, the King became separated from his entourage, and although his horse returned, he did not. We searched for weeks but eventually resigned ourselves to the possibility that he'd been killed. Finding no trace of either the King or his clothing we presumed that he'd been caught unawares by some beast of the forest, for there are many dangers in Eldane. Then, two years after his disappearance and quite unexpectedly, I might add, King Athelstone appeared at our city gates. Still dressed in the same hunting clothes, he looked to be totally unharmed."

"Where had he been?" asked James, eager to hear how this story might connect to his dad's disappearance.

"He said that he'd lost his memory," Mendel replied, "but this was not the truth." He looked up at James. "He was, and still is, an impostor, a Hedra wizard called Dendralon Pendragon. Even now, he uses his dark Hedra magic to wear our dead King's skin. He is intent on leading our people to their doom."

"Is he the one...?" began James.

"That you call the stranger?" said Mendel splashing to the surface. "Yes, and he was the one who sent me here, James. We have to get back to Denthan to stop him before it's too late."

"And my dad?" pressed James.

Before Mendel could answer, an irate voice called up from the bottom of the stairs. "James!"

It was his mum.

The surface of the bath rippled.

"It's time for church. Now! And don't force your feet into your new shoes!" she shouted.

James often wondered if his mum was really a witch. She always seemed to know what he was doing. He looked down at Mendel. "I have to go out for a while."

"But you can't!" Mendel protested. "I'm not sure that it's safe."

"I haven't got any choice. Besides, I won't be safe from mum if I don't go right now."

Mendel swished his tail in annoyance. "Be careful. The reason you felt strange when you wandered into the stone circle yesterday was because something else has come through the gateway. Dendralon will have sent others to do his dirty work. He needs to finish me off before I find a way to return and expose him. It was only because of my position in Denthan, my high standing, that he couldn't kill me there. He would have lost the trust of the High Council. He had to settle for a morphic banishment."

"A morphic what?" James shook his head in frustration.

"James, who are you talking to?" His mum was standing at the front door, waiting on him.

"No one, mum," he lied. Mendel continued talking to him as he made his way down the stairs. "A morphic banishment is when you're sent through a gateway in the form of an innocuous creature to live out a pitiful life on some other world. Dendralon will know by now that you are helping me, James. Be careful. Be very careful..."

"I need to go," James answered, a mixture of fear and frustration building in his chest.

Interpreting his words as a question, his mum clipped him round the ear. "Of course you need to go. Idiot. We always go to church."

* * *

As his mum drove the short distance to the church, James felt the wizard's presence fade away until finally all connection with the little goldfish was lost. While James felt some relief at this, he mostly felt a growing sense of dread. He had to get back home again as fast as he could.

As they made their way through Drumfintley he soon saw the familiar red sandstone spire of St. Donan's Church. People were already filing inside the grand building, and as the car door swung open, James could hear Mr. MacNulty thumping out some hymn or other on the pipe organ. Over by the graveyard, he spied his Aunt Bella talking to her cronies, her best Sunday hat sitting perched like a bird's nest on her blue rinse perm.

Seeing them coming, she waved. "Cooeee! James! I've got your favourite crunchy rolls." Then she winked with such enthusiasm that her hat almost slipped off her head.

James, remembering he had to go to her house for breakfast, forced his lips into an unconvincing smile and gave a pained nod. Visiting Aunt Bella meant that indigestion and daggers from his mum were sure to follow, especially when certain bodily noises were impossible to stifle. Even worse were the cuffs round the ear when he tried to drop pieces of half-burnt tattie scone or fried haggis under the table to Edwina, Aunt Bella's smelly dachshund.

He sighed. Aunt Bella's attempt at kindness was bad enough. Worse, though, was the way people at church acted around them since his dad's disappearance. They were all sympathy, smiles and smarm, and too many of them not meaning a bit of it.

"Are you coping alright? Do you need anything?" People always asked James's mum the same thing and she always said the same thing in response, "Fine, fine, we're fine."

Things weren't fine and his mum *did* need stuff, but she was far too angry and proud to admit it. Most of that pride and anger came from her conviction that James's dad had gone off with some other woman, leaving her to deal with the embarrassment. By now her anger toward his dad had grown to such proportions that she seemed ready to lose it. James could only hope that she was able to hold it together long enough to get through church and lunch.

So far, so good, he thought when he saw his mum stop to talk to Father Michael.

It was while the vicar was nattering to his mum, that James noticed something strange. High above him, at the top of the church tower, something moved beside the gargoyle. *Perhaps it's just a bird*, he told himself. But when he heard a strange creaking sound and saw pieces of dirt and dust drift down onto the churchgoers below, he stepped back for a better look.

Concentrating hard, he screwed up his eyes and focused on the massive gargoyle that sat on the west face of the tower. After a long moment, James was just about to move on when the stone creature shifted. James almost screamed out loud, clapping a hand over his mouth just in time.

His mum threw him a withering glance and then continued her conversation.

James tried not to look up for a few seconds, but when he did, he saw the gargoyle's head twitch as its surface changed from unyielding stone into soft, black fur and grey, leathery skin.

For a split second, the morning sunlight caught the movement of its broad shoulders as it edged itself over the parapet, trembling with the newness of life, quite shocked to be alive.

Not as shocked as the churchgoers would be if they looked up, thought James. But none of them did. Not a single one of them seemed to notice the dust raining down on their heads. No one saw the animal crawling head first, like some giant bat, straight down the west wall of the church tower.

"Mum," James interrupted, grabbing her hand. "Mum, I think we should…"

His mum's deep brown eyes blazed with fury. "James! Don't be so rude. Can't you see I'm talking to Father Michael?"

The vicar, a small man in his forties, smiled down at James and continued to listen as his mum.

James couldn't believe it. Although the gargoyle was about the same size as the tiger he'd seen at the zoo, it clung, without effort, to the vertical sandstone wall right behind his mum and Father Michael. Its horrible canine face was fixed in a hideous grin and James could feel its dead eyes burrowing into him. A sudden coldness kissed his heart. A million goose bumps raced over his skin, stinging his arms and legs as he watched the gargoyle prepare to jump, its muscles rippling, its small, leathery wings glistening in the sunlight.

Thud!

The gargoyle landed heavily on an old, ivy-covered gravestone directly behind his mum and Father Michael. It rose up on two legs, stretching to the full height of the church door.

Still, no one ran or screamed. Only James seemed to be aware of the danger.

On its hind legs the gargoyle was less agile, but that didn't stop it for long. It soon began to stumble awkwardly towards him, lurching and growling as it moved.

James froze, gripping his mum's hand even tighter.

As the monster grew steadily closer, James noticed the twisted horns that covered its neck. Like tiny, black knives, these spikes pushed out from the creature's fur as it moved, sprouting from its chest and arms as it shuffled closer.

Stunned, James gulped as the gargoyle's wings dropped down under their own weight. Sticky and cumbersome, they grew more engorged with every step.

"Mum!" James screamed, pulling away from her.

Suddenly alarmed, Father Michael tried to stop James from running away, but in the moment of blind panic that followed, James brought up his knee with the swiftness of a third-dan karate champ, and felled the man.

"Uuhhhhhh…" the poor vicar moaned and fell to his knees, clutching his middles.

* * *

Cathy Peck froze in shock while the churchgoers, confused by the commotion, instantly decided that Father Michael had said something inappropriate to his mum and had suffered the consequences.

"Serves you right, you fiend!" scolded Ephie Blake, failing, as usual, to keep her tone subdued.

Father Michael, still unable to breathe, tried to defend himself. He raised a finger, opened his mouth, but only managed a small squeak.

* * *

James was, by this time, more than four hundred yards away from the church. Something inside told him he had to lead the creature away from his mum. Good or bad, she was all he had left.

Too scared to look back and too full of fear to wonder or worry about Father Michael, he could only think about the gargoyle. Mendel, the wizard goldfish, had been right. He *was* in great danger.

His chest was getting tighter by the second, and he'd left his inhaler beside his bed.

When he finally reached Willow Terrace his eyes filled with tears. He was so near his home, yet he knew he couldn't go any further. He could barely breathe.

James turned round, preparing for the worst.

But there was nothing there.

Where is it? He wondered, frantically searching the road. There was no sign of a snarling face, no jagged quill-like spikes. Nothing.

There was no sign of any mass terror back at the church either.

The monster had disappeared.

Then, above him, he heard the flapping of wings. Beyond exhaustion, James couldn't bring himself to look up.

There was a loud scream. A rush of air hit his face. His chest burned in agony. His head pounded. Through a fog, he heard himself say, "Stwwwonerwwighwwtww!"

He felt dizzy and sick.

"James! James…!" His mum's voice called out from somewhere in the distance. "Jamzzzz…"

A black mist smothered his senses.

CHAPTER SIX

THE JOURNEY BEGINS

Even standing outside, Cathy Peck could hear Joe and Helen Harrison, Craig's younger brother and sister, arguing over which cartoon channel to watch. She pressed the doorbell and listened, irritably, as it whirred, clattered and eventually made a small ding.

She saw Craig's mother, Jean, through the frosted glass and felt a little surge of adrenaline as the door swung open.

"Hello, Cathy!" Jean greeted, a nervous smile spreading across her freckled face.

Cathy didn't know Jean particularly well, but she knew that David was bound to have met her at one of his Scout meetings. Everybody knew good old David Peck.

"It's good of you to stop by!" Jean prattled, obviously unnerved by the sight of Cathy standing outside her door. "I met David recently—at the Fintleyshire Pets Gold Cup. He gave me some good advice on hamsters. What breed to buy, how long they lived, the best kind of cage, that sort of thing."

Bewildered and not particularly interested, Cathy nodded.

"We bought a Chinese Orange as a birthday present for Wee Joe. He called it Mufty," Jean finished.

Nonplussed, Cathy nodded again. "Sorry to disturb you, but I just wanted to know if you had noticed James acting strangely or anything…" Cathy immediately caught the stunned expression on Jean Harrison's face. She looked like a startled hare. Cathy knew why, of course. Her husband "situation" was the talk of the village. "I mean, I expect he…eh…has been acting…, that is… What I'm trying to say is… You know, with his father running off like that, but…" With Jean's wide sympathetic eyes staring at her, Cathy was finding it hard to say what she really wanted to say.

Seeing Cathy struggle, Jean's expression mellowed even more "You look worried. You'd better come in," she said. She led Cathy into the living room and sat her down. She poured some coffee and then eased herself into her chair, all ears.

Munching on a chocolate teacake, Cathy reeled off the church incident, explaining how James had run out of the church grounds after felling Father Michael.

"Why on earth did he do that?" asked Jean, moving over to the drinks cabinet.

Cathy ignored the question. "Then I found James on our steps, unconscious, lying beside a pile of sand. Goodness knows where that came from." She told Jean how she'd phoned Doctor Miller and how he'd said that James was probably suffering from something called Delayed Stress Syndrome. "I even caught him wandering around in the front garden last night at four in the morning.

"Oh, dear," whispered Jean.

"He seems fine now, but I just wondered if Craig had noticed anything out of the ordinary."

Jean placed the bottle of port on top of the drinks cabinet and popped her head into the hall. "Craig! Darling!"

Craig trundled into the front room, and when questioned, explained that James was fine under the circumstances, perhaps a bit hyper, but basically normal enough.

* * *

In number 45 Willow Terrace, James heard someone banging up the stairs.

The voice was familiar. "James, are you up there? Your mum's in our house asking questions about you." Craig barged into James's room and continued, "I only managed to escape by telling them I had to go spray Bero." He held up a can of orange flea spray. "Last week he was just jumpin' with the little blighters. He's okay now, but the mums don't know that." He grinned.

"Well, now that you're here," began James.

"Never mind that. What a classic." Craig performed an over exaggerated bow. "I'm not worthy."

James screwed up his face. "What are you on about."

"I'll need to make a note," continued Craig, "if I ever want un-grounded, I'll get myself straight along to church and kick the vicar in the unmentionables. Brilliant!" He collapsed into a fit of giggles.

"Not funny," mumbled James. He turned round and pointed to his messed-up bed. "Sit down. It's time to let you in on a few things."

"About time too!" Craig complained, glancing at the old, tin bath. "Your mum's right, you know. You've been acting totally weird for the last few weeks but, what with your dad doing a runner and stuff, it's only to be expected."

"He did *not* do a runner!" James realised that he was holding his inhaler like a small dagger. He took a deep breath in an attempt to calm down. "Just listen! Don't speak—if you can manage that—and try to be open-minded." James pulled a green rucksack out from under his bed and headed over to the tin bath.

The floor creaked as Craig followed. "What's that?" he asked, flicking his fingers towards the bath.

James stepped over the remains of several unfinished model spaceships and crouched down. "This is Mendel."

"What! You call your bath Mendel?" asked Craig.

"Don't be stupid. The goldfish in the bath is called Mendel." James already sensed that trying to explain the whole scenario was going to be a disaster.

"Look, this fish," James whispered, pointing down at a clump of plastic weeds, "is Mendel. He's a wizard sent here from another world called Denthan, and he wants us to help him get back." James paused for effect. "Craig, are you listening?"

All at once, Craig's right eye narrowed, his left eyebrow jumped up and his head jerked back. "James, I hate to say it, but I think your mum's right. You're gone man, gone." Craig made little circles with his finger at the side of his head.

James flushed. "Listen. Yesterday I found a weird footprint up on the moor, beside the Jesus Rocks."

"So?" said Craig, already poking his finger into the water.

"Well, it was weird for two reasons really. It was huge with on-ly three toes and it looked as though whatever made the print had crushed a little animal to death."

"So?" Craig asked again, making circles in the water with his finger.

James was getting annoyed with his friend's indifference. "Well, at first I wasn't sure if it was a weasel or a stoat, but…"

"Ah, that's where I can help," Craig interrupted, a sly grin forming on his freckled face. "A weasel is weasily identified, but a stoat is stoatally different. Get it?"

"Hardee-har-har!" James snapped. "You're not taking me seriously, are you?"

"No," said Craig. He dipped his finger further into the cold water of the old, tin bath then began wiggling it around. He paused. "Hey, that's my crystal under there, isn't it?"

"Don't touch it!" James cried, sensing that he was going to need Mendel's help with this. He would never be able to explain everything. "Look, my dad might be caught up in this whole thing."

Craig pulled his hand out of the bath and flicked some of the water onto James's face. "Wake up and smell the roses, James! Your dad's run off because your mum's a psycho-fruit, and you, my Scottish numpty, are losing it, big time."

James tensed as his head began to pound. He heard himself say, "Swnwwakewwwrithewww!"

Craig frowned. "Why are you trying to sound like you're underwater? What the…?"

Suddenly, Craig's hands began to twitch and his forearms started to shake. James saw his friend wince as his skin turned a bright yellow and then yelp when each arm transformed into a twisting, spitting snake. Black tongues flicked in and out of the snakes' yellow-scaled mouths and their fangs dripped pus-coloured venom as they spat and snapped round Craig's horror-stricken face.

"James!" screeched Craig. "Stop them!"

"Eh," James replied nervously, the wizard's voice echoing in his head. "Mendel says they can't harm you."

"What? Just stop them!" Craig looked totally manic. Then, just as James thought Craig was about to pass out, he felt the knocking sensation build inside his head again. "Swwnuffww Swnwwakeww."

The yellow scales turned pink, the snakeheads changed back into fingers, and the writhing, reptilian bodies jerked back into the shape of two, quite normal, arms.

Tiny beads of sweat rolled down Craig's forehead and onto his cheeks as he stood transfixed, staring in stunned silence at James. "What h…h…h…happened?"

James watched as Craig glanced down at his arms before gingerly peering over the side of the tin bath. Mendel was swimming in lazy circles, looking entirely innocent. With little effort, his shimmering orange tail slowly propelled him between the plastic castle and a clump of fake weed.

"I must have caught whatever you have. Or...or...it's some kind of illusion, right? Or a...or a..." Craig gave up and dropped to his knees.

"Now do you believe me?" James knelt beside his friend and stared with him down at the pulsating ball of gold and orange. "This is Mendel. He can do magic and he talks to me. That is, I hear him in my head and, well..."

Mendel chose that moment to speak up. "I believe you can both hear me now."

Craig and James looked at each other.

"Craig," Mendel continued without waiting for confirmation, "everything James has said so far is true. We need your help."

Craig began glancing round the room, searching for the source of the voice. James knew that he was having trouble connecting the goldfish in the bath to the sounds in his head.

Mendel spoke again. "I have to ask you a question."

"Fire away," said Craig, in a shaky voice.

"When you dug up the crystal, did you expose it to the sunlight?"

"No," he lied.

"Did you touch it with your bare hands?" pressed Mendel.

James saw his fins tense.

"No," Craig lied again.

James turned his friend about to face him. "This could be important, Craig."

"Well you never said anything about not touching the bloody thing nor exposing it to the light, did you?" Craig accused, quite sulkily.

"Think. Yes or no?" James knew the look on his friend's face. He'd seen it too many times. James held his gaze, patiently waiting for Craig to crack. He always did.

"Fine! Yes, yes, yes, bloody yes. So what?"

Mendel's voice, when he spoke again, was sombre. "Look carefully at the surface of the water and you will see why this is so important."

James massaged his temples as the knock, knock, knocking sensation began again. The words, "Wwwvisionwwpoolwww," spilled easily from his lips.

In response to his command, the surface of the bath water turned blood red, flashed blue, then transformed into a smooth mirror. For several moments, silver streaks of mist swirled over the surface until a small flash of lightning lit up the water.

They were soon looking down at a crystal clear picture. It showed a blond, messy-haired little boy wearing a pair of brown shorts and a blue jumper that was too big for him. Beside him a tall, solid-looking, blond girl in jeans and a pink hooded sweatshirt, was sticking her tongue out.

"It's Wee Joe and Helen!" Craig exclaimed. "And they're in my room mucking about with my TV! Just wait until I get my hands on those little brats," he growled, clenching his fists. "I could have sworn I hid the batteries for that remote."

In the vision pool, Helen had just snatched the remote from Wee Joe's small hands.

"Mum!" Wee Joe bellowed like a wounded cow. "Mum! Helen has…"

"Shhhh, Joe! Look at me!" Helen pleaded. "Look at this!" Having snatched the remote, it suddenly dawned on her to that there might be consequences. She immediately stood on her head in an effort to reverse Wee Joe's screams of pain to screams of laughter. "Look! I'm a big, fat, farty pig," she said, in a piggy voice. "Ssnnyorrrt! Nkuuk!"

There was a small zapping sound and the picture in the vision pool shifted to Craig's downstairs living room. There, Jean, Craig's mum, seemingly embarrassed by the interruption upstairs, put on a false, posh nanny tone. "Helen, Darling. What are you doing?" Flushing pink, Jean smiled at Cathy and mouthed the word "sorry" several times—a word which, the boys knew, had never featured in Cathy's vocabulary.

By this time, back in the upstairs bedroom, the three-year-old Joe was screaming with laughter, the remote returned to his grubby little fingers, plus two Blackjack sweets and a promise from Helen that he could use her Winky Doll for target practice for the next three days.

With a resigned shake of his head, Craig acknowledged, "Yeah, that's my lot alright." The picture became fuzzy, there was another small zap and the picture switched back to his mum and Cathy Peck nattering in the living room again.

Craig's mum began, "Oh, Constable Watt's alright, just a bit on the keen side. I'm sure he doesn't really think that you had anything to do with David's disappearance, not directly."

Cathy Peck let her teaspoon clatter down onto the saucer. "What do you mean, 'not directly'?"

Jean eased back. "Well, you know what men are like. They need their space and..."

"Space?" Cathy's voice became threatening. "As far as I'm concerned, the sooner James and I move on the better!"

Jean flushed. "I'm sure there's a..."

"There's a perfectly reasonable explanation?" finished Cathy. "For his sake, he'd better be dead. Because if he's just up and left, I'll kill him! Slowly..." she added, twisting the wrapper of her second chocolate teacake until it snapped in two.

"This is better than any TV show I've ever seen," breathed Craig.

James shook his head. "That's enough, Mendel!"

The fish wizard cleared his throat. "As you wish, James."

There was a small flash on the surface, then a luminous digital clock appeared at the bottom of the picture and began whirring through the seconds.

"Just say when!" Mendel pronounced.

"Eh? When!" Craig blurted out.

The picture froze. "Now I'm going to ask the most important question of all: How long?"

James gulped. "What?"

"How long do you want the loop to run?" said Mendel.

"The loo..." James began.

"The time loop," said Mendel impatiently. "Thirty minutes is the maximum. I'll fix it at that." The moment Cathy Peck bit into her second chocolate teacake the picture froze. It was 19:15:01, exactly.

"Now that you've marked the beginning of the loop," Mendel explained, "the seconds will tick by until 19:45:01, at which point time will return to 19:15:01 and begin again. Simple, right?"

"Eh, nope." James shrugged. There seemed to be nothing simple about it.

Mendel appeared to roll his large, fishy eyes. "We need to get to the Jesus Rocks. They're the gateway I talked of, the one that leads to my world. If we don't get there soon, both our worlds could be at risk, especially now that Craig has, rather stupidly, revealed his inner thoughts to our enemy."

James fixed his best friend with an accusing stare.

"By setting this time loop," Mendel continued, "we have given ourselves the perfect alibi. No one will know we're even gone." The wizard looked up from the bath. "I'm just trying to make things a little easier with your parents. I'll look after you. I promise."

James figured it out. It was Sunday, the twenty-second of June, and apparently, until Mendel broke the spell, the half-hour loop would continue to repeat itself. While time repeated itself in the Harrison living room, the boys and Mendel could make their way, undisturbed, to the ancient standing stones on Bruce Moor.

"What about transport?" asked Craig, pointing down at Mendel. "How do we get him out of the bath and up to the Jesus Rocks?"

James looked round his room then reached under his bed until he found what he was looking for. "We could fill this see-through water wing with some of the bath water and put him inside. Then all we have to do is slide him over my arm," suggested James, slowly slipping into a 'maybe that does sound kinda daft' voice.

"I don't think so," Mendel replied.

Craig too looked puzzled by the suggestion. "How would we get him inside the bloomin' thing in the first place?"

"Well, I don't know!" said James defensively. "I guess that's why the stranger, I mean Dendralon, sent him here as a goldfish. Not too easy to get around."

"Not too easy at all," Mendel agreed. "But Dendralon had no idea I would meet you two."

"Sounds like an anti-dandruff shampoo," Craig remarked.

"I'm sorry?" The little fish pushed to the surface.

"Dendralon," said Craig, "It sounds like something Mum would buy. 'Dendralon, guaranteed to revitalise limp and lanky hair!'" Craig grinned. "You've got to laugh, haven't you?"

Before James could explain that it was no laughing matter, they all stopped talking. Something was moving on the stairs outside James's bedroom.

Bang! Thump!

James spun round.

Craig shouted out. "Bero! It's only Bero. He must have followed me here."

Bero lumbered over to Craig and licked his face.

"Yuck," Craig sputtered. "Your breath stinks, ye old fur ball."

In response, Bero wagged his tail even more vigorously than before. Soon his whole back end joined in on the reunion celebration. His big paws dug into the pine floor, shaking the ornaments and pictures.

"There is another way," said Mendel, cutting through the racket, "I could Mind Merge with the dog."

"No you could not!" protested Craig. "I'm not having a half fish, half dog pet. And... and I bet it would hurt him too." All three of them, including Bero, looked down into the tin bath in disgust.

"I've got it!" cried James. "What about Mum's brandy barrel?"

"What?" Craig looked down at James. "You're being a numpty again."

"No, I'm not. Dad brought the barrel back from Switzerland. He'd been on one of his trips abroad. You know, she actually threw it at him, along with her wedding rings and his coat. One of the rings hit him in the eye."

Craig looked over at James. "And you still wonder why your dad has beat it?"

James ignored him. "Bero could wear it round his neck and come with us. Like one of those Saint Bernard dogs."

"And I would be where, exactly?" Mendel questioned.

"You'd be inside the barrel, of course, safe and sound," finished James, a little smile beginning to dimple his cheeks.

This idea wasn't much better than his last, but they decided to give it a try. So while Bero stood still, they strapped the unwanted gift round his big, furry neck.

Inside his new home, a dull, off-brown, plastic barrel, about four inches in diameter, Mendel tested the walls for any leaks or holes. "I suppose it will do," he admitted. There was even a small piece of see-through plastic, embossed with "Wundadoz Chemicals," against which he could push a googly eye or flick a golden fin.

At first, his little splashing noises made Bero sniff and cock his crooked ear. But after a few minutes, the old dog accepted his new collar and began to wag his tail again.

The boys beamed down at the plastic barrel.

"Let's go," said James.

CHAPTER SEVEN

ANOTHER CLUE

Carrying provisions that included a small tub of fish food, the flea spray—just in case, as Craig put it—and, of course, the blue crystal, James, Craig, Bero, and Mendel all passed through the corrugated underpass that led up to the moor. As they climbed up the forestry track, the sun slipped a little further down the evening sky and the temperature dropped. They were making their way up to the standing stones on Bruce Moor where James had panicked the day before and where Craig had found the blue crystal.

James and Craig knew them as the Jesus Rocks, as did everyone hereabouts. Long ago, some spiritual vandal had painted "Jesus Saves" on the side of the biggest standing stone. Oddly enough, through the years, someone always refreshed the paint whenever the words faded or became obscured by moss and ferns. Hence, the name 'Jesus Rocks' had stuck for the five-thousand-year-old, higgledy-piggledy gathering of stones on the moor.

Still bathed in the summer sunlight, Drumfintley lay below the stones, spread out like a miniature patchwork quilt. The moss-covered houses, the church—missing one gargoyle—and the little green and white village hall were all tinged with an eerie mist that had drifted up from Loch Echty.

James saw a big lumbering heron heading towards St. Donan's church spire on its way to Loch Echty. He was sure that this was the second time he'd seen the same bird flying overhead in exactly the same manner as before. What's more, although they'd been walking for at least an hour, the sun didn't seem to have made much progress across the summer blue sky. It had dropped closer to the horizon but now it was back up again, and, although it had cooled several times, it was now warming up again.

"Weird!" James exclaimed. "The spire, look at the church spire! In about two minutes you'll see that big heron twist away from the rectory and veer upward to keep from smacking into the church tower. Just watch!"

Craig looked down at the spire. Sure enough, after about two minutes, the big grey heron adjusted its flight just in time to avoid narrowly missing the church spire.

"How did you know that?" asked Craig, sounding bemused.

"Quite simple," answered Mendel in stereo, or triploid, if you included Bero. "The Time Loop is now fixed."

James instinctively looked down at the plastic barrel to speak to Mendel. "What do you mean?"

Mendel explained. "When we initiated the time loop, the process set off a reaction that spreads out from the epicentre in the same way that ripples do when you throw a pebble in the water. It's called Nester's Time Loop Paradox."

"You mean the whole world will eventually repeat itself?" asked James, his grey eyes widening.

"Yes, James, that is correct. The thirty-minute loop will spread outward from Craig's front room until everything repeats at thirty-minute intervals. We are now two minutes into the third loop."

"So that means it's seventeen minutes past seven again?" James loved puzzles.

"Well done," replied Mendel.

"That poor bird will be knackered," said Craig, who always worried more about animals than humans.

"Never mind the heron, what about the mums? All that coffee. And all those biscuits!" James sniggered.

"They're gonna be humongous," laughed Craig, his familiar freckle-faced grin growing ever wider.

Ahead, the path ducked into the trees and disappeared amongst the greens, browns and blacks of the forest. It would be another quarter of a mile in the darkness of the wood before the path opened up onto Bruce Moor. It was the first time since the underpass that the boys had left the comforting light of the evening sun. As soon as they entered the shadows of the woods, they began to slap their foreheads and scratch at their bare legs.

"Stupid midges!" cried Craig, snapping off a fern to use as a makeshift fly swatter.

But he was no match for the tiny man-eaters who were already feasting on the band of travellers. From May through October, the nasty flies swarmed and bit their prey, and dusk was one of their favourite times to dine. Although the boys were used to them, they still hated the little terrors with a vengeance.

"Argh!" Craig blurted. "That was a big one!" A small trickle of blood trailed down his bare leg.

Moving faster now, James began to feel nervous. In the dark woods the shadows took on a life of their own, and the old larch trees creaked and moaned like wailing witches. The forest floor was covered with decaying brown needles that felt spongy beneath their feet, the thick layer forever damp in the dank atmosphere of the forest. Even on the brightest day, there were parts of Tank Woods that remained in complete darkness.

"Oouch, ya..." James nearly said a bad word, but slapped his own face to swat a midge, interrupting himself. A little drop of blood began its journey down his left cheek before dribbling into the side of his mouth. "They're not midges!" he exclaimed. "Do you think they're Clegs? I hate Clegs," he whispered, suddenly realizing he was making a lot of noise.

Before Craig could answer, Mendel's voice filled their heads. "Run, boys! Run as fast as you can!"

Shocked into action, the two boys bolted. Even Bero kept up with them; he seemed to be under attack, too. These pests were neither midges, nor the normal blood sucking Clegs that sometimes plagued Scottish forests. Bigger and noisier than either insect, this new attacker's menacing drone was loud enough to fill the entire forest with its threatening sound.

Mmmmmmmmmmm...

Above them, a hundred thousand flicking antennae sensed the miniscule change in temperature caused by the meal passing below and the noise grew louder still. When the nearest tree shed a writhing skin of insects, Bero started to bark at it frantically and the whole wood suddenly came alive. The air was thick with insects.

"Com'on Craig, run!" shouted James. He felt something on his arm and glanced down to see one of the culprits up close for the first time. Looking like no fly he had ever seen before, it more closely resembled a huge, furry moth with curved, jagged teeth. James could actually see the white mandibles searching his skin, testing for the best place to feed.

"Giant moths! Gia…." Craig screamed. But these fearsome creatures were not moths, either. They had long, skinny legs that trailed behind them and shining red eyes. There appeared to be millions of these eyes, and they glowed like devilish fireflies in the black of the forest.

Sensing great danger, the boys tried to run faster, but the monsters swarmed round them, hitting against their faces, making it nearly impossible to make any headway. The continuous drone of the huge squadron of insects filled the boys' heads.

"Mendel!" James shouted, flinching as a soft, warm wing filled his mouth.

"Yuk! Ti! Ti…" James spat out the wing, then pinched the fleshy insect body before the creature climbed back into his mouth. The soft sac burst and yellow fluid, which tasted of candy pear drops, exploded his mouth. "Yuucckkkk!"

"Swwa…" Mendel tried to say the spell, but wasn't able to force the words from James's lips. As the seconds passed, the swarm continued to bite and tickle and deafen. "Swwarmm…"

James couldn't push the word out. Again, he tried, "Swwarmmwwkwwiwwllww!"

James felt faint, but he knew he had to keep going. With only fifty yards to go, Mendel's powerful presence filled his head once more. "Swarmkill!" As Mendel pushed the spell from James's lips, the knocking sensation, a dull, persistent pain from which it was impossible to escape, clouded his senses.

Finally reaching the edge of the forest, the two boys and Bero leapt out onto the Moor. Their flailing legs kicked in mid-air before they landed on a deep, brown, scratchy bed of heather. Rolling and tumbling, they thumped to a stop in one big panting, sweating, drooling pile.

The swarm had disappeared.

My inhaler! thought James, as he fumbled for his rucksack. "Where is it?" He was beginning to panic. "Where's the rucksack?" James looked at his clothes. His jumper was torn, his shorts were in tatters and a mass of tiny cuts covered every inch of his skin. James could see that Craig had suffered too. His thin football shorts had given him no protection whatsoever.

"What was all that about?" Craig sounded dazed and frightened.

"That was Dendralon's work," Mendel answered. "He knows we're coming to the gateway. He is determined to stop us. For the moment, however..." He splashed about in the barrel, "we are safe..."

"Wooow..." Craig whispered. "A talking fish, time loops, and now man-eating moths!" Craig was almost delirious. Then he saw something worrying. "Hey! Wh...what's Bero doing?"

Bero was heading back into the forest.

"Bero!" Craig shouted, close to tears. "Come back! Bero, come..." His voice grew weak as Bero plodded back without pause into the dark forest.

Several birds flew up from the trees; Woodpigeons, Rooks, even a startled Tawny Owl drifted into the air as the old dog retraced his steps.

"Agh!" Craig cried out suddenly. "They're back! Get off!" He slapped violently at his leg, but it was only a harmless green-bottle, drawn to the mixture of blood and salty sweat that covered his legs.

"No, they've really gone," said James, "whatever they were." He coughed and shuddered convulsively before taking a long, slow breath. "Don't worry. Mendel's with Bero. He'll be okay."

"Those birds that flew out of the woods," said Craig, still straining to catch sight of his pet. "Why didn't *they* scram when those mutant moths appeared?"

"Because no one ever seems to see or hear these creatures apart from..." James wheezed painfully, "those who can hear Mendel."

"How comforting." Craig picked a piece of grey wing off of his shoe. At that moment—to the boys' amazement—Bero strolled back out of the forest. His tail twirling like an old propeller. He sauntered towards them and placed the familiar, green rucksack at their feet. Thanks to Bero they had their food, the blue crystal, and more importantly, James's inhaler back in their possession. Grabbing the rucksack, James dug deep inside and snatched the little, blue puffer. He tried his best to breathe out then, closing his eyes, he pushed down on the puffer and inhaled. He held his breath for as long as he could before releasing the excess white mist from his open lips. Feeling a bit better, he looked down at the barrel strapped round Bero's neck. "I could really do with some of your magic again, Mendel."

"We're nearly there, so let's keep moving, boys," said Mendel. "Dendralon knows we're getting close."

"Wait!" James held up his left hand.

Craig sighed. "What now? You've had your puffer."

James bent down and snatched up a piece of green and brown checked velvet cloth about the size of a hanky from the heather. He rubbed it between his thumb and forefinger before flinging it to the ground as though it had burned him. He stepped back, still staring down at the scrap.

"It's probably just a coincidence," said Craig.

"It's dad's lens cleaner for his binoculars," said James dully.

Craig screwed up his face and rubbed his legs. "I recognise it from your room, but how could the police have missed it? I mean, they searched up here for days."

James placed the rucksack beside the lens cleaner and picked up the cloth again. "I have to go back and tell Mum about this. I have to go back and tell the police!"

"Wait!" Mendel sounded concerned. "It could be a trick to delay us. The gateway can only be used at certain times and…"

"Dad!" James shouted, scanning the horizon until his gaze fixed on the Jesus Rocks. He felt a tinge of fear as he recalled his experience on the moor the day before. He felt, however, that today was different. Birdsong was everywhere and he could feel the summer breeze on his face. "Maybe dad's come back," he said.

"James, we have to go now, or it will be too late to save my people." Mendel waited.

"Maybe your dad's gone through the gateway already," suggested Craig.

"Maybe," said James, sceptically. He clutched the green rucksack and looked at the standing stones up ahead.

Somewhat hesitant now, they made their way across the remaining patch of moor and stopped short of the stones. James looked for the footprint and the body of the stoat, but he found nothing to ever suggest that they had been there in the first place. There was, though, a feeling about the standing stones that made him uneasy.

Bero put his tail between his legs and whined.

Craig knelt down and stroked the old dog's head. "There boy, try not to worry. We've got a goldfish to protect us." There was more than a hint of sarcasm in his voice.

The old dog cocked his head and the water in the barrel sloshed to one side. A sliver of gold moved slowly past the little window, until a large, disapproving, fishy eye pressed against the plastic and stared up at Craig.

Mendel was not amused.

CHAPTER EIGHT

THE GATEWAY

Back at Craig's house, Wee Joe and Helen had now watched the same cartoon episode twice, but in the five minutes before the show began they were about to realise, for the third time, that the remote control was dead. The two batteries were missing.

"Where are the batteries?" said Helen, "They were on the bedside table. Right here!" She pointed to the white table, then bent down and scowled at Wee Joe. "Think!"

Wee Joe returned the scowl then smacked her across the face with the remote.

"Agghh…Mum!" Helen shouted downstairs. "We can't find the batteries for the remote, and Wee Joe's just hit me!"

"They'll be wherever you left them," Jean insisted.

"How helpful," snarled Helen. "Not!" She twisted a strand of her bobbed, blond hair round her finger in frustration. "Joe, you're a vicious little…"

"Mum!" Wee Joe screamed. "Hewens annoywing me."

"What?" roared Helen, her little freckled nose scrunching up. "You little dweeb!"

Jean stood up, sensing an impending fight. "Helen?" She buttoned her mohair cardigan, looking exactly like a soldier preparing for battle. "Excuse me, Cathy, I'd better go and find those batteries before World War Three breaks out." Jean thumped up the plywood stairs followed by Cathy, who said she would help search.

Jean tried her best to keep her calm. "Helen, have you looked under the beds yet?" she said, in a sing song voice.

Helen shrugged and gave her a puzzled look.

"I'll look in this cupboard," volunteered Cathy. But as she did a shower of toys, games, and dirty washing fell over her head and shoulders.

Mortified, Jean tried to distract Cathy from the mess by asking her to look behind the curtains.

She glanced back to see Jean kneel down and look into her daughter's screwed-up face. "When did you last see them, Helen?"

"I don't know!" cried Helen, shooting her mother one of her death-glares.

Cathy would have landed her one right there and then, but Jean only smiled.

"I've seen dem!" shouted Wee Joe. They'd all been ignoring them. "I've seen dem!" he screeched again in frustration.

The whole hunting party stopped and turned to look at Wee Joe. "Where?" they all asked at once.

"In my dweam," he said proudly.

"What!" they bellowed in exasperation.

"Well, you asked if anyone had seen dem, and I have," said Wee Joe, now in a sulk.

While they all stared at him in disgust, Mufty, the hamster, continued to pile more shredded paper on top of the two, tube-shaped objects that had magically appeared in her cage the day before.

* * *

High on Bruce Moor, James stepped into the stone circle and ran his hand over the fading graffiti on the largest stone. On it, the words, Jesus Saves, were barely visible. He screwed up his eyes.

"I'm starving," complained Craig, digging into James's rucksack. James glared at his friend. "What are you doing?"

"I'm hungry, and so is he!" Craig shook the rucksack in Bero's direction.

"Well, tough luck!" James was still holding his dad's lens cleaner. "Bero can wait!"

"If it wasn't for Bero," Craig growled, "you wouldn't have your stupid rucksack!" Craig was tired and sore, as well as hungry, but a bit of him knew he shouldn't have shouted the last part.

Mendel intervened. "We will eat later. Right now we need to find an inscription." James jerked the rucksack free from Craig and knelt down to look inside the barrel. "You mean apart from the white writing?"

"That's correct," said Mendel.

"But we've been coming here for years and we've never seen any inscriptions." James gave an exasperated sigh. This seemed like such a waste of time.

But after seeing Craig move over to a rock and start to examine it, he decided to give in and follow his friend's lead. First, though, he made sure to tuck his dad's lens cleaner safely into his rucksack.

Together the two boys traced every stone in the circle with their fingers, hoping to find an indentation or an irregular piece of granite. Soon frustrated, Craig banged his fist on the biggest stone. "Nothing. Not a jot."

"Please, keep looking." Mendel sounded calm, but they could tell by the way he kept a googly eye pressed against the window of the barrel that he was worried.

They scraped the moss away from the base of the stones, and even climbed on top to see if there was anything there. Bero dug too, snuffling round the bottom of the stones and scraping at the wiry heather. But still they found nothing.

"I thought the crystal was the key," James grumbled, staring at his scraped knuckles.

"Let me explain," said Mendel. "We have the blue crystal key and I know in which direction it has to be set." James followed Mendel's gaze as he adjusted the angle of his golden eye against the little window. "North-by-North-East," continued Mendel.

"You mean toward Ben Larvach?" asked James.

"Indeed," agreed Mendel, "but we also need the correct incantation to activate the gateway."

James lowered his gaze and stared down at the hole where Craig had found the blue crystal.

"The cloth!" exclaimed Craig. "It was wrapped in a blue cloth. Would anything have been written on the cloth?"

"Not as such." Mendel hesitated for a moment then splashed loudly. "Craig, trace the graffiti with your finger again."

"You mean the 'Jesus Saves' bit?" Craig clarified.

"Yes. Is it hiding something?" asked Mendel. "Try looking beneath the letters."

Craig's fingers dug round the faded white paint. "You're right! There are other words, other shapes underneath."

"Show me!" Mendel demanded.

The boys found several more shapes on the stone's surface and transcribed them in the soil at the bottom of the stone. Within the first "S" of "Saves," a smaller inscription revealed itself, "Sevaasuusej."

"Is that a real word?" asked Craig.

"Of course it is," James scoffed.

Craig suddenly looked the way he had on his first day at Drumfintley Primary School, when he'd asked to play football with the local kids. "No chance, Sassenach," had been their reply. Craig's smile slipped to reveal a little hint of sadness.

James recognised the same hurt look he'd seen on Craig's face that first day and felt ashamed of himself for acting like such a know-it-all.

Mendel laughed. "Ha! The incantation was here all along, scribbled on these rocks of yours! Jesus Saves, extended by the more ancient Denthan double vowels 'aa' and 'uu' would read, Jesuusaaves, when read right to left. The word, sevaasuusej is Denthan, although I don't know how you knew that, James."

James felt another tinge of guilt.

"It's Denthan alright," said Mendel. "An old dialect, but Denthan nonetheless. It means 'pass through.' I should have remembered the gateway's password but it's been a good two thousand years or so since I've used this one."

"Two thousand years?" echoed James disbelievingly.

"Two thousand and twenty-two, to be precise," said Mendel smugly. "Now, shall we get started?" Not waiting for an answer, the fish started issuing orders.

Following Mendel's instructions, James placed the blue crystal on the ground and pointed it north-by-northeast, towards Ben Larvach. Then he uttered the magic password they'd just uncovered, in that strange fishy way that meant magic was afoot, "Swwewwvwwaaswwuuwwsewwwj!"

At first, nothing happened. Soon, however, the ground began to shake violently. Within the stone circle, spindly blades of grass began to flutter, caught in a sudden rush of air. Bero yelped as the turf peeled itself back like skin, making a horrible ripping noise. They all tried to jump high enough to avoid the sod as it folded away from the rock beneath, but the sudden movement took their feet away, knocking them backwards onto a clear, glass-like sheet that now completely filled the middle of the stone circle. Lying on top of the cold film of glass, they remained as still as they could, suspended above an inky black abyss that seemed to stretch down below them into oblivion.

Just like the day before, the birdsong stopped and the breeze disappeared. Then something even worse happened. There was a loud bang! A thousand hairline cracks began to spread over the surface of the glass.

"Don't anybody move," pleaded James.

Bero, for some unknown reason, seemed to be enjoying himself. He began to wag his tail, and it slapped hard, *thud, thud, thud*, against the fragile crystal surface.

"Bero! Don't do that…" Craig whispered as loud as he dared.

Crack!

The glass beneath them exploded into a fine dust, and they fell, and fell, and fell…

As they spiralled downwards, helpless, unable to breathe, the bright circle of Drumfintley sky above them flashing ever smaller until it disappeared completely.

As darkness closed round him, James imagined he was looking down at the gaping hole in the centre of the Jesus Rocks. Like someone rolling out a giant carpet, the turf replaced itself and, in seconds, nothing looked different.

Under the deep blue, umbrella sky, the highland breeze flicked trails through the wiry grass. The skylarks sang as they rose up into the air then fluttered back down to earth.

Everything was set back in its proper place.

For now.

CHAPTER NINE

THE CAVES OF DENTHAN

James was the first to wake. He yawned and rubbed his eyes as they adjusted to a faint glow that seemed to be coming from the sand at his feet. "Where are we, Mendel?" he whispered.

"Not where we should be," answered Mendel. "I think we are in some kind of tunnel system that runs under Denthan, perhaps under the great Forest of Eldane itself. Dendralon must have changed the portal position. This is not where I came through."

Craig moaned and rolled onto his elbows. "Dendralon? The hair guy? Where?"

He was about to tag on another stupid question when James shouted out, "Look! Footprints!"

Craig peered down. "Yeah, could be... "

"Dad? Dad!" James stood up, his voice echoing along the tunnel system.

Mendel splashed in the barrel. "Be quiet James. We don't know what dangers may lie ahead." His golden eye pushed against the plastic window and flicked down at the sandy loam floor. "I'm sorry to disappoint you, James, but I'm sure these are the footprints of *Sygentius trolificus*. Don't you recognise them from the moor?"

"You mean Sleven?" James sighed and placed his foot against the prints. "Yeah, I can see that now," he remarked, trying to stifle his disappointment.

"Who's this Slever?" asked Craig. "He sounds as though he's got a drooling problem."

"His name was Sleven," James corrected. "He was a Swamp Troll with size twenty-eight feet and a fondness for squashing stoats."

Craig looked absolutely befuddled.

"But you're not wrong about the drooling bit," James added encouragingly. Craig still looked bewildered.

"Sleven's dead," clarified Mendel.

Craig knelt down to peer into the little plastic barrel. "How can you be sure that the prints don't belong to James's dad? They might be four or five prints together in a clump."

Mendel splashed. "Because, Craig, Sleven was a nine foot tall Swamp Troll with three toes, not to mention the fact that I am an expert at tracks. I can identify over one million…"

"Alright, alright, but James's dad might have injured himself up there." Craig pointed up at the jagged ceiling. "That grass flipped back pretty roughly, you know. It could easily have whipped off a couple of his toes."

Shaking his head at his friend's attempt to defend his reasoning, James kicked the sand until he obliterated the prints.

Mendel responded, "I'm quite sure it was Sleven. It's his master, Dendralon, we need to focus on now. His capacity for evil is unsurpassed, and he will not stop until he saves himself and his Hedra race from certain extinction."

"Great. Can't wait to meet him," drawled Craig.

James threw him a quizzical stare.

"Only kidding." Craig stood up.

"Let's start walking," suggested Mendel. "I'll tell you more as we go."

The boys started down the tunnel, following Bero and the little, swaying barrel. Mendel continued, "Dendralon can use the gateways just as easily as I can, and he may send more than the hapless Sleven or a few Zental Moths next time. I've already explained his trickery to James."

Craig looked across at his friend. "Thanks for sharing everything with your best mate," he said sarcastically.

James protested, "It's not like that. I haven't had the time. I don't even know what a Hedra is yet."

"Sure ye don't, numpty!" Craig shot back.

"I don't!" said James.

"The Hedra are a race of reptilians that evolved, without interruption, from the early Saurs of Denthan," Mendel hastily explained.

"You mean dinosaurs, right?" asked Craig, really starting to regret his involvement in this whole weird experience.

"That's correct. But whereas your planet experienced a global extinction sixty-five million years ago, ours did not." Mendel's voice deepened. "Dendralon's plan is to betray my people. He is determined to save his own race at the expense of all others."

"That sounds a bit mean," said Craig.

Mendel ignored Craig's understatement. "If I could return to my true form, I'd regain the full extent of my powers. Then I'd be able to save my people. But there is only one place in Denthan where I can do that."

"Where's that?" asked James.

Mendel splashed some more, causing Bero to twitch his ears. "Above, in the Forest of Eldane on an island called Senegral, there grows a sacred tree called the Eden Tree. If we ever get separated, you must meet me there."

Craig's eyes widened. "What do you mean 'separated'? I thought you were going to look after us."

"I have every intention of looking after you, but..."

"But what?" asked Craig, anxiously looking back into the gloom.

"Well, it's better to be safe than sorry," answered James, sounding slightly pompous and not really knowing why he'd just said what he had.

"We need to press on," urged Mendel. "We'll discuss this more later."

As they shuffled along in the darkness, the dank roof dripped water onto their hair and clothes. The smell in the tunnel reminded James of old churches—damp horsehair and musty pews, with just a hint of woodworm.

"Which way do we go now?" James asked, seeing a labyrinth of caves and tunnels stretching out ahead of them.

"Follow the dog," Mendel told him.

The boys weren't convinced that Bero would really know where to go either. But they followed the old mutt anyway, through high-roofed chambers as big as cathedrals and through tiny, little corridors that made their footsteps echo until the sound blended into one long clatter. Finally, after much crouching and scraping of skin, they stood up to find themselves in a truly massive cavern.

Craig cricked his neck as he tried to pick out the ceiling. "I bet you could fit the whole of Drumfintley in here."

"And most of Loch Echty," added James, staring round him in awe.

Behind the fearless Bero the boys walked quite a distance into the chamber before they noticed a large door ahead of them that appeared to be glowing even brighter than the sand. Flanked by two oversized torches, the gigantic wooden door must have stood at least fifty feet high, with several thick belts of rusting metal banding across the length of it. As the three of them stood there staring up at the door, they felt the pull of the light drawing them nearer and nearer.

"It's a door!" Craig hissed.

"Duh, you think?" James muttered irritably. He hated it when Craig stated the obvious: it's a lovely day; that's a big tree; it's raining outside. James wanted to shout, 'Of course it's a bloody door!' But instead he said, "Do you feel that?" He searched for words to describe the magnetic pull of the strange amber light. "The way it's drawing us closer?"

Craig reached out for something to hold onto. "Yeah, I can't stop my legs. I don't like this one bit. Mendel, what's happening?"

"Just follow the dog," Mendel dictated. "I think I know where we are." James noted from the wizard's tone of voice that he didn't sound too pleased.

The boys did as they were told, but soon stopped to gape at a huge statue. The stone creature leered down at them, a malevolent frown marring its face. Positioned in a recess next to the giant door, it was almost hidden from sight. Its horned head, James decided, was that of a bull or buffalo. He could just make out a pair of beady eyes, barely visible beneath a deeply furrowed brow.

"Why have we stopped?" whispered Craig, gazing dreamily at the effigy.

"Is it a man or a giant or...?" whispered James.

"*Homo minatorres*, known in the legends of your world as the Minotaur," answered Mendel.

"Looks nothing like a Minotaur," said Craig. "This one's all hairy, and its head looks more like a pig with horns than a..."

"I can assure you," interrupted Mendel, "that it is a Minotaur! A distant relation of yours, in fact."

James tittered. "Look Craig, it's got your ears."

"Hardee-har-har!" Suddenly self-conscious, Craig pawed at a large freckled lug.

Mendel once again ignored them. "Wiped out along with the Neanderthals and many other sub-species, it was branded as a monster and destroyed."

"I can understand the monster bit." James reached out and touched the ugly, stone creature but, as he did, the strange amber light that had drawn them to the door disappeared.

"Why did you touch it?" Mendel roared.

"Why not?" yelped James, startled.

"Always, always ask if it's safe first." Mendel sounded like he was biting his lip in an effort to control his anger.

"And was it?" Craig wondered aloud.

"Was it what?" demanded Mendel.

James looked back at his freckle-faced friend as he rephrased the question. "Was it safe to touch it?"

Creeaak!

"There's your answer!" Mendel cried, his voice barely audible above the deafening, creaking noise that filled the cave. The huge door cracked and creaked as its ancient iron braces stretched. Almost immediately, the air went from smelling like "stale church," which was quite nice, to "stinking toilet," which was not. Frozen to the spot, they stared at the straining door. Several bands of iron buckled away from the ancient wood and the massive, square door swung open.

"Through the door," ordered Mendel. "Now!"

Cracks and bangs echoed round the big chamber like explosions. For a split second, the boys could only stand there and gag at the smell, but when they saw Bero bounding forward, they dashed after him, not wanting to be left behind.

Surprised to find that his breathing was regular and controlled, James felt a rush of energy and power—a power he hadn't felt since Mendel's spell had opened his airways that morning. Despite his fear, he revelled in a feeling of freedom, freedom from the ever-present weight on his chest that had stifled him in Drumfintley.

"I can breathe..." he shouted after Craig and Bero. "I can breathe!"

"Maybe not for much longer, ye numpty!" yelled Craig.

They heard heavy footsteps behind them. Craig tugged at James's shirt and pulled him onwards. The stench was getting worse. They cut round a corner and skidded to a stop. They'd come to a dead-end, a solid wall with three doors set into it.

"Now what?" blurted Craig.

"Go through the middle one!" snapped Mendel.

Bang-slide-crunch. Bang-slide-crunch.

Stone on stone. Something extremely big was moving along the tunnel behind them.

"Quick, push the middle door as hard as you can!" yelled Mendel.

They both leaned against the door, pushing as hard as they could.

It wouldn't budge.

Their fear hung in the stale air like treacle. It slowed them down and cluttered their thoughts.

Bero barked. "Woof!"

They tried again, and this time Bero joined in, putting his full weight against the heavy middle door. As he pushed, his big paws scratched against the grey wood. He panted and yelped and they strained and heaved.

At last, the door began to move.

An ominous shadow filled the tunnel behind them. Two horns stretched along the wall, followed by the distorted silhouette of a big, black, bulky body, a jagged club lifted high above its head. Horrified, they stared at its flickering shadow easing along the wall of the tunnel until massive and lumbering, the Minotaur came into view. Seeing them, it snorted loudly, its' wide, dripping nostrils flaring. More stone than flesh, it leered at them with its black, piggy eyes.

Seeing the beast before them, James felt his legs turn to jelly. Any remaining strength was ebbing away.

"It can't see us," whispered Mendel, "but it can hear your steps and smell your breath." The boys gave each other a wide-eyed look then immediately covered their mouths.

"One last push!" shouted Mendel.

Ignoring their aches and pains, the two boys slammed their backs against the door and pushed with their legs.

There was a loud crack as the door gave. It swung open, and they all shot through, spilling onto the floor on the other side.

Thump!

The door slammed shut behind them.

"Yes," panted James, "we did it." He shut his eyes, but goldfish-wizard's voice cut short his relief.

"Get up! Keep running," shouted Mendel.

As James and Craig hauled themselves forward again, the door behind them burst into a thousand pieces, a giant club appearing through a flurry of wooden splinters.

Bero took the lead, racing round corners until he arrived at a seemingly endless set of stone steps. Without looking back, they all raced up, two at a time, until the boys began to overtake Bero.

"He's not so good on stairs anymore," Craig wheezed.

James could see Bero's back legs wobbling.

"Uurrgghhuu!" the Minotaur bellowed up at them and smacked its club down hard on the bottom step.

Standing about twenty steps beneath them, the monster moved awkwardly as it attempted to place its oversized, clumsy stone feet on the ancient stairway. Growing impatient with this method, it shifted its weight to its back foot, brought the club back behind its head, and threw it.

Whistling up the stairs like a cannonball, the club smashed into the ceiling above them sending a flurry of shattered stalactites down upon their heads.

James leapt aside as debris crashed all around him. Through the roar of falling stones, he heard Bero howling woefully, "Yow! Whooo! Oow!"

And then all went quiet.

Dust hung in the air like a thick, grey curtain, choking and blinding him at the same time. He coughed. "Craig..."

The Minotaur roared up at them, "Uurrgghhuu!"

"Bero?" James's heart pounded hard in his chest. Somewhere in the confusion, not too far below them, James could hear the Minotaur moving. He heard Craig call out, "Bero!" But there was no sign of the old dog, or of Mendel.

James rubbed his eyes and shook his hair free of stones and muck. "Craig, come on!" his best friend was only a few yards away.

Bang! Bang! Bang!

Closer than before, the huge, stone beast moved clumsily below them steadily advancing on them despite its ungainliness.

Realising Mendel had disappeared from his thoughts, James groped for Craig's arm. "Get moving up the stairs. I can see the Minotaur. It...it's crawling towards us."

Through the dust and fallen rock, the Minotaur struggled forward. Although it looked like a mass of moving stone, it stank like something long dead. James winced as the stench of rotting flesh caught in his throat. Yellow liquid dripped from the monster's nostrils and splashed onto the steps.

The boys looked behind the beast for Bero, but their hearts sank when they saw the great piles of heavy stone that littered the stairs.

James clawed at Craig's grey jumper. "I can see a door above."

Craig held back.

"Craig, for Pete's sake!" snapped James.

"Yes, but Bero…!" Craig, looked as if he was about to give up.

James found Craig's hand this time, and he yanked him upright, pulling him roughly up the stairs.

"Move!" James cried out as the Minotaur's giant hand slammed down, right where Craig had stood moments before.

The boys raced up the stairs as quickly as they could. They were making headway again.

"There's a door up here," gasped James.

Having gained about fifty yards on the lumbering monster, they reached the door and pushed it as hard as they could.

It held fast.

"It's hopeless." Craig slumped against the door.

"Get up!" James shouted, taking over. "Look around! Look for anything that might help." He saw something that resembled the font in St Donan's church. James peered across into the still water. "It's a key," he whispered. When he realised that Craig was nearer to it, he shouted, "Get the key, Craig! It's in the font!"

"You get it!" Craig barked back.

James pushed past Craig and put his hand into the water.

"Awch! It's boiling hot. I…I can't reach it." James pulled out his hand and shoved it into his armpit, gripping his throbbing fingers tightly with his upper arm.

The Minotaur crept closer.

Thinking quickly, James pulled off a chunk of damp, brown moss from the wall and wrapped it round his hand. As he turned, about to try for the key again, he saw something that made him hesitate. Two letters had been carved into the back of the door—D. P.

"Craig, look at this! D.P. David Peck. Dad must have been through here, too."

"Don't be a numpty!" his friend grumbled. "It could be Dimple Pukepants for all you know. Just get that bloomin' key!" Craig glanced nervously back and forth between the letters on the wall and the Minotaur.

This time, James plunged his hand even deeper into the well.

"Got it!" he shouted triumphantly, brandishing a strange bronze key.

"There…there's the keyhole, on the bottom left," said Craig, pointing to the spot.

James fumbled with the key as the Minotaur moved to within six feet of the boys.

The key sunk home. It turned.

The door, caught by some unseen draught, flew open and a current of air pulled them through.

Blinded by the incredible brightness beyond the door, they stumbled forward and covered their burning eyes.

The Minotaur roared.

James sensed its stinking mass above them and ducked…

Bang!

As if being blinded wasn't bad enough, the explosion above their heads deafened him. James dived to the ground, his senses numbed.

Fragments of finger and horn covered his clothes. Wincing, James was aware of a descending yellow cloud of dust. He rolled over, still shielding their eyes from the incredible light, and bumped into Craig.

"I can't see!" Craig sobbed.

James dared to open his eyes a little more, but the burning light made him bury his face in his hands for a second time.

Slowly and fearfully, the two boys pulled themselves to their knees, both covered in a sulphurous, yellow dust. Small tear tracks ran over their fingers and down their cheeks like little streams. Behind them, a moss-covered door stood wide open and a trail of dirt and debris disappeared into the blackness beyond.

Realising what must have happened, Craig hid his face in his hands and sobbed hard. James found his friend's mop of dusty blond hair and pulled him close, wondering what they were going to do now. "Craig," he started hesitantly, "I think Bero's gone."

Craig shook his head. "Bero's not gone. He can't be."

James saw the pain in his friend's face. He wanted to comfort him. "We'll go back and look for him." His eyes were acclimatising to the new light and he was beginning to focus on the strange landscape.

He glanced up at the sky and took in a sharp breath. "Craig…Craig, look!"

"What is it?" muttered Craig.

"There are two suns in the sky!" James tried to stand. He wasn't sure if he was seeing things right.

"Of course there are two suns in the sky. This is Denthan," said a voice.

The two boys nearly jumped out of their skins.

"Bero!" They both shouted with joy as, out of the dust and darkness, the old Golden Retriever plodded towards them, his little plastic barrel still intact and his old feathered tail thrashing behind him in a display of utter delight.

"Who is Dimple Pukepants?" asked Mendel, sounding intrigued by the name.

Still half blinded by dust and tears, Craig laughed and told Mendel about the D.P. they'd found carved on the wall inside the cave.

"My dad's left his initials as a clue!" James pushed Craig to the side and knelt down beside the little, plastic barrel. "It's just the kind of thing he would do. Tell him Mendel. Tell Craig that's what it will be!"

Mendel soon dashed James's hopes by explaining that the initials could also stand for Dendralon Pendragon. "I'm not saying it wasn't your dad," he added hastily, "I just think we should consider all the options before jumping to conclusions."

James slumped down and sighed in despair.

Craig shook more Minotaur fragments from his hair. "Why would the grand master of evil, or whatever he is, take the flipping time to scratch his initials on a bit of old rock? You would think he had better things to do."

"When a wizard carves his initials by a doorway or near a ford," said Mendel, "it is a sign that he has set magic in motion to guard that spot. This was a case in point. Don't you see James, that if you hadn't opened the door in time…?"

"You mean you didn't do any magic to protect us?" asked James, stunned.

"Sorry," began Mendel, "but coming through a gateway to another world is quite a draining experience. Besides, there's nothing wrong with getting a bit of luck now and again."

"Luck?" echoed Craig.

"Oh, yes. And the fact that I knew Minotaurs cannot exist in daylight." Mendel's golden fin flickered past the window of the barrel as he somersaulted inside. "Oh, it's good to be back home in Denthan!"

James could almost hear Mendel smile.

Brushing themselves down, they stared, once again, at the breathtaking views before them. The two suns threw a wondrous light over a beautiful land. Blue mountains rose in the distance, higher than any James had ever imagined, and an immense forest filled with peculiar looking trees and vines stretched on and on as far as they could see.

They had made it to Denthan...wherever that was.

CHAPTER TEN

DRUMFINTLEY AND THE CLUES

It was Trinity Sunday and the twenty-four hour clock on the crusty-brown oven had just clicked over to 17:15. Father Michael was having a bad day. Things were not going well, not well at all. Having taken his position as Priest-in-Charge only nine months ago, he was struggling with the depressingly low attendance at the eleven o'clock service and the increasing mountain of paperwork in his study. But those problems weren't the worst of it. It was the people in Drumfintley, his 'flock', always suspicious, always thinking the worst.

Everyone here seemed to have a massive chip on their shoulder and it was wearing him down. In his sermons, he had hinted strongly that it was much better to be positive about others, much better to think well of your fellow man. But so far, there was nothing to suggest that his congregation was listening.

He thought he might go for a walk to clear his head. Perhaps he would regain his confidence through some spiritual contemplation, something he desperately needed after the incident with Cathy Peck's son, James. Kicked in the unmentionables in front of the whole congregation. Why? He had startled the boy, but why would the little rotter...?

Clang!

Michael nearly jumped out of his skin. "What the heck...! Mr. MacNulty?"

"Ywes Favar," the voice drifted in through the open kitchen window.

Michael leaned out. "What's that noise...and why are you talking like that?"

"Twalking wike what?" Mr. MacNulty was rummaging through some old bikes and bells in Michael's garden shed.

"Twalking, I mean, talking like that?" replied Michael.

"I cwanny fwind ma teef!" MacNulty struggled to stay on his feet as Patch, Michael's Jack Russell pup, jumped round him in little circles, barking excitedly.

"Patch! Come here! Leave Mr. MacNulty alone." The little black and white pup did a half twist in mid-air, then latched her teeth onto the sleeve of MacNulty's tweed jacket.

"Patch, stop that!" scolded Michael. But the reprimand went unheeded as all three of them became distracted by a large, grey heron flying overhead. Disturbed by the commotion below, the bird corrected its flight, soaring just ten or so feet above their heads, only narrowly missing the church tower as it flapped onward. Watching its antics, both Michael and MacNulty noticed at the same time that something was missing from the top of the west-facing parapet.

"Bwoody Vwandwals!" MacNulty ranted, enunciating as best he could without his teeth.

Michael looked round, shielding his eyes against the evening sun, then stared back up at the tower in disbelief. "What kind of vandals would steal a half-ton gargoyle from a fifty foot tower? They'd need a helicopter."

The combination of Patch swinging from his sleeve along with trying to look up for too long made MacNulty sway, then tumble backwards over a pile of old, paint pots.

Clatter! Bang!

"Eeek! Oow!" An old paintbrush, with solid white bristles, ricocheted off his balding head.

Patch, seemly satisfied, released her grip on his sleeve and scampered back up the garden.

Once she was well hidden in the rose bed, the little dog resumed gnawing on poor, old MacNulty's false teeth.

* * *

The two suns of Denthan shone down on the new visitors: a small boy with a biggish nose and a slight stoop; a tall, skinny boy with blond hair and a myriad of freckles; and an old Golden Retriever with a bent brown ear and a plastic barrel strapped round his furry neck.

James, the green rucksack between his knees, produced his dad's chequered lens cleaner. He teased it between his fingers and held it up to shade his eyes from the intense light. He could never let something rest once he'd set his mind on it. "You can both believe what you want," he muttered, half to himself, "but I know that my dad's been here. I just know it."

Craig and Mendel were both preoccupied. Craig was busy checking Bero's back legs for any damage he may have suffered in the Minotaur's tunnel, while Mendel was busy getting his bearings. With a swish of his fishy tail, he headed for the window. His gills pulsed rhythmically.

"Where now?" asked James, still annoyed with them both.

"Well," Mendel pondered, "I believe we should walk into the trees ahead and look for the path that bears south."

Ahead of the boys, the strange forest seemed to go on forever. Long, mossy strands covered the trees, with only the odd, palm-sized leaf poking through the dense foliage. It looked impenetrable. Where they sat, close to the top of a small valley, there was little or no shade. The twin suns seemed to cancel out each other's shadows, filling the place with a strange, unfaltering light.

"It's just like the kind of light you get on stage," said Craig. "Remember James? Like the pantomime we had last Christmas. The one where you forgot your lines."

"Mmm..." James mused, looking round. Where they sat, the vegetation was sparse and the grass, woody and tough.

Behind them, the moss-covered door had disappeared. There was no sign of the black opening in the cliff, or, for that matter, the yellow dust that had covered them when the Minotaur exploded.

As the boys' eyes adjusted to the light, they began to see all sorts of creatures around them. The first ones they noticed were funny bird-like animals jumping from bush to bush. Resembling small geese with enlarged beaks, they sported red-feathered, vestigial wings that flicked and fluttered about as they clumsily hopped across the ground on two ungainly legs.

"Dodos?" wondered Craig. Shading his eyes, he blinked uncertainly at James. "They kinda look like the ones in your Extinction With Distinction book." He turned to the little barrel. "They aren't dangerous, are they?"

One of the creatures bounced a little closer.

"Not at all," said Mendel. "You are looking at a Quezta, *Queztala invigouralis*. In fact, it shares the same gene tree as your Dodo. But this variety managed to survive and become more successful due to its unique defence mechanism."

"Which is?" James queried.

"Which is to spit Penturic acid at any attacker," said Mendel. "As long as you don't make any aggressive movements, you should be fine."

"I thought you said they were harmless," accused Craig, inadvertently inhaling a floating clump of Bero's fur as he petted the dog's coat. "Phe, phe..." Craig gagged then choked, spitting the yellow fur ball from between his teeth.

The little dodo-like Quezta, along with several more of its inquisitive friends, jerked upright and turned its head to get a better look.

"You stupid boy!" Mendel scolded.

"I only coughed, for God's sake!" protested Craig.

Immediately, four or five Quezta surrounded him. The nearest one, standing only a couple steps away, spat a jet of green acid several feet up into the air. Both boys jumped to their feet.

Mendel splashed inside the barrel. "Don't let that liquid get on you! It'll burn straight through you!"

Alarmed, Craig and James leapt back even more, dancing this way and that, as the Quezta shot green jets of acid at them from several directions.

"Whatever you do, don't run," Mendel warned. "Just walk calmly towards the forest."

"That's easy for you to say," snapped Craig, still darting about. "It just missed my leg."

"Walk!" Mendel's normally rich voice had gained an octave, making him sound exactly like an over-anxious parent. The tone reminded James of his own father. Pictures and memories of his dad flashed through his mind, fortifying him as he struggled to keep himself from running off in a mad panic. A splash of acid landed near his foot and he ended up stumbling the last few yards to the edge of the forest, hoping all the while that the birds wouldn't give chase.

At last, when they got far enough away from the Quezta to feel safe, they stopped and looked back. One of awkward-looking birds, who'd been unfortunate enough to get acid sprayed over his back, was now the subject of their interest.

"Yuk! Look at that poor thing," said Craig, scrunching up his eyes.

"Poor wee things, are they?" scoffed James. "I don't think so. That could have been one of us." He was about to chastise Craig for starting the trouble in the first place, but decided not to bother. They'd been lucky this time, and it was a relief to get into the shade of the forest. He didn't want to stir things up again.

Mendel advised that they put some distance between themselves and the 'harmless' Quezta, so they kept walking for another hour. Unable to see any sign of a path at first, they had to clamber and squeeze through the undergrowth for almost a mile. Despite their struggle, James continued to be amazed that he could breathe so freely in the Denthan air.

"There!" Mendel's triumphant voice filled their heads as they broke through a rough patch. "The path to Gwendral."

"To where?" enquired James.

"Gwendral, the magical city that holds the key to all our survival." Mendel sounded excited. They heard him splashing about beneath Bero's chin. "Stop for a moment, and I'll tell you more."

The boys were exhausted and gladly sat down on a nearby log. "Don't get me wrong," said James, "I'm tired and I want to rest, but I thought you said that we had to get to a place called the Eden Tree?"

"That's right, James, but a little clarification might be expedient at this stage."

"Expedi-what?" queried Craig.

"Worthwhile," explained Mendel. "Can you see the large circle of red on the Eastern horizon?"

The boys nodded.

"That's Tealfirth. It's the larger of our two suns." Mendel sounded sad. "I'm afraid it's dying."

"But you've got one spare," said Craig, pointing to the other smaller sun setting in the West.

Mendel puh-puhed against the plastic window of his barrel. "I have studied supernovas in other galaxies, and my calculations tell me that Denthan will not survive because Tealfirth isn't going to die quietly; it's going to explode. We will have to use the city to rescue as many as we can before that happens."

James frowned. "How can a city rescue you from a world that's going to explode?"

"Gwendral is a huge gateway," Mendel told him, "and could be used to save all those who are inside the city walls by transferring them to another world."

"You mean," said James, "it's like a huge ark?"

"And that's why Dendralon wants to take control of it!" exclaimed Craig.

"Exactly!" exclaimed Mendel. "But there are a few other issues to resolve apart from changing back into my own form and convincing my people that King Athelstone is, in fact, the impostor Dendralon."

"What would they be then…" pressed Craig, teasing Bero's fur, "these other issues?"

Mendel cleared his throat. "Well, we need to get hold of three unique crystals so that we can turn the city into a functioning gateway. The Salt Trolls, the Osgrunfs and the Hedra each have one."

The boys looked confused.

"They are the three most ancient races besides the Manimals, and…"

"Hold the bus!" cried Craig. "We know Dendralon's one of these reptile Hedra things but what the heck are Manimals?"

Mendel laughed. "I am one. But that doesn't really help, does it? We look a bit like you, Craig."

"Poor things." James shook his head in sympathy. "Hardee-har-har," grumbled Craig.

"But with some modifications," Mendel interjected.

"Modifications?" echoed James.

"Well, due to the brightness of our suns, our eyes are different than yours—they are slitted like a cat's and mostly white. Other than that, we pretty much evolved from similar creatures."

"Ooo, scary!" said Craig. "So why can't you do all these things you have to do as a goldfish? Defeat Dendralon, get the crystals and stuff…?"

"I'm simply not as powerful in this form. That is, I can perform my magic much more effectively as a Manimal. And to defeat Dendralon, I will need to perform the most powerful magic that I can muster."

James looked concerned. "And how long have you got before you have to change back into your own form, defeat Dendralon, and get the three crystals you need to operate the ark?"

"To do all three? I'm not sure. A week, a month, a day…"

"A day? Well, that's just fantastic, isn't it?" James slumped down off the log onto the ground. "And you've forgot about number four."

"Number four?" Mendel repeated.

"Your number four, but my number one." James sighed. "I need to find and rescue my dad before this planet blows to smithereens."

Mendel sighed. "Ah, of course."

Craig shook his head.

"What are you shaking your head at?" asked James, weary of his friend's lack of faith.

"You don't even know if he's here," pressed Craig.

Mendel's voice was sharp. "No need to start that now. Let's move on. We have to quicken our pace."

"Oh, come on," whined Craig. "Bero needs a drink, and I'm exhausted."

Mendel released a stream of bubbles. "But it's only ten more miles to the Eden Tree."

"We need to rest!" the two boys shouted in unison.

Mendel appeared in the window of the barrel. "I suppose it'll be dark soon," he relented. "We should be relatively safe here."

"Relatively safe?" James looked into the trees and wondered where his dad could be. He had the lens cloth and he'd seen his dad's initials in the Minotaur's cave. *I hope he's alright.*

As they explored their camp, the woods grew steadily darker, though the twin suns still winked through the mossy hue that laced the barren branches above their heads. It wasn't too cold at this point, and the boys had found a small stream for Bero. They splashed each other with the clear water and, with a sense of freedom, realised that they didn't have to wash or even brush their teeth.

"It feels like we've been running and screaming non-stop since we left my bedroom," James remarked with a grim smile.

"We have," said Craig, grinning as he turned his attention to Bero and Mendel. "Are you absolutely sure we're safe here?"

"The woods don't seem very welcoming," added James.

Bero gave him a quizzical look, and there was no reply from Mendel, so they opened the green rucksack and rummaged about.

"Mmm…" James produced two caramel logs, and they began to munch on them, wondering if Mendel was in a huff at their refusal to go any further, or just sleeping. They drank their juice, ignored the apples, and shared a piece of cold chicken with Bero. James sprinkled some fish food into the barrel and looked down at the goldfish that had taken them so far from home.

"I miss my mum," said Craig as he snuggled into Bero.

"I miss mine, too," sighed James.

Craig shot James a puzzled glance. "But she's always shouting and screaming at you."

"Yeah, I know. But I still miss her." James felt weird defending his mum. He could hear her now in his head, "If you would just behave yourself and keep your room tidy, I wouldn't have to shout all the time!" James looked across at Craig and felt a pang of jealousy. His best pal had a dog to cuddle, and a dad, even if he was in the Navy and a mile under the Arctic Circle. At least Craig knew, within a few thousand miles or so, where his dad was.

As the suns set and the forest darkened, a tremendous racket filled the evening air. Grunts, squeaks, growls, and some totally indescribable noises made the boys feel fearful and homesick. They prayed nothing would appear out of the dim light between the trees. No creature that made the sounds they were hearing now could possibly be good news.

But after an hour, when nothing particularly nasty revealed itself, the din became part of the background noise and they fell into a deep, dreamless sleep.

* * *

High in the main citadel, on a balcony that led off from the main Council Chamber, Cimerato, a young captain in full armour, looked out over the colourful buildings below. The city of Gwendral, bathed in fading sunlight, shone pink and gold above the treetops of Eldane. Each of its spires, studded with glittering gems, stretched high above the cobbled streets below.

In the distance, tiny flying reptiles could be seen spinning down over the rooftops, while fragile plumes of chimney smoke sailed skyward only to dissolve in the evening breeze.

It was still warm in the purple glow of the two suns. The larger of the two, Tealfirth, sunk slowly behind the jagged peaks of the far off mountains to the east of the city. To the west, the smaller sun, Zalion, had almost reached the surface of the Gorton Sea, its reflection shimmering on the still waters. Both suns would set at the same time, and both suns would rise on opposite horizons a full nine hours later.

In the Council Chamber behind Cimerato, discussions about the Hedra, the reptilian race who normally lived in the southern marshes, were in full flow.

The captain reluctantly stepped in from the balcony just in time to see his father, Lord Eldane, come into the room. The important figure stepped forward to stand within a semicircle of scales that fanned outward to face the Chamber. There, he directed his speech to the Council members occupying the ornate wooden seats in front of him. Behind him was an ivory throne where the tall, black-robed figure of King Athelstone sat watching everything as he tapped a gnarled stick on the floor and fidgeted distractedly.

"They have gathered, I'm told, by the thousands," said Lord Eldane, "and are only two days away, or less. They have Raptors and siege weapons." He cleared his throat, then continued, "We have not had to defend our beautiful city for more than a hundred years and we have to ask ourselves, are we prepared to do so now?" His disquieting words echoed round the Chamber with its lofty ceilings and serpentine carvings.

While Lord Eldane had spoken strongly and clearly, there was a trace of wariness in his voice as he turned to face King Athelstone. "My son, Cimerato, has seen all this with his own eyes."

On hearing this, Cimerato walked into the main Chamber and made his way to the throne. The still handsome King Athelstone eyed the young man he'd put in charge of preparing the defences.

"Please carry on, Father," said Cimerato, bowing briefly to his King before sitting down. He was a good six feet tall, his muscles tensing beneath his yellow armour as he placed the tip of his curved sword on the floor. He rested his hands round the leather hilt and took in the scene.

Athelstone shifted in his throne, his long, black hair framing his face. He scratched the skin on his forearm, and then stood up. He, too, was an imposing figure, taller even than Cimerato.

"I think your father has said enough, Cimerato." He grasped Lord Eldane's shoulder causing the old man to wince. Athelstone glanced over to see Cimerato's reaction and smiled at what he saw. "We are running out of time, and the Hedra are at least fifty thousand strong!"

"We still have time!" proclaimed one of the younger Councillors. He stood up and bravely faced King Athelstone. Cimerato watched Athelstone's eyes bore into the young Councillor and knew what would happen next. The poor man promptly shut his mouth as he sat down heavily in his seat, his young face looking pale and wizened. Cimerato felt his frustration build as he saw how the whole Council now tried to avoid Athelstone's gaze. He wasn't the only one to regret the day they'd welcomed their lost King back into Gwendral.

Cimerato remembered how their missing King had appeared back in their city after an absence of two years. Everyone thought he'd been killed or had disappeared for good. Many now wished he'd stayed away.

Cimerato recalled how King Athelstone had blamed Mendel for the evils that now plagued Gwendral, and how, little by little, he'd turned the main families against the wizard, eventually convincing the Council that Mendel had to go. When Mendel in return claimed that their King was an impostor, Cimerato knew something would have to be done. They could not execute him, he had helped his people for too long, but finally the Council agreed to banish Mendel from Denthan for ever. He was sent through one of his own gateways, in a form that meant he could never return.

Strangely, ever since Mendel's banishment, sightings of Tree Trolls and Centides—the giant predatory insects that inhabited the darkest parts of the Forest of Eldane—had increased. This had caused panic and most of the city blamed the Council for being too hasty with Mendel. And now, with a great army of Hedra amassing to the south, the future of the city looked grim. It all seemed very odd, very suspicious. Worse, the Council seemed unsure about what to do in response.

Although Athelstone still looked as calm and serene as he always had, as strong and fit as the day he'd disappeared, there was something about him that wasn't quite right. A few were even suggesting that perhaps Mendel had been correct about the King. Where before Athelstone had been a calm and wise leader, he was now prone to violent mood swings. Indeed, more and more often lately, he audibly hissed with rage when any dissenters dared to cross him. Today was no exception for, as Athelstone set his strange stare on Cimerato, he cracked his gnarled staff against the scaled floor and said, "Come closer, Cimerato, Son of Eldane."

Cimerato had been told of Athelstone's announcement in advance and he dreaded the Council's reaction when they heard the news. He had never truly trusted Athelstone since his return and had almost sided with Mendel, but his father had implored him to stay silent.

When Cimerato was asked to join his father on the scaled semicircle that fanned out from the throne, the Council members began to murmur and shuffle about nervously in their seats. All sound and movement ceased immediately when Athelstone fixed his cold gaze on them.

The King began, "The Osgrunfs have been seen in the east, gathered in a great herd that stretches far back into the Forest of Eldane. To the west, the Gorton Sea bubbles with Salteths and Salt Trolls."

Mumbles and mutterings once again filled the grand Council Chamber.

Athelstone walked forward to the edge of the scaled semicircle on the floor and raised both hands. "I have reluctantly decided that the complete evacuation of the city is our only option. We must leave Gwendral."

The Council Chamber fell silent once more as everyone stared at the King in disbelief.

Cimerato's father, Lord Eldane, was visibly shaken. "I know we discussed this privately, but we can't just abandon our city to the hordes…"

Athelstone's Manimal eyes, white, with a single vertical pupil, flashed with a sudden fury.

"We have no choice, Eldane," Athelstone ground out the words impatiently as he stepped past the old man and his son to address the Councillors. "Hedra, Osgrunfs, Salt Trolls, all marching this way. My information is that they are all determined to take Gwendral. All because of Mendel's stupid prophecies. We cannot defend ourselves properly with only three thousand soldiers to protect the city. Think of the women and children. We must keep them safe." He paused. "I can tell that you are not happy about this, but there is little choice. We can either welcome the idea of living in a new city or sit here and wait to be slaughtered. I have already instructed my soldiers to open the secret tunnels that lead north to Nordengate. We will have to use them now if we want to survive."

When Cimerato saw the look of utter despair on his father's face, he knew that he too would have to challenge the King. Abandoning their great city was unthinkable. Knowing that he was possibly putting his life at stake, he stepped forward to address the Council…

CHAPTER ELEVEN

EETHAN

Having admitted defeat in the hunt for the batteries, the women resumed their conversation in Jean's living room.

"Not in my backyard, not in our school, not in Drumfintley!" Cathy Peck declared passionately. She was onto her favourite subject: the downward spiral of standards at the local school. "If we get the city intake here in Drumfintley, like they say we're going to, I'm sending James off to Balfinty instead. Drumfintley's had it. The place is going to be overrun by bullies and thugs—"

"And that's just the teachers!" Jean finished, biting her bottom lip in an effort to suppress a smile. To distract herself, she returned to the drinks cabinet and grabbed the bottle of port. "A tipple?" she broached.

"No, no. I better not. Well…maybe just the one," Cathy promptly decided. She had never known a day like this, not that is, since her husband's disappearance. One wee glass shouldn't hurt; it might even steady her nerves.

Jean glugged the Tawny Port into a large glass. "I mean, Mrs. Galdinie said we're getting another one hundred kids from Greenloch this year. They're just so…" Jean was a terrible snob. "Well, just so common," she finished lamely.

Cathy glowered at her.

"Oh, dear…" She handed Cathy a large glass, "didn't you come from Greenloch?"

Cathy took a big slurp of Port. "Yes…but things were different then."

Jean quickly changed the subject. "I meant to thank David for getting me the hamster for Wee Joe's birthday."

"Mmm…" Cathy's frown became more pronounced.

Bang!

A deafening thud shook the thin ceiling above their heads and a shower of dust drifted down into their glasses.

"Helen?" Jean immediately stood up.

"Now what? Why is it, any time I'm on the phone or with visitors, they decide to wreck the place?"

* * *

Upstairs, Wee Joe had dislodged the bowling ball from the top shelf of his big brother's cupboard while trying to borrow a game. After the ball hit the floor, something fluttered past his face. It was a funny looking piece of blue cloth that would be just perfect, he decided, for tying up Helen's beloved Winky Doll. He snatched it up and started working on the doll.

That's when things took a turn for the worse.

As he struggled to make a knot—he'd never done one before—his skin began to sting. It felt just like a nettle rash. He frowned. Then, to his amazement, the cloth began to melt and blend into the plastic surface of the doll. When the scrap had disappeared entirely, the toy began to glow a funny, bright blue colour.

Realising something was up, he shouted on his sister who, in turn, shouted on her mum.

"Mum! Joe's messing up my stuff!" She was looking forward to getting him into trouble.

But as she moved closer to see what he was up to, she stopped dead in her tracks. Both she and Wee Joe's mouths fell open at the same time. The Winky Doll, that Helen had once known and loved, had changed into something quite different, something quite unnatural. It was alive. There it stood, in the doorway of the cupboard, blinking and rubbing its eyes. The creature smiled up at Wee Joe and Helen, winking at them and clapping its hands excitedly.

"Mummy!" Wee Joe and Helen called out at the same time as they backed away from the cupboard. They were unsure what effect their shouting might have on the hairy, pixie-like creature. It still bore some resemblance to the Winky Doll, though it was taller and much uglier now.

They watched, mouths gaping, as the little creature's neck and body momentarily pulsated like a boa constrictor swallowing dinner.

When it had stopped convulsing, the doll stretched its arms and legs, just as one might do after waking from a long sleep.

Looking more alert now, the strange creature jumped out of the cupboard and ran past them into the hall. It skidded past the hamster cage and bounded up onto the windowsill, naked apart from a small piece of pink cloth that had once clothed the doll. It sat down with a thud.

Wee Joe pointed as he gave Helen a kick to get her attention. "Wook! Its head is awll flat and squished." The creature was still changing shape.

Helen didn't want to look. She had already seen enough when her doll had changed shape right before her eyes. She trembled and wondered what was taking her mum so long.

"Wheere ees Mendel?" it asked in a high, husky, voice, which faded into a wheeze.

Startled, Helen and Joe took a step back.

"W…w…who?" Helen stuttered, not quite believing that what she was seeing, and now hearing, was actually real.

"You're bad!" Wee Joe pointed up at the creature accusingly, impatiently brushing his overlong blond bangs out of his eyes with his other hand. "You're a gobwin."

"Hee hee hee… Not exactleee, leetle one," it replied.

The hamster wheel stopped spinning and there was a rustling sound in amongst the shredded paper. Wee Joe saw the creature glance across at the cage.

"You better weeve Mufty awone!" Wee Joe warned, "or you'll get a smwack!"

The creature only sniggered.

* * *

Panting from their second sprint up the stairs in five minutes, Cathy and Jean threw the bedroom door open.

"Where are you?" called Jean. "Helen! Wha…?" Jean stopped mid-sentence as she spied the blue-skinned creature, tapping its' heals against the wall under the windowsill. It was picking its nose with a strangely elongated thumb.

"Argghhh!" Everybody screamed at the same time, including the creature.

Everyone, that is, except Wee Joe, who calmly picked up the TV remote control.

The creature, about two feet in height, was a bit shorter than Wee Joe. Full of determination, and lacking any fear, Wee Joe pulled the little blue doll-thing down off the sill by its' left leg and smacked it, full force, in the face with the remote.

All those video games he played were actually coming in handy, thought Helen.

"Eeeeghh! Leetle bratee!" The creature cowered underneath the swinging curtains. "Whatcheee do dat feer? Eeeeghh...!" It whimpered and scowled, baring its little needle teeth at Joe, before fixing its sorrowful gaze on Jean. "Don't let leetle bratee hurt Eethan. Eethan wants to help ees!"

Jean looked at the blue creature with his strangely familiar pink loincloth and checked her empty glass. "What?"

"What?" Eethan mimicked Jean's surprised tone and giggled riotously.

"Mendel, ees used thee Creestal, haseent eee?" he continued, still making no sense whatsoever.

"Who?" Cathy was swiftly regaining her composure. "What are you? Where did you come from? And who is Mendel?"

Eethan looked confused for a second then replied, "Blue Man, Denthan, and ee fish... at dee moment," he added. He broke into another fit of giggles.

Wee Joe was about to give Eethan another smack with the remote, but Jean intercepted the weapon mid-swipe. "No, Joe! It's not nice to hit peop... eh... things."

"I ees Blue Man. Not thing!" Eethan corrected. "Yee know Mendel, so you do. Yeees do." Eethan pointed an accusing, spindly finger at Cathy.

"The only Mendel I've heard of is that genetics bloke..." said Cathy, remembering something from her school days. Then she thought for a moment. "You don't mean that stinking fish James has got in his room? He's in big trouble for that too. Thinks I don't know about it, but..."

"One en dee same!" Eethan clapped his hands and little blue sparks pinged out from his fingertips. "One en dee same!" he repeated excitedly.

"What do you want with a goldfish?" she demanded.

Thoughtfully, Eethan clawed his chin with his long fingers.

When he didn't answer, Cathy snapped, "You can have the stinky thing!"

"Stinkee es nice. Mee likes stinkee!" Eethan slapped his thighs and vibrated with laughter. He plumped down on a pile of boxed games.

Helen began to titter.

Jean threw her a "don't you dare" look.

Cathy thought it was a good look and wondered why Jean didn't use it more often.

"Tell dat goblin not to sit on my stuff or I'll hit him again!" Wee Joe reached for the nearest hard toy, which happened to be a small, wooden sword.

"No!" Eethan and Jean shouted at the same time as Cathy, foolishly, bent down to pick the creature up. Eethan, however, was too quick. Giggling, he ran between her legs and raced down the stairs.

"Bero!" Jean shouted. "Where's Bero?" Neither Jean nor the kids had seen the dog for almost an hour.

"Craig took him for a walk. Went to spray him, or something," remembered Helen, her eyes still on the blue creature as he bolted out the front door.

Jean stopped at the front door with the others and watched as Eethan hopped and skipped down her path. At the gate, he skidded to a halt and smiled back at them. Then, pointing up at the hill above Drumfintley, he squeaked, "You must follow meee! Jeesus Savees!" He motioned them to follow him, then shot off in a blur in the direction of the underpass.

They all stared after him in disbelief, wondering whether or not the whole episode had perhaps been a hallucination. Wee Joe, however, was looking elsewhere. Cathy followed his gaze to see what could possibly have distracted him. There, next to the church tower, a big grey heron was flapping erratically, seemingly off balance as it narrowly avoided smashing into the spire.

It was almost half past five.

CHAPTER TWELVE

A SLIGHT DELAY

It had become extremely cold during the night and a thin layer of frost had covered the boys' clothes. Fortunately, Bero was able to keep them warm enough so that they slept right through till dawn.

Now, however, their teeth chattered and there was a chill in their bones as a bitter morning breeze blew through the trees. Shivering, the boys opened their eyes to see little brown patches on the forest floor. Fingers of sunlight had found a way in through the branches to melt patterns on the frosty earth. All kinds of insects, bigger than anything they'd ever seen at home, fluttered round the giant trunks and burred between the branches. James thought he spotted several of the "moth creatures" that had attacked them in Tank Woods.

"Flateria zentalophus," Mendel remarked, already darting past the little window in his barrel. He'd read James's thoughts. "Harmless enough. Well, typically."

Craig yawned. "Mendel, you know that James thinks you make up all those Latin names and stuff. Don't you, James?" Craig winked at his friend and rubbed his cold, bare legs while Bero's tail gave its first wag of the day.

Mendel pushed an angry eye against the window. He focus on Craig. "They are not Latin names! The nomenclature predates Latin by over twenty thousand years!" Mendel sounded most miffed. "Where do you think Latin came from in the first place?"

"I don't know," shrugged Craig, not caring in the slightest.

"Craig…" James cautioned.

"Zental Moths are only dangerous when they swarm round their queen," snapped Mendel. "They were sent to Drumfintley to scare us off. Dendralon knows that Sleven has failed him so now he will take other measures to delay us, or better still, kill us if he can."

Finished with his lecture, Mendel splashed about more vigorously than usual before finally settling down.

As the suns eased themselves above the eastern and western horizons, the frost on their clothes slowly melted. They were walking again, heading for the Eden Tree. Peculiar puddles of fog floated round their ankles, obscuring the forest floor. It made their progress both slow and painful. The boys moaned about their various cuts and scratches as they stumbled onward.

It was James who heard the distant rumbling first. Like far off thunder, the sound rolled, stopped, and then drummed once more. With each boom, the noise grew louder making Bero whimper. He tucked his tail between his legs and flattened his droopy, mismatched ears.

"Mendel, what is that?" asked James, unsure if it was thunder or an earthquake that he was hearing.

Mendel stopped splashing about and listened. "Osgrunfs, I shouldn't wonder."

"Os-whats?" asked Craig, grimacing as a sharp branch jagged his shin under the layer of fog.

"Osgrunfs, which means we need to be ready." Mendel began mumbling to himself and James soon felt the "knock, knock, knocking" sensation that meant magic was a-brewing.

"Swwawwrdlive, Firewwtwwongueww!" he bubbled.

Craig stared at him incredulously.

Then James said, "Spwwearwliwve, Gwwreewwnwwormww!" He sounded out the garbled sounds, though the words, Swordlive, Firetongue, Spearlive, and Greenworm were clear inside the boys' heads.

At first, the fog swirled round their feet in circles, then it began to spark and crack like drips of water hitting hot oil.

Craig looked frightened as the fog rose over him and gathered round his right arm. "No more snakes, please!" he yelped, staring hard at James.

The same crackling fog, however, shot up James's back then wisped down his right arm. It spun faster and faster around his hand. "Mendel!" he cried. "What's happening?"

Craig felt something heavy land in his hand, but it was there for only a second. Feeling as though he was being scalded, he screamed and let it fall.

James was experiencing the same problem as his friend. He, too, yelped in agony and let the heavy object drop from his burning hands. Both boys were almost in tears with the pain.

"Quickly. Put your hands in the stream over there," Mendel directed.

Craig and James both crawled across and knelt down. They plunged their stinging hands into the cold water. To their relief, the pain immediately subsided. Feeling better, they drew their hands out of the stream and peered down at them. In the centre of Craig's palm a picture of a green serpent had been burned, or possibly tattooed, into his skin. On James's palm there was a red bird-like creature with a lion's head. You could see every feather and claw in great detail. It looked incredible.

"My mum will kill me!" blurted James. "She hates tattoos!"

"What a shocker," mocked Craig. "My dad's got one, a big anchor with the letters, 'JC' written below it."

"Yeah, but your dad probably wasn't eleven when he got it!" James started to moan.

"Boys!" Mendel shouted. "We must focus!" The trees were really shaking now, showering them with dead leaves and branches. The fish-wizard's voice was tired, weakened by the magic he had just performed. "The Osgrunfs are getting closer," explained Mendel. Hold up your hand, James, and say the word Firetongue." He directed Craig to do the same, but to say the word Greenworm, instead.

James looked at Craig for a second, then said the strange word. "Firetongue!" About three yards away, the heavy object that he had dropped to the ground shot up from the mist and landed squarely in his hand, settling easily in his grip. It was the most beautifully made sword he'd ever seen. The graceful shape of the red bird-like creature was etched into the dull grey metal of the blade. A lion's head faced toward the tip of the sword, its mouth open as though about to bite, while its mane swept back down the blade, giving one a sense of speed and grace. The creature's tail feathers formed a Celtic helix that swirled down the remainder of the blade and onto the hilt. The handle, covered with soft, red and gold leather, balanced perfectly in James's hand. It seemed to mould itself to his fingers. James knew the sword should be heavy—he'd heard the thud when it hit the ground—but to him it felt as light as a feather.

Behind him, there was another low rumble followed by a resounding crash that made the whole forest shake uncontrollably for several minutes. Finally, the quake stopped and in the relative silence he heard Mendel shout out, "Quick Craig, say your word!"

"Oh…eh. What was it again?"

"Greenworm!" Mendel cried hoarsely, his patience waning.

"Greenworm!" hollered Craig, looking a bit sheepish.

A stick-like object rose from the mist of the forest floor, flew over to Craig, and settled in his right hand. Lifting it high, Craig stared in amazement at the spear now sitting in his hand. It was about four feet long and in the dim light appeared to be metallic green, with a dragon-like serpent etched masterfully on the spearhead.

"I wanted a sword!" complained Craig, a cheeky grin spreading over his freckled face.

"For goodness sake, Craig," Mendel exclaimed. "Just get down!"

Bero, on hearing Mendel say the word 'down', plumped to the ground behind a fallen tree. Craig and James quickly followed suit. Seconds later, the whole forest shook again. This time the deep bass of the rumbling noise vibrated in their stomachs and made them feel sick. Peering out from their hiding place, the boys watched in horror as thousands of hairy creatures thundered past them like a herd of stampeding wildebeest.

There was a blur of steel and hair for about twenty seconds, and then the strange beasts just stopped. Without warning, a stench, which vaguely resembled the odour of putrefying cheese, hit the boys like a tidal wave. It caught at the backs of their throats, making them want to gag. Both boys quickly pinched their noses to shut out the rancid reek and wondered why it was that so many creatures on this world smelled so bad.

Through the rootlets and ferns, they could see the growling mass of evil standing only about ten feet away from them. There were hundreds, maybe thousands, of the creatures. *They look like oversized sloths*, thought James. Their bodies even had the same slouching posture and snub-nosed faces. Long, greenish-brown hair covered their whole bodies. It poked out here and there through openings in their strange armour.

James felt his palms go moist when he spied the Osgrunfs' long, hooked claws. They hung down from the ends of their hairy limbs like grotesque, unkempt fingernails. Amazingly, these misshapen hands managed to hold all manner of weapons—swords, pikes, maces, even double-headed axes. The weaponry chinked and clanged as the panting beasts attempted to get their breath back and prepare for the next charge.

Completely terrified, the boys pushed themselves flat against the forest floor, not daring to move or even breathe.

Clouds of flies buzzed and pestered the Osgrunfs, making them snap at each other in frustration.

A shout cut through the din - "Harka!"

The harsh voice came from a giant of a creature that stood a good head and shoulders above the others. Not only was his crimson armour shinier and in better condition than the rest, it was also more elaborate. An assortment of deadly spikes and hooks jutted out from the elbows and knees. James reckoned that the beast's shield was the size of his kitchen table back home. The creature's spiked axe had to be at least twelve feet long.

This must be the Osgrunf leader, thought James. When he approached, the huge throng made way for him, clanking and clattering as they scrambled to make room. He was very close to the boys now and they both noticed something familiar hanging round his hairy neck. It was a blue crystal, similar to the one they'd left in Drumfintley. It shimmered enticingly in the light coming through the canopy above.

Walking through the ranks, the Osgrunf leader appeared to be inspecting his army's armour and weapons, poking at a pike not held high enough or a badly skewed helmet. Finally, seemingly satisfied with what he saw, the beast took a deep breath and called out once more, "Harka!"

Almost before the cry left his mouth the whole herd—for that is what they looked like to James—began to move as one.

For quite some time, their thunderous charge shredded branches and tore through the undergrowth like a tornado as wave after wave passed the boys' position.

"Well, that was bloody scary!" breathed Craig when the last of the Osgrunfs had finally disappeared.

James stood up and stared down at the red sword in his hand. Cautiously, he tapped it against the bark of the fallen tree they'd hidden behind. He stared, open-mouthed, as sparks of crimson whizzed up amongst the flying woodchips.

"Don't play with that!" snapped Mendel. "If you only knew what you were holding you would…"

"I would what?" challenged James, smarting at the reprimand.

"You would show a lot more respect for things…" Mendel's words trailed off again as the roar of the Osgrunf army faded into the forest. "They're heading straight for Gwendral," he muttered, half to himself. "Dendralon's obviously no fool."

"Hey, that big one had one of your crystals round his neck," Craig pointed out.

"He is called Hushna. He is the crystal barer for the Osgrunfs." He circled for a moment in the barrel. "Dendralon must have tricked them into attacking the city of Gwendral," he continued after some thought. "The Hedra wizard must know how to operate the magic scales. This is not good."

James lifted his gaze from his sword and stared into the plastic window of the barrel. "Scales…? Do you think he's going to try and turn Gwendral into a giant portal using the crystals."

"Very well deduced, James!" said Mendel.

James felt slightly mollified for getting snapped at earlier.

Mendel's voice was unsteady, as if he'd just received bad news. "He needs Hushna's crystal to operate the gateway. But why," he pondered, "has the whole herd gone to the city in full battle armour? What has Dendralon promised the Osgrunfs to lure them to the city?"

The boys had no clue what Dendralon may have told the Osgrunfs, nor what relevance any scales had to the operation of the ark-like city of Gwendral, but they did know that they didn't want to see any of the Osgrunfs, especially the leader, Hushna, ever again. To avoid that, Mendel advised that they wait for the smell and noise of the Osgrunfs to completely fade before moving off.

While they waited, Craig examined his spear. James could tell he was uneasy. He knelt in front of the barrel that hung under Bero's chin. "Mendel, it probably hasn't crossed your mind at all, but I'm not too comfortable holding this thing." Craig tapped the spear against a moss-covered stone. "I mean, I don't really know how to use it and I'm not sure that I want to either."

"What do you mean, ye numpty?" James yelped, swinging his sword. "These are great!"

"Firstly," Mendel cut in, "let me explain where we are. The Forest of Eldane is one of the most dangerous places you could possibly imagine. For over thirteen thousand years this forest has stood between the cliffs of Nordengate, behind us, and the steppes of Gwendral ahead. As the first saplings pushed their way up through the cold soil, long dormant creatures began to stir and venture above ground, the Osgrunfs being one of the first to appear. They were one of the few races that were able to adapt to the bright light. Extremely powerful, they are hated and feared by all, even the Hedra. You will need some kind of protection against them, for we are sure to encounter them again. Secondly, don't worry about using your weapons, as they will do the work for you. If you hurt or kill anything, it will be the work of the magical weapons, not you."

"Oh, and that makes it alright, does it?" said Craig. "Kill, guilt free, or your money back, is that it?"

"Look, my boy." Mendel's voice sounded sharp. "If a Hedra were to pop out of the forest now and attempt to chew your head off, you're telling me you would refuse to defend yourself on moral grounds?"

"So where do the Hedra come from, then?" asked James, anxious to dampen Mendel's anger. He glanced nervously round the undergrowth before lifting up his rucksack. It was time to get moving. Besides, Mendel was starting to sound a bit too much like his mum, and that was never good.

"The Hedra, as I've already explained, are reptilian creatures. They've lived in the southern marshes for many years now. Their correct name is *Hedritica nubula...*"

"Do we really need to know the Latin names for every bloomin' thing?" Craig hated what he thought of as useless details. "I mean, it's all very interesting and stuff," he went on, the bored look on his face belying his words, "but I'll never remember any of it anyway, so what's the point?"

"*Nubulatis!*" Mendel finished stubbornly, ignoring Craig's plea. Splashing his tail, he issued a disparaging, "Harumph!" and fell silent.

"I think he's in a huff," whispered Craig to James.

"Yeah, nice one, numpty," James whispered back.

In silence, the two boys and the dog trudged onward. They followed a faint pathway that headed southeast, toward the small sun Mendel had called Zalion, which was also hopefully in the same direction as the island of Senegral and the Eden Tree. After about a mile of scrambling over fallen trees and jagged vines, James turned to Craig. "I can't believe how great this feels. Back home I could never have made this hike without using my stupid inhaler every five minutes."

"I suppose I just take breathing for granted," Craig replied, suddenly stopping and kneeling down. Something had caught his attention. "What's this?"

James quickly joined his friend. There, amidst the leaves and brush, was a shiny piece of metal. Caught in a slender ray of sunlight, it glinted and winked invitingly.

"Is that what I think it is?" asked Craig.

James felt his pulse quicken. "Yes. Yes it is." James tentatively touched the piece of metal, then pulled it free of the dead leaves. It was a little silver-coloured compass, hinged in the middle, with a sharp pin on one end and a pencil holder on the other.

"It's my Dad's," whispered James, his eyes welling with tears.

"It does seem a bit out of place here," Craig acknowledged. "But you can't be entirely sure it's your dad's, can you?" He sounded almost smug about it, which, of course, annoyed James even more.

"I am absolutely sure it's his," he snapped, "because I bought it for him." He searched out Bero. "Mendel!" James lifted the barrel up until its plastic window was just a few inches from the metal compass. "It took me ages to find him a compass with a brass hinge like this. It's Dad's—the one he always uses when he's orienteering. I've seen him use it tons of times. I just know he's here." James stood up and scanned the forest. "Dad!" His small voice could barely be heard above the general din of screeches and howls that surrounded them.

Mendel floated over to the window of the barrel to take a look. "We don't use such instruments in Denthan, so…" He tilted slightly to stare up at James.

"So?" repeated James.

"So, one logical explanation may be that your father is here after all," admitted Mendel.

"I knew it." James smiled as he sucked on his thumb, having pricked it with the needle-sharp pin. "I was right!" he cried triumphantly. A heartbeat later, he realised that this meant his dad might truly be here in this strange world—a world that was about to blow up—and they had no idea where he was. Suddenly, James didn't feel so elated.

CHAPTER THIRTEEN

THE TUNNELS

After a few moments spent searching amongst the gravestones below the church tower, MacNulty decided that whoever had stolen the missing gargoyle must have had the transport needed to take it away. Really, he had other things to do besides worrying about a stone statue—like finding his teeth, which were still missing. There was also the matter of the Jesus Rocks on Bruce Moor. It'd been six years since he'd renewed the words on the biggest stone.

Giving himself a mental shake, the old man lifted the fresh can of white, all-weather emulsion paint from the highest shelf in Father Michael's garage and prepared to start work. He would continue to take care of things up on the moor, just as his father had, and his father's father before that.

* * *

Father Michael, too, had made up his mind. It was just after five and far too nice an evening to waste at the police station filling out forms. He would report the gargoyle theft tomorrow. Right now he would go for that relaxing walk he'd promised himself, and get in the right mood before bell ringing practice later that evening.

Using his trusty hickory walking stick, he pushed the garden gate open and shouted to Patch, "Here girl!"

Patch lifted her muddy muzzle from the rose bed and bolted across the lawn to join Father Michael. Her stunted tail was a blur as she sniffed at anything that looked remotely interesting. Still just a pup, she almost tripped Michael several times, weaving between his legs and snapping at his heels.

Passing the Peck's house, Michael felt a pang of embarrassment recalling the incident at the church earlier. He noticed a strange pile of sand in the Peck's garden and wondered briefly if Cathy Peck was going to mono-block her driveway. Seeing the sand lying there, a flash of suspicion about her husband's disappearance niggled at him, but he quickly pushed the thought out of his mind.

Things like that just didn't happen in Drumfintley.

Continuing on his way, he had the funny feeling at the back of his neck that someone was watching him. Glancing back, he saw the front curtains twitch at number fifty-four. A brief glimpse of a treble chin told him it was Miss Blake, the churchwarden's sister. *She must have been watching me the whole time,* he thought. She watched everything, taking notes in her little black book from morning till night. He normally felt quite sorry for her, but after today… when she'd called him a 'fiend', in front of the whole congregation, he felt annoyed and hurt. Until that moment, he'd found her quirky, funny, even likable, but now he didn't know what to think. What would make her say such a thing, especially after James Peck had attacked him out of the blue like that? The boy's kick had hurt, but not as much as Ephie Blake's jibe.

* * *

Ephie Blake, wrapped in her favourite pink dressing gown, gripped a pen in one hand and a bar of homemade tablet in the other. Crumbs of the sugary substance covered her face and clothes, possibly because she was struggling to write, eat, and hold the net curtain open with her head, all at the same time. She knew Father Michael was up to no good, and she didn't want to miss anything.

"No shadow of a doubt!" She coughed out some tablet and continued mumbling to herself, "That man is a philanderer!"

"Now, Sis," Kwedgin Blake interrupted, using his most subservient voice, "so far, he's been a good man to the people here and…"

"Do not…" Ephie paused for another mouthful of tablet, "interrupt me when I'm right!" When she saw Kwedgin cower like a child, her eyes narrowed with satisfaction.

"He's after that Peck woman, and her poor husband not even cold!" she snapped.

"We don't even know if he's dead for sure, Sis," Kwedgin ventured. "It's only a missing persons enquiry. He's just missing."

"He's dead, I tell you! And I'm not going to let the new vicar make things worse for that poor woman!" Opening her wardrobe, she yanked out a green-waxed coat and pulled it on. At the same time, she flicked the matted, furry slippers off her feet and adjusted her hair. Heaving a martyred sigh, she rummaged around until she produced a humongous pair of powder blue jogging bottoms.

Kwedgin began to untangle the flex of the Hoover. "Where are you going, Sis?" he asked tentatively.

"Never you mind. Just make sure you vac the stairs and get some of that ironing done!"

"You and Cathy Peck must be related," he muttered as he hauled the vacuum over to the stairs.

"What!" Ephie Blake stared at him open-mouthed.

"Umm... I said you're going to get constipated," Kwedgin struggled, his face reddening. "I mean...eating all that tablet."

"I heard what you said. I am nothing like that woman," she shouted, packing her pockets with several more bars of tablet. "And you're lazy! Sure as fudge. Bone Lazy! Anyway, Kwedgin you're the one who promised to do the ironing."

"I promised nothing of the kind," he argued feebly.

Ignoring his grumbling, she whisked past him and thundered down the narrow stairs in hot pursuit of Father Michael. "Constipated, indeed!"

She slammed the front door shut behind her.

* * *

Loosening his dog collar, Father Michael took one last look down Willow Terrace before turning the corner that led to the underpass. The dark corrugated tunnel had been built at the same time as the dual carriageway and was about twenty yards long. It led to the farm track that wound up the hillside, through Tank Woods, and eventually onto Bruce Moor. The bypass overhead was extremely dangerous, always busy with tourist traffic heading north. Judging by the excessive amount of noise above, today was no exception.

Michael picked up Patch to ensure that the little Jack Russell didn't cut her paws on the broken glass that littered the dank floor of the underpass and made his way down the tunnel. He was almost through, when he stopped in his tracks. There was something up ahead. Frightened, he sucked in a lungful of stale air and rubbed his eyes. He was positive he'd seen a something jump across the patch of light that marked the end of the tunnel.

"I must be imagining things," he whispered to himself, struggling to keep hold of Patch who had become quite wiggly all of a sudden.

With a bark, she managed to wriggle out of his arms and fly up the remainder of the tunnel, yapping and growling until she disappeared into the bright light at the end. Then, two or three seconds later, he heard a sharp hissing sound, and she dashed back towards him. She ran as fast as her little legs could take her, squealing and yelping the entire way.

"Patch?" He tried to catch sight of her in the darkness, but the little dog found him first, jumping straight back up into his arms.

"What was it, girl?" Patch whined and snuggled beneath Michael's black jacket.

Cautiously, Michael moved forward, toward the end of the tunnel. Patch's little heart pounded furiously against his. He almost turned to go back towards Drumfintley and safety, but then regained some courage and walked forward again. He couldn't afford to let the local yobs get the better of him.

He had just reached the opening at the end of the tunnel when a small voice from behind him shouted, "Boo!"

Michael cried out, "Arghh!" He crouched down, squinting over his shoulder.

"Yip! Yip! Yip!" Patch barked and growled up at the roof of the tunnel.

"What's going on?" Michael shouted, spinning round. "Where are you?" he demanded, steadying himself against the cold, ridged wall of the tunnel. "I don't think your prank is funny in the least!" he scolded, trying to sound brave.

"Over heeere!" the voice whispered.

He jerked his head back and looked up at the corrugated ceiling of the tunnel. To his complete amazement, a tiny blue man, wearing nothing except a pink piece of cloth clung to the roof above him. The material fluttered in the summer breeze that wafted through the corridor.

"Neeece to meeet you, Fatheeer!" Michael gulped.

Above Michael and Patch's head, the little, blue man began to dart this way and that, sticking to the corrugated ceiling like a spider.

"Have eee seeen Mendel?" Eethan directed the question at Michael but immediately answered it himself. "No, ee don't sense eet! No."

"Have…?" the little blue man started, then screeched, "Eee!"

* * *

The vicar and his dog had vanished. "Theeys gone!" Eethan dropped to the tunnel floor and began muttering to himself. "Eee…what? What's Mendel done?" He began to titter and clap his hands. "Ah, yes! Loop dee loop…loop dee loop!" Eethan's voice echoed down the metal tunnel, eventually fading into the noise of the traffic outside. He turned and raced up the farm path that led towards Bruce Moor and the gateway known to the locals as the Jesus Rocks.

It was Trinity Sunday and it had just gone a quarter to six.

CHAPTER FOURTEEN

THE CENTIDES

In silence, the boys picked their way through the undergrowth, often passing through golden shafts of light that crisscrossed the forest floor. The occasional giant bug fluttered round their heads before flying off, while unknown creatures continuously slithered out of their way. Large moss-covered roots rising up out of the earth meant they had to scramble and climb more often than not to make any headway. After an hour of hard going, Craig noticed that Bero's back legs were beginning to play up.

"What happened to the path?" asked Craig. He knew that Bero couldn't keep up this pace much longer.

James shrugged and Mendel did not reply. Not even one moody splash or grumpy blub. "What's wrong with you, Mendel? You're not still in a huff, are you?" Craig knelt down and tapped on the barrel.

James slid to halt beside Craig. "He doesn't like that. You know he doesn't," he warned.

"Do you think he knows where we are?" said Craig.

"Of course he does," answered James. "He's probably just sleeping or thinking. You know how he gets." James pointed to a brighter part of the forest up ahead that seemed to be a little less dense.

"There's an opening across there. What to do you think, Mendel? Should we head that way?" James bent down and stared into the barrel, but there was no reply. Instead, his question was met by a drool-laden lick from Bero. "Yuk! You know, Craig, your dog's breath really stinks."

Craig laughed. "Yeah, it's great, isn't it? You know, if I was your dad, I would have gone that way too." Craig pointed to the clearing James had spotted. "We've got your sword and this." He gave his spear a violent shake.

"Hey, watch what you're doing with that thing!" exclaimed James, his gaze still fixed on the bright patch ahead. He sighed. "You might be right. Let's give it a try."

For about a mile, the going was much easier. But it wasn't long before they realised that the trees were growing thicker once again. The forest was becoming even darker than before. They also began to notice large, sticky patches on the forest floor.

Craig prodded the clear, gelatinous goo with his green spear. "Yuk. What is that stuff?"

James shrugged and they continued walking, more cautiously now. Step by step, the number of blobs grew in number, forcing the boys to adjust their stride and zigzag. It was only when James happened to look up that he saw what may have been causing the mess.

Suspended above their heads, hundreds of glossy, black pods hung down from the canopy like giant cocoons. Swaying slowly in the breeze, the pods were held fast to the highest branches by long strands. Mirror-like, the pods reflected the colours and shapes of the forest around them, making them virtually invisible.

James bent down and shook the barrel. "Mendel! Wake up!"

"What...? Be careful!" Mendel's voice sounded both angry and groggy at the same time. "Never shake a goldfish unless you want to kill it," he scolded as he swam up to the plastic window. "Why did you leave the path, James? Why?"

James looked up at the pods. "We tried to ask you, but we thought you must have been tired or..."

"It was my idea," Craig intervened, coming to James's rescue. James gave his friend a grateful look.

"I might have known," Mendel muttered. "Let me get my bearings." The wizard noisily sloshed about before pushing the familiar orange and black eye up against the plastic window of the barrel. James could actually see him squinting up at the black pods to see for himself.

"You dim-witted oafs...!" Even though Mendel could see through James's eyes, sometimes he needed to be certain. "Those are *Scolopendra*. But unfortunately for us, they are of the Denthan variation."

"*Scolowhatta?*" attempted Craig, his freckled nose wrinkled up in confusion. "Sorry, mate, none the wiser!"

"They're Centides," Mendel explained.

"Oh, I see," said James, stupidly pretending that he knew exactly what Mendel meant.

"You haven't got a blinking clue what he's on about, have you?" demanded Craig, squinting at James. He raised his spear and pointed at one of the pods.

However, the weapon shimmered, made a little "puhh" noise, and then vanished.

"My spear!" he shrieked.

"Oh no, not now…" James looked down at his sword only to see it do the same thing. "Mine's gone too!" he said anxiously.

Together he and Craig kicked about in the leaves, searching frantically for their lost weapons.

"You can stop doing that," Mendel assured them. "Your weapons are still close by. All you have to do is say your magic words and your sword or spear will be back in your hands ready for action."

"Whaow!" Craig smiled and clapped his hands.

Mendel flicked his tail. "Shhh! Keep as quiet as you can. We do not want to disturb them."

Peering round them, the boys could see that nearly every tree had at least five or six smooth pods hanging heavily from its branches. James moved closer to the nearest black shape. Its surface was like polished marble and his reflection, bent and distorted, was just like it had been in the Hall of Mirrors at the Easter fair.

The pod twitched.

Craig whispered sharply, "James, did you see that?"

James, his face still only inches away from the pod, appeared not to have heard.

"James. Look ou…"

"Ughhh!" James gasped as black powder shot out of the pod directly into his wide eyes and gaping mouth. A second later, a vicious pair of orange pincers attached to long tentacles burst free of the pod and whizzed past his ears. Without warning, the stalk that ended in the two pincers hit him in the chest and pushed him to the ground. The pincers snaked back over his face and began to close around his throat. Trapping him as they closed, they burrowed deep into the soil on either side of James's neck.

"Ughh! Help! Kuu! Kuuh!" he spluttered, choking from the black dust. Not only was he pinned to the ground, he was struggling to breathe and completely blind.

Bero, the only one not stunned into immobility by the surprise attack, barked loudly, then bounded forward. He sank his teeth into James's sleeve and pulled with all his might. Struggling, the dog shook his furry head and dug his paws deep into the leaf litter. He had managed to move James a couple of inches when a second, much bigger set of black-tipped pincers burst from the top of the pod and thudded deep into the ground at the precise spot where James's legs had just been.

This time, Bero gnawed at the tentacle holding James down by the throat. His sharp teeth made quick work of the thinner appendage.

James sat up. His eyes stung like mad. He was wheezing terribly and felt completely disoriented, but he knew it was up to him now to get away from the pod. Using his feet and elbows, he managed to back pedal while Bero continued to pull on his sleeve. Together, they succeeded in getting another few feet away.

With a tearing sound, the pod ripped from top to bottom spilling its wet, orange cargo, squirming and squealing, onto the ground. Warm, black liquid seeped over James's feet and legs as he slipped and struggled a few more inches away.

Mendel shouted out, "Craig! Say your command word. Say it!"

"I...I...can't remember it. You s...s... You say it!" Craig stuttered.

"You have to!" Mendel screeched.

"Greentongue," he tried. "No...no... Um, Greenbums? Argh! Not even close!" He moaned, then his face brightened. "Greenworm!" The spear magically appeared in Craig's hand just as the fully emerged Centide rose up on several sets of legs. The deadly pest attempted to pull its sharp pincers free of the soil, the segmented antennae on its terrifyingly large insect head flicking and writhing with the effort. Triumphant at last, the giant insect clicked its black-tipped mandibles together and began to advance.

James had slid back a good ten feet by now, but had stopped, unwittingly, directly beneath another swinging pod.

Now armed, Craig ran forward, his spear swinging in a perfect arc before him. With no chance to change his mind, the spear's razor-sharp tip slashed between two orange and black segments, cutting the first giant centipede in half.

An eerie cry echoed throughout the forest as the Centide's two halves thrashed about like headless chickens, spilling black, steaming liquid all over the forest floor. Looking away from the horrible sight,

Craig saw that the second Centide had begun cutting through its pod. Soon its many legs were free from the black sack that hovered above James's head. It was preparing to drop.

Without any conscious command on his part, the green spear shot from Craig's hand and plunged deep into the black sack.

Inside, the creature convulsed, jerked twice, and then stopped moving.

Mendel's frantic voice filled their heads. "Run! Now!"

Craig pulled James to his feet and dragged him along. Hundreds of the twitching pods hung over their heads, heaving and writhing. It felt like they were running through an horrendous children's adventure park, only the obstacles were not squidgy, foam rubber animals, but stiff, shiny pods holding the deadliest of cargos.

"You've triggered an emergence!" announced Mendel excitedly. "Each pod has a receptor, which reacts to carbon-dioxide and temperature change. They're releasing pheromones. They're actually talking to each other!"

The boys couldn't believe it. In the middle of complete chaos the little fish was trying to give them a natural history lesson on Centides.

"You gormless guppy!" Craig screeched. "There's nothing wonderful about it!" He was hauling James along while his spear sliced and stabbed at the creatures reaching down. "Do something, you useless old fart!"

The black dust from the hatching pods was beginning to blind and choke Craig. He was having trouble breathing and he could hardly see a thing. Sharp, poisonous mouthparts reached out, searching for flesh. He could hear them clacking and hissing as, behind them, hundreds of legs fumbled onto the forest floor for the first time.

Craig began to panic. "I can't see! I can't bloody s—"

The ground beneath them suddenly dropped away.

Bero barked as they all tumbled over the edge of a ravine. Landing heavily on their backs, they began to slide on the moss and mud, picking up speed as they fell. Faster and faster, they tore down the slope until... "arghhhh!" they kicked in mid-air.

Just when they thought they were done for, they splashed into something cold and wet and fast moving. It was a river, and unfortunately for them, it was in full spate. Caught in the roaring torrent, they were swept downstream like a bunch of bobbers. Half submerged, the boys and Bero tried to push themselves away from the jagged rocks as best as they could, cutting their hands on the sharp edges.

The cold water soon washed the black, stinging powder from their eyes. They could now see, but they were choking, swallowing water as they struggled and kicked like mad to keep their heads above the heaving surface. After what seemed like hours, but was probably only minutes, they were thrown up onto a small, shale beach. Completely soaked through and numb with cold, they huddled into each other for warmth as they searched the slopes of the ravine. Thankfully, there was no sign of the Centides.

Bero shook himself, giving the boys one last dousing. Less weighed down by water now, his tail began the familiar, silly wag they all knew so well.

James pulled himself further up the shale beach then rolled onto his back. "Craig, are you okay?"

Without looking at James, Craig nodded his head and gave him the thumbs-up. "A little soggy, but I'll dry!" He flashed a familiar toothy grin as he reached out to pet the waiting Bero.

James stared at his friend's hand as it teased Bero's fur. Something's wrong, Craig. Something's missing." He studied Bero for a moment before realising what it was. "Mend...Mendel?" James threw himself towards the big Golden Retriever and felt for his collar. "Where's the barrel?"

Craig's grin faded as the boys looked at each other in disbelief. The barrel was gone. In unison, they started shouting for Mendel, keeping it up until they were hoarse. But there was no reply.

James looked at Craig hopelessly. "Now what do we do?" He was scared. His throat ached and his eyes still stung.

Craig shrugged his shoulders and cuddled into Bero's wet fur. "I shouldn't have called him an old fart," he muttered.

"Maybe not your best idea of the day, no," agreed James.

Craig sighed and flopped back onto the shale beach. "We're in big trouble now, old pal. Big trouble..."

CHAPTER FIFTEEN

THE CITY OF SPIRES

Dendralon closed his eyes and formed a picture in his mind of the Gorton Sea. The immense body of water stretched out toward the western horizon. Like an endless mirror, it merged seamlessly with a cloudless sky. A few small ripples lapped against the dark brown beaches that stretched north and south as far as the eye could see. Only a spattering of islands marred the horizon.

Below the tranquil surface, something moved. In a straight line that stretched over two miles back into the depths, the water bubbled and boiled, the disturbance growing more intense as it neared the shore. Far beneath, thousands of strange beasts stirred. Long lines of Salteth, the warrior slaves of the Salt Trolls, followed their underwater pathways to the shore. Rising to the surface, they snapped and gargled. Soon they would have to depend on their rudimentary lungs to survive.

The Salteth were smallish creatures, about three feet high with had crested heads, tiny holes for ears and smooth, green skin. In their webbed hands, they carried kelp nets and hooks made from sharpened coral. On the shore, they wove in and out amongst their hulking masters, the Salt Trolls, who stood more than twenty feet high. This type of Troll was often said to be the most hideous of all. In the bright morning light, the leathery, skinned giants blinked their great orb-like eyes. Their grey flesh was covered in flaking crusts of salt that dropped off as they walked. They supported themselves on long jagged spears made from the saw teeth of Gnarwhales. The stench of rotting fish that preceded the horde wafted high over the city walls of Gwendral, a terrifying warning of what was to come.

A mass of bodies, they clambered up the wet sand and scrambled over the rocks heading straight for the City of Spires. The bigger Trolls often flicked the puny Salteth out of the way or simply crushed them under foot. High-pitched whines echoed over the beaches as the trampled Salteth squirmed in pain; a live snack for the Salt Trolls, but more often eaten by their own in a few awful moments of frenzied feasting. Swarms of flies hung in a permanent cloud above the sea creatures, drawn to their deathly stench.

Dendralon opened his eyes and smiled to himself. As he had foreseen, the Denthan city of Gwendral was in complete and utter panic. The mass evacuation was gathering momentum.

Hordes of fierce Osgrunfs, some fifteen thousand in number, had already taken over the fields surrounding the city walls.

The dark wizard closed his eyes again, anxious to see more. Centides, just recently released from their pods, had gathered round the edges of the Osgrunfs' camp while several lumbering Tree Trolls congregated at the tree line, wary enough to keep their distance from the clawed Osgrunfs in their spiked armour.

From the south, the reptilian Hedra had pushed north and now covered the entire ridge, south of the main gates, impatiently awaiting their chance to retake the city that had once been theirs. For generations, their need for revenge and their hatred of the Manimals had never faltered. Now, the Hedra looked west towards the sea, to where more than twenty thousand Salteth and their lumbering Salt Troll masters hissed at the skies and shook their bleached spears in defiance.

All was going to plan...

* * *

Back in Drumfintley, all was about to change...

Having run downstairs to put on the children's coats and shoes, Jean turned to Cathy. "That Eethan thing wants us to follow him."

"Yes, but should we take the kids?" Cathy hoped Jean would say no.

"We have to. I can't leave them here alone!" argued Jean, lifting Bero's lead from the hook in the shoe cupboard and stuffing it in her pocket.

"Well, c'mon then, let's get after him," Cathy grumbled.

"What about James and Craig?" asked Helen, her blue eyes still wide with excitement.

"He's got dem!" Wee Joe's comment made them all stop for a second.

"He could be right," remarked Jean.

"Oh, that's just great," said Cathy sarcastically. "I'll check at my house on the way."

They hurried out through the front door and up the path after the little, blue man.

* * *

Meanwhile, Ephie Blake was panting and puffing up the slope towards the corrugated underpass. She'd seen Father Michael disappear into the blackness ahead and wanted to catch up before he got too far. As she sorted her hair, she heard his little dog barking like mad at something or other. The racket was amplified and distorted by the tunnel. She heard Michael criy out.

"Oh, dear, what's happening?" Ephie whispered to herself in blind panic. She called out, "Who's there?"

"Ephie Blake!" a harsh voice called back. Ephie almost jumped out of her skin.

* * *

Cathy Peck had reached the slope that led up to the underpass ahead of the others. She smiled to herself at Ephie's reaction then turned to Jean. "No sign of the boys or Bero at my place."

Still trudging past Galdinie's shop, Jean struggled with her two kids, begging Wee Joe to please walk on his own. "I've carried you for the last two hundred yards. Darling, please!"

"Up on yous head! Up on yous head!" Wee Joe repeated with unfaltering zeal.

"But darling," Jean whimpered. "Mummy's tired!"

Cathy shook her head in disbelief, then turned to see Ephie Blake edging back out of the tunnel. She put her hand on Ephie Blake's shoulder. "Who are you spying on this time, Ephie?"

"Spying, spying? I'm not spying on anybody!" Flustered, the large woman reached into her pocket for some of her sticky tablet, now thankful she'd grabbed a handful of packets on her way out of the house.

As they gathered round the entrance of the tunnel, Cathy saw a small dog run out, heading straight towards them. "It's Patch!" cried Helen.

One second later, Cathy and Jean were back in the comfort of Jean's living room having just put down their coffee and bit into their second "Tea Cake."

The thirty-minute time loop, set by Mendel, had run its course. It was once again 17:15:01 on Sunday, the twenty-second of June.

* * *

Eethan knew how to stop the time loop. Immune to its repetition, he ran up the forestry track and through Tank Woods as fast as any startled hare. Out into the orange twilight of Bruce Moor he sprung, leaping high above the heather as he bounced and scampered onward to the Jesus Rocks. As he ran, his shape changed again. He bore little resemblance to the toy that had given him life. His blue skin shone in the twilight as his fine, downy hair began to slough off, then blow away like dandelion seeds, leaving a little white trail behind him. Stepping inside the Jesus Rocks, he chuckled and muttered to himself as he made his way towards the biggest stone.

For several seconds, he sniffed and scampered about until he found the blue crystal, still pointing towards Ben Larvach. Eethan picked up the shining gem, placed it on the palm of his hand and then waited.

After some time, the crystal, like snow, melted into his skin until, finally, with a hiss, it was gone.

"Uhhh...!" he groaned. This part always stung painfully, but it also made him feel dizzy with exhilaration.

He thought back to the time when Mendel had found him on Hushnish Beach, far to the west, on the Isle of Harris. Outcast and alone, he'd been attacked by his own kind for refusing to drown the sailors who struggled near the rocks.

From the start, Mendel had found Eethan fascinating. The wizard was amazed to see magic flow so easily from the little blue man. A mutual respect blossomed between them and their ensuing adventures had made them the best of friends.

While his thoughts drifted peacefully back over the years, Eethan's body began to shake and change once again. His skin stretched over his muscles and his bones creaked and groaned as they lengthened. Within seconds, he stood his full three feet.

Feeling much better now, Eethan glanced down into a peaty puddle to check on his reflection. His face had returned to its typical

light grey colour. A shock of snowy white hair had replaced the doll's
curly locks and now drooped lazily over his left eye. His body, though
still blue, glittered red and gold in the evening sun.

"Eeeestephie nan ta chee la!" His hand placed on the Jesus
Rock, Eethan shut his black eyes and whispered the phrase twice more.
The third time he said the words, a huge crack of thunder signalled the
end of the time loop. A sudden gust of wind rattled through the heather and bushes as it swept down the hillside. Like an old steam train,
time pushed forward, eventually getting itself back on track. In Drumfintley, the seconds ticked forward once again.

Down in the valley the heron flapped past the church spire for
the fourth time, but on this occasion, instead of starting all over again,
it sailed off into the cobalt sky above Loch Echty. A relieved cry
rasped from its throat and it ruffled its feathers as though somehow
understanding it was finally free from any further delay.

* * *

Cathy, Jean, and the kids were once again at the entrance of the corrugated tunnel. An officious but wary Ephie Blake took her place bedside
them.

Eethan knew that fate required everyone to attend, and he
chuckled as he waited for them all to arrive at the Jesus Rocks.

* * *

In Denthan, everything was also racing towards its rendezvous with
fate. Using the semicircle of stone scales in the Council Chamber,
Dendralon had created a vision pool to watch the unfolding events
outside the city. The Osgrunfs were growing restless, but Hushna, their
giant leader, kept them in check under his "Harka" command. Swarms
of flies darkened the skies above the stinking beasts as they squatted in
the great Plain of Gwendral. Always on edge and eager to charge, they
crouched in their dirty, battered armour and bickered with each other.
Their supplies dwindling and the sight of Gwendral goaded them, filling them with a mixture of frustration and excitement. For over one
hundred years, this high speed, nomadic, berserker army had never
known defeat. They viewed the other gathering hordes with complete
disdain and a ravenous hunger. Fifteen thousand strong, the powerful
Osgrunfs could easily turn upon these lesser beasts and, like a battering

ram, push through any resistance they might offer. If their wait was too long and their patience tested too far, perhaps they would.

Using magic, Dendralon had called Hushna to arms. Speaking to him in a dream, Dendralon told the Osgrunf leader that the gates of Gwendral would open wide for his race, and that all the powers and treasures within would be theirs alone. Dendralon grinned as he watched Hushna looking across at the other armies while fingering the blue crystal that hung round his neck. He had told Hushna that there would be a great gathering of the races and to wait for his signal before acting. Having travelled far and long, the Osgrunfs were ready—ready for battle and for reaping their just rewards.

Satisfied with what he saw, Dendralon turned his attention to the massive Salt Trolls. They had now reached the city walls, their loose skin dropping to the soil in huge lumps as they walked, only to be swiftly replaced by the hardened scales that would protect them from Denthan's twin suns. Huge shark skins, draped over their broad backs and shoulders, were used as a kind of armour and as an occasional food source. Typically, however, whenever the mood took them, they just picked up the nearest Salteth and swallowed the tiny creature whole.

Sintor, King of the Salt Trolls, had dreamt the same dream as Hushna. In his dream, Athelstone had peeled his Manimal skin away from his reptilian face and revealed himself as Dendralon, the ancient Hedra necromancer of old.

As he watched, Sintor was sharpening his whale-tooth spear. He had a blue crystal like Hushna's, but this one was set in a thick bronze bracelet that dug into the scaly flesh round his huge wrist. Dendralon saw him look up at Tealfirth. He knew that the heat would intensify and that the Troll King would not be able to keep his army at bay for much longer.

The Salt Trolls' slaves, the Saltheth, were forever pouring seawater over themselves to preserve their fragile skin, which had never truly evolved a remedy for the burning heat. Ceaselessly, they snapped and hissed at each other in bad temper, their foul mood having much to do with their discomfort and hunger. The situation was so bad that the putrid parasites actually fought each other over the right to eat the Trolls' sloughed-off skin. Dendralon knew that like the Osgrunfs, both the Salteths and the Trolls had no regard for the other races of Denthan and would start to grow restless if the gates did not open soon. In fact, judging by the numerous fights breaking out, it appeared as though their tempers were already close to breaking point.

Dendralon's own race, the Hedra, was a different case altogether. The Hedra King, Feldon, had organized the reptilian creatures into alternating rows of infantry and archers, extending all the way back to the edge of the marshes. To the southeast and southwest of the gates, there were numerous spearmen and chariots to guard the army's flanks. Lookouts had been posted and were constantly scanning for any sign of trouble from the Salt Trolls or the Osgrunfs.

Before he'd donned King Athelstone's Manimal skin, Dendralon had paid a personal visit to Feldon and hammered home to him the importance of victory. Besides Dendralon, Feldon was the only one who knew the truth about Tealfirth; that the largest sun of Denthan was dying. He, too, recognised its flares for what they truly were—the death throws of an ancient star.

Because the Hedra had felt Tealfirth's heat longer than any other race on this planet, it was easy for Dendralon to convince Feldon to follow his plan. "There is space for only so many," he'd explained", and since we were the first to evolve, we should be the first to escape. Our ancestors built Gwendral, and therefore, it is only right and fitting that we and our kind should be the ones to escape and rule other worlds. With my power and magic, we will forge a new beginning."

The three crystals, which included Feldon's own, were all within reach now, and soon Dendralon would be able to shed his degrading, and increasingly disgusting, disguise. Within a day or so, the Manimals would empty into the underground tunnels like the true vermin they were, and the Hedra would take over the city.

CHAPTER SIXTEEN

THE SECOND GOING

At the same time Patch bolted for the exit leading to Drumfintley, Father Michael almost slipped in his efforts to follow the little pup. Breathing heavily, he felt his way along the metal sides of the underpass.

Now that the time loop was broken, Michael was finally able to leave the tunnel. To his surprise, a crowd of people were gathered at the entrance, staring at him suspiciously.

Cathy Peck immediately began to interrogate him. "What's going on? Are you alright? Is Patch okay? Have you seen James and Craig?"

She's like a headmistress on adrenaline, thought Michael, still reeling from his encounter with the little blue man.

"Well," he began. "Well, I'm not sure, really..." He noticed that his hands were shaking. To make matters worse, at that moment a violent rush of air roared out of the tunnel behind Michael, ruffling what little hair he had, spraying everyone with bits of sand, and making the children wince. It blew for several moments before finally dying away, leaving an eerie silence behind.

With everyone staring at him, Michael discovered that he still couldn't find the necessary words to describe what he'd just seen. But as it happened, he didn't have to say anything because Wee Joe did it for him. The little boy looked up at Cathy and asked, "Did the wee blue dolly man bite him?"

"It bites?" gasped Michael.

Ephie Blake stamped her foot. "What's going on here? I demand to know the truth!"

Michael looked on in horror as Patch interpreted the large woman's gesture as a threat and proceeded to sink her sharp teeth into

Ephie's powder blue joggers. Latched on tightly, Patch jerked and bucked as Ephie tried to kick her off, screaming like a banshee. The dog seemed intent on removing the pants altogether, but Michael grabbed the pup just in time and pulled the blue joggers free from her little teeth.

"Unhand me, you fiend!" Ephie shouted at the vicar, struggling desperately to heave her joggers back into place.

"I was only trying to help," protested Michael, blushing a co-lour only a few shades darker than Ephie's bloomers.

"As sure as fudge you were! I know what you're trying to do!" Ephie threw the remains of her bar of tablet at the vicar and gave a little 'ha' of delight when it pinged off his forehead.

"Awch! Why...is everyone giving me such a hard time today," yelped Michael.

"Oh shut up. And as for you, Ephie!" Cathy had dismissed Mi-chael with a flick of her fingers, "Nobody's interested in re-moving your joggers, I can assure you. So shut up and help, or bog off!"

"Now, now!" Michael laughed nervously. This was the most humiliating scene! "Patch, for goodness sake," he cried, seeing the dog go after Ephie again. "Leave Miss Blake alone!" He knelt down and picked up the little Jack Russell terrier.

Jean moved forward and quickly explained that Craig, James and Bero were missing. "We think Eethan has something to do with it."

"Eethan? Who's Eethan?" Ephie demanded to know.

"He's a little blue man!" Cathy answered angrily. "So are you going to help look for the boys or not?" she challenged, throwing Ephie a nasty smile. Everyone knew that Ephie hated her first name.

Ephie blushed and gave Cathy Peck a hateful stare. Giving an irritated sniff, she nonchalantly tried to flick her permed hair back to show she wasn't bothered. In the end, she heaved her joggers up even higher and moaned, "I'll come. Of course, I'll come." She began dip-ping into the pockets of her Barbour jacket for more sweets, only to look up a see that the rest of the group had already moved on. "Wait for me!"

Cathy assigned Michael the task of baby balancing while Ephie, once she'd caught up, held Helen's hand, more for her own balance than out of any sense of duty. Up in front, Cathy and Jean led the way toward Tank Woods. Ahead of them the forest looked dark and forbidding. A woodcock zigzagged low across their path, causing Patch to yelp and pull on her lead.

"Are you sure the boys are up there?" Michael asked, steadying himself on a stone dyke as he rearranged Wee Joe.

Cathy Peck turned to face the Reverend. "We're not sure where anyone is. We're just looking, okay?"

"Eh… What Cathy means," Jean cleared her throat, "is that we think Eethan…"

"De Gobwin," Wee Joe interpreted, helpfully.

"Yes. The blue creature," Jean pressed on. "We believe he said something like Jesus Saves."

"Well, he certainly sounds like a good chap," mused Michael. He nodded his approval and caught Cathy's arm just as she slipped on a moss-covered stone.

Behind him, Ephie muttered, "As sure as fudge," at least a half dozen times in succession. He quickly let go of Cathy's arm.

"Ave you got any den?" enquired Wee Joe. Perched high on Michael's shoulders, he could see quite a bit.

Ephie wasn't too comfortable around children. "Pardon, dear?"

"Fudge!" Wee Joe lowered his hand in anticipation, ready to accept.

"N…n…no!" Ephie lied, slipping her hand in her pocket. She fingered the several bars of tablet.

Although Tank Woods looked sinister, the path evened off a bit, making the going a little easier. Here and there, they saw a muddy paw print and what looked like the marks made by two sets of trainers. It was hard to be sure, though, as the forest floor appeared to be littered with of a mixture of pine needles and dead moths.

They pressed on.

* * *

Further up the hill, Archie MacNulty had just negotiated the little fern-lined path that skirted Tank Woods, when he stopped in his tracks and took a sharp intake of breath. "What the…!"

His gaze had settled on a little, blue man standing, bold as you please, in front of the Jesus Rocks. No more than three feet high, the creature pointed straight at Archie and smiled. MacNulty didn't want to breathe or even admit to himself that he saw what he did. Nonetheless, he stepped forward, his hand tightening round his paintbrush. He checked his poacher's pocket and, sure enough, his favourite ferret, Sarge, was still curled up inside nice and warm. It gave him a strange sense of comfort to know Sarge was still there, not that the little animal would be much good against this thing.

"Don't bee freetened old manie! Eee em also a Gatekeeper. Eee knows eets secrets!"

Eethan's screechy voice drifted across the heather and his odd laugh caused Archie to twitch and spill a large slop of "all-weather" white emulsion paint down the left leg of his tweed trousers. "Aachhh!"

He didn't let it distract him for long, though. His curiosity kindled, he continued to move closer to the little blue creature, flicking blobs of white emulsion off his leg as he hobbled along. "G…g…gatekeeper?" he jabbered, still holding the paintbrush out in front of him as though it were a sword.

Eethan grinned, and at the same time, a child's voice sounded from somewhere in the woods behind them.

* * *

"Der eating me, mum, der eating me!"

"Now, now darling, they're only midges," soothed Jean.

Cathy had taken Wee Joe from Father Michael, out of some sense of latent guilt for the incident with James earlier in the day, and was beginning to regret it.

"I said der eating me." Wee Joe dug a sharp little knee into Cathy's left ear.

"Oh shut up and stop moving about, or I'll eat you!" snapped Cathy. She was too tired to even attempt to be polite about it.

Helen laughed, Jean fumed, Michael cringed, and Ephie continued to toy with something in her pocket. Cathy knew what she was doing, trying to snap off a small piece of tablet in her pocket without the children noticing. *How pathetic*, she thought.

Michael was the first to see MacNulty. He waved and called out to he gardener, "Archie!"

Ephie Blake promptly forgot about her hunger pangs and midgie bites. Mouth agog, she stared at what could only be described as a little, blue man. He had an odd, greyish-coloured face and a shock of white hair. Naked apart from a small piece of pink cloth, he waved gaily at Michael, tittering like some old man "in the know." Next to him stood the church organist, Mr. MacNulty. The old man had one trouser leg rolled up and was holding something in his left hand that looked remarkably like a small, dripping dagger.

"I knew it!" shrieked Ephie. "You've lured me here as some kind of human sacrifice. You're all evil!" The word evil echoed round the standing stones. She swayed and fell back into Michael's arms.

"Oh! I can't hold you. Help. Too heavy!" Michael teetered.

Eethan doubled over with laughter as he watched Michael and Ephie fall backwards onto the scratchy heather.

"What do you mean, too heavy?" Ephie howled as she scrambled free from Michael's grasp and pulled herself to her feet. "Don't you dare paw me again, Reverend! That's the second time…"

Cathy shook her head. "Paw you? Why would anyone want to do that? Nobody's in the least bit interested in you, you daft woman." Scowling, Cathy stepped round Ephie and marched ahead until she faced Eethan. "Where's my James?" she shouted. "Have you got him? Is he alright?" Her voice wavered a bit on this last query.

Eethan considered her questions for a moment. "In there." He pointed to the middle of the stone circle before scratching his head and continuing, "No ees not got eem, and yees; at least, ee think so!"

Cathy frowned. "Don't get smart with me, you…"

The group moved closer to the stone circle, except Archie who had loosened his sopping trousers and was now attempting to remove them.

"What is this?" Ephie screeched. "Some kind of weird ritual? Get your trousers back on!" she ordered.

"Twhere cwovered in pwaint you stwupid wuman!"

"What'd he say?" Jean asked, as she pulled Helen to her and held her close.

Michael answered for him. "It's his teeth. He lost them this evening."

With a curse that came through surprisingly clear despite the lack of teeth, Archie MacNulty pulled his sodden trousers back up again. "Women!" he grumped, swatting the paint off his leg with a clump of heather.

They were all now standing in the middle of the stone circle watching Eethan as he headed toward the Jesus Rock. When he reached the stone, he put his hand on it and looked out towards Ben Larvach.

Cathy noticed that his hand was beginning to glow.

"Ees might find dees a bit strangee, but Mendel and dee boys need us!" Eethan's wispy voice was just audible above Patch's constant yelping.

"Shush, Patch!" Michael picked the pup up, but she wouldn't stop barking. The little animal knew something momentous was about to happen.

"Shut up!" Cathy screamed at the dog and the pet stopped her yowling instantly. Not because of Cathy, but because the grass under everyone's feet was moving, sloughing away from the rock and soil like a banana peel.

As the centre of the circle detached itself from the bedrock, Eethan muttered a strange word that sounded something like,"sausages, or perhaps, sevaassuusej."

He repeated it over and over while everyone else stumbled about, screaming at the top of their lungs as they crashed to the ground. All, that is, except Wee Joe, who clapped his hands and screeched with laughter. "Yippee! Again! Again!"

Completely terrified, Patch bolted out of the ring of stones.

In an effort to avoid standing on the mutt, MacNulty fell backwards, rolling out of the circle and cracking his head on a rock.

Shins and elbows banged and bruised, everyone lay motionless on a huge circle of glass inside the stones, suspended high above a fathomless black void. Patch and MacNulty were nowhere to be seen.

"Everybody needs to geet up and jump up eeen down! Eeh hee!" Eethan's black eyes sparkled in the evening light as he skated from the outer edge of the glass circle to its centre.

Clutching Helen, Jean's eyes widened. "Are you mad?"

"Don't you move an inch!" Cathy shouted. She watched, incredulously, as Ephie shifted her considerable weight in an effort to stand up...

Crack!

"Arrghhh..." they all screamed at the same time.

"Dees es deee best bit!" Eethan stamped his feet on the glass surface and Wee Joe happily copied.

The circular pane, thoroughly weakened now, shattered like fine crystal. In one big whoosh, they plummeted downwards, spinning and spinning, into the darkness below. Air rushed past their faces, masking Ephie's screams and Wee Joe's laughter.

It wasn't long before they were all engulfed by complete and utter darkness.

* * *

Rising to his feet, MacNulty looked round him in stunned disbelief. He wondered if he might be losing his mind. Tentatively, he ventured forward in the dim light. "Ish anyone were?" He waited, but there was no reply. Even though he knew the others were somewhere else by now, he called out one last time, his voice echoing over the deserted moor. "Favwer Michael!" As he reached for the comfort of his faithful, prize-winning ferret's warm fur, he saw two figures emerge from Tank Woods.

It was Sergeant Carr, closely followed by Constable Watt.

"Don't move an inch, MacNulty!" Sergeant Carr ordered, then beamed down at the young Constable. "We've got the old poacher this time, ferret and all!"

* * *

Far away in the blackness, Cathy Peck managed to push a name from her lips before passing out.

"James…"

CHAPTER SEVENTEEN

THE BEACH AND THE HILL

In the Forest of Eldane, two cold, wet, tired boys sat on the shale beach by the river. They'd waited over three hours for a barrel containing a small goldfish to appear in the water beside them, but it never did. Mendel was gone. Exhausted after their lucky escape from the Centides, they finally gave up and settled down with Bero in a copse of ferns and fell asleep.

Hours later, James felt Bero tense beside him. The retriever issued a low rumbling growl. He sat up, immediately hearing what Bero had heard. A distant drumming sound echoed through the forest.

Bang. Bang. Bang.

He shook Craig, and his friend reluctantly opened his eyes. "James?"

James, still half asleep, thought he heard something else. "Mum?" he whispered.

Craig screwed up his face. "Get a grip! It's me, not your Mum, ye numpty! Listen!" Craig pointed into the dense foliage. "That racket's coming from over there."

"But I could have sworn I heard her voice," said James. The sound of his mum's voice, calling out for him, still rattled around in his head, even above the noise of the drums and the rushing river.

James pushed himself up onto his elbows and blinked in the dappled sunlight, a look of sudden realisation crossing his face. "I don't believe it."

"I know. Some alarm clock. It's probably those Osgrunf things again." Craig stood and went over to splash his face in the cool river water. Bero soon joined him and began to drink.

"Never mind that. Where's my green rucksack?" James stood up and looked round in a panic. "We've been so bloomin' busy looking

for Mendel we've lost the rucksack. Craig, check the beach!" The boys
began scouring the shale bank, but there was nothing there. James felt
close to tears. "It's gone, gone just like Mendel and now we are totally
and utterly…"

"No, we're not!" Craig said firmly. "We're alive and so is Bero,
and it looks like you might even find your dad, so don't go getting all
depressed on me. I can't stand it when people get all depressed on
me."

James knew Craig was right, but he couldn't help himself.
Sometimes there was this unbearable weight pressing down on him
that he just couldn't shake off. "I know but…" James froze, an idea
forming in his head. "Craig, can you remember your magic word?"

"What? You mean, Greenworm?" From out of no-
where, the green spear appeared in Craig's hand. It glittered in the sunlight, as beautiful as ever.

James pointed to the river and said, "Put it in the water." Craig
glanced down at James. "What for?"

"Maybe Mendel will sense it," he explained, growing excited,
"or…hear it, or…"

"Let's see." Craig lowered the tip of the spear into the water
and waited. Nothing happened. The river continued on its course, refusing to give up its secrets. Only the distant banging of drums and the
occasional birdcall interrupted the silence.

"Duh. What did you expect?" said Craig, shaking his head.
Crunch!
Something stirred on the opposite bank, something big.

A strange booming call came from the trees across the river,
"Ssslathat?"

James took a step back. "Get that spear out of the water.
Quick!" The hackles rose on Bero's neck as the boys edged away from
the riverbank one step at a time, keeping their eyes on the shuddering
trees. James whispered, "What have you done?"

Craig gave James a withering glance. "What do you mean, what
have I done? You're the gormless git who told me to put the spear into
the water in the first place." Suddenly the whole bank began to vibrate
beneath their feet.

"That's definitely not Mendel," Craig stated the obvious once
again. They watched in horror as the trees across the river started to
bend and snap under the weight of something very heavy.

"Ssslathat?" The strange cry echoed across the river again.

On the far bank, a large moss-covered tree snapped in two and splashed into the water exposing a pair of huge, purple eyes set into a face the size of a small car. James couldn't believe what he was seeing. It looked like one of the Trolls in a book he'd seen at the library. Its fingers were easily the size of James's legs and its teeth were like sharpened stakes. The strange skin that covered the beast was almost black with just a few tiny patches of orange. It resembled the gnarled bark of a dying tree. Cocking his huge, bald head in their direction, the Troll pushed another tree down into the water in order to get a better look at the boys. The gigantic beast was now in full view, yet somehow seemed to blend in with the forest.

"Not Ssslathat! Manimals!" he roared.

He jerked his head back, sniffing the air. James remembered the much smaller Swamp Troll doing something similar before it leapt off his mother's roof. He took another step backward, feeling sick to his stomach. With each jerk of its giant head, the beast bellowed out a strange cry. "Kak. Kak!" Snapping off a sizable limb from the straining tree, the Troll put a bark-covered foot into the river.

Having edged a good ten yards back from the riverbank by now, the boys slipped and stumbled over clumps of ferns. "Firetongue!" James shouted, suddenly remembering his word. He glanced down at the red mark on his right palm and waited for the sword to appear. When it did, it immediately began to flick and jerk in the direction of the Troll creature.

"Do we sit tight or run?" whispered James. Then he gasped. "Bero!"

The Golden Retriever had rushed back down to the beach to face the creature, barking and growling for all he was worth.

"You stupid dog!" James cried. He could hardly believe what he was seeing. He glanced at Craig. "What does he think he's doing?"

Craig stared at Bero in disbelief and whispered, "I don't know. He must think it's some kind of big stick or something!"

"You've got to be kidding me…" James crept toward the edge of the bank, his legs shaking fiercely. The Troll was easily thirty feet high and only needed three steps to cross the river. Seeing Bero down below, it laughed, exposing more of its splintered teeth.

"Not Ssslathat. Dinner!" He reached out towards Bero. His long nails, like carving knives, were only inches from the old dog when a green spear flew past Bero's brown, floppy ear and sunk deep into the Troll's right eye.

"Aaaaaarghh!" As the giant writhed in pain, James lunged forward and grabbed hold of Bero's collar. "Come on boy!" He tried to pull Bero back up the beach but Bero dug in, barking and growling more viciously than before. Panicking now, James looked up to see the Troll clawing at his eye in an effort to dislodge the spear.

"Let's get out of here!" James yelled.

Craig hesitated. "He's got my spear!" he moaned.

"Never mind your ruddy spear," shouted James. "Just move!"

The Troll screamed out in anger and began running toward them. Clumsily, he thumped his huge club down onto the shore sending sand and stones flying into the bushes behind them. They would never get away in time.

Before he knew what he was doing, James found himself running up the makeshift club until he reached the point where the half-blind Troll gripped on, his log-like fingers wrapped tightly round the end.

"James?" Craig yelled hysterically. "Have you gone off your rocker?"

Brandishing Firetongue, James lashed this way and that, hacking through the Troll's fingers. After a few moments, the club, along with several sliced-off fingers, splashed into the river. The Troll roared in agony.

James twisted away from the screeching giant as it grasped at its stump, landing on his feet at the river's edge.

"Sssslathat! Ssslathat, my brother. They've blinded me!" The sheer volume of the Troll's voice shook the forest, sending flocks of birds and bats soaring into the air.

Craig pulled James from the water and yanked him back up the beach. "There's another one."

"What?" James felt dizzy.

Craig continued pulling Bero and James away from the beach. "There's another one and it's coming our way fast!"

Crashhh!

A second Tree Troll thundered through the forest on the opposite bank. "Ashthat!" it bellowed. "Who has wounded you?"

This must be Ssslathat, thought James. He was even taller than his brother and full of rage. Oddly enough, he wore a crest of ferns on his balding head that made him look like a punk rocker. It would have been funny if James weren't so scared and in the process of running for his life.

Howling with anger, the second Troll threw its massive spear across the river. Lucky for them it fell short, splashing into the water a few feet from where they stood. The force of the giant spear hitting the river caused a wave of muddy water to rise up and drench them. Bero shook hard.

Reaching his brother, Ssslathat put a hand out to steady him as he screamed a curse across the river. He did not attempt to chase after them, however. James wondered why. "Do you think he's too scared to cross?"

"Yeah, right!" Craig frowned and shook his head disdainfully. "Bero, come!" he commanded, yanking his old, furry pal away from the river. Before long all three were running through the Forest of El-dane again, ducking branches and constantly checking behind them for the Trolls.

At last, exhausted, they slowed and bent double.

James had a piercing stitch in his side but he forced himself forward up a steep incline. The boys and Bero scrambled over patches of bare rock and soon climbed high above the trees. The desire to stop and rest was almost overwhelming, but a Troll-like wail in the distance made them quicken their pace even more. Panting hard, they clutched at ferns, strands of moss, and whatever else they could find to pull themselves up the hill as fast as they could.

Halfway up, Craig tugged on James's tattered sleeve. "Wait. Bero can't climb that fast. Slow down!" They waited nervously while Bero caught up.

Eventually, the boys reached the top of the hill. Slowly turning about, they braced themselves for the worst. But there was nothing there, no crashing branches or thundering steps, just the distant shouts of the fern-headed Ssslathat and the moans of his wounded brother, Ashthat.

Realising they'd not been followed, James's panic eased. "I still can't believe I can breathe so well," he remarked, half expecting his asthma to seize him the moment the words were out. "It's like a miracle!"

"It's a miracle we're breathing at all after your little stunt back there," said Craig.

"I...I don't know what came over me," said James, moving over to sit against one of the large stones.

"Quite impressive, all the same," admitted Craig, giving his friend a grin. "So now what?"

James looked round. Denthan's twin suns were setting along the eastern and western horizons and the world was growing dark. His stomach rumbled as he realised he'd not eaten all day. "Look, there's a city across there." He pointed it out. "That must be Gwendral."

"Wow!" Craig knelt down beside James, his eyes wide with excitement. "Check out those spires. Do you think they're made out of real gold?"

James squinted. "It's possible." He saw something moving outside the city walls. "Is that grass or...?"

Craig stood up for a better look. "It's not grass, it's living."

The plain before Gwendral was alive with hordes of weird creatures.

"It's those smelly Osgrunfs," said Craig.

"And look...at the edges! Those are the—" he didn't want to say the word. James shuddered at the sight of the hideous, giant insects that had attacked them earlier.

Craig nodded. "The Centides. Brilliant. I wish Mendel was here."

James stared in disbelief. The seething mass of monsters stretched all the way across the huge Plain of Gwendral, extending from the edge of Eldane to the still sea that shone crimson in the distance. James's shoulders slumped. He felt exhausted from all the running they'd been doing and weak from hunger. "There must be a good fifty thousand or more of them down there."

Craig grimaced. "How do you work that one out?"

"Well, I've been to the Hampden Park football ground to see Scotland…"

"What? Get whipped by England?" Craig finished, smiling down at his friend.

"Hardee-har-har! Anyway, as I was saying, Dad told me there were more than fifty thousand people there that day." James shrugged, reaching down to pet a delighted Bero.

"There's a lot more than just Centides in amongst that lot," said Craig. He stared out at the scene, his expression bleak. "You think your dad's here on Denthan, don't you?"

James pinged a bug off his shorts and looked at his knees. "I know he's still alive." He closed his eyes and thought about how much he had suffered since his dad's disappearance. The worse part was missing him so much. But he also hated how his mum never wanted to discuss it. He sighed dismally. Everyone else in Drumfintley was discussing his dad's disappearance, so why couldn't she?

Craig was one of those kids who always tried to make light of a bad situation, but the complete unreality of the sight below them had put him off kilter. "Look James, part of me still thinks this is some kind of dream, okay? But it hurts every time I pinch my arm so it must be real. Anyway, I know you want to believe your dad's in this place, but I just can't see how he could have got here. I mean, without Mendel. Don't you think he just got fed up with…"

James preferred Craig's stupid jokes to this. He put his hand up to call a halt to his friend's whitterings.

"Well," pressed Craig, "with your mum going on at him all the time… Don't you think that he probably just needed some time to himself or…"

James stiffened. "Mum's been on his case for more than twenty years, so why would he run away now? Besides, she can be kind sometimes." James saw Craig's shocked expression. "She can!" he persisted.

"If you say so." Craig lowered himself to sit down.

"And what about the compass and the lens cleaner?" James continued.

"Yeah, well, that's funny, isn't it?" Craig gazed out at the minarets and towers of Gwendral. "Why would the police have missed the lens cleaner? They searched Bruce Moor for days."

"Well, we found it easy enough," replied James. "Maybe something picked it up and dropped it again."

"Like what?" asked Craig with a frown.

James bristled. "Like a stoat or a weasel. I don't know."

A mischievous grin replaced Craig's freckled frown. "So a weasel stole your dad's lens cloth and then dropped it back beside the Jesus Rocks again? You'd think he'd keep it for his own little weasel binoculars."

"Shut up," snapped James. "Okay, explain the silver compass then. Dad always took it with him when he walked the moor."

"Maybe a weasel found that too. I bet he wanted to use it to find his way about when he went through the gateway. You know, to hunt down the creature who squashed his best mate, the stoat."

"Now you're being facetious," spat James, using the biggest word he knew.

"Fa-what-tiuos?" asked Craig.

"It means 'bloody stupid'!" James inadvertently gripped his sword a little tighter and twisted its point into the sandy soil.

As an only child, James just wasn't used to being pushed to the brink of breaking point, not like Helen and Wee Joe probably were. Pouting, he stretched back and gazed at the vast expanse of glistening water in the distance, determined to ignore Craig.

"You know, it's kind of weird," said Craig, "but right now I've got this really powerful feeling of déjà vu. It's like I've been here before or dreamt it or… Oh, I don't know. But I look at the city and I just feel like I've seen it before."

James, still silently seething, twisted round to look at the city of Gwendral, with its golden minarets and towering spires. Suddenly, he felt it too. He stared so long that his eyes glazed over and the city blurred into a mishmash of amber, gold and crimson blotches. "Yeah," he whispered. "There's something familiar about that city. There shouldn't be, but there is." He yawned and gathered in his legs until his chin rested on his knees.

Bero and Craig were already sleeping.

CHAPTER EIGHTEEN

THE BETRAYAL

Growing increasingly uncomfortable in King Athelstone's tightening skin, Dendralon stood on the highest balcony in Gwendral and surveyed the land. The wind swept through his long black hair as he looked beyond the Osgrunfs and Sea Trolls to his Hedra army massing on the southern ridge.

"Sir, I think it's a message bearer." Behind him, a tanned soldier pointed ahead to a small, flying reptile. Beating its fragile wings hard against the breezes that swirled round the citadel, the creature squawked with frustration before landing on the balcony. Dendralon knew the messenger had come from Feldon, the Hedra King, so he waved the Manimal soldier away, then removed the tiny note from the reptile's left leg.

"Ashthat and Ssslathat, the two Tree Trolls, have arrived at our camp as planned. But on the way here, Ashthat was blinded by two small Manimal boys and a yellow beast. Ssslathat wants revenge and can think of nothing else until he gets it. We think the boys may be on the Hill of Dunnad. What are your instructions?"

Dendralon scanned the forest until his eyes rested on the rocky knoll. Feeling a frisson of disgust, he stuck his finger into his right eye and peeled back the white Manimal lens. Able to use the full power of his Hedra infrared vision, he focused in on three faint red glows. He couldn't sense Mendel. He instantly knew that there was a connection between the strangers and the meddlesome wizard, though.

"Argh!" he roared angrily and brought his hand down so hard on the balcony that a small chunk of Manimal skin fell off.

Hearing the cry, the soldier poked his head through the black curtains in alarm, but his master waved him away again. Quickly, Dendralon scratched out his reply to Feldon. When he was done, he tossed the reptile off the parapet where it spun down between the spires before righting itself to flap back over the city wall. Dendralon's message read: This is Mendel's doing. Take fifty of your best warriors and kill the boys and their beast. Do not fail.

Eyes narrowed, he watched the reptile glide towards the Hedra camp. When it appeared to be safely on its way, Dendralon looked again into the Forest of Eldane at the small, rocky outcrop known as Dunnad. Staring at the eerie red light cast over its summit, he thought back to the small boy he'd met in Drumfintley—the one Sleven had failed to eliminate. That would not happen again. This time his Hedra kin would finish the job properly.

Behind him, the curtains twitched once more. "Sir," the soldier announced, avoiding his King's stare, "the Council is asking for your advice."

Dendralon adjusted his voice to a more Manimal-like tone and snapped, "Out of my way." He stepped through the doorway and swept past the red-plumed soldier. It was time to speed things up. He needed to retrieve the crystals now and speed up the evacuation of the city.

Time was running out.

* * *

On the southern ridge, above the Plain of Gwendral, the Hedra camp heaved with activity. Huge piles of black-bladed pikes and swords lay ready to be sharpened by the reptilian armourers. Over-laden wagons, drawn by large, hideous reptiles, creaked through the camp, whips cracking as the Hedra drivers guided the beasts through the chaos. Deep in the centre of the reptilian horde was King Feldon's tent, surrounded by many other smaller black tents, all of them boasting the bright green flag of the Hedra.

Not far from Feldon's tent, a Hedra guard called Jal yawned and blinked his yellow-slit eyes. The two setting suns coloured his grey, scaly skin with a spattering of pink and orange highlights. His armoured chest was adorned with a green dragon clutching the twin suns of Denthan. This too glinted in the fading light.

Hunger gripped the giant as he stood still as a statue facing the city of Gwendral. And only a moment ago, his wide, reptilian eyes had caught sight of a flying reptile, its fragile wings flapping in the distance.

The little, purple reptile flew unsteadily over the city walls and now, between the Hedra tents and fluttering flags.

His heartbeat quickened as it flapped closer and closer to him. His tongue flicked from his lips and took in the creature's scent. He glanced round but no one else had spotted the little flying serpent. It was his.

As the flyer jerked its way over the guard's head, Jal's long black tongue shot up and wrapped round the little reptile's left wing. There was a small "Eeek!" as it disappeared into his mouth. Pierced by his poison-laced fangs, the helpless creature was instantly paralysed. It wasn't long before a succession of tiny spines was guiding the meal down Jal's bulging throat into his large, acid-filled stomach.

* * *

Dendralon was delighted to see a real sense of panic building in Gwendral. In the main Council Chamber, Lord Eldane spoke for the second night in succession. "What conspiracy is this?" he demanded. "The city is completely surrounded. Along with the Hedra to the south, there are now Salt Trolls and Salteths to the West. And if that weren't bad enough, we have Centides and Tree Trolls creeping out of the Forest of Eldane to join the ranks of the Osgrunfs and Hedra. Why have all these creatures decided that they should come here? And why now? Something strange is going on." He sat down beside his son, looking stunned by this turn of events.

Since many of the Council members had already left for the tunnels, the Chamber was half empty.

Dendralon stepped onto the serpent-scaled patch of floor before the throne and addressed the remaining few. "You simply have to accept the facts. Whether we want it to or not, our city is going to fall. It is madness to stay! I plan to remain in the city with my elite guards. We will hold off the hordes and allow you all to escape. It would be such waste to let your own kind perish when they can flee to safety." He stopped and looked directly at Lord Eldane.

Cimerato rose to his feet. "Did you just say, 'your own kind'? Are we to understand that you are not one of us?"

Dendralon cursed himself for making such a stupid slip. "Everyone knows who I am, Cimerato. Why do you pick up on such a triviality? These are times of great pressure. Surely not you, nor anyone here, could doubt that I am your King, Athelstone of Gwendral, son of

Elvana and Dersarius, sixty-third Lord of Denthan." Deciding that attack was better than defence, Dendralon watched to see how the remaining Councillors would react. Everyone, apart from Cimerato, bowed his head respectfully.

The young Cimerato changed tactics. "Many of my soldiers would gladly stay and fight to the death if they must. We could use the dragons of Hest against the Hedra."

"What?" Dendralon scoffed. "Twenty ancient serpents that can hardly get off the ground? If you want the Hedra archers to have some good sport, so be it!" He tapped his gnarled staff on the stone floor. "Enough, Cimerato."

Cimerato stepped forward. "My father says that you were once a brave and valiant warrior. You also have great magical skills at your disposal." The whole Chamber echoed with the sound of the Councillors' anxious mutterings. "So why now do you shy away from the fight?"

Lord Eldane, shut his eyes and shook his head at his boy's folly.

"Discretion is the better part of valour, my boy," Dendralon answered, working to stay calm. "At times like these, you must listen to our head and not your heart. With age, you will understand. Wisdom comes with the years that may yet visit you, Cimerato." Seeing the Councillors nodding in agreement, Dendralon pressed home his point. "Time is running out. We never saw this coming—it took us all by surprise. All we can do now is save ourselves and regroup." He turned back to face Cimerato.

The young man was flushed with rage. "Mendel would have foreseen this!" he shouted.

A thin smile lifted Dendralon's dead Manimal lips. Cimerato would not let this go; Dendralon was going to have to do something about him. He turned away from the troublemaker and closed his white Manimal eyes. Seconds later, beads of sweat began to drip from Cimerato's handsome face. He grasped his forehead in pain.

"Not feeling well, Cimerato?" Dendralon's tone was conciliatory. Cimerato dropped to his knees. "You are not the great King Athelstone of old."

He clasped his head in his young, scarred hands, gritting his teeth in pain.

Lord Eldane rushed forward to steady his son. He glanced up at Athelstone. "Please! Stop this!"

Dendralon's magic had made Athelstone's Manimal skin flush with vigour and he suddenly looked very powerful. He shook his head in false pity as Cimerato's limp body slumped to the floor. "I did not know Cimerato had a weak heart. Stress is a very dangerous thing." Dendralon studied the Council members to see what their reaction was, but no one looked him in the eye.

Lord Eldane alone shook with fury. "It's not his heart!"

Feeling more energy than he had for a long time, Dendralon wanted to tear off Athelstone's dead skin and reveal who he really was. He wanted tell everyone how he had captured and killed their pathetic King, then turn them all into stone. Instead, he found an inner strength that made him calm and focused. He dared not harm the old fool. Not just yet. There were still too many Manimals left in the city.

The spines in his throat fell flat to allow him to produce the Manimal voice he'd practiced for so long. "My elite guards are already manning the main gates. I strongly advise that you leave the city before it's too late. I may yet save Gwendral, but the magic I need to perform is new to me and completely untested. We cannot rely on it. I refuse to risk twelve thousand lives, so go!"

Eldane spoke, shakily. "We will make sure it happens, King Athelstone. Tonight. But my son…" Lord Eldane's voice trailed off into a whisper as he made to follow Cimerato who was being carried from the Council Chamber.

Reading the old man's thoughts, Dendralon said, "Your son will be fine. Now go." Then, turning away, he made for the black curtain that hid the balcony beyond.

* * *

Deep in the belly of the city, Cimerato regained consciousness. Far from being in the physician's quarters, he was lying alone in a dank, musty cell. Some dark magic had possessed their King or, worse still, Athelstone was an impostor.

He peered through the barred window overlooking the creatures on the plain below and wondered if Mendel was truly gone forever. He should have supported the wizard when he'd had the chance. He'd fallen under the spell of this so-called Athelstone, feared for his father's safety, and had voted for Mendel's banishment.

As a boy, Cimerato had played in Mendel's gardens, and he remembered now how the old man had smiled whenever he'd asked him about some book or strange creature. Always categorising and often lost in his old manuscripts, Mendel had never failed to listen and answer a curious boy's many questions. Cimerato's eyes filled with tears. He wished Mendel were still here to help them. The old wizard would have known what to do. He would never have left the city.

With a despondent sigh, Cimerato eased himself down onto the cold floor of the cell and tapped his fingers on the wooden door. To his surprise, someone else tapped back...

CHAPTER NINETEEN

THE SECOND ARRIVAL

Michael was the first of the group to open his eyes. The smell of dank church vestry filled his nostrils, and for a moment he thought he had fallen asleep in St. Donan's. It was a familiar smell, a reassuring smell, which made sense being that he'd spent most of his forty-two years exploring churches and graveyards.

His mother and father had lived with the Reverend Ash in the vicarage of Burton on the Wold. Initially employed as a housekeeper, his mother had managed to get his father the position of gardener and they soon became a proper unit, moving from church to church as a family of sorts. They even holidayed together, doing exchanges with other vicarages. Every year there was a new rectory to explore, a new church spire to climb, a new graveyard where Michael could run wild and play hide and seek with his brother and sister. He remembered the long, sunny summer days clambering up yew trees and playing bish-bash with Reverend Ash, a   keepy-up version of badminton using wooden bats and a shuttlecock. It had been a wonderful, spiritual time.

As an adult, Michael had tried teaching for a while, but found the job too stressful. So, in the end, he had simply slipped back into the life he loved, albeit as priest-in-charge at St. Donan's.

When he thought he heard his gardener,   come-organist, MacNulty, calling his name, Michael's belief that he'd been sleeping in the church was only reinforced. "MacNulty?" he called back, sitting up.

"Wh…where's MacNulty?" Ephie asked as she straightened her overstretched joggers.

"Wakee, Wakee! We ees here!" Eethan's high-pitched voice echoed gratingly round the tunnel as he paced back and forth in front of them. The little blue man counted the group with a big, toothy grin. "Ees one missing. Thee one weeth the painty brush. Neever mind."

With this, he disappeared down the dark tunnel in front of them. Oddly, the sand at their feet emitted a faint glowing light which was the only thing standing between them and utter darkness.

Michael got up to follow.

"Please, wait!" moaned Ephie, feeling her way gingerly along the tunnel.

Eethan doubled back and waved them on. "Ceemon!"

"Where the heck are we?" demanded Cathy.

"You weell see!" Eethan replied enigmatically, before hurrying on ahead.

Not having much choice, Ephie, Michael, Cathy, Jean and the kids all scrambled to keep up. For what seemed like hours, they stumbled along the cramped confines of the tunnel system before finally stepping into a vast underground cavern. Apart from a stone plinth, the giant cave was empty. A dim orange light coming from a crack in a nearby medieval-type door illuminated the grey platform. It appeared as though someone had left the Chamber in a hurry, forgetting to close the huge door behind them. Eethan scampered ahead and slipped through the opened door, beckoning to them with three wiggling fingers before disappearing into the orange glow.

Excited, Helen and Wee Joe ran ahead. "Come on, Mum! There might be another big slide like the last one."

"I hope not," Jean replied. "My stomach's still fragile after that drop." But the kids weren't listening. "Helen? Joe! Wait on me, please!" Jean ran after her kids, leaving the rest behind.

Cathy pointed at a large footprint in the sandy floor. "What's made that then?" She turned to Michael.

"Something big and heavy, I would say," answered Michael, looking grim. He felt a strange attraction to the orange light that shone from the door. "Look, Cathy, there are more of them! Paw prints and two sets of smaller footprints." Michael looked over at Ephie for confirmation, but she seemed distracted.

"Greedy guts is too busy hunting for more tablet in her coat," sneered Cathy. She knelt down on the sandy floor. "I'm sure those are James's trainers. I'll kill him!"

Michael didn't think the marks she was examining looked anything like human footprints. He watched as she stood up and pushed on in a strop.

"Come on, Miss Blake!" Michael tried to get Ephie's attention as he followed after Cathy.

"Mmm, what?" Ephie couldn't walk and search her pockets at the same time.

"We're moving on," he said. Michael quickened his pace and Ephie followed suit. "Are you okay?" he said after a moment.

"Mmm..." replied Ephie, already munching.

Michael tried to keep the conversation going, "I think MacNulty must have jumped clear of the stone circle in time, though I'm sure I heard his voice when I first woke in the tunnel."

Ephie was panting again and seemed in no mood for conversation.

Eventually, the grumbling adults and excited children reached three doors set in the cave wall. Helen was first to stop. "Which way should we go now, Eethan?"

Instead of answering, Eethan lifted his left hand above his head and called out, "Ee tra shee lan!" Immediately, the door to the right began to vibrate. Its wooden panels began sliding over each other like worms in a jar, only these worms had sharp little teeth that gnawed and snapped at each other.

Helen grasped her mother's hand. "Are they snakes, Mum?" Everybody looked at Jean for an answer, but jumped back in fright when the door on the left exploded into a thousand shards.

"Good God!" Michael grabbed Ephie's arm and pulled her back. He muttered a prayer for their protection.

"Dis is great!" Wee Joe flicked some sawdust from his face as the centre door opened inward. The familiar orange glow spilled onto the stone floor in front of them.

"Eee! Don't ee touch the snaky door! Eet's the bad one!" Eethan moved forward and passed through the middle door, followed closely by the kids.

"I can't go any further!" Ephie cried as she clutched Michael's shoulder and dug in her nails.

"Where are you going to go, Ephie?" Cathy mocked.

"I can't stand snakes! They're too close...they..." Ephie's grip tightened further still.

"Oww, Ephie, my shoulder!" Michael gasped. "It's just an illusion," he told her, hoping she would loosen her grip.

Ephie was shaking. "But they look so real."

"Dee are!" Eethan added, unhelpfully. "But dees not snakes, dees Vileworms; Dendralon's nasty pets. Come, now!"

The door to their right, now a mass of slippery, giant worms, hissed and spat vile pus at them as they ran through.

Cathy caught Ephie's sleeve and dragged her through the door, kicking and screaming, before unceremoniously dumping her on the tunnel floor. "Pathetic," hissed Cathy before striding ahead to catch up with the others.

Only Michael held back for the terror-stricken Ephie. Reaching down, he took her hand in the darkness and pulled her to her feet.

Ephie struggled ahead, sobbing and muttering her regrets at coming along.

The rest of the group marched along through twists and turns for what seemed like miles before coming to a halt at the bottom of an old set of stone stairs. Seeing the steps in the gloom, Jean let go of Helen's hand and lifted Wee Joe down from her shoulders. "The roof's collapsed," she whispered. "Look at the mess."

"There must be a thousand tons of rubble," said Cathy, staring at the pile in shock. "James!" she shouted up the stairway. "James!"

"Craig?" shouted Helen.

Helen's little voice brought tears to Jean's eyes.

Helen turned to Eethan. "Where's my big brother? Are they here, under the rocks? James and Craig and Bero. Are they all dead?"

"Can't bee..." Eethan paused for a moment and then said, "No, can't bee! No smelly smell!" He smiled reassuringly and then began to climb the stairs. "No smelly dead smell, little one," he shouted back. "Wee must go up. Wee must!" With a decided nod, he spun round, hoisted Wee Joe onto his scrawny shoulders, and leapt up the shattered stairway.

Jean was first to move, but soon the others began to pick their way through the broken stalactites and smashed rocks. "Eethan! Joe!" she called out, growing worried. "Wait a minute..."

For her part, Ephie clutched at her chest and complained of heartburn, asking if anyone had anything to help.

Cathy's eyes narrowed. "That's what you get for stuffing so much tablet into your fat gob! Mrs. Galdinie says you buy two-dozen packs a week."

Ephie stepped back from Cathy. "Well, I have never been so..."

"Serves you right!" snapped Cathy.

"That's not very Christian, Cathy!" Michael scolded as he fished about in his pockets. He soon produced a filthy, square antacid tablet.

"But it's dirty!" Ephie exclaimed in disgust.

Cathy clenched her fist. "Do you want the bloomin' thing or not? You are an ungrateful cow!" She pushed past Ephie, leaving her to gape while she began her climb.

"Up we go!" said Jean brightly, trying to ease the growing tension. "Eethan says that the kids are alright, so let's try to stay calm and get along with each other." She gave Cathy a meaningful look.

"Ha!" Cathy sneered.

Ephie pursed her fat, petulant lips as though she wanted to say something, but on seeing Cathy's scornful stare, decided not to push it.

Peace somewhat restored, the group carefully picked their way through the rubble until they noticed the small stone basin at the top of the stairs.

"I think it's a font!" exclaimed Michael. "In fact, it's rather like the one in St. Donan's!"

"Michael, ask me if I care!" snapped Cathy.

Michael frowned. He'd only been trying to make conversation.

"Now, now… Let mee see." Eethan moved round the edge of the basin. "Ees a test. But theeres no key! Wee needs the key!" Eethan began to examine the floor, only to discover the letters D.P. carved on the wall.

"You mean this one!" Helen pointed to a small bronze key still protruding from a keyhole at the bottom of the door.

"Yees! Yees!" Distracted from the carved initials, Eethan gave Helen a pat on the back. "Good girlee!" The key hung out of the keyhole at an angle, so he pushed it home. *Clunk!* As soon as he turned it, noises began to echo up from the bottom of the steps.

Ephie clutched her chest. "Something's coming up the stairs!"

"What could it be?" Michael's question hung in the air, unanswered.

Whatever it was, it was large and it was moving towards them through the dust and gloom. Eethan glanced once more at the D.P. inscription and shook his head. "Eees beeen protected."

Cathy whispered, "Whatever that thing is, it doesn't seem too friendly." It was one of Cathy Peck's few understatements. The monster following them was a giant of a creature. It had red, matted fur that covered its long-limbed body and a small horn protruding from its forehead. In the darkness of the passage, orange highlights sparkled in its malevolent eyes and glinted on it sharp, black teeth. The thing struggled to make headway up the narrow section at the bottom of the stairs, growling and bellowing with each step.

"Dees ees bad news," hissed Eethan.

Helen stared at the beast while Eethan fumbled with the key. "Look at its eyes! There are four, no eight. It has eyes everywhere!"

"Baccckkk…" the creature screeched up at them before falling heavily.

Eethan gulped. "Ee must've turned ee keey the wrong weey. Oopsie!"

Cathy gripped Eethan's scrawny arm. "You mean you made this thing appear?"

Eethan continued to fumble with the key. "Nobodee's perfect, nice laydee! Now help push!"

They all leaned on the door and shoved hard, but it wouldn't move.

"There's a wock jamming it!" cried Wee Joe. The smallest of them, he was able to reach into the hinge and flick it out of the way.

At last, the door began to move. But the creature, having climbed over the rubble, was now leaping the stairs ten at a time and getting close.

"Quick Eethan. Open the bloomin' door!" Michael didn't often swear, but felt certain the moment called for it.

"Eet's a Mertol," explained Eethan. "Ees not an easy beastie to kill. Eees not." Leaving the door, the little man faced the howling beast. Holding his left hand high above his strange, plumed head, he muttered, "Sith tan eech tan!"

A flash of blue light shot from Eethan's hand and hit the Mertol right in the face. Momentarily halted, the red-haired beast stretched his neck and closed his eyes in pain. Pointing a clawed hand at Eethan, the Mertol barked his own charm in return, "Seethh! Baaacckkk!"

From an opening on the right side of its cheek, a small, red ball shot out and slammed into Eethan's skinny chest. The speed of the attack took Eethan by surprise and he was thrown back against the door behind them. The impact was so hard that the door opened even further and now a thin beam of bright sunlight streamed through. Seeing that the door was moving, the frightened group all pushed for dear life, apart from Ephie, who just stood there emitting a constant, high-pitched wail. The sound seemed to both annoy and distract the Mertol, who rubbed his eyes and twitched his fur in little spasms.

Another red ball shot from a different "eye" and smacked into Ephie's mouth with a thud. "Eeeeeeeee—Uffff!" She immediately froze and then, horrifyingly, began to change. Her skin and clothes began to shine like wet rubber and her body wobbled like a giant jelly mould. Disjointed, her bottom lip hung down until it bounced off her considerable chest. It looked as though she was melting.

"What a hideous sight!" Jean whispered in terror.

"I kind of like it," said Cathy, grinning.

"That's mean, Mrs. Peck," remarked Helen with a frown.

Despite what had happened to Ephie, the group continued pushing on the door. It opened bit by bit until light poured through the gap, temporarily blinding them. The bright light soon fell upon the Mertol. The creature yelled out.

Squinting, everybody turned expecting their pursuer to scream or turn to stone but the loathsome beast only blinked and gave them an evil, toothy smile. Two small, black balls shot out from what they could now tell were holes on the sides of his face, bursting above their heads and showering them with a fine, black powder. The last thing they heard was the "Baacckkk" sound of the creature as it began laughing.

CHAPTER TWENTY

LOST AND FOUND

As the twin suns of Denthan rose over Dunnad Hill, James and Craig slept soundly. Cuddled into their beloved Bero, sleep helped them escape their hunger and took them home again to the people and places they already missed so much. James dreamt he was walking over the hills with his dad. His mum was in the dream too, but she looked different. She was dressed like a warrior or...

The boys were rudely awakened when their heads knocked off a big sandstone slab. Their 'pillow', Bero, had shifted.

"Bero! Watch it!" they moaned, still groggy.

By way of an apology, Bero licked their faces, then blew-dry the sticky drool with his own brand of stinky dog breath.

"Yuck, Bero, that's absolutely minging." James grimaced, shading his eyes against the intensity of the early morning suns.

"Yep, he stinks alright," said Craig, "and now so do we. But who cares, eh?" Craig laughed. "Your mum can't tell you off or ground you, so why worry?"

"Yeah, but guess what?" James grumbled.

"What?" Craig enquired.

"I don't like smelling like a dead badger! I'm tired, starving and..." James hesitated, looking behind him, "and I wish you'd stop being so cheery." He paused again. "Did you hear that?" Not giving Craig a chance to reply, James said his special word and the intricately etched sword appeared in his right hand, twitching menacingly. "Get your spear ready!"

Hesitantly, Craig whispered, "Greenworm?" He wasn't sure if the spear would come or whether it was still lodged in the Tree Troll's eye. But thankfully, as soon as Craig said his word, the spear was there in his hand. Surprised to see that it wasn't covered in troll gunk, he tested its weight. The green spear balanced beautifully and shone like polished bronze in the weird, Denthan double dawn.

Ready for combat, the boys ventured out from their sleeping place. They edged their way down the rocky knoll, hoping nothing in the forest below had seen or heard them. They soon realised, however, that their path was blocked. Hundreds of snakes and lizards were using the knoll as a warming site, and not a single one of them looked friendly.

Craig grabbed Bero by the scruff of the neck and jerked him to a halt. "Whoa, boy. They might bite."

James stuck his sword into the ground and hunkered down to take a better look. Some of them had spines covering their backs while others had curved horns on top of their heads.

"They're all awake," said James.

"Yeah... Now what?" said Craig.

Sensing the intruders on the knoll, the reptiles slithered toward the boys, hissing and spitting, their scaly skin glistening in the eerie light.

"They look a bit like iguanas without legs," whispered Craig.

"Shut up, Craig. Just get ready to use your spear," snapped James.

"Has your mum been giving you lessons?" said Craig.

"What kind...?" But before James could answer, the squirming mass spread out around them in a deadly arc, moving quicker than the boys had thought possible. When they were within a few feet, the snakes rose as one and struck out, forcing them to retreat back against the sheer face of the rocky knoll.

James almost lost his footing. "We have to attack now," he shouted to Craig, "or they'll be no way out of here. They're closing in too fast."

Craig nodded. "I suppose we don't have much choice. Let's head for that big tree over there." He pointed to a huge, misshapen tree off to their left.

Giving each other a subtle nod, both boys jumped forward swinging their weapons like ancient warriors. Longer than James's sword, Greenworm proved the more effective weapon. It swung with barely any effort on Craig's part, slicing in deadly arcs as it cut through the moving mass of fangs and scales. Jets of black, serpentine blood spattered the boys' faces and pattered across the dry ground. A path of wriggling tails and writhing limbs marked the boys' gory progress.

They were almost at the gnarled tree when one of the snakes got too close to James.

"Watch your back, James!" Craig hollered.

A large black and red cobra, its body as thick as a drainpipe, lunged at James's heel.

Deftly, James sidestepped it, but it lunged again, nearly catching hold of his leg. This time James slashed at it with his sword, but his arm was growing tired and he missed. The serpent hissed and attacked again, flicking its barbed tail at Bero. The dog yelped and bounded out of reach.

Craig was busy fighting to his own battle so James was on his own. Gripping the hilt of Firetongue tightly in his two hands, he waited for the next strike.

"Watch out, James!" Craig yelled again, distracting his friend.

James spun round as the snake lunged.

By itself, the crimson sword, Firetongue, flicked backwards and buried itself between the snake's nostrils, slicing its head in two. *Was he trying too hard?* thought James. *Could the sword actually do all the work for him.*

"There's another one!" Craig shouted.

This time Firetongue swung out to slash at a three-headed lizard. There was a gurgling sound as putrid yellow pus foamed hideously from three headless necks.

Not long after that, the snakes began to retreat. Perhaps they had sensed the futility of their attack. Whatever the reason, Bero and the boys were able to make their way down the knoll without any further threat.

When they reached the gnarled tree. Craig came to a stop. He was shaking. "We had to do that, didn't we?"

James was too busy scrambling down the dirt track they'd climbed up the night before. "I can't hear you," he called, rushing towards the tree.

Craig steadied James as he came to a stop. "I said, I didn't like killing those things!"

"Well, *I* didn't like the thought of being lunch, okay!" He shrugged Craig's hand off his shoulder.

"Okay, so maybe you've got a point, but look..." Craig skidded on a patch of slime. "Why can't we just stop for one moment? We've been running and fighting since we set foot in this crazy place."

James pretended not to hear him. He only wanted to put some distance between himself and the bloodbath back on the knoll.

Craig gripped onto a thick strand of moss. "He's nearly eighty years old!" he shouted.

"Who is?" said James, tripping over a rootlet.

"Bero is! In dog years. He's an old codger, you know, so we should stop," said Craig. Before James could answer, Craig fell onto his back and began to slide down the side of the knoll. He grabbed at ferns and strands of moss to try and stop himself. "Help!"

"I think... we've come down... the wrong way!" James yelled. He too was flat on his back and gathering speed. The hill dropped away even more.

"Whoah!" Craig fell forward, shouting the whole time, his yell stifled by the thick hanging moss that slapped against his face and filled his mouth. Finally, he landed at the bottom of the hill in a heap of arms and legs.

James thudded to a halt a few yards to Craig's left. He was surprised to see that Craig was licking his lips, a delighted look on his face.

"The moss!" barked Craig. "It's delicious!"

James watched as Craig pulled some more strands of moss from the nearest tree. He winced as Craig stuffed a handful into his mouth. "Don't be daft. It could be poisonous."

"Look, numpty boy, I'm starving and I'm having some more." He squeezed some of the grey fibres into a ball. "Here boy!" he called out to Bero who had just caught up. "Let's see if you're braver than numpty boy." Craig tossed the ball of moss towards Bero who caught it mid-air and gulped it down. "Starving all this time and we were completely surrounded by the bloomin' stuff," shrieked Craig.

Sheepishly, James put a small piece to his lips. It tasted of melon. "Hm... Not bad."

"Not bad?" said Craig. "It's bloomin' wonderful!"

James gulped down another piece and was soon tearing strands from the surrounding trees just as voraciously as his friend.

Half an hour later, and full to bursting, they lay back under the huge, gnarled tree that spread out above them. The Denthan suns had crept a little higher and the air had grown hot and heavy. Gigantic Insects and strange birds fluttered through the canopy above while, at their feet, bright yellow flowers, that looked like overgrown daffodils, grew in clumps between the buttressed tree roots. A purple plant with shiny blue berries helter-skeltered down from the overhanging branches far above.

James let loose a large burp, feeling satisfied and relaxed for the first time in days.

"I wonder how many times the heron's flown by St. Donan's spire now," he remarked, rubbing his full stomach.

"Yeah," said Craig, "and I wonder how many chocolate tea-cakes our mums have eaten!" He sniggered, already doing the arithmetic. "Last night was our second night here, right?" He turned to James.

"I think so, but we did have a kip on the beach for a while." James began counting up the hours too. "An hour and a half to the Jesus Rocks. Goodness knows how long in that cave. Say two hours?"

"I suppose so," agreed Craig. "Then another two hours before first nightfall here."

"Maybe." James began writing with his finger in the dirt.

"No, that's right enough, and add eight hours for our sleep that first night in the forest."

"Mmmm. Say twelve hours by the time we'd seen the Osgrunfs and escaped the Centides." Craig began munching on the moss again.

"You forgot the Tree Trolls," James reminded him.

"How could I forget them?" Craig chuckled. "And last night we slept for, say another eight hours?"

"And it's about three hours since Bero cracked our heads," announced James. "Aha!" He sat up at the same time as Craig, both of them blurting it out at the same time. "Thirty-six and a half!"

Craig clapped his hands "Ah, but remember Mendel set the loop at thirty minutes, so that makes…"

"Seventy-three teacakes!" They said before bursting into fits of laughter.

"My mum's got to be at least eighteen stone by now!" said James. He could hardly say the words for laughing.

Suddenly his expression sobered. He tugged on Craig's filthy shirt-sleeve. "Did you hear that?"

"What?" Craig was still giggling.

"I thought I heard my mum shouting!" James rubbed his ears.

"Not again. What is it with you?" asked Craig.

"No!" James interrupted distractedly. "I heard her shouting 'run.'" He peered through the mass of twisted branches and vines. "I think…"

"I think you've eaten too much of that dodgy moss." Craig stood up and stretched. Then he froze, his hands still high above his head. "Hey, there's something in the ferns!" he whispered. "Look, Bero's wagging his tail at it."

James could hear it now too, a high-pitched chattering. He wondered if he should summon his sword but for some reason decided not to. He gripped Craig's arm and whispered, "There must be some friendly creatures in Denthan, right?"

The chattering noise grew louder and the ferns around them began to twitch. Little sparks of light began to dance between the fronds.

Bero snapped at them. Strangely, though, he continued to wag his tail.

Out of the corner of his eye, James noticed a figure emerge from the ferns. A short, balding, yellow-skinned man stepped out onto the path.

The boys swung round to face him.

He smiled and bowed politely before saying, "I am Landris." His eyes were completely black except for a pale blue, horizontal slit. James saw that his thin, angular eyebrows had the same blue tinge. He was dressed in a neat, brown jacket and a pair of bottle-green trousers. Smiling again, he asked, "And you are?"

"Eh…James…James Peck," said James.

Craig moved forward and caught hold of Bero's collar. "This is Bero, and I'm Craig."

"And you are lost, are you not?" asked Landris.

"We are," replied James. "And there's someone else who's lost too."

Craig gave James a puzzled stare.

James continued, "that is to say, we've become separated…" James tried to sound calm but inside his stomach was churning, "…from the person we were with," he finished.

"He's in a barrel," Craig explained. "He's a talking fish!"

James couldn't believe Craig had just blurted it out like that. He felt a flush of embarrassment when Landris's eyes twinkled.

"Hmm. Well, as this is not a good place to be chatting, we will go somewhere slightly safer. Then you can tell me all about your problems. Come!" With that, he slipped back into the ferns and disappeared.

As soon as the boys ducked into the ferns behind Landris the ground fell away. "Not again!" cried the boys, but it was too late. Bero barked loudly as they all tipped forwards down an unseen slope. Before long their screams of alarm turned into yelps of exhilaration as they shot down a smooth slide into the darkness. After a few minutes, their descent slowed and all three landed gently on their feet inside a candlelit chamber. Brightly coloured tree roots and faded tapestries depicting battles, weird-looking cities and beautiful landscapes decorated the small room.

The yellow man, Landris, was waiting for them. "Not exactly our most luxurious accommodation," he explained, "but a place where we can talk safely."

Landris used a crooked, glowing twig to light the way and they followed after him, wondering what kind of creature he was and where they were. In silence, he led them to a bigger chamber where several other yellow-skinned creatures were standing around chattering to each other. They all stopped talking when the James and Craig entered the room.

The boy's arrival did not create too much of a stir. It was Bero who really held their attention. The creatures all stared in wonder at the dog and begged the boys for permission to pat the retriever's soft fur.

"What is it?" a younger version of Landris enquired.

"It's a dog!" Craig declared proudly.

"A dog. A dog…" The creatures repeated the word over and over until their high-pitched babble filled the chamber.

"Silence, please!" Landris shushed them and ushered the boys toward an elaborately decorated door at the back of the hall. When they reached it, he said, "We need to show you something. Young Garlon here found it." He pointed to the creature that had asked about Bero. Garlon grinned and gave them a little wave.

"It was washed up on a small cove," explained Landris, moving behind a low table. He began rummaging for something in a drawer. "Garlon is convinced that he heard a voice in that place, and when you mentioned a barrel and a talking fish, I thought I might be able to solve your puzzle." He rummaged some more. "Aha!" he exclaimed. He held up a weird-looking bag and placed it on the tabletop. The boys stood motionless, watching closely as the yellow man lifted a familiar object from the bag and placed it in front of them.

"The brandy barrel!" both boys shouted at the same time.

James was first to pick it up. He turned the trinket over and peered through the cracked plastic window. "Mendel?"

"Someone spoke to me," Garlon said. "I heard them!" But the creature's words fell on deaf ears. James was too busy peering inside the barrel. He issued a loud gasp and then held it up to the light.

"He's not in there, is he?" asked Craig.

"It's empty," said James. He tossed the barrel over to Craig.

Craig examined it thoroughly.

"What's wrong?" Landris asked, signalling the young root-dweller to stand back.

James turned on the younger creature. "You couldn't have heard him!" he accused. "He's not there." James grew tearful and sat down on a small, wooden stool. In just a few moments, wild exhilaration had turned to complete despair.

"I wonder where Mendel is now," said Craig, thinking out loud. "He's either been eaten, or he's gotten his little brains dashed out against the rocks in the river, and then been eaten."

James looked up at Craig through tear-blurred eyes. "Why do you always do that?"

"Do what?" asked Craig, totally oblivious to the fact that he'd just made matters worse.

"Oh, never mind. Even if Mendel hasn't been splattered against a rock or been swallowed whole, the barrel's totally useless now anyway. Look, it's cracked."

James shook his head despondently. When Landris moved over to touch his arm sympathetically, James could only flash him a tight-lipped smile and pull back, feeling suddenly awkward and stupid.

Landris stepped back, his weird, blue eyes luminous in the strange light. "I'm really sorry about your friend, but tell me again, boys. What did you say your friend's name was?"

"Mendel," answered Craig.

Landris and Garlon looked at each other and nodded.

"And the wizard shall return to the Eden Tree," whispered Landris, pointing to an old book in the corner of the room. "That is what it says." He closed his eyes and smiled happily.

"Hey, that's right!" exclaimed Craig, pulling on his friend's dirty sleeve. "Mendel said that if we ever became separated we were to meet him at the Eden Tree."

James fingered the broken barrel. "On the Island of Sen...Sen..." James couldn't remember.

"Senegral," finished Landris. "Yes, we must all go there soon."

James was confused.

Before we leave, however, there is more that I must tell you. And, perhaps, once you've eaten and rested a little, you may feel at ease enough to tell us how you came to be here in the great Forest of Eldane."

"And," added Garlon excitedly, "how you came to know one of the greatest wizards of all time."

CHAPTER TWENTY-ONE

THE MERTOL

Exactly one hour before the boys woke up on the knoll of Dunnad, Jean's eyes flashed open in sudden panic. "Helen? Joe?" Her voice was groggy as she tried to get her bearings. "Helen! Joe!" She peered through the gloom and saw four cages.

She tried to focus, tried to get some idea of what was going on, but the brilliant light to her left dazzled her, nearly blinding her with its intensity. A constant rumbling noise, like the roar of a crowd interspersed with strange yells and unearthly screeches, made her wonder if she was still sleeping. After a bit, though, her eyes adjusted to the light and she saw that she was in a large, open cave. However, she soon realised something else...

She was trapped. Imprisoned in a rusting cage, with no way out. "I must be dreaming," she groaned, her head thumping painfully. "Oh God, please let me be dreaming." Unfortunately, she was quite sure that she was not. The breeze blowing on her face and the foul stench seemed to confirm that, sadly, she was quite awake.

She glanced round some more, hoping to get her bearings. In the distance, bathed in a strange unfaltering light, she could see the jewel-encrusted spires of a beautiful city. It must have been about a mile away, but she could still make out the city walls and a jagged outline of minarets. She counted nine tall towers. The biggest tower of all, an enormous, white citadel, stretched skyward like a giant mast pointing to the heavens.

"It looks a bit like the cathedral in Barcelona," remarked Michael.

"Michael, where are you?" Jean cried, relieved to hear a familiar voice.

"I'm here, in the cage behind you. Isn't that the most wondrous sight you've ever seen? Those spires! And the citadel…!"

Momentarily distracted by Michael's descriptions of the architecture, Jean suddenly snapped out of her trance-like state and sat bolt upright. "The children!" she cried. "Where are the children?"

"Umm…I'm not sure," admitted Michael, somewhat hesitantly. "But Eethan's over there, tied to that spit thing, and Cathy is in here with me. I think it's morning, but I'm not sure how long we've been here." Michael's voice sounded weary. "Could be hours, could be days…"

"Ees nearer to thirtee hours," bleated Eethan.

* * *

Hearing the others talking, Cathy opened her eyes and sat up. After shaking her head to clear it, she immediately began to test the cage for flaws or weak points. "We have to snap out of it, people! We have to find the kids and what's left of Ephie, if anything."

For the moment, Cathy's challenge hung in the air unanswered. Something had caught Jean and Michael's attention. She followed their gaze.

Just above the city, a grey and white dragon flew, flapping its large wings slowly and rhythmically. They could hear it barking and yelping like a giant dog as it came towards them. Eventually the winged creature reached a long ridge packed with hordes of reptilian beasts waving black and green flags. Just as it was passing over them, a giant arrow flew upward and pierced the dragon's underbelly. Attached to the arrow was a rope which in turn was anchored to some kind of machine. The attackers wound the rope tight, hauling the convulsing beast down, screaming and flapping frantically, onto the ridge below.

That's when the stunned observers realised that there was someone on the dragon's back. Whoever it was fell off as the creature spun to the ground, its wings now frozen in death. There was a sickening thud followed by a huge, horrible cheer. A deafening drumming began, and the clash of metal on metal merged with the roars of the baying creatures.

"Helen? Joe?" Jean stared blankly at the patch of sky where the dragon had flapped its last flap and began to weep.

"Theey're not heer, Jeannie!" It was Eethan, who still swung beneath the spit, desperately trying to free his hands. "Eeee! That's eet!" Eethan had freed one hand and now waved it above his little shock of white hair. "La chee cha sag!"

A blue flash of light spread round him and he was suddenly free. He scrambled up the nearest wall and scuttled, spider-fashion, across the roof of the cave. "Wee ees lucky," he continued, "that dee Mertol has eaten alreadee!" He pointed to a pile of scaly, flesh-covered bones on the floor.

Jean fainted.

"No ees not the children. Not! These ees Hedra bones." Eethan sounded annoyed.

"What in God's name is a Hedra?" asked Cathy, her voice wavering.

Eethan began to open the other cages, choosing to ignore Cathy's question for the time being. Then, after throwing open the last rusty door, he jumped across to a large table and lifted a black saucepan from the debris. He flicked it the right way up and began filling it with water, which he poured from a rusting jar. "Wees been sleeping a long time, en already, Dendralon's evil ones have filled dee valley. They ees everywhere! Only Mendel can save our world now." He paused and stuck his thumb up his nose.

"I wish you wouldn't do that," Cathy grumbled.

"I ees looking for clues!" protested Eethan.

"What, up your nose?" Disgusted, Cathy pushed past Michael and jumped down from the cage.

Eethan just chuckled and told them all to come closer. Jean was coming round, and Michael was busy reassuring her that her children would be okay. In the meantime, Cathy confronted Eethan. "Look, if you can do all this magic, why can't you just get rid of those things down there?" She pointed to the valley below.

"Can do a few trickees that Mendel taught me but ees not enough…" He winked cheekily at Cathy as he dipped his middle finger into the saucepan. A blue flash shot across the surface of the water, soon fading away to reveal a very disturbing scene.

"There!" Michael pointed to the unmistakable figure of Ephie Blake. She'd appeared on the surface of the water. "She's in trouble!" he gasped.

Jean, fully awake, pushed past the Reverend to get a better look. "I have to see my children. Where are they? Oh my God…" Jean's voice fell away as the horror of the scene unfolded.

Ephie looked totally worn down, her rosy cheeks had turned white and tears filled her eyes. It was obvious that she was close to breaking point. "No! No No!" she cried. "Not again, please! Please, not again!"

Cathy felt a pang of regret. "Poor sod," she muttered.

In the picture that shimmered on the surface of the saucepan, Ephie's face drooped and her voice wavered piteously. "You promised me that was the last time. You promised!" Ephie seemed to give up, then. Letting out a small whimper, she began, "Two little mice, Tiffy Toffy mice; having adventures and never thinking twice..."

"That's Wee Joe's favourite song!" Jean exclaimed, tears of relief rolling down her face. "He must be making her sing it!"

As the picture panned back, they saw Wee Joe, singing along with poor Ephie. They saw Helen too, although she looked as fed up as Ephie did.

"Helen hates that song," Jean explained. "She's heard it so many times."

"The kids are fine," said Michael.

"Yes," whispered Jean.

"So how did Ephie survive?" demanded Cathy. "She went all gooey, like she was made of rubber."

"Ees all an illusion!" Eethan replied, grinning broadly. "Good though, eeh?"

Michael shook his head. "I thought she was dead." He let out a pent-up breath as he stared hard at the kids. "So where are they? I can't tell."

Like a bat, Eethan scampered up onto the ceiling and looked down at Michael. "Ees another cave, en look, behind theeem, eets dee Riveer Leevan!"

"Well, I can't see any sign of that Ape Thing so they must be safe!" said Michael.

"Thank God," murmured Cathy, who had moved in closer to get a better look at the vision in the saucepan. The walls of the children's cave ran wet with damp, and strands of moss hung from the ceiling. Behind them, she could see the river.

Deep in concentration, Eethan began fiddling with his left nostril. "I ees not sure where de Mertol ees."

Cathy bristled at the sight. "Will you please stop that disgusting picking and...!"

"Baacckkk!"

The grinding sound of a heavy stone door being pushed open followed the horrific cry. Tins and pans clattered at the back of their cave.

"Run!" Cathy's voice cut through the din. Her shout ricocheted out of the Mertol's cave, sending several birds flapping from the trees.

The Mertol hesitated for a second before picking up a gigantic wooden table. With a terrifying scream it launched it across the cave. "Baacckkk!"

The table smashed into a huge stalactite, which shattered into a hundred pieces, showering them with dust and limestone. Coughing and screaming Cathy, Jean and Michael ran out into the dazzling sunlight.

Eethan, however, remained in the cave. Scampering across the roof above the Mertol's head, he made a spider-like dash for the open door at the back of the cave.

* * *

Out in the sunlight, Cathy saw that Michael had doubled back towards the cave. "What are you doing, you idiot? Watch out!"

Michael's manoeuvre had brought him to within feet of the Mertol. The beast brought his massive, red fist down to crush him.

Cathy circled back and yanked on his black flannel jacket, pulling him out of the way just in time; the giant fist missing him by inches. Losing his footing, Michael rolled down the slope, tearing his black suit as he fell. Jean and Cathy chased after him, down the tree-covered slope, unwittingly heading straight for the reptilian Hedra army in the valley below. The Mertol screamed again, but then turned unexpectedly and leaped back into his cave. Cathy supposed the beast must have seen Eethan.

* * *

Eethan knew that magic was always drawn to magic, so he tried to remain as still as possible. Below him, the Mertol searched the cave. Creeping along the litter-strewn floor, the creature's heel caught the saucepan and knocked it over. The enchanted water splashed over the floor of the cave causing sparks and flashes of electric blue to swirl round the Mertol's feet.

"Baacckkk!" The beast called out again as he stumbled over the debris in the cave and then crashed into one of the swinging cages.

Clinging to the vaulted roof, Eethan scampered through the open door and into the secret passage that led down towards the children and Ephie. In seconds, his eyes adjusted to the dark and he was able to put a good distance between himself and the Mertol. Moving quickly, he soon arrived at a dank, moss-covered cave.

"Eethan!" exclaimed Ephie, her bloodshot eyes wide with relief.

With a flick of his wrist, the door on their cage sprung open and the captives leapt out. Knowing enough to keep quiet—even Wee Joe—Ephie and the kids followed Eethan out of the shadowy river cave. The dark green river oozed past them as they made their way along its slippery bank, ducking through the strands of moss that hung down like lacy veils from the branches above. They walked for several hundred yards before Eethan guided them into a clump of ferns.

"Sit," Eethan motioned to them as he pointed to the ground. "Everyone sit still. Don't ee move, make sounds or singy songs."

Ephie wiped the sweat from her brow and patted Wee Joe on the back. "Don't worry. No singy songs. We promise. Right?" She smiled weakly at Wee Joe who stuck his tongue out and made a farty sound. "Pthuuuuuuw!"

Ephie's brow wrinkled, then she leaned across to whisper to Eethan, "I'm so glad you came when you did. That thing was very gentle with the children, but..."

"Dee Mertol doesn't harm little ones," Eethan interrupted with a grin. "No, neever. Only eets you for dinneer, Eeeephie." The little blue man chuckled at the horrified look on her face, then faded back into the bushes.

* * *

"It's Ephie, not Eeeephie," bleated Ephie, "whatever you are." She sighed and looked round, still trembling from their ordeal.

"Eeeephie. Eeeephie!" Wee Joe called out, adopting Eethan's pronunciation. She began to fumble frantically in her deep overcoat pockets for some more tablet to shut him up. She had to find some! She was willing to give the whole lot to him—anything. She didn't want Wee Joe to draw the Mertol to their position.

As she dug about, she wondered if the others—especially Father Michael—were okay. She didn't know why, but she was beginning to change her mind about the new rector. She shoved some tablet into Wee Joe's sweaty little hands and passed some over to Helen. Blessed silence descended as they stuffed their mouths with the sweet, flaky fudge.

* * *

On lookout duty, Cathy was first to spot the Mertol re-emerge from the entrance of his cave. The creature looked very angry. Its appearance was so sudden that she didn't have time to duck and was spotted. She muttered to herself as she scrambled down the hill to where Michael and Jean were hiding in the bushes. Their eyes widened when they saw, first her, then the Mertol. They braced themselves as the beast balanced at the top of the slope and took aim. A small ball whizzed from one of the pouches in his left cheek and exploded above Cathy's head.

"Baacckkk!" They heard his eerie cry above them.

"Hold your breath and run!" Cathy shouted at them as she rushed past. Pinching her nose, she slipped and slid down the slope. The others followed, running until the black cloud of dust disappeared.

"Baacckkk!" The Mertol cried out again and beat his chest in frustration as he chased after them.

Now a good hundred yards ahead of the beast, Cathy, Jean, and Michael veered to their right, a move that took them away from the army on the ridge that had killed the dragon. They were soon skidding down a slippery, muddy path on their backsides and gaining momentum. With a screech, the three flew through the air and then plunged into a cold, sludgy river that was a disgusting shade of green.

Sitting in water a foot deep, Michael clutched at his shoulder. "This isn't going to do my arthritis any good whatsoever!" he groaned.

"Neither would that thing's teeth," Cathy snapped. "You're a typical, wuss of a man who doesn't know how to put up with a bit of..." But Cathy was interrupted by the cry of the Mertol behind them; he sounded like he was in pain.

"What's happening to it?" Jean stood up, but soon crouched down again when a black arrow zipped into the river just inches from her leg.

"Swim! Now!" yelled Cathy.

More arrows zipped into the water where they'd stood just seconds before. Further away now, the Mertol's angry cries changed into a series of grunts and screams, as if the creature was under attack.

Frantically, Jean, Cathy and Michael kicked themselves round the bend of the river. Their arms and legs heavy with fatigue, they pushed deeper into the dark Forest of Eldane.

* * *

Eethan passed Cathy, Jean and Michael, unseen, on the opposite bank. He soon arrived back at the small cave by the river where the Mertol had held Ephie and the children. He knew he had to close this particular exit before the Mertol returned, so with a wave of his hand, he muttered his magic and the ceiling collapsed in a roar of rock.

* * *

Cathy could see that Jean was struggling against the weight of her sodden mohair cardigan. "Take that bloomin' thing off!" she snapped. But just as she was going to help her with it she heard a familiar voice.

"Psssst!"

She saw the little, blue man standing on the riverbank waving them in. Doing as they were directed, the three adults dragged themselves out of the river. Exhausted and soaking wet, they followed Eethan into the forest without a thought of where he was taking them. Their brains were too numb.

"Mum!" Helen jumped out from a clump of ferns and threw her arms round Jean's neck.

"Helen! Joe!" cried Jean in stunned delight. All three burst into tears as they clung to each other.

"My back is killing me!" Michael complained, his eyes screwed up tight in pain as he shuffled across to a patch of grass to sit beside Ephie.

Cathy just shook her head and lay back on the damp grass. "Men!" She sighed as she stared up at the patches of blue beyond the canopy, her mind drifting to thoughts of James and the man who had deserted them in Drumfintley more than three weeks before. Her energy seemed to ebb away and a terrible emptiness took hold of her. *All men are pathetic*, she decided. They never stop moaning and are useless when they fall ill or have aches and pains. At least I won't have to listen anymore to David moan about his heartburn or his back or his lack of sleep. A small tear rolled down her left cheek, but she quickly wiped it away before anyone noticed.

In the distance, they could still hear the muted screams of the Mertol. "Ee thinks the Mertol's having a bad day," Eethan tittered. "Ees probably trapped by Hedra archeeers."

Hearing this, Cathy snapped out of her daze, remembering what had happened to the dragon. She sat up and pointed at Eethan. "Never mind the Mertol. He'll distract those things from us. Let's focus on the important things. When are we going to find my son? How much time do we have before that thing or those weird reptile things come after us again? And what can we eat around here? I'm starving."

Eethan simply glanced once over his shoulder at her and answered all three questions in his sing-song voice, "Soon, not much, and this!" He stood up and offered her some moss, a cheeky, needle-toothed smile spreading across his leathery face.

Cathy jumped up and grabbed Eethan by the throat.

Michael stood up. "In God's name, Cathy, leave him alone!"

Cathy glanced sideways at the Reverend and saw that he was shaking with rage. Apparently, the man had a bit of back-bone after all.

"No violence in front of my children, please!" said Jean pulling the kids closer to her. She shot Cathy and Michael a pointed stare.

Cathy let go of Eethan's neck and whispered, "Pathetic. You're all bloody pathetic." Free from her grip, Eethan clutched his throat and coughed. Undaunted, he managed to blink out another smile. "Ees nice. Try some." He waved the moss at Cathy again, but not for long. Ephie snatched it from Eethan's fingers and stuffed it in her mouth.

"Mmmmm. It's delicious!" Her plump cheeks regained some of their colour and she sighed in ecstasy.

"Mossgeld," explained Eethan. "Eees full of veetameens, so eet ees."

"Yummy!" said Wee Joe, pulling a strand from the nearest tree.

"It tastes just like melon candyfloss!" cried Helen, already chewing on the sticky strands. Soon they were all pulling strips of Mossgeld from the trees. Eethan disappeared for a moment, returning with a cup-shaped leaf filled with water, which they passed round. Only Cathy remained sitting, her back to a tree, staring blankly into the distance. It was Michael, forever the peacemaker, who crouched down beside her and offered her some water, but she didn't even acknowledge him. Instead, she continued to look ahead into the gloom of the forest, oblivious to all, alone in the prison of her rage.

After they'd eaten and rested, Eethan explained what they must do. "Wees have to build a raft and go upstream, away from all dee bad things. Wees have to start now. I theenk Mendel will take dee boys to dee Eden Tree and that's furtheer up dee Reever Levan from heere!"

Jean, Michael, Ephie and Eethan all began gathering the necessary logs and vines to build the raft while the kids amused themselves playing with the ropey moss.

Cathy continued her sulk and did nothing to help.

It was Helen's voice that eventually cut through her angry thoughts. "It's ready, Mrs. Peck. Come and see it. We're all waiting on you."

Cathy looked up to see them arranging themselves on the raft. Moored to an overhanging branch, it bobbed in the green waters of the River Levan. Ephie sat at the front of the craft with Michael, while Jean and Eethan manned the rear.

Befuddled, Cathy took Helen's little hand and walked down to the beach.

Helen addressed the tight-lipped onlookers. "I think she's sorry." She smiled up at the blank-faced Cathy. But Cathy had neither the will nor the energy to acknowledge the little girl.

There was an uneasy silence as the raft moved out into the green water of the river. At first, the raft began to drift the wrong way, caught in a slow current that would have led them back towards the Mertol's cave. But once they got their rhythm, their makeshift paddles began to propel the craft upstream, further into the forest.

Eethan beamed. "Ees not too deefeecult, eh?"

Adjusting their strokes to counter the current, they slowly began to move away from the caves of the Mertol and soon passed close beneath a rocky knoll.

"Ees called Dunnad," explained Eethan.

Cathy was just about to tell Eethan to quit yapping all the time when she felt a tingle down her spine that caused her to gasp. "James?" She blinked up into the morning light that flickered down through the canopy.

"Why did you shout on James, Mrs. Peck?" Helen enquired.

"Um, no. It was nothing," said Cathy, suddenly annoyed a herself.

It felt cooler now beneath the overhanging branches as they paddled deeper into the shadowy Forest of Eldane. Wee Joe's little voice echoed out over the green waters, "Two wittle mice, Titty Tatty mice, having adwentures and never finking twice…"

CHAPTER TWENTY-TWO

THE YELTAN BANQUET

Deep below the Forest of Eldane, Landris was keen to exchange information with the boys as soon as possible and, in order to induce a more convivial atmosphere, he'd prepared a special banquet.

They sat down to steamed river fish, grilled rootlets, golden-spotted mushrooms, purple Mossgeld, and an interesting array of little drinks that were all laid out in concentric rings across a beautiful hardwood table. The boys were at the far end, seated beside Landris and Garlon.

They were busy filling their wooden plates with various pieces of fish and fruit when Craig asked, "What do you guys call yourselves then?"

James's eyes widened. He thought this was a bit cheeky. "He means…" he interjected, feeling embarrassed. "If that's not too rude a question…"

Landris laughed and cut another slice of pink flesh from the scaled monster on the table, then dipped it into a shallow bowl of boiling spiced oil. "We call ourselves Yeltans, but we are known as Root Dwellers, Tree Pixies, Yellow Imps—"

"Or an appetizer, if you're a Hedra!" Garlon interrupted. The Yeltans all began laughing, except Landris who gave Garlon a stern glance.

James found the array of small glasses that littered the huge table-top intriguing. Yellow, green, and even black liquid filled these delicate crystal goblets and the Yeltans seemed to pick certain colours to go with certain courses. Craig was the first to try one.

"Gonie huv some, James!" announced Craig, in his most annoying, phoney Scottish accent. "Ish wan tastes jist like bubblegum! Try it!" Craig slid over a small glass containing a thick yellow liquid.

James shook his head disdainfully at Craig's attempt at the accent before cautiously taking a sip. He shivered as the drink filled his nose and mouth with the flavours of bubblegum and creamy chocolate. "Whaow! It's delicious!" Reaching for more, he soon caught up with Craig, drinking four in a row.

"So what's this called, Landris?" Craig held up a glass of the bubblegum drink and started to giggle.

"That particular one is called Lugpus," answered Landris.

"What-pus?" Craig cried, then laughed loudly, his eyes tearing up.

Landris explained, "We harvest it from the ears of an animal called a Yukplug then leave it to cool in the river for at least two days."

By now, James was in fits of laughter too. "That's totally gross!" he guffawed, spitting some of the liquid onto the table.

"James! Manners!" Craig patted his friend on the back as he roared and slapped his knee.

It didn't take long for the boys to realise that the laughter was becoming painful.

Landris signalled to Garlon. "I think they've had a little too much." Garlon nodded then looked down the table at the two helpless boys, who were literally shaking and unable to get up. Lying on his back, Craig did a good impression of Mendel's bubbly fish voice by pinging his lips and attempting to talk. "Who's a pwwwetty bwwoy wen? Who's a pwwwetty bwwoy?" Garlon laughed and, moving closer, produced a crumpled, cloth bag from his red belt. He nipped a pinch of yellow powder from the bag and blew it straight into their faces.

Instantly, their laughter stopped. Somewhat bemused, they got to their feet and picked up their chairs. James looked round expecting to see accusing stares or looks of outrage, but there were none. Everybody continued talking and eating as if nothing had happened. Only Landris addressed them. "It does that!" he said quietly. "It makes you giggle, but if you take too much, you begin to laugh and laugh until..."

"Until what?" asked Craig, a small snigger escaping before he managed to cover his mouth.

"Until it becomes necessary to take the anti-mirth powder," Landris told him.

"Mirth pow— Can we have some? The Lugpus, I mean. It would be great in school..." said Craig, winking at James.

"Only if you take some antidote as well," said Landris. "Many creatures have literally died laughing." He smiled and signalled to another Yeltan. "Bring the boys some Lugpus and anti-mirth powder."

James wiped his eyes and asked, "What is the antidote, exactly?"

"Anti-mirth powder? It's other name is Nose-squeeze. It's from the same animal," explained Garlon. "But it's left to dry in the sun for two days until it becomes a powder. But don't ever take the anti-mirth powder before first taking the Lugpus or you'll probably jump off the nearest cliff in a fit of depression."

"You said the animal this stuff comes from is called a Yukplug?" Craig looked at Garlon and Garlon nodded back with a smile. His strange blue eyes sparkled.

"What does it look like, this Yukplug?" Craig, ever curious, was anxious to see the creature that could actually produce such weird stuff.

"I will show you," said Garlon.

Craig's eyes widened when the young Yeltan took his hand and led him from the table. "Bero, come boy!"

James and Landris got up and followed after them. Soon they were all standing outside in an arena surrounded by huge roots. "These are the stables," Garlon told them.

"Stables? You mean you can ride them?" Craig had two years of riding lessons under his belt. "Can I have a go?"

James hiccuped before saying, "Craig's a bit of a show-off."

"A show-off?" enquired Landris.

"You'll see," James told him.

While James was about the same size as the Yeltans, Craig was almost six inches taller and perhaps a bit too big to ride the creatures comfortably, but he was determined to give it a try.

"It will be a doddle!" Craig announced, sounding smug. He moved round the fence until he was standing only a few feet away from the nearest beast.

James tugged at Landris's sleeve. "Watch this!"

Covered in long brown hair, the Yukplugs looked like a Woolly Mammoth crossed with an ostrich—their long necks covered in feathers.

James called out to his friend. "They look just like two-legged highland cattle!"

Craig was mesmerised. The Yukplug stood some six feet high on its thick scaly legs, including its head and neck. Its long ears began to flicker as Craig drew closer. A single white horn peeked through its woolly mane and a set of wet nostrils flared and dripped yellow blobs onto the sand. Craig wondered how best to approach the beast. He looked across at Garlon for some advice.

Babbling in Yeltan, Garlon jumped into the pen. The Yukplugs instantly began braying like donkeys. Then, running with unexpected agility, Garlon jumped straight onto the nearest woolly back. Holding the white horn with his left hand, he grabbed a tuft of wool with his right and kicked his heels. The animal shot forward and circled the pen. It galloped towards them at breakneck speed then, with only feet to go, he spun the beast round in front of James and Landris, showering them with sand.

"Garlon!" Landris checked him. "You are being a show-off!" He grinned at James, who grinned back.

Garlon looked perplexed.

Stale air, smelling a lot like a hamster cage, wafted over them from the nearby Yukplug. The scent immediately reminded James of Craig's house and of his dad, who'd been the one to get the hamster for Wee Joe. The memory made him sad all of sudden. Feeling more sober now, he was just about to ask Landris if he or his kind had seen any signs or heard of any news about his father when he noticed Craig stroking the Yukplug's mane.

"Look, it likes me!" Craig giggled again until the Yukplug sneezed, covering him in yellow drippy snot. "Argh! Yuck! No. What the...?"

James's face brightened again. "Serves you right, ye numpty!"

"They know when other creatures still need a little more anti-mirth!" Landris chuckled, giving James a pat on the back. While Craig chased after the Yukplug, James turned to Landris. "I've been meaning to ask... Have you found anything else in the forest, I mean, apart from Mendel's barrel?" Landris raised an eyebrow so James tried to explain, "You see, my father is missing and we found his compass in the forest. I don't suppose anyone's seen him?"

Landris looked concerned. "Well, we've just picked up some clothes that look similar to your own. But..." the Yeltan frowned. "It is not so much what we've found but where we found them that concerns me."

Across the paddock, Craig yelped. He was perched on a Yuk-plug and holding on for dear life. Already on the move, the Yukplug made small purring sounds as it tried to dislodge its tall, unfamiliar rider. But Craig was good. He held on and steered the animal this way and that until it cantered over towards James.

"This is fantastic! It's much more comfortable than the ponies I've ridden back home." Smiling like a Cheshire cat, he bounced up and down on the Yukplug's soft matted wool.

Still thinking about what Landris had said, James felt his chest tighten and, for the first time since he'd arrived in Denthan, he felt a horrible shortness of breath. Ignoring Craig's excitement, he turned to Landris. "Please... Tell me what you've found."

"Shouldn't we wait until Craig joins us?" asked Landris.

"We don't need to," persisted James. "Please, just tell me."

Landris signalled to Garlon to get Craig off the Yukplug. "I'd much rather show you both."

Garlon jumped off his beast and motioned Craig to do the same.

"Oh, come on. I'm just beginning to get the hang of it," complained Craig, a mixture of confusion and frustration on his face. He slid off the Yukplug and walked over to James and Landris. "That was great fun." He patted the Yukplug's mane. "What's the matter now?"

James answered, "The Yeltans have just found some clothes. They might be something to do with Dad." James saw a flash of irritation in Craig's eyes.

Back inside, the Yeltans led them to the chamber where they'd first entered the caves. Mendel's broken barrel still sat on the desk. Walking past it, Landris stretched up to retrieve a small cloth bag from a high shelf. "I hope you are prepared." Landris looked grave. James was almost in tears when Landris opened the bag. The Yeltan tipped a blue cagoule and a neckerchief onto his desk. James stared down at the familiar items for a second then turned to Craig. He couldn't speak.

Frowning, Craig wandered over to the table and picked up the blue and white Scout neckerchief. "It's the fifth Drumfintley Scout's colours, alright." He looked closer and his face paled. "The leather woggle—it's your dad's, isn't it?"

"Yes, but it was hanging on my wall when i left. My dad didn't have it with him when he disappeared. What's going on?" James looked over at Landris's strange face. "Where did you find them?" he breathed.

"We found no trace of your father," Landris replied. "Only the clothes, but…"

He turned to Garlon who added, "They were found at the entrance of a cave, a Mertol's cave."

James and Craig didn't know what a Mertol was, but it sounded bad. Bero licked James's hand.

Landris continued, "The Mertol is a magical creature that ranks Yeltan as one of its favourite dishes."

"You think it's eaten his dad, don't you?" Craig blurted.

Landris and Garlon said nothing.

James looked sick, then suddenly brightened. "Wait a second… Mendel told me that he was certain my dad was still alive! Before he told us about Dendralon."

Dendralon's name caused Landris to gasp. "Why do you say that name?"

James sniffed. "Well, Dendralon is the one who banished Mendel while disguised as a King. I think that's what Mendel said anyway."

"King Athelstone? An impostor? Amazing! You must tell us everything," instructed Landris, beckoning Garlon to come closer.

"Well," James began, "Mendel told us that this Dendralon was a kind of reptile."

Landris nodded. "Dendralon is an ancient Hedra wizard, but we thought he was dead."

James wiped his nose with his sleeve. "Well he's not dead. I've met him. And he has apparently disguised himself as the King of Gwendral to trick the people in the city into leaving. He wants to use the place as a giant gateway, but only for his own kind."

"I can't believe it," said Landris. "You mean he's found a way of doing this?"

"I suppose so," replied James, giving a little shrug.

Craig moved forward. "You see, your sun is dying, and Mendel says that Denthan will…" He scrunched up his freckled face as he searched for the right word, "explode?"

It wasn't the right word. Landris and Garlon began wailing like a pair of strangled cats.

"Or… or…" Craig motioned for calm. "Mendel could be wrong, of course," he continued unconvincingly. "At least James's dad looks to be safe enough though, eh?"

The wailing continued.

James never failed to be amazed by Craig's lack of tact. "Look," he interjected. "If we ever got separated Mendel told us to meet him at the Eden Tree. So why don't we just go there now?"

The Yeltans still looked distraught. "We must tell the Manimals about Athelstone. This makes perfect sense, perfect sense." Garlon and Landris proceeded to babble to each other in a high-pitched language that the boys could barely hear. Bero seemed to hear it, though. Whenever they started up their strange mutterings, his tail began to wag.

Finally, Garlon calmed down a bit. "The Athelstone of old would never have banished Mendel. We always knew this, but never realised that Dendralon Pendragon was the one controlling the strings. If he has truly returned, we are in grave danger. He is probably the most powerful wizard ever. It took a hundred years to defeat him the first time around."

"Well that's a pity," remarked Craig. "According to Mendel we've got about a day and a half."

The Yeltan's wailing began all over again.

"Nice one Craig," sighed James, covering his ears. "If we ever make it out of here, you should really consider joining the Diplomatic Service."

Ignoring him, Craig was just about to say something else to the Yeltans, but James, deciding his friend had said more than enough, gave him a swift kick.

"Argh! Owww…!" The wailing Yeltans, who must have thought Craig was commiserating with them, grabbed him and hugged him and wailed even more.

Other Yeltans had gathered at the doorway by now, no doubt drawn by all the caterwauling. James tried to get Landris and Garlon's attention. "We have to get going!" he yelled. "There's no time to waste!"

After another few minutes of wailing, the terrible noise died down to a more manageable moan. Landris shook his head. "I'm sorry James, you are right, of course. We need to leave straight away. If Mendel has truly come back with you to save us, we have to go now." He heaved a shuddering sigh.

Craig took hold of Bero's collar. "We did mention the bit about Mendel being a fish, didn't we?"

"I think Landris heard you the first time you blabbed it out," James snapped.

As they set out, James wondered if maybe Landris knew more about Mendel's banishment than he was letting on. He even wondered if the Yeltan might have been part of the group that had made the decision.

As they made their way deeper into the Yeltan labyrinths, James noticed a large room off to their right containing piles of golden armour and small spears. He nudged Craig, who, when he saw it, asked Landris what it was.

Landris told him that it was their armoury. He had stopped to explain this in front of a large tapestry, which now caught James's attention. "What do those pictures show?" he asked, pointing to them.

Landris turned round. "This tapestry depicts the arrival of the Dragons of Hest, which happened almost three thousand years ago. That," Landris pointed to a blue-cloaked figure seated on the back of one of the many white dragons, "is Mendel."

James reached out and touched the woven cloth, tracing the bumps and fibres with his fingertips, hoping to get a better look at the blue-cloaked figure. But there was just not enough detail. Mendel was only a tiny part of an enormous landscape. The epic scene depicted the city of Gwendral, surrounded by a host dragons that chased and torched a massive army of dark, grey-skinned, reptilian people.

Landris said, "The Hedra fled from the city, disappearing into the Southern Marshes."

Standing further back, Craig noticed a smaller blue figure sitting next to Mendel, his hand raised above his snow-white hair in an odd gesture.

Garlon traced his fingers over the tapestry too. "The small creature you see beside Mendel is called Eethan Magichand. He was a powerful sorcerer and is still worshiped by the Yeltan race. Mendel and his friends have already saved us once. Let us hope our great wizard can do it again."

CHAPTER TWENTY-THREE

THE BEGINNING OF THE END

As the tapping sound outside his cell door grew louder, Cimerato's pulse quickened in readiness. Gwendral's jails were set deep within the foundations of the city, well below the splendid minarets and citadels. There was little hope of escape. Cimerato decided, in the dank confines of his cell, to take any chance offered to him, however slim it might be. If this was a guard, he might still think the prisoner was unconscious, at the very least, drowsy. Cimerato must ready himself to attack if he was to have any likelihood of getting out of this fetid cell.

A key turned in the lock, and the door creaked open. As quietly as possible, Cimerato moved back against the granite wall and waited for the door to open further. It swung inward and the light of a flickering torch filled the room.

He was about to spring forward when he heard a familiar voice call out, "Son?"

Cimerato paused. "Father?" He edged forward. "How did you get down here with Athelstone's guards everywhere?"

"They are not all his guards. Not yet." Lord Eldane signalled his men to help escort the still-groggy Cimerato out of the cell. "Come!"

Following his father and the guards down a set of dark, slippery stairs, Cimerato soon realised that they were heading toward the underground sewers that lay deep beneath the city. "What's your plan, Father?" he panted. His father's personal guards came to a halt beside a small, rowing boat.

Short of breath, Lord Eldane wheezed, "We must get out of the city!"

"We can't just leave everyone behind!" Cimerato protested. "Where's mother? What about the children?"

Lord Eldane climbed into the boat and began to untie the ropes. "You must come now. They have already left for the tunnels that lead to the Nordengate Mountains. As soon as Athelstone used his dark magic on you I knew, in my heart, that he was not the same man we all once loved and trusted. I should have known that when he banished Mendel." He sounded ashamed, for he had been one of those who had sided against the wizard.

Cimerato kept his silence as he boarded the craft. There was nothing he could say that would alleviate his father's shame.

As they took their seats, Lord Eldane made sure he was sitting close to his son. "I've had news from the Yeltans, over near Dunnad. A small reptilian flyer arrived at my window carrying a scroll bearing the seal of Landris."

Cimerato knew that whenever the Yeltans had some useful information for the Manimals they rarely sent messages by flyer, preferring instead the pomp and ceremony of official visits. "What does Landris say?"

"He says that he has found two small boys and a yellow creature, called a dog. He writes that these boys are not from our world; that they've travelled to Denthan with Mendel, no less."

"Mendel!" Cimerato punched the air excitedly, causing the small boat to rock and pitch perilously. "I knew he'd find a way to get back!" Reaching out, Eldane steadied the boat and the guards began to row. "Apparently, the boys transported Mendel back to Denthan inside a small barrel, which they'd suspended round the neck of this dog creature."

"Ingenious! But can Mendel do his magic as a fish? I thought Athelstone had purposely changed him to stop him performing his magic."

"Hmm. Yes." His father frowned, quickly veering away from that subject. "It's unclear from the message, but Landris says that Mendel and the boys have become separated. The Yeltans asked that we meet them at the Eden Tree on Senegral Island."

Cimerato knew his father was holding something back. The old man's eyes darted about, unable to meet his son's scrutiny as he busied himself unnecessarily with his robe.

"Father, Landris told you something else in his note, didn't he?" The old man's fingers became tangled in his purple robe. With a sigh, he leaned over and whispered so the guards wouldn't hear, "Landris has said to take great care around King Athelstone. He is, as Mendel claimed all along, an impostor. The boys have told Landris that Athelstone is actually Dendralon Pendragon."

Cimerato felt his stomach lurch. He knew, all too well, who Dendralon was. As a child, whenever he had displeased his parents they would say that Dendralon's ghost would come and steal him away. "You mean we've banished Mendel, one of the truest men Gwendral has ever known, on the advice of a Hedra wizard? Worse, this traitor has persuaded us to abandon Gwendral so that all he has to do is open the gates and let his Snakemen walk into the city. How could we have been so stupid?"

"Shhhh," Lord Eldane hushed his son. They would soon be beneath the city walls. "If Athelstone is indeed Dendralon, he must possess very powerful magic to have made such fools of us all for so long."

"He does look exactly like Athelstone," Cimerato admitted, feeling a rage rising in his chest.

Lord Eldane sighed. "Son, we have something much more deadly than Dendralon to worry about."

Cimerato didn't understand.

"Time itself." Eldane moved closer to Cimerato in the darkness of the wet tunnel. "Mendel told these boys that Denthan might only have a few days left before Tealfirth explodes."

Cimerato blinked. "Then we'd better get to the Eden Tree fast, don't you think? Mendel would never have returned without a plan. There must be a way out of this."

"There is," whispered Eldane. "Landris has said that Dendralon knows of a gateway that can transport thousands at a time from this world to another. They say that he is going to save his own kind at our expense."

Cimerato mulled this over as they passed under the city. Sticking to the shadows, the boat edged its way nearer to the River Levan. Slowly, and with muffled oars, the little boat glided under the ridge where the Hedra had gathered in such great numbers. The small party of Manimals could hear them screaming and banging their war drums above them. The bloodthirsty yodels made them all shiver with dread.

The Hedra sounded ready for war.

* * *

Determined to make sure nothing could go wrong with his plan, Dendralon stepped off the royal boat that had taken him under the city and scanned the sewer area, looking for weaknesses.

"Sssire!" hissed Jal, bowing low as Dendralon passed. He recognised the Hedra wizard immediately. Even though Dendralon was still hidden beneath the straining Manimal skin of King Athelstone, Hedra could always sense Hedra, no matter how well they were disguised.

Jal was one of King Feldon's most trusted guards and had come to greet Dendralon. Jal's torch lit the way up the steps that led to the Hedra camp above them. He stopped to let the dark wizard proceed, but to his surprise, Dendralon turned and slapped him across the face with a small, needle-spiked dragon whip.

"Get more guards down here, you idiot!" Dendralon hissed in his own Hedra voice. "We don't want any Manimal worms escaping this way." Having delivered his order, Dendralon waved Jal out of his way and grunted disparagingly. As he moved on, Jal's flickering tongue caught the stench of Manimal in the tunnel. Dendralon's magic was struggling to keep Athelstone's skin from rotting.

Jal called after the retreating figure. "Yes sire, I will call more guards to man the sewers." But Dendralon was already gone.

Back down at the underground river, Jal stood looking into the darkness and cursed the dark wizard King under his breath. Hunger pains took hold of his stomach. His last meal, a small reptilian flyer, had been many hours ago. He looked up at the steps on the opposite side of the river and called to the solitary Hedra guard. "Go now and get more sentries down here. Move!"

The guard nodded and scampered up the wet steps to do as he was bidden.

* * *

"What was that?" Cimerato asked. He'd thought he'd heard some kind of scuffle ahead. "Slow down. Quiet!" He took command of the group. "I'm going to scout round this next bend," he told them. Cimerato turned to his father's guards. "You four, stay here with the boat and my father. You and you, come with me." He unclipped his yellow armour and slipped into the cold water along with the two guards and swam round the bend in the river.

There they saw a small jetty and beside it, a large Hedra guard who looked agitated and restless.

Cimerato swam closer and noted that there were no other guards, just the solitary Hedra giant positioned on the right-hand bank, guarding a set of slippery stairs that disappeared behind him into the darkness. Turning to swim back to the boat, he noticed the giant moving towards the stairs, muttering to himself and belching loudly before disappearing from view.

Once Cimerato reached his father's boat, he gave them the news. "Row very quietly," he told them as he climbed in. "There was just one Hedra guard. He's gone now but he may return at any time."

The rest of the guards climbed in and the boat edged round the corner of the underground river. It soon passed the stairway and drifted out into the night.

Only ten more minutes and we will be in the estuary of the River Levan, thought Cimerato.

When they reached the great river, he said to his father, "I saw a Dragon pulled down by the beasts on that ridge this morning. Why did someone try and fly over the ridge?" Cimerato stared up at the dark mass of granite above them.

Lord Eldane scanned the night sky. "There must have been at least six attempts to cross the city walls on the Dragons of Hest. Only one succeeded. One! Some of your richer relations foolishly thought it would be safer than the tunnels."

"That guard back there... I'm sure he had the green serpents of King Feldon on his breastplate." Cimerato looked up at the thousand camp fires dotting the ridge, then back at the City of Spires' moonlit silhouette. The city looked impregnable from this angle. "If we take turns rowing, we should reach the tributary that leads to the Island of Senegral by daybreak." Cimerato closed his eyes as he pictured his mother making her way through the old tunnels that led to Nordengate. No one had been in those tunnels for centuries. He worried, and wondered what dark creatures might linger there in the black pools.

* * *

Having forgotten his rations pouch, Jal doubled back to the bottom of the stairs to fetch it. When he crouched to pick it up, however, he thought he saw the outline of a small boat fade into the inky night. In an instant, he switched his eyes to infrared. The insects and bats working the dark tunnel were transformed into a mass of flying dots and traces that made it difficult to focus. Before long, though, he saw what he was looking for. In the distance, eight faint red, glowing figures, that could only be warm-blooded Manimals, had slipped past on a rowing boat.

If I confess this to Dendralon now, I'll be soundly punished, Jal realised with a shudder. *No, I'll say nothing*, he thought. *Why should I risk my neck any more than I have to?* He started back up the stairs, having convinced himself that he was doing the right thing. When he reached the top of the stairs, he heard voices and froze.

"What do you mean you never got my message?" Dendralon raged. "I ordered you to find the boys and kill them!"

"But, sire," exclaimed King Feldon, "we never received the message!" The Hedra King did not like being humiliated, especially in front of his entourage.

Dendralon continued his attack. "I sent it last night, attached to the reptile flyer that you sent to me!"

"But it never returned," said Feldon, shifting nervously.

Hidden in the shadows of the stairwell, Jal gulped as he remembered his snack from the night before.

Dendralon waved Feldon's guards away and continued in a low voice, lest any would hear other than Feldon himself. "In two days, I will give the command to open the gates. Later that same day Tealfirth will die and our world will be no more!"

"What?" Feldon's slit pupils expanded and blackened in fear. "As soon as that?"

Dendralon gave him a cold smile. "I have already given the order for a mass evacuation of the city. Even now, they scamper like rats." He leaned closer still. "Remember Feldon, only those inside the city of Gwendral will survive the holocaust. Once I have the three crystals in place, the city will transport our race to another world. The Hedra will be the only Denthan survivors."

"As it should be." Feldon's nostrils flared with satisfaction at the news.

Dendralon glanced down at the blue crystal that hung round Feldon's neck and smiled. "Don't shoot their tired dragons down from the sky anymore, let them flee. Save your weaponry." Dendralon scratched at a peeling patch of pale skin. "In two days time, once the Salt Trolls and Osgrunfs have wiped each other out, you can simply walk into an empty city. Have patience, but be ready to move at a moment's notice."

Feldon nodded.

"I have work to do," continued Dendralon, "so I must go. While you wait, I want you to take care of those boys. I cannot risk any interventions by that persistent fool, Mendel. Is that clear?"

Feldon nodded once more and in a blink of an eye, Dendralon disappeared in a swirl of black mist.

Jal continued to watch, still somewhat bemused, as Feldon summoned his captain, a savage fighter called Telan, and explained what had to be done. "Make sure that all Hedra have gathered on the ridge. Tell them to stop wasting ammunition on old dragons." Feldon looked at the spot where Dendralon had stood, his long tongue flicking in and out of his mouth, attempting to sense the wizard's presence.

Seemingly reassured that Dendralon was gone, Feldon gave his next instructions. "Take a troop into the forest and make sure that the archers who fired on that useless Mertol show you where they saw the Manimal woman in the river. Take the Tree Trolls with you and find those boys. Make sure you kill all of the Manimals, young and old!" Telan made to bow, but Feldon put the point of his sword under Telan's chin, forcing him to lift his head again. "Be sure to kill the Mertol this time too. He failed Dendralon. If he had done his job properly, the strangers would not have entered the forest. Also, once the Tree Trolls have done their work, get rid of them too. Got that?"

Jal suspected that Dendralon would look well on such thoroughness.

Feldon motioned Telan to leave and then called out. "Jal! Jal! Where are you?"

Jal pressed himself against the wet wall as King Feldon shouted down the stairwell that led to the underground river.

"Sire?" To Feldon's annoyance, Telan was still in the room. "Sire, the Mertol killed twenty of our archers today. Its magic is dangerous and unpredictable. And how exactly do you kill a Tree Tro—?" The guard stopped mid-sentence as Feldon whipped round and gripped his throat.

"Sssssssssss. I thought I told you to go. You do not think. You just do!" Telan shut his scaly nostrils tight as Feldon's dank breath washed over him. The Hedra King moved even closer to the captain's face and hissed, "Go!"

The Hedra officer tripped backwards, struggling to breathe. He bowed awkwardly, then fell out into the warm night air. Jal could hear Telan's voice outside. "Where are the..." he coughed, "the Tree Trolls?"

Not wishing it to appear that he'd listened in on the various conversations, Jal waited a few seconds before slipping from the wet passageway into Feldon's tent. Feldon looked up when his bodyguard entered. "Ah, there you are, Jal. Come here." He sat Jal down, his voice was soft when he spoke. "Telan has just left."

Jal smiled. "Yes, my Lord, I noticed."

"He won't be coming back again. Ever." Feldan tilted his head and looked Jal straight in the eye. "Understood?"

Jal blinked his yellow-slit eyes. "I don't quite follow, sir." Jal had, of course, heard everything, and did follow, but he liked to play dumb. He was less of a threat to the King that way.

Feldon smiled at Jal. "Once Telan has carried out his tasks, I want you to kill him."

"Tasks, my lord?"

"Listen carefully, Jal, and you will understand. I want you to go with Telan—tell him I sent you. Tell him to relay every instruction I've just given him to you. Remind him that he will need more than twenty archers to overpower and kill the Mertol. The useless ape failed to guard the gateway into Denthan and has displeased Dendralon. Only after he has carried out all my instructions are you to kill Telan. Got that so far?"

"Yes, sire."

"And then you may come back and tell me when all is done." Feldon had used Jal for missions of this nature many times.

"Another clean-up, Lord?" remarked Jal with a smile.

"That's it, a clean-up. You're good at cleaning up, Jal, but..." Feldon turned to pour himself a large glass of red liquid. "Make sure you return within two days."

"Do we attack after this, my Lord?"

"Something like that. I'll need you back at my side by then, so just make sure you're here when I need you." Feldon drank deeply from his chalice and waved Jal away with a flick of his taloned hand.

Jal bowed then made his way out into the main Hedra camp. In these last desperate hours, he would have to look after himself. From a young Hedra, Jal had devoted his life to the King, doing his dirty work, protecting him. But that, Jal knew, did not mean Feldon would be doing him any favours in return. When push came to shove, the Hedra King would think only of saving his own skin.

* * *

The Tree Troll, Ashthat, sat sharpening a large tree trunk, a task made more difficult by the huge patch covering his blind eye and his currently unusable hand. As he attempted to work, driven purely by thoughts of revenge, his brother, Ssslathat, poured a great bowl of oil over his blooded finger stumps. Already, green shoots had pushed through the ends of his severed fingers, bending and flexing as they grew.

"You two!" Telan pointed at the Tree Trolls. "Feldon has agreed to assist you in your hunt for the little boys who wounded you."

"They had magic on their side!" protested Ashthat in his deep, woody voice.

"If you say so," Telan mocked.

By this time, Jal had caught up with Telan and his crew. As he had done all his life, he listened carefully, but appeared to hear nothing. He was particularly intrigued by Telan's next instruction. "We'll sniff them out for you, but first you must help us."

"Help?" Ssslathat's massive frame creaked as he straightened up. Telan flicked his black tongue nervously. "Yes, help. You must help us kill a Mertol who has failed in his duties." Although he tried to hide it, it was obvious to Jal that the Hedra captain was intimidated by the immense size of the Trolls. He wondered how Telan was going to manage getting rid of two of them when the time came.

"Ha! Ha!" Ashthat, still gripping his wounded hand, roared with laughter at the suggestion.

"This is not a joke," Telan insisted. "If you want our trackers to help you, then you must kill the Mertol. That is our condition!"

"It is not easy to kill a Mertol," said Ssslathat.

Ashthat let his half-sharpened spear fall to the ground and stood up. He put a heavy hand on his brother's shoulder and said, "I will kill the Mertol. The request for revenge is mine, therefore so too is the condition!"

* * *

On the River Levan, Cimerato gazed up at the star-filled sky and listened as his father told him more about Mendel's prediction. "Mendel warned the inner Council that Tealfirth would explode and wipe out Denthan. But Athelstone argued that Mendel's calculations were wrong, then accused him of scaremongering to retain power. We didn't want to believe Mendel, even those who knew and loved him. We listened, instead, to Athelstone; we preferred to believe him. It wasn't long after that when the attacks on our outer villages began.

Athelstone blamed Mendel for these too, convincing us that it was the wizard's experiments that brought this evil upon us. We stupidly believed the soft words of Athelstone and agreed to banish Mendel. But, the sun flares and heat storms continued. In the confusion, the banishment went ahead and we justified it to ourselves, mainly because we did not want to face up to our own fears. I'm sorry, Son..." The old man gripped Cimerato's arm. "Do you remember how that terrible heat storm hit the city just at the point when Athelstone banished Mendel?"

"I remember," Cimerato replied.

"Well, its arrival upset Athelstone considerably and we suspected that all did not go according to plan."

The glow of several far-off campfires lit up the sky as their boat headed further up the river.

"I've been thinking about the last words Mendel said to me," mused Eldane. "He said that if he could return to Denthan, he might be able to save our people by helping them escape through a huge gateway to another world."

"But a gateway can only take a few people at a time," Cimerato pointed out.

"That's what I always believed. But after reading the Yeltan letter, I think now that Athelstone, or should I say Dendralon, has found the giant gateway that would be capable of taking thousands."

"But Dendralon has sent everyone into the tunnels, away from the city," Cimerato argued. "He could just have left us alone to our fate and escaped through his gateway. Why invite the Hedra? Why are the Osgrunfs and Salt Trolls here? I don't understand. He seems to be making things difficult when it could all be so easy for him. Why come back to Gwendral in the first place? Unless..." Cimerato gripped his father's arm. "Gwendral... The gateway must be in Gwendral."

"Exactly."

"But mother and the children and..." gasped Cimerato.

Lord Eldane waved a finger at him. "I've told everyone to wait in the tunnels. They will walk only a mile or so before stopping. They are to wait there until further instructions."

"What instructions?" Cimerato saw nothing in his father's eyes that suggested he had any kind of plan. "You don't know, do you?"

Eldane sighed. "All I know is that Mendel is our only hope now. We must believe that he has managed to return somehow and that he is somewhere in there waiting for us." He pointed ahead into the dark forest.

The muffled oars beat out a steady rhythm as they distanced themselves from the city, passing by the Knoll of Dunnad before slipping into the leafy shelter of the Forest of Eldane.

* * *

Several Salteths were arguing over the remains of a dead comrade who'd been squashed by one of the Salt Trolls, when they saw something that made them screech and jump back from the campfire. Before them, a ghostly, black-cloaked figure stepped out of the flames and dark smoke. They dropped their weapons and ran blindly, tripping over other sleeping Salteths, which caused an even greater commotion than before.

Dendralon addressed the nearest Salt Troll in his distinctive, deep hissing voice. "Sintor!"

Sintor, who'd been watching the quarrelling Salteths with some amusement, shrunk back from the strange apparition that had interrupted his pleasure. With a grunt, he raised himself up, soon standing high above Dendralon. "Why does King Athelstone visit my camp?" he boomed.

"I wear the dead King's skin, Sintor, but I am someone else. Surely you can recognise my voice from your dreams?"

Sintor squinted at him. "Dendralon?"

Dendralon opened his robe and pulled a strip of rotting Manimal flesh away from his serpentine scales. "Very soon now, I shall be free of this." He tossed the fragment amongst the Salteths, who screamed and kicked, until one emerged triumphant with the small morsel in his mouth.

Sintor ignored his noisy slaves. "Why are we not in the city yet, Dendralon? Why have you deemed it necessary for my kin to fry in the heat of day for so long? Why?" he bellowed.

Undaunted by Sintor's aggression, Dendralon stepped forward. "As you know, only some will share the treasures of Gwendral. The stars have foretold it." Dendralon peered steadily at Sintor, his dark eyes unreadable. "You are to destroy the Osgrunf hordes. They are not worthy to pass through the ivory gates of Gwendral." Dendralon pointed up to the black ridge in the distance. "King Feldon and his Hedra army will help you."

A displeased murmur grew amongst the Salt Trolls who had overheard Dendralon's words and they raised their massive Gnarwhale spears. Not intimidated in the least, Dendralon shook his long, black hair from his hood and continued, "I will weave magic that will help you in your fight, but I need something of yours to protect you from my spell." Dendralon lifted his right hand above his head and whispered a small charm.

The trees that had sheltered the sea creatures from the intense heat of the day began to sway and bend in a sudden breeze. The Trolls looked about in fear, then let loose a mighty roar, preparing to attack the wizard at Sintor's command. But the Troll King only held up a hand, staying them.

Dendralon pointed a long finger at Sintor. "I need your crystal."

Sintor had worn it since birth. "But why?" he growled, not liking this request at all. The blue crystal was his badge of Kinghood. Set in a bronze wristband, the talisman shone amber and cerulean blue in the light of the campfire. For an instant, a flash of light from the crystal lit up Dendralon's face, making him squint. Sintor shielded the crystal with his massive, wrinkled hand.

Dendralon held out his hand. "I will, of course, return it after the massacre."

A younger Troll, who'd been watching, hissed his disapproval, "This is trickery, Sintor! Do not trust the words of this necromancer in disguise. I can smell his Hedra stench!" The dissenter was about to say more, but fell mute as Dendralon fixed his gaze on the young Troll's large silhouette. He moved his hand back and forth in front of the unlucky creature and, slowly, the brute's skin began to tighten. The fire that had brought Dendralon to their camp leaped free from its embers and snaked up the legs of the screaming giant until the flames covered him completely. After several horrifying moments, there was a sickening crack and the fire snuffed out. The Troll stood motionless, little traces of white smoke seeping from his charred form. There was a quiver and a rumble, and then his body simply exploded, black dust showering over everyone.

The Salt Trolls stealthily began to back away from the wizard, keeping their eyes lowered. All, that is, except Sintor, who remained where he was, dazedly wiping away the black dust covering his craggy face. "Take it!" he finally hissed. "Just take it!" With a grimace of remorse, he dropped the heavy bracelet into the wizard's outstretched hand.

"Do not worry, Sintor, you will not regret this," said Dendralon. "Now, be ready to attack the Osgrunfs. They were never invited to this place."

Sintor turned, and without looking back at Dendralon, barked the commands to his horde. "Get ready for battle!"

With the Salt Troll crystal tucked safely into his pocket, Dendralon slipped between the ranks of the stunned sea creatures and disappeared into the night.

* * *

Dendralon knew he had to move fast, especially now that Mendel might have returned. Using his magic, he soon entered the part of the Plain of Gwendral occupied by the Osgrunfs. Beside a make-shift tent, he spied their leader sitting on a large throne covered with animal skins.

Dendralon's voice interrupted the din. "Hushna!"

The oversized Osgrunf turned to face the wizard, then called for wine. "Wine for the dream-maker. Wine!" Hushna's blue crystal swung on a heavy black chain round his neck. It sparkled through the matted hair that partially covered his armour. "You're not looking your best, Dendralon." Hushna had met the wizard in his disguise before.

With a wave of his flaking hand, Dendralon declined the goblet of wine. "Sorry, Hushna, there is no time to make merry. Not yet. I have come to warn you that the Salt Trolls are planning to move on the city first. They too have had a dream that tells them that the city is theirs. And they are greedy for the treasures within."

"What!" Hushna stood up at once and beat his chest armour with a black hooked claw. "You have betrayed us?"

"I have not," Dendralon lied. He moved in close and whispered into Hushna's ear. "I suspect Mendel summoned the sea creatures here before his banishment." Dendralon spat on the dirt. "I will help you fix this."

Hushna growled at the Osgrunfs that stood beside him as they snarled and jostled to make way for their King and the black wizard.

"What do you have in mind, Dendralon?" Hushna asked, growing agitated when Dendralon beckoned him closer.

Speaking in a low mutter, the dark wizard gave his instructions. "You must attack the Salt Trolls first, and as your reward, we will give you half the treasure of Gwendral. My Hedra army will help you. The stars have foretold our victory. It will signal the dawning of a new age."

Having got what he wanted, Dendralon quickly stepped back. "I must leave now. Time is short. Remember, attack just after sunrise. I am depending on the legendary fury of your army, Hushna." As Dendralon turned to leave, he checked the blue crystal hanging on a thick, black chain round the Osgrunf leader's neck. Dendralon stared at it for a moment, then, satisfied that it looked genuine enough, backed away with the true gem tucked safely in his pocket. Dendralon knew Feldon, the Hedra King, had the third and final crystal. It was the oldest and most important one of them all. With all three, he could operate the greatest of the Gateways. Once events were set in motion, there would be no one to stop him. The appearance of the hideous Salt Trolls and fearsome Osgrunfs at the city gates had been enough to clear the city of the Manimals. Now he would let these armies of Denthan destroy each other. Soon Gwendral would be back in the hands of its original builders, the Hedra.

CHAPTER TWENTY-FOUR

THE BATTLE OF THE BREAK

Ethan slept soundly on the little raft. His disgusting choking noises only interrupted by lengthy pauses, during which, the only two awake, Cathy and Michael, wondered if he was still alive. Normally, however, a loud snort followed by a noise like a vacuum trying to suck up a pint of drool, would signal the blue man's continued existence.

"I'm beginning to feel quite queasy," said Michael, as he paddled in the darkness.

"He's disgusting," Cathy agreed. "Maybe I should give him a dig in the ribs before something out there hears him." She pointed into the gloom of the forest.

"No, let me," the Reverend quickly volunteered. "He might scream out if you, um... hit too hard."

She shrugged. "Whatever."

Nodding grimly, the vicar moved over next to Eethan. "Eethan!" he whispered into the little man's ear, then instantly drew back.

Cathy felt the chill of the night seeping through her coat. "What's wrong now?"

"His ears smell rather ripe," Michael grimaced as he shifted away from the little, blue man.

Cathy lifted her oar out of the water and cracked it against Eethan's skull.

"Eeee! What ees eet, nastee woman?" screeched Eethan.

"Wake up. All that racket you're making is going to bring all the beasties out of the forest," complained Cathy.

"What rackeet? Eethan rubbed his head and muttered something in a strange tongue.

"Mum?" Helen stirred briefly, but fell back to sleep.

"See," spat Cathy, "you're going to wake the kids. Just pick up an oar and row." She gave Eethan a quick kick to the shin.

"Eee! Nastee woman…" Quite awake now, Eethan mumbled to himself as he slipped into the water. Holding on to the back of the raft, he started to kick and they began to move a little faster.

As the night sky assumed the blood-red hue of dawn, the raft moved into a much wider section of the river where the current pushed more forcefully against them. They were struggling to make any headway.

"Wees need to turn een there!" Eethan splashed Cathy's face and pointed to an offshoot, which seemed to lead deeper into the forest.

Cathy's eyes flared with anger as she considered giving Eethan another, harder, crack with the oar, but on seeing that the current was stronger still, she shook Jean and Ephie awake instead. "Rest time is over, you two. You have to help paddle!"

* * *

James and Craig stood beside the Yukplug pen with Bero, mesmerised by Denthan's spectacular double dawn. For the first time since they'd arrived in Denthan, they noticed a few clouds gathering overhead.

"We're ready, Garlon," said James, spotting the young Yeltan. He saw that Garlon and Landris now had a sizeable entourage of Yeltans with them. Each carried a couple of bags and two small spears.

"Good morning, boys," greeted Landris. He narrowed his strange light-blue eyes. "Be careful not to touch the spear tips. They are laced with poison."

"Right." James took a step back.

"Are you both happy to travel by Yukplug?" asked Landris.

"I am," said Craig, "but what about Bero? He would never be able to keep up with those things."

"We could leave him here until we get back," James suggested. "Back from where?" snapped Craig. "Besides, he's come this far." Craig tensed. "I'm not leaving him now."

"Fine!" James looked across to Landris and shrugged. "No Yukplugs, then."

"No problem," said Landris. "We will travel underground."

"How long will it take to get there?" Craig couldn't help thinking of Bero's shaky back legs.

"About three hours, all being well," said Landris . He went on to explain what their route would be. "We will skirt the Centide breeding grounds then travel north to a place known as The Break. It's an off-shoot of the River Levan. For a brief time, we'll need to go to the surface. After that, we'll head deeper into another tunnel system that will lead us to the Eden Tree, which grows on a small hill."

"On Senegral Island?" asked James.

"One and the same," said Landris. "We will travel up under the hill, to the roots of the Eden Tree itself."

"I was there last year!" exclaimed Garlon.

"On your fiftieth birthday," reminded Landris.

"Fiftieth!" The boys blurted it out at the same time. James was amazed that the young-looking Yeltan was so old.

Garlon laughed. "That's nothing! Mendel is said to be more than twelve thousand years old."

James and Craig's eyes widened and Craig gave James a friendly punch on the shoulder. "Un-bloody-believable! You've got a twelve thousand-year-old goldfish, mate!"

James rubbed his shoulder. "I wish. It would be a lot bloomin' easier with Mendel here now."

Standing in line, they waited to drop into the chute that would take them to the necessary tunnel. When it was their turn, they made the leap and flew down the slide. "Ooohhh!" James cried out. "This is great!" He loved slides and roller coasters. Moving at high speed, they eventually landed with a bump in the darkness. There was a click off to their left and light filled the tunnel.

Craig turned to James and whispered, "Electricity?"

"I don't think so, somehow. Look!" James pointed to the Yeltans at the front of their group. They held the same glowing branches they'd seen the day before.

Even though the boys ducked low, the ends of long roots clawed at their hair and clothes as they moved through the cramped tunnel system.

In such a dusty, confined space James marvelled at how easy it was for him to breathe. "I still can't believe I've not coughed or wheezed once since we've been in Denthan." He tried not to think of the lost rucksack and the inhaler inside. Just remembering he didn't have the thing was enough to send him into spasms.

"Just as well," said Craig, "now that you've lost your inhaler. I mean, normally you'd have keeled over by now. I mean, I wouldn't rate your chances here if..."

"Craig!" James exclaimed. "I'm trying not to think about it, for Pete's sake!" James forced himself to think about his dad instead as he plodded on. His dad would have loved exploring the Yeltan caves and the strange Forest of Eldane. Then he remembered Landris producing his father's scout clothes and his good mood melted away.

Deep in his heart James knew that his dad was still alive. He just knew it. *But did his mum? Did she even want his dad to be alive?* Bent double as he navigated the narrow passage, his thoughts drifted to the time when she'd been locked in a toilet on the intercity train between Glasgow and London. His dad had slept through the whole thing. "Six hours and forty-five minutes of hell," his mum had screeched. In his mum's case, it probably had been hell. She was claustrophobic. When they'd finally arrived at his Auntie Bella's she'd recounted the whole sordid affair at least ten times. "He did it on purpose, Bella. I know he did," she'd moaned, "He likes to get back at me now and again, see me suffer. He knows I can't stand small spaces."

The story in turn reminded him of the shout he'd heard on the hill the morning before. He was sure he'd heard someone yelling the word 'run', and it had sounded just like his mum. But then, it couldn't have been. She was on teacake number one hundred and thirty two or something, safe and sound back in Drumfintley.

James tried to get Craig's attention. "How many teacakes are they on now, back at your place?"

Ahead of Bero, Craig chuckled and shook his head. "I don't know, hundreds..."

"Oofff!" James clutched his eye. "Watch where you're pinging those ruddy roots. That hit me right in the face, dunderhead!"

Craig just laughed as he let another one fly.

"Hey!" yelped James.

* * *

Telan, Ssslathat, Ashthat, a whole troupe of Hedra light infantry, and Jal had finally tracked the boy Manimals' scent and were now following it to its source. The two Trolls walked through the river while the Hedra jogged along in the forest. Since the Hedra already knew where the

Mertol's cave was, having lost twenty men there the day before, they soon reached the spot.

Nearing their prey, the trackers separated into two groups.

Ashthat, along with one hundred Hedra, veered east to the Mertol's cave while Telan, Ssslathat, Jal and the rest of the party pushed north along the River Levan. It was this column that locked onto the scent of the Drumfintley party first.

The lead Hedra's tongue flicked excitedly back and forth in the morning air. "Sir, we are close!" He pointed to a small, shale beach. "It is not the boys; it is the second Manimal party!"

Swords drawn, Telan and twenty fighters crept up the bank and then leapt into a shadowy grove. As they hacked at the hanging moss and jabbed into the thick ferns, they soon realised that their prey had moved on. "Look… There were one, two…four adults, two children and…and that." The tracker pointed to a small, three-toed footprint.

"What's that?" Telan asked.

The Hedra shrugged and flicked his tongue, savouring the scent. "Come, we have to catch up with the others." Telan ran back down the beach but stopped as his eyes caught sight of something. He picked up a smooth-white, shiny piece of paper. He held it up to the light and saw some tiny brown grains clinging to the folds and creases. He was completely mystified by the symbols written on the edge of the waxy paper, which read: Galdinie's Hand Made Tablet. For a moment his long, black tongue probed the creases, then he threw his head back in a hideous laugh. "Ha! As ssssweet as honey! They're going to taste good with this running through their veins!" The rest of the Hedra laughed too as they splashed back into the river to join Ssslathat and the remainder of their column.

* * *

Near to the Mertol's cave, the other group of Hedra formed a semicircle behind Ashthat. The hulking Troll blinked his one remaining eye, then jerked his head back and issued a deep, eerie cry that echoed over the hillside. "Kak! Kak!" He was summoning the Mertol to battle. Crumpled Hedra lay scattered round the cave entrance, victims of the previous day's battle. The stench of death wafted down through the ferns to the nervous Hedra below. All had slipped feather-light bows from their backs and, with arrows notched, waited for any sign of movement.

Ashthat came to a halt at the opening of the cave and sniffed the air. His heavy limbs creaked as he crouched down low to peer inside.

He saw a few mangled cages hanging from the roof and a shattered table lying in pieces on the damp floor. As his one remaining, purple eye acclimatised to the darkness, he realised that nothing breathed life in the cave. The Mertol had gone. He backed out of the entrance and looked down the grassy slope at the terrified Hedra. "Nothing there. It's gone! Kak!" He turned, ran, and with an amazing leap bounded over the ducking Hedra. "Back to the river!" he cried. The Hedra sped after him through the forest not wanting to lose sight of the Troll who could cover such huge distances with every step.

It wasn't long before Ashthat had caught up with his brother and the rest of the Hedra. He explained how he'd found the Mertol's cave empty.

Telan cursed. "King Feldon will not be pleased if we return without the Mertol's scalp." He scratched his scaly head. "There is nothing we can do now but go after the Manimals. They are more important."

The troop headed out, a wave of water pushing ahead of the two Trolls as they marched upstream toward the beginning of the tributary known as The Break. Drops of rain began to fall round them and steam rose up from the forest canopy.

"I hate the rain!" Jal blinked as the raindrops intensified.

Telan shouted up at the Trolls. "What can you see up there?"

Ssslathat creaked as he bent down to speak to the Hedra captain. "The river continues onward, but I can see a smaller offshoot to our left. Which way?" he croaked.

Telan flicked his tongue in the rain. "I don't know. I can't smell anything in this muck! Just stick to the main river and look for any sudden movement. They can't be far now."

* * *

Eethan swam round to the front of the raft, then disappeared beneath the clear water.

Jean quickly woke the children. "Helen, Joe, it's morning!"

"Where's the nose-picker off to now?" Cathy punched Michael's shoulder.

"Ow! I don't know." Michael rubbed his shoulder.

"Why are you always hitting people?" said Ephie.

"Oh, shut up, Ephie! Can you see the nose-picker or not?"

Ephie stretched over the side of the raft just as the rain began to fall and looked into the water. "I'm not sure. I can't really see anything for the rain drops."

"Move out of the way, you useless…" Cathy hissed.

Startled, Ephie pulled herself back from the edge.

Cathy peered over the side herself and muttered, "Go nibble on your tablet. That's about all you're good for."

"Well I think…!" began Ephie.

"That's just the point. You don't think at all, do you, Ephie?" Cathy was now completely at her wit's end, the combination of tiredness and worry had frayed her nerves to breaking point. She was slipping into manic-tyrant mode and now the whole boat seemed to be avoiding her gaze.

"I wish she'd stayed in Drumfintley," sulked Ephie.

Michael nodded. "I'm beginning to have some very unchristian suspicions about Cathy Peck and her husband's disappearance. She seems capable of anything."

Cathy felt the frustration build inside her and was just about to lay into Michael when there was a sudden splash.

Eethan's wet mop of hair appeared through the raindrops on the surface of the river.

"Eethan! What were you doing?" gasped Michael.

"Listeeening. There ees big trouble coming soon. Wee must hide somewhere."

They squinted at the high cliffs that rose above them on their left and then peered into the dark forest to their right. Rain stung their faces, jabbing at their skin like needles. The pretty pink dawn had turned into a dull, drab morning. The trees of Eldane swayed in a sudden breeze.

"Stop!" Cathy cried. She stood up, making one side of the raft dip below the surface. She pointed to the rocky slope beneath the cliff. "Stop paddling now!" Already wet through, Cathy plunged into the river and swam for the bank.

"She has definitely flipped!" exclaimed Jean as she attempted to shelter the kids under her dripping mohair cardigan. "What does she think she's doing?" When Cathy eventually appeared, about ten yards from the shore, she began wading towards a large group of rocks.

"Is she leaving us?" asked Michael.

"I hope so," whispered Ephie.

Cathy lunged forward and picked up something floating near the moss-covered boulders. It was a small green rucksack, bashed and heavy with water. She held it above her head like some kind of trophy and shouted back at the raft. "It's David's rucksack! James had it!" She found the zipper and jerked it open. Water poured out, along with various sweet wrappers, two uneaten apples, and an empty juice bottle. In the front zipper, she found James's inhaler and, to her surprise, a rusting can of flea spray. Written on the small label inside the bag was the name, David Peck. Gazing skyward, her eyes blazed as the rain splashed her face. "David! Where are you when we need you?" Her voice echoed off the high cliffs that stood proud against the blackening sky.

Scared and cold, she hugged the rucksack close to her chest, relieved that the rain hid her tears. She thought of David and sadly, the last words she'd ever said to him. *Go on your walk! You're never really here anyway, even when you are. So why don't you just disappear forever!*

"Anger management... That's what she needs!" said Jean, confiding in Ephie."I saw a program about it on the telly!"

Cathy screamed when Eethan's blue hand clasped her leg from beneath the water.

The little, blue man, who seemed just as at home under the water as he did walking upside down on the roof of a cave, smiled his cheeky smile and pulled her back towards the raft. "Wees have to keeep going, beeg danger's coming."

Cathy stuffed the bits and pieces back into the rucksack and waded through the shallows without acknowledging him. She just stared into the distance until she had to start swimming back to the raft.

Helping her aboard, Michael placed his soggy, black jacket round her shoulders. "Are you okay, Cathy?" He looked at the little, green rucksack. "James had this with him, didn't he?"

His question hung in the air, unanswered. Cathy was staring at something behind him, her eyes widening.

The raft jolted as a large wave lifted the bedraggled crew a good two feet above the river and then slapped them back down again. They all screamed, waving their arms in an effort to keep balance.

Jean pulled her soaking cardigan around her neck and teared up. "This has got to be some kind of nightmare, right?" she sobbed.

"What in God's name is that?" bleated Michael.

Helen peeked out from under her mum's mohair cardigan. "Giants? They look like giants." She turned Wee Joe's head to see, as he was looking in the wrong direction. Behind them, where they'd turned left into the smaller tributary, two gruesome heads bobbed up and down above the treetops.

"Are they made of some kind of wood or...?" Jean stopped when she saw the first thick leg splash into the river. It looked like a tree, but it moved like something living. The first giant she spotted had a gnarled, shiny head and a patch over his right eye. The second giant sported a Mohican-type hairstyle composed of green ferns.

"Mum! Dat one's a punk rocker!" cried Wee Joe. "They're cool."

His big sister, Helen, wasn't so sure they were 'cool' at all. Her face was pale, making her freckles stand out even more than usual.

"Paddle quicklee en smoothlee, and don't make anyee more noisees!" whispered Eethan. He slipped into the water and kicked with renewed vigour. The raft moved much faster now, and soon gained an extra twenty yards on the giants behind them.

"Tree Trolls, theys ees. But dee rain is heelping us just now." Eethan glanced behind him and saw the Trolls stop and look up the tributary towards them.

"Kak! Kak!" The bald one jerked his head back, his nostrils pulling in the damp air. With a satisfied nod, he bellowed, "There! I can see them!"

A swarm of serpent-like creatures, dressed in armour, poured round the bend. They milled around the crested Tree Troll's legs like ants.

Everyone on the raft froze, too afraid to move.

Barely a second later, a terrible scream resounded from the reeds at the mouth of the tributary. The bald Tree Troll was lifting a long, sleek boat out of the river. Gleefully, he threw it back down into the water, where it hit the surface hard. Someone was struggling in the water. He picked the unfortunate creature up, and examined him with his one good eye. "It's a Manimal guard!" it roared.

Next to him the other troll crushed the craft beneath his huge gnarled foot.

The serpent creatures cheered.

Grinning, the bald one closed his thick fingers round the guard and tossed his lifeless body into the river. There was a splash, and another cheer.

Jean began to sob as she pulled the kids back into her damp cardigan. Only Eethan continued to kick with all his might as they edged round a bend and slipped out of sight.

* * *

When Cimerato heard the thunderous shout from the river, he blinked his eyes open. Not even the relentless roar of the downpour could have stifled the pathetic cry of the guard.

"The boat!" Lord Eldane sat up.

"Shhh, Father!" he hissed. "Get down and keep still!" Motioning to the others to stay where they were, Cimerato crawled through the nest of ferns that hid them to see what was going on. He sighed in despair. Fragments of their boat floated out in the river while a troupe of Hedra and two Tree Trolls searched the trees around him. The rain grew heavier and the ground began to turn to mud as he crawled back into the fern grove where they'd slept.

"Tree Trolls and Hedra…lots of them," he panted. "They'll be here in minutes. We must move now."

"Move where, Son?" said Lord Eldane.

"We must go deeper into the forest and find somewhere to hide," said Cimerato.

Crunch!

A huge foot stamped down behind them throwing mud all over them. One of the guards bolted. Ssslathat immediately scooped him up and threw him back towards his brother. "Is this one of the Blinders?" he bellowed.

Ashthat caught the terrified guard and held him up by his leg. He blinked his one purple eye and shook his massive head before opening his needle-toothed jaws.

In one gulp, the guard disappeared.

"Not a blinder," said Ashthat, wiping his ragged lips with the back of his hand. "These are Gwendralin morsels. Kuh!" he coughed then picked some of the guard's clothing from his teeth.

As Ssslathat snapped trees and crushed bushes with his club Cimerato and his men crawled away from him like snakes, pulling themselves through the mud and rain.

Ssslathat roared and tossed a small tree he'd plucked from the muddy earth into the river.

Telan had to duck to avoid the discarded tree but was soon beside the Trolls, hacking at the undergrowth along with fifty Hedra soldiers.

Jal stood motionless on the corner of The Break. Two translucent red films of skin slipped over his yellow reptilian eyes. "There's another orange glow at the edge of the trees," he shouted.

Cimerato heard him and froze. His heart pounded hard against the inside of his breastplate.

A third guard had been spotted, but only after he'd dealt with two Hedra scouts, slashing them down with his curved Gwendralin sword. Unfortunately for him, Ashthat's club found its mark, squashing the guard flat into the mud.

Cimerato winced, fearing the worst for the rest of them. Then he remembered an old trick he'd used to spy on the Hedra. "Scoop up the mud and cover yourselves. Be quick about it!"

The others copied him then remained as still as they could under the debris and foliage. The cool mud would protect them from the Hedra's infrared vision but they could still be stumbled upon or crushed to death by one of the Tree Trolls.

Ssslathat's massive foot crashed into a tree near to where they lay, showering them with leaves, branches and rainwater.

The sharp spike of a broken branch pierced the mud inches from Cimerato's left ear but he remained completely still. The Hedra were everywhere. Any movement would be fatal. The Trolls seemed to be moving back towards the river, muttering to each other in registers too deep to understand. Hedra tongues flicked in the rain, trying to pick up some trace of scent, their eyes scouring the wet foliage for some telltale glow or movement.

Cimerato, Lord Eldane and two guards lay absolutely motionless, plastered in mud and hidden by the debris left behind by Ssslathat and Ashthat. One guard, however, was missing.

The Hedra were still searching, stabbing the ferns with their short swords and prodding the thick bushes with their steel-capped bows only feet from where Cimerato and the others lay.

"Telan!" one of the Hedra called out. "Look what I've found!" Cimerato saw the Hedra soldier bend down close to where his father lay. His reptilian tongue flicked over his father's face in hungry anticipation, but Eldane remained totally still, his eyes fixed on a spot behind the Hedra. "You might be a bit tough when I chew on your old hide tonight..." hissed the Hedra soldier, lifting his pointed bow for the killing strike. "But I've had worse."

Shhhunk!

From behind, a curved Gwendralin sword sliced through the Hedra soldier's neck, relieving him of his head...and his hunger. The missing guard had crawled up from the riverbank in time to save his master. Without concern for his own safety, he kicked the severed head away from Lord Eldane's hiding place and began pulling the corpse back toward the river. He was nearly there when twenty Hedra rose out of the water in front of him.

The exposed guard skidded to a halt, dropping the body. "I will not surrender, so give it your bessst..." Before he could finish his sentence, twenty arrows flew fast and furious from the Hedra bows. Courageous to the end, the guard toppled over, his face, even in death, fixed in an expression of defiance.

* * *

"Keep him alive!" Telan shouted as he scrambled through the undergrowth, but he was too late. "Fools!" The Hedra had seen their dead comrade and revenge had raced ahead of reason. Telan slapped the nearest Hedra across the face. "We could have made him talk. Are there any more?"

"No, sir. Just the four," answered Jal. Staying well away from the fray, Jal had spent his time scanning the area while the others searched. The rain was beginning to ease and further down the tributary to their left, a glint of sunlight had caught the surface of the water. He was certain that he'd glimpsed another boat before it edged round a bend. He was also sure he had seen more than four people in the boat that had just been destroyed, the night before, meaning there were probably more Manimals hiding in the undergrowth. For now, he would hold his tongue; he would wait and see what would happen first.

"Let's go this way," Jal suggested, pointing down the tributary. Without waiting for a response, he began to move forward.

"Why?" shouted Telan.

Jal could tell that Telan, a captain, resented a common guard telling him what to do, even if he was one of King Feldon's personal minders. "Well, if I was going to skulk off into the forest, I would go down here. That's why."

Ashthat looked worried. "This inlet leads towards the Eden Tree. We don't like that place. It's forbidden!"

Telan glanced up at Ashthat and hissed, "I'll tell you what is, and what is not, forbidden!" He signalled his troops and they fell into line. "This rank," he pointed to the archers who'd killed the last guard, "will stay here. Let nothing pass in or out of the tributary until we return, and search the ferns again! I am sure you dolts missed something!" The disgruntled rank of archers nodded. Without the protection of the full Hedra brigade and the Tree Trolls, those that stayed behind were vulnerable.

Ashthat looked back at his brother. "I have to find the Blinders." With a deep sigh! he turned down the tributary that headed toward the Eden Tree.

Reluctantly, Ssslathat followed.

CHAPTER TWENTY-FIVE

FURTHER ON, ROUND THE BEND

"I'm bored Mum. I want my toys!" Wee Joe, oblivious to any danger, tugged at his mother's tattered skirt, but Jean was transfixed as she stared blankly into the mishmash of trees behind them. "We're in real danger here, aren't we?" she whispered anxiously to Cathy.

"What a stupid question. Of course we are, and so are all our children." She turned away rudely and addressed Eethan. "You there!" Cathy directed her anger at the little blue man. "What were those tree things doing?"

Eethan winced in a sudden shaft of sunlight and continued to kick his feet in the water. "Wees better keeep going. They weel soon catch up with us."

The raft turned round another bend in the tributary and a strange island came into view. The gorge they travelled through opened out and they gathered speed as the current pushing against them eased.

Eethan climbed out of the water, onto the raft, and said to Michael, "You must keep on going to dee tree." Eethan pointed to a giant, copper-leafed tree in the centre of the island. It stood high on a grassy knoll, twisting upward towards the brightening sky.

"The reever is eeasier now, so you should bees okay. Stop when you reachees dee Island. I will go en deestract dee Tree Trolls." He brushed past Cathy to speak to Wee Joe. "Lookee after your mummy, Wee fighteer Joe!" Eethan winked at the small boy then dived into the river.

"Where is he going now?" Cathy's eyes were wide with disbelief. "And he never even answered my question."

"Calm down, Cathy!" said Jean. "You're scaring the kids and…and just making things worse!"

Ephie, who had just found one last bit of tablet deep in her pocket, tried to distract the kids with it. "Joe? Do you want some tablet? What about you, Helen?" Her ploy worked at first but soon the kids were fighting over the last bar.

"She got de biggest bit!" yelped Wee Joe.

"Liar!" Helen ripped the last piece from Wee Joe's fingers and he began to scream like a stuck pig.

"Shhhh! For goodness sake!" hissed Michael, glancing anxiously around.

Ephie fumbled with the wrapper. "Here, I'll split it again. Try and share. Please!"

"Everyone shut up!" Jean stamped her foot down so hard on the raft that two of the moss strands that held the whole thing together snapped. The strands whipped past Cathy's face and she fell back onto her elbows.

The raft slowly began to drift apart.

"Nice one, Jean!" cried Cathy, surprised at the outburst.

They all stared at Jean as two of the main support logs drifted away from the raft. A third log broke free and they all scrambled to hold onto each other as the raft broke apart.

"Grab on to something that floats. Ahh!" Michael fell backwards, cracking his head on a green, slimy log before sinking beneath the surface of the river.

"Michael!" Ephie jumped straight in after him.

Cathy sighed with frustration as Ephie kicked deeper into the blackness. "He'll be okay. What are you…?" She soon realised, however, that Ephie may have been right to go in after Michael. He wasn't anywhere to be seen and the weeds were thick in this part of the river. She turned to Jean, "Ephie was a champion swimmer when she was young. When she was thin," she added. Cathy peered into the murky water, shielding her eyes.

"There! She's got him," gasped Jean.

Ephie had grabbed onto Michael's jacket, pulling him to the surface with several strong kicks.

"Ahh! Ach! Ach!" Michael coughed and spluttered as murky green water spewed out and dribbled down his chin. As he worked to free himself, however, more weeds wrapped round his legs. He began to panic.

"Don't fight it!" shouted Cathy.

But they were sinking again. Struggling to keep her head above the water, Ephie gave Michael a brisk, stinging clip across the face and regained control.

Cathy, along with Jean and the kids, clung to what remained of the raft while Ephie and Michael treaded water. In the commotion, they'd drifted close to the green, grassy hill. Cathy looked up at the huge, copper-leafed tree. It towered above them, shading the olive-green waters.

"I can touch the ground now!" spluttered Michael.

Ephie stood up and spread her arms for balance. She swayed for a few seconds, letting the twin suns throw down their warmth on her full face. Michael tried his best to support himself as he made for the riverbank. The rocks on the riverbed were slippery, causing him to stagger and stumble. When he was on a more even patch, he turned to his rescuer. "Th…thanks, Ephie!"

"No problem. Well, I mean…" Ephie was confused when she saw the genuine gratitude in Michael's eyes.

"Oh, come on," interjected Cathy. She hated unnecessary soppiness. "There's a time and a place for that kind of guff."

"Thanks…" Michael wiped at the water from his face and stared straight at Ephie. "Your eyes are very beauti—"

"Pardon?" Ephie's face turned puce.

"I'm terribly sorry. I didn't mean to… I mean, I'm sorry…"

"Don't be." Ephie gave him a small smile.

To Cathy's disgust, Ephie seemed about to make the most of the compliment when the Helen interrupted the tête-à-tête. "You pushed me!" she barked, splashing Wee Joe.

Wee Joe spat at her. "Did not! Pigface!" Like most three-year-olds, Wee Joe had the voice of a town crier and his screech sent three snow-coloured birds flapping skyward.

Cathy scowled at Jean. "Will you keep those brats quiet?"

Jean ignored her and the commotion caused by the kids. "Michael, are you alright?"

"Yes, thanks to Ephie," replied Michael.

In the shallows, Ephie blushed as she struggled with her sodden, powder blue joggers.

Cathy Peck turned on Michael. "Will you two cool it? Pull some more of that candy floss stuff off that tree and give it to the kids instead of standing around gawping like a pair of love-struck school kids."

Michael picked up his soaking wet jacket from the edge of the river and reached for the nearest strand of mossgeld. "I am not ashamed to show a little human kindness, Cathy."

Just as Cathy was about to start on him, another wave pushed down the river, tossing fragments of their raft towards them. The others just made the shore as the debris smashed into the rocks beside them. Jean's eyes widened. "They're coming again!"

"She's right," said Michael. "The same wave hit us just before we saw the giants the last time."

Instinctively, Cathy picked up Wee Joe, grabbed Helen's hand and began to move. As they all slipped and skidded on the wet grass that sloped up to the Eden Tree, she growled, "I thought Eethan was going to do something about those…" she searched for the right words, "Trolls!" She set Wee Joe down and pointed him and his sister in the direction of the tree. "Get under the big tree. Hide amongst the roots."

As the kids ran for the safety of the Eden Tree's giant roots, Cathy rounded on Jean. "Shift yourself, and look after your own kids for a change!" Cathy snapped some ferns from the surrounding foliage and thrust them into Jeans' hands. "Hide the kids with these."

* * *

Next to the River Levan, Cimerato and his entourage lay motionless in the cold mud. Still covered by broken branches and foliage, a sense of hopelessness washed over them when they'd heard the instructions given to the Hedra archers. If the rain stopped, and the Hedra archers covered every inch of ground as they'd been instructed, the small group would be discovered and killed. They would have to move. Cimerato slowly turned his head towards his father. He was just about to tell him to make a move when he felt something slippery grab his ankles.

"What the…!" Cimerato stifled the cry just in time. He looked down to see a small pair of muddy, yellow hands pulling on his boot. Turning his head to see what was going on, he soon saw that his father and the two remaining guards were also being dragged along under the fallen debris, away from the Hedra guards. Strangely enough, his father had a smile on his old face that shone through the mud and muck.

They'd been dragged a good fifty yards away from the Hedra and had dipped down into a green, leafy grove, when a low babbling sound came to their attention.

Cimerato caught hold of his father's sodden, purple robe. "Yeltans?"

"And not a moment too soon," added Lord Eldane.

The Yeltans stood round the dishevelled Manimals and waited until their leader, Landris, stepped forward. To his relief, Cimerato recognised at least three of the Yeltans from past meetings in Gwendral. He sat up when he saw Landris. Lord Eldane blinked the mud from his eyes and was just about to speak when Landris put a small gnarled finger to his lips. "Not here," he whispered. He pointed in the direction of a mossy, earth-covered hatch.

Making haste, they slid through the opening and fell down into the darkness until they ended up piled on top of each other at the bottom of the chute. Trying to stand, Lord Eldane struck his head on an overhanging root.

"It is a little cramped, Lord Eldane," Landris apologised, "but hopefully better than being roasted over a Hedra spit." Landris smiled as he and the other Yeltans bowed respectfully.

"Quite. Thank you, Landris." Lord Eldane bowed back.

Standing to the left of the Yeltans, were two boys—one was taller with blond hair and freckles; the other was smaller, with a biggish nose and a slight stoop. The strangest things about the boys were their eyes. Coloured and round, they were not like any Denthan eyes he'd ever seen. Other than those oddities, they looked like Manimals, even though they wore strange white shirts and short leggings that shone like silk.

"Stendelburgh United," said the taller boy, a cheeky smile on his face.

The smaller boy shook his head. "He won't know what you're on about. He doesn't care what football strip your wearing."

Cimerato peered over the small boy's shoulder to eye the hairy animal behind them. "This is a...?"

"Dog," answered the taller boy. "My name is Craig, and this is James." he nodded at smaller boy. "Are you from Gwendral?"

"Yes, we are from Gwendral. And you are?" asked Lord Eldane. He'd just addressed the yellow-furred creature, known as a dog.

"Eh, that's Bero. He can't speak. But he's from Drumfintley, and so are we," said Craig, patting Bero's head.

One of the guards, caked in mud, was the first to reach out and touch Bero's brown ear. "He has the face of a dragon." He smiled up at Cimerato.

Cimerato looked at the Yeltans standing round them in the gloom and, to his surprise, saw that they had their elaborate war spears with them. Being a peaceful race, the Yeltans rarely carried weapons of any kind, shunning conflict whenever possible.

"We heard the sounds of battle and saw Ssslathat and his brother searching for you," Landris explained. "I'm so sorry we did not reach you in time to save the others."

Lord Eldane shook his head. "We should have been more careful."

"Did you say, Ssslathat?" asked James.

"Did he only have one eye?" Craig enquired.

"Yes," Landris answered. "Ashthat, brother of Ssslathat wore a patch over one eye."

"They said they were looking for the Blinders," Cimerato interrupted, turning to the two boys.

"Well they attacked us first and…" Craig defended himself.

"Who are you, anyway?" The smaller boy piped up quickly, as though trying to steer the conversation away from his friend.

"Your eyes are almost pure white," the other one interjected, looking at Cimerato's eyes. "Are you blind?"

"I don't think he's blind," said James. "He has a slit pupil like a cat."

Cimerato grinned. "I am Cimerato, son of Lord Eldane." He nodded towards his father. "These are our two remaining guards."

The guards nodded at Landris and the boys.

"We are trying to reach the Eden Tree." Cimerato turned to face Landris. "As, I assume, are you. My father recounted your letter to me last night. If Mendel is back amongst us, we owe him our help. I only hope that he can save us in the little time we have left. We should try and reach the tree now, before the Hedra get there first."

"I couldn't agree more, Cimerato." Landris signalled to his kin and they immediately began to march. The Manimals followed first, leaving the boys and Bero to keep up as best they could.

* * *

James nudged Craig. "What did you have to tell them about the Trolls for?" He was looking at Craig's muddy shorts as they struggled along the low tunnel after the Yeltans, and not particularly liking the view.

"I was only being friendly," Craig whispered over his shoulder.

"You only told them that we're the Blinders, or whatever those Trolls called us. And Landris knew their names and everything. They're probably friends of theirs, or something."

"Friends?" Garlon had overheard James's whispers. "Friends? Those two have eaten more Yeltans than…than I care to think about. They are no friends of ours, James."

James felt embarrassed, but less so when Garlon added, "In fact, I was wondering if you could tell me more about your fight with them. If we ever survive this disaster, I could do a tapestry of it. It sounds as though you gave a good account of yourselves." With a grin, Craig assured the little creature that he would tell him everything. James only groaned.

After twenty minutes of crawling through the narrow Yeltan tunnels, they entered a high-roofed cave that smelled of herbs and spices. Landris pointed to a set of ornate ladders. "That is our way up."

Garlon spoke excitedly, "This is where I had my coming of age ceremony."

Landris put his finger to his lips to signal silence. "These stairs lead to the island of Senegral where we will find the Eden Tree," he informed them.

"Please Landris, can I speak to Cimerato?" asked James.

Landris gripped the ladder. "If you must, but time is not on our side."

James turned to Cimerato and asked quickly, "Have you seen or heard of anyone else like me, here in Denthan? Perhaps with my kind of eyes. I'm looking for my father."

Craig widened his eyes so that Cimerato could be reminded what human eyes looked like. This annoyed James immensely, but persevered, nonetheless. "I came here, mostly, to find him, you see. Obviously, I'm sad about your predicament too, and Mendel seemed to need me for his magic but…"

Cimerato patted James's shoulder. "I'm sorry boy, but there have been no reports of anyone else like you here in Denthan. But just because I haven't heard anything about your father doesn't mean that he isn't here."

James felt quite inadequate standing beside the big warrior. "Well, I just wondered, that's all."

Landris addressed Lord Eldane, "I've already told the boys that there are more of their *kind* in the forest. There's a good chance that James's father is amongst them."

Craig touched James's arm. "More of our *kind*? He never said that, did he?"

James shrugged, looking just as confused. "There were the clothes, my dad's compass and his lens cloth, but no real explanation for them."

Lord Eldane, a man who looked to be about two hundred years old, placed his hand on James's shoulder. "Well, if Mendel brought you here, anything is possible. However," the old man turned to face Craig, "I don't understand how you two managed to lose track of the most powerful wizard our world has ever known."

All eyes were on the boys.

Craig raised a blond eyebrow. "What I can't understand is how you lot were stupid enough to banish him in the first place!"

There was an awkward silence at the bottom of the Yeltan ladder. Eldane, Landris and Cimerato were all struck dumb.

James, well used to Craig's lack of diplomacy, winced as he grabbed hold of the ladder that stretched upwards. For once, though, he actually agreed with his friend. "You tell 'em, Craig," he said in a low voice as he began to climb the ladder.

Landris called after him, "James, wait! One of us should check that it's all clear first. The Trolls could be waiting or…"

But James had reached the top of the ladder and had already slipped the rusty bolt that separated the world above from the world below. Sunlight streamed down into the Yeltan chamber. He pushed against the hatch with his shoulder until the heavy lid fell open, thudding onto the ground. Dust showered down on the onlookers below making them cough and cover their eyes. Excitement building in his chest, James pulled himself through the opening and glanced up to see that he was kneeling between two giant roots. Like the buttresses of a cathedral, they rose above him, supporting the trunk of an enormous tree that must have stood well over two hundred feet tall. It had to be the Eden Tree. He tried to concentrate, see if he could sense Mendel. He knelt up and closed his eyes. He listened for the deep reassuring voice, but there was nothing.

CHAPTER TWENTY-SIX

THE EDEN TREE

C athy heard a dull thump. It had come from the direction of the Eden Tree. She hesitated, turned to the rest of the bedraggled group and motioned to them to wait. She could still hear the disturbing grunts and howls of the god-knows-what down in the river behind them, but it was the expression on Jean's face that really threw her. Jean Harrison should have had the terror-struck expression of someone about to be torn apart by a giant Tree Troll. Instead, her face wore the look of someone who'd just won first prize at the village raffle. Jean's eyes had widened and now a beautiful smile lit up her face. Cathy felt quite sure the woman had lost her mind. "Are you daft, or something?"

"Mum?" a voice called out. Cathy spun back round to look behind her.

"James?" Cathy felt her legs give. She saw her dishevelled son peering over the nearest giant root of the Eden Tree. Seeing he was safe, she couldn't help herself; the words just began spilling from her lips. "What do you think you've been up to? We've all been worried sick and..." but for once, her lips quavering, Cathy fell silent. Without another word, she ran to James and pulled him close. Holding him tightly, she kissed his dirty face. She shook with relief at seeing him again, alive and well. "James, where have you been?"

Her sobs set James off too. Under the shade of the huge bronze-coloured tree, he hugged her back, tears spilling down his cheeks. He was part of her. She knew his smell and he knew hers. She drew back and wiped his tears. By now, four or five strange yellow faces had appeared between the huge buttress-like roots. Seeing them, Cathy gripped James's arm.

"Owww! Mum?" James turned to see the Yeltans. "It's okay, Mum."

Not sure which way to run or what to say, Cathy could only watch as a tall man, covered in mud, came into view. He was obviously some kind of soldier; she saw hints of yellow armour shining through the caked-on dirt. A large, curved sword in his hand glinted in the sunlight. "James, don't move," she whispered.

"They're friends," he told her and she relaxed a little bit, still holding him tightly.

James sniffed back a tear. He held her tight, as if he did not want the moment to end.

* * *

Everybody—Ephie, Michael, Jean and even the strange onlookers behind the roots—seemed to respect the private moment between Cathy and James, but it was short-lived.

In the river below, James heard a huge splash and quickly pulled free of his mother's arms. A few seconds later, the Tree Troll, Ssslathat, rose up from the waters below, his ridiculous green crest waving in the breeze. An evil smile twisted his splintered mouth. "Blinder! Blinder!" he bellowed in his deep, woody voice. Then he called back for his brother, "Kak! Kak!" jerking his hideous head back in a series of creaks that sounded like a huge timber door being ripped in two.

Scared stiff, Wee Joe and Helen peered out from gaps in the ferns. The Yeltans swiftly ducked back behind the tree's giant roots while Cimerato crouched down low. Unfortunately, James, Cathy and the Drumfintley contingent were totally exposed. They stood for a moment on the grassy hillside, like statues, unsure what to do.

Ashthat appeared beside his brother, crying, "Kak! Kak!" Both Trolls jerked their hideous heads back in joy at finding their prey.

Ssslathat was the first to move. He grabbed a small tree, ripped it out of the earth and smashed it against the hillside as he advanced. In two steps, Ssslathat had come twenty feet closer. He ignored the panic stricken adults. He was after one of the little ones, one of the 'Blinders'.

On seeing James, Ssslathat let out a terrible roar that shook the ground they stood on. He began to close in. "I'm going to tear you apart, Blinder. I'm going to squish you flat!" He thumped his fist down and smashed a rotting tree stump. Ssslathat twisted round to look down at his brother behind him. "Come, Ashthat, this kill is yours."

James and his mum edged back towards the roots of the Eden Tree. Without once taking her eyes off the Tree Troll, Cathy whispered, "Blinder? Why did he call you that?"

"Eh, now's not a good time to explain, Mum. Trust me," answered James. He was looking at something down at the river.

Hundreds of grey-skinned reptilian creatures had gathered round Ashthat. Hissing and flicking their tongues in anticipation, they swarmed round the monster like worker bees round a queen. In the dazzling light of Denthan's twin suns, their black armour flashed menacingly as they moved forward. Most of them had drawn their metal-tipped bows, and James heard the sound of a hundred black arrows clicking from their sheaths. Out the corner of his eye, he saw Landris issuing orders to his own fighters. He was amazed to see the calmness on the little creature's face. When Landris raised his hand, fifty Yeltans immediately rose up from behind the roots of the Eden Tree. When he lowered his hand and said, 'Now!', the Yeltan spears flew into the air.

The Drumfintley group ducked as the shower of spears soared over their heads. In the confusion, Michael, Ephie and Jean found themselves being dragged behind the roots of the Eden Tree by the Yeltans. James and Cathy, still trapped by Ssslathat, had no choice but to run the opposite way, towards Helen and Wee Joe who were still hiding in the ferns.

There was a shrieking noise as the Yeltan spears struck home. Six dug into the wooden hide of Ssslathat, three hit Ashthat's face, and twenty Hedra dropped to the ground, killed instantly by the Yeltan poison that laced the spear tips. The rest of the missiles either fell short or simply failed to find a target.

Unharmed by the pinpricks in his tough wooden hide, Ssslathat charged. He reached down to snatch up James, but James wasn't going down without a fight. He had already said his magic word to retrieve his small, crimson sword, and with a yell, he leapt up onto the Troll's swinging arm. With the power of Firetongue racing through him, he soon reached the Troll's shoulder where he jumped higher again, twisting in mid-air before plunging his sword deep into Ssslathat's right eye. *If they were going to call him Blinder*, he thought, *he might as well live up to the name.*

"Arrrrghh!" The Troll crashed backwards and landed on his brother, knocking him back on top of the advancing Hedra. James just managed to leap to the ground and roll out of the way before getting crushed by a flailing arm or leg.

"Watch out, you fools!" Telan snapped at his Hedra brigade. "Fall back!"

"Blinded! Blinded!" Ssslathat covered his wounded eye and screamed in agony. At the same time, Ashthat struggled to regain his feet, his huge legs crushing another group of Hedra coming up on his left.

"Get back, I told you!" roared Telan.

Ashthat was finally able to stand. "You will die now!" he bellowed, full of rage and revenge. "All of you!" Straightening up to his full height, he jumped over the squirming body of Ssslathat and lunged up the hill, his club raised high, ready to crush James.

But James was already racing back to his mum. He had just reached the cover of the Eden Tree when Ashthat's club smacked hard into the ground behind him.

Further back, Landris addressed his soldiers. "Don't waste your spears on the Trolls. Aim for the Hedra!" He lowered his hand a second time and the last of the Yeltan spears arced towards the retreating Hedra. Another twenty or so screams rose up from the bushes on the riverbank, echoing all round them.

One of the cries had come from Captain Telan who fell at Jal's feet. "Telan?" Jal caught hold of the Hedra leader's arm but seeing that he was quite dead, released him to drift away on the slow current.

Unaware of anything else going on around him, Ashthat moved closer to the Eden Tree and slammed his huge wooden club down into the dirt a second time. It narrowly missed James's mum but, unfortunately, landed on three Yeltan spearmen who were trying to scramble back to the open hatch.

James saw Father Michael and Ephie Blake, disappearing below ground into the Yeltan tunnels, but the Yeltans were finding it hard to restrain Craig's mum. She was shouting out for Wee Joe and Helen. *What are they all doing here,* he thought.

Ashthat stepped round the trunk and spied James. "Blinder!" he roared.

James looked over his shoulder and into Ashthat's one remaining eye.

"Blinder!" Ashthat bellowed again. He lifted his club, and with a wicked grin, brought it down. The large piece of wood whistled through the air as it headed directly for James's head.

"No!" Cathy screamed at the giant Troll. She grabbed James by the shoulders and yanked him backwards.

A few feet away from them, the massive weapon thumped dully against the ferns and mud. The earth heaved upwards throwing James and Cathy away from the Yeltan escape hatch.

As he was falling to the ground, James spotted Craig's mum as she slipped free from the Yeltans.

"You missed me!" he shouted, hoping to distract Ashthat. The giant roared in frustration and began to raise his club again. Behind him, Jean dragged Wee Joe and Helen out from a clump of ferns and back to the hatch.

He caught hold of his mum's arm. "Keep moving!"

But the slippery mud on the knoll made it difficult to move and they soon fell. Even with his sword, James could find enough purchase to stand fast.

Ashthat readied himself to make the final blow…

* * *

"Shut the hatch!" Landris shouted as Jean and the children landed heavily beside him.

"No! Let me past. James is still up there." It was Craig, his voice full of anger and panic. Then he realised who it was that'd come down the ladder so roughly. "Mum, Helen, Wee Joe! What are you all doing here?"

"We's been wooking for you, stupid!" said Wee Joe.

Craig beamed at his little brother, scrunching Wee Joe's hair before leaping up the Yeltan ladder. "I'll be back in a minute!"

"Craig! Get down here now!" Jean, still shaking from fetching her two younger children, watched in horror as Craig pushed the hatch open and jumped free.

Above ground, Craig landed right beside Ashthat's left foot.

Incensed, Ashthat screamed down at Craig and tried to stamp on him.

"Argghh! You're the one who took my eye! You will pay for…" Ashthat never finished the sentence. Springing to his feet, Craig slammed his green spear into Ashthat's gawping mouth. It sliced off one of the Troll's jagged teeth before flying deep into the back of his woody throat.

Dropping his huge club, Ashthat clutched his throat with his splintered fingers. "Guuurrgg!" He dropped to his knees. "Hhh! Gugg!" The hideous noises that followed sent the Hedra cowering further back into the river. His brother, Ssslathat, looked up the hill, but clutching his eye in agony, retreated with the Hedra.

"Brother! Ashthat?" Ssslathat shouted up at the Eden Tree. "We were warned not to come here! It was forbidden! Ashthat, come awayyyy..." His voice trailed off into a deep, wooden sob.

* * *

Standing in the river, Jal looked up and pointed to a Gwendralin Captain who'd just appeared from the giant roots.

The Hedra watched as Cimerato edged past the wavering Ashthat and ran towards the small brown-haired boy that had blinded Ssslathat and what looked like a Manimal woman.

"Fire at the Manimals!" Jal pointed up at the figures on the mound. "We cannot return empty-handed!"

As one, the remains of the Hedra brigade let loose their black arrows at Cathy, Cimerato and James.

Cutting through leaves and shattering branches all around them, the black cloud descended. One arrow grazed Cimerato's cheek and many more would have found their mark but for the boy. His sword whizzed with lightning speed deflecting the arrows an instant before they hit their target.

Jal shouted at his soldiers, "Stand fast! They have Ashthat behind them, Ssslathat is with us and there are only three of them." He held up three scaled fingers. "Three! We are still over a hundred strong!"

The Hedra line wavered. Then, slowly, they all slipped their round shields from their backs and began to walk through the murky, green water again. Ssslathat lingered near the far bank as the Hedra regrouped and advanced.

* * *

Back on his feet, James's sword glowed with the fury of the fight. It seemed to feed on danger, gaining extra speed and power the worst things got. His arm, on the other hand, had just about had it.

James felt his mum staring at him and he turned to face her.

"James, where in Heaven's name did you learn to do that?" She shook her head in disbelief as she picked bits of shredded arrow from her long, black hair.

"It's not really me, Mum," said James. "It's the sword." He spotted Craig moving behind Ashthat and jumped up to meet him. "Nice one, Craig."

Craig tapped his lips twice. "Keep it down! He's not dead yet, numpty!"

Ashthat was still coughing and hacking beside the Eden Tree as he struggled to steady himself against the thick trunk.

Craig glanced at the advancing Hedra before pointing up at the Eden tree. "We have to get back to the hatch!"

"What about Ashthat?" James saw the giant stagger, cough one more time, and then fall.

Craig shook his head. "Just be careful. I lost my spear in his mouth and I'm not sure when it will appear again." As if to prove his point, he repeated the word "Greenworm," several times and stared down at his empty hand.

Cathy came up the hill behind Craig, who blushed and winced at the same time. "Eh. Hello, Mrs. Peck," he said.

"Don't you 'Hello' me!" she hissed. "What have you got yourselves into?"

James could tell his mum was going to go off on one. "Mum. Please. Not just now." His voice rose higher with every syllable he spoke, his face flushing with embarrassment.

Cimerato grinned and waved them on.

Cathy rounded on the smirking soldier. "And you can take that stupid grin off your face, whoever you are!" Cathy pushed past Cimerato and grabbed James's arm, hauling him up the hill towards Ashthat, who was now lying motionless at the foot of the Eden Tree. She ignored a Hedra arrow that just missed her foot. It sunk deep into the turf.

"They're advancing again," warned Cimerato, "so let's be quick before one of their archers gets lucky. They never were the best of shots." Cimerato moved ahead of them with his sword at the ready.

As Cathy neared the crumpled heap of Ashthat, she gripped James's hand so tight it hurt. "Is it dead?"

The Troll didn't move.

James wasn't sure.

Another arrow smacked into a branch just above Craig's head. "We've got no choice," said James, "we have to move round him." He stared at the troll's open mouth, his huge wooden fist still buried in his throat. As they passed, he couldn't help staring at the Troll's strange bark-like skin. Gnarled, metallic lumps lined Ashthat's hide and patches of moss and orange algae grew between the folds of his tough skin. When he saw the long, dagger-like fingernails, each at least a foot in length, he shuddered. But the Troll's mouth was even worse. It was full of row upon row of razor sharp teeth, like those of a shark.

As they inched towards the safety of the open hatch, the stink from the felled Troll's mouth was overpowering. James could see Landris, willing them forward. Ashthat never moved, nor even appeared to breathe, as they walked briskly round the hulking beast.

Cimerato was already at the hatch, but as he turned to climb down he shouted out, "Watch out!"

Ashthat rolled with incredible speed and smashed his fist down in front of them. James and Cathy stopped dead, shocked by the sudden change in the creature.

"Not so fast Blinders," he gurgled, the words barely discernible. The Troll pulled himself into a kneeling position.

James lifted his sword, but Ashthat's branch-like arm shot out and caught his mum by the leg.

Still gurgling, the Troll stood up, holding Cathy against his huge belly. James's heart nearly stopped. He couldn't speak.

"Put that cursed sword of yours down, Blinder, or I will squash her dead... Now!"

James dropped the crimson sword and heard it clatter against a gnarled root before it disappeared.

"Magic swords won't hurt us now, will they…Kak, Kak!" muttered Ashthat. Cathy squirmed as Ashthat jerked his head back in an evil laugh. He flicked her over to his other hand, then his splintered fingers closed round her writhing body.

Cathy tried to speak. "R…run, James!" She was losing consciousness.

"Mum!" he screamed. He could see Landris and Cimerato through the Troll's legs, hear the hisses and shouts of the Hedra as they climbed up from the riverbank below. Their black arrows were thudding into the earth around his feet.

James felt his chest tighten. There was no way out of this.

* * *

Jal knew they still had a chance to kill the Manimals if he got his soldiers up to the top of the hill right away. Still in the river, Ssslathat seemed reluctant to follow them.

"I have the Blinders, Brother!" Ashthat stood up to show his brother below. As the troll nearest to James called out, he dangled his mum in mid-air, swinging her like a rag doll.

James was looking round for help when a cry echoed up from the river, "Baacckkk!"

Before Ssslathat could turn to see what it was, an apelike beast leapt up out of the water and onto the Troll's back.

"Argghhh!" Ssslathat screamed as the Mertol sank his long, glistening black teeth into the Troll's woody hide.

Jal looked back to the river. "It's a Mertol!" he exclaimed in disbelief. "It must have followed us here." Jal glanced back and forth between the fight in the river and the Eden Tree.

The Mertol was pounding on Ssslathat's back and biting his neck and shoulders. The wounded Troll, totally unprepared, was fighting to keep his balance, still clutching his eye. Finally finding his feet, the Troll tried to swing round and pull off the attacker, but he couldn't reach. Strips of woody hide flew off the Troll as the Mertol tore into him.

Jal gasped as, by chance, Ssslathat grasped a handful of red fur and, in frenzied desperation, spun the Mertol, who was only half his size, over his head. The Mertol hit the river with a tremendous splash. As he was struggling in the water, Ssslathat lunged forward and grabbed the Mertol's arm, throwing him back behind him this time, toward the trees on the far bank.

Seeing that things were going better for Ssslathat, Jal urged his troops forward.

* * *

But the Mertol was not finished. Mesmerised, James watched from up on the hill as the beast, his red fur dripping with green river water, lunged to his feet and raised his ape-like hands high above his head. Ssslathat, hearing the splashing water roared out and turned to finish off the Mertol.

But it was too late...

A small, black ball shot out of the Mertol's right cheek and whizzed right past Ssslathat's head. The Troll looked surprised, swinging round to see who the beast was aiming at. It was his brother, Ashthat.

Ashthat screamed as the ball swooped up the grassy knoll, flattened itself to resemble a shining blade, then sliced cleanly through his neck. A look of shock spread over Ashthat's face as his head slowly fell backwards and then rolled off his massive shoulders. His fingers spasmed and loosened. Cathy dropped to the ground as the decapitated Troll's limp body sank to its knees then, like a felled tree, slammed into the ferns and roots.

Before the earth had stopped trembling, a second ball shot from the ape-like creature's face, this time aimed at Ssslathat himself. Ssslathat, stunned by his brother's demise, lost his footing in the river and stumbled. The second speeding ball missed Ssslathat's head by inches, whizzed through his green crest, and then continued up the hill. It flew over James's head and smashed into the Eden Tree. In an instant, green sparks shot up the huge trunk and the whole tree burst into flames.

James heard an unearthly cry coming from the river below. "Noooo!" Shaking with uncontrollable hatred, the Tree Troll turned to face the Mertol. "You have killed my brother!" With a roar Ssslathat rushed at the creature and landed heavily on his chest. The weight of the Troll forced the Mertol back under the water, his matted body disappearing beneath the foam. The writhing beast attempted to rise up from the waters, but Ssslathat reached out and thumped his jagged fist down on the Mertol's back. He fell back into the river again and Ssslathat forced the Mertol's ugly face under the water until the ape creature stopped struggling.

With a wail of sorrow that sounded over the roar of the burning Eden Tree, James watched Ssslathat charge up the small, fern-covered hillside towards him and his mum, who was lying motionless on the ground. Determined to reach his fallen brother, Ssslathat trampled several more Hedra as he bounded up the hill.

By this time, Ashthat's body was burning as brightly as the Eden Tree. Strange green flames sparked and popped as the fat beneath Ashthat's wooden hide caught fire. Above them, the hanging moss burst into flames. Crackling like burning lace, flecks of the glowing fibre floated down the hill and onto the Hedra.

James felt the heat intensify. He hauled desperately at his mum but he could barely make her budge. Craig tried to keep the burning moss from landing on her, beating it away with his hands. Suddenly, Cimerato appeared beside them. With ease, he picked up Cathy and began running back to the open hatch. Craig and James stumbled after him, dodging a storm of floating embers.

Ssslathat slid to a halt in the face of the inferno and screamed up at the smoke-filled sky.

"Hurry!" Landris shouted. The Eden Tree was burning now too, dying just like Denthan's tired sun, Tealfirth. Slamming the hatch shut behind them, the three slid down the ladder, landing roughly on the floor of the chamber below.

"Mum... Mum, are you okay?" James coughed as he crouched down to look at her. Cathy's eyes were closed, her face pale. A sizable crowd of Yeltans gathered round him, babbling wildly as tears traced down his sooty cheeks. "Mum!" he shouted.

"Shhh! Be quiet!" James rounded on the Yeltans. "I can't hear if she's breathing or not!" He could barely hear anything. The crackling noises and the thump and crash of falling timber on the ground above them was growing louder by the second. The heat was becoming un-bearable. He felt his lungs begin to constrict.

"We have to leave here now! Those bigger branches are going to drop and trap us," yelled Landris. He motioned to Cimerato. "Pick her up and come!"

The frightened group followed after Landris, coughing and babbling as they moved down the passage away from the Eden Tree. James felt an unbearable sense of hopelessness bear down on him as he staggered after Cimerato and his mum, his throat tight with fear.

Hearing a thundering crash above them, Helen screeched and the Yeltans began their dreadful wailing.

* * *

Above ground, the island of Senegral burned with a ferocious intensity. Jal steered the inconsolable Ssslathat away from the flames while the Hedra retreated back into the river. Smoke from the fire blew into their faces and stung their reptilian eyes.

Once they reached the water, Jal searched for the Mertol, but there was no sign of the creature. The Mertol had either drowned and been swept away by the current, or he had crawled into the trees to die.

Behind Jal, Ssslathat cried out for his dead brother and smashed his giant fists into the river. "Ashthat! Ka! Ka! Ashthat…"

"There's no time for that just now," hissed Jal, "we need to move." They had to get further away from the furnace; retreat from the floating cinders that showered down like flecks of burning snow. Stunned, Jal shook his head in disbelief as he waded away from the blaze. "I have never known such a defeat," he muttered, "Yellow devils; Manimal children with magic swords; and then the Mertol." He fixed his gaze on the grief-stricken Troll and sat down with a thud on the opposite bank. He splashed water into his stinging eyes. "Half the brigade dead and nothing to show for it. I cannot return to Feldon." Jal glanced up through the smoke at their largest sun and spat.

A wounded Hedra soldier approached Jal and after a brief bow, whispered in the ancient Hedra tongue, "You are correct, sir. We cannot return without a hide or a head as some proof." He surreptitiously eyed the wounded Tree Troll.

"Hmmm…" Jal considered the situation. "The brother is probably burned beyond recognition, so we can't use him."

"And the Manimals will have perished with him," added the wounded Hedra.

Jal nodded. "Still, as you say, we need proof. We will wait a little longer just in case the Mertol returns. If the Troll kills the beast, we'll use its head as our trophy. If not…" He glanced over at the moaning Ssslathat. "There is always your suggestion."

"Of course," agreed the soldier, smiling.

"Whatever we do, though, we must keep moving.," said Jal, "for I can assure you that our doom is sealed if we do not return to Gwendral very soon." Jal shielded his eyes against the reddening sun, just visible through the grey smoke, and wondered how all this was going to end.

CHAPTER TWENTY-SEVEN

THE RETURN TO GWENDRAL

Ephie Blake knelt over Cathy and immediately began mouth-to-mouth resuscitation. The tunnel where James's mother lay was narrow, but at least they were all well away from the heat and devastation of Senegral Island. They were, in fact, under the river itself. As James numbly watched Ephie working on his mum, the cold, green water of the River Levan dripped down his neck from the leaking roof.

Father Michael held Cathy's wrist, checking for a pulse and issuing encouragements. "Come on, Cathy. Breathe!"

James was now convinced that his mother was dead. Ashthat had squeezed the life out of her, and what was worse, James hadn't reacted quickly enough to stop him from doing so. He was the one to blame for his mum's death. He stifled a sob.

At the same time, Ephie paused to wipe a tear from her eye. "It's no good."

"What? No! Keep going!" shouted James.

Ephie looked up at James and sadly shook her head.

"Please, Miss Blake, try again. Please!" James felt Bero's cold, wet nose push against his bare leg.

Ephie sighed, her shoulders drooping. Then, with a determined nod of her head, she pinched Cathy's nose and took another deep breath. Three short blows made Cathy's chest rise again and this time, to everyone's relief, she began to cough and sputter. Her eyes blinked open. "Cugh! Cugh! Agghhh...!" She seemed to recognise the sizable outline of Ephie Blake leaning over her.

James braced himself for her inevitable reaction.

"Yuck! Get off me you tub of lard!" Cathy slapped Ephie across the face.

"Mum! No. She...she saved your life!" James was crying with relief but red with shame.

In the bright light of the Yeltan torches, Ephie nursed her stinging cheek. "What did you just call me?"

Michael stepped forward to comfort Ephie. He was shaking with anger. "I think you owe Ephie an apology, Cathy!"

Jean appeared out of the gloom, holding Wee Joe over her shoulder. Amazingly, the little boy had fallen fast asleep. "Everybody just calm down. Getting angry isn't going to help," she said, "We're not exactly in a normal situation here and we must do our best to stay focused." Jean edged nearer to Michael and whispered, "What will these people think of us?"

Helen nuzzled in beside her mother. "Mum, why is James's mum always so angry? She's such a pig to everyone."

Everyone looked at Helen.

Right there and then James knew that she'd said aloud exactly what they were all thinking. He cringed with the shame of it all.

Even Landris, who'd known the conscious version of Cathy for less than ten seconds, nodded his head in agreement. "Truth often spills from the lips of the young. However we have to get going right now."

Garlon edged his way forward. "The tunnels beneath the river are not safe."

Landris waved them on. "I would prefer to get back to our home. We've lost too many in this struggle; I don't want to lose anymore."

James's voice cut through the gloom. "But what about Mendel? We've got to go back and look for him. He said he would meet us at the tree!"

Craig edged forward. "There is no Eden Tree anymore, mate."

"It's not safe!" Landris exclaimed. "There are Hedra everywhere and..."

"We've not got time for safe," interrupted James. He felt totally drained, both physically and emotionally, but he wasn't going to give up now. He looked into his mum's eyes. "Mum, I think dad might be here somewhere. He could be up there right now." James pointed to the low, dripping ceiling above his head.

Cathy Peck's hazel eyes narrowed. "Son, your dad isn't up there. Your dad is in deep..."

"Deepest France?" finished Craig, a toothy white grin creasing his dirty face. "You see, Mrs. Peck, I've told James not to worry too much. Mr. Peck's probably just bird watching in the south of France. "

Cathy Peck drew Craig a deadly stare.

Craig moved off and muttered, "Getting the first bit of peace he's had in the last twenty years."

James jabbed Craig in the ribs. "Not helping." He pointed to the tunnel ahead. "Landris, where does that tunnel lead to?" The dark passage veered off to the right and James could see the rungs of another ladder.

Landris put his yellow hand on James's shoulder. "It leads up to the forest opposite the island. It would take you right into the middle of the Hedra. Please take my advice…"

But James had already made up his mind. He looked back at his mum. She seemed confused and disoriented. "Are you okay, Mum? You see, I have to go…"

"You aren't going anywhere!" Cathy was still weak and not quite sure where she was, but her voice was as strong as ever.

"But Mum…" James pleaded. Half hero, half kid, James felt torn in two. He knew that Mendel was the key to his dad's safety, the key to all their safety. The goldfish was the only chance they had of surviving this mess. "I know that if we don't find Mendel, we'll all die," he said simply.

Cathy raised herself up on her elbows. "Don't you dare move an inch, James Wilson Peck!"

"Wilson?" Craig snorted.

"I'll be back soon," he told her, then, ignoring Craig and avoiding any eye contact with his mum, he dashed off down the tunnel towards the ladder.

"James!" Cathy's furious voice filled the tunnel, but James pushed on regardless, never once looking back, knowing full well that he was in serious trouble when he got back. If he got back…

Cathy pulled herself up into a sitting position, but instantly winced in agony and clutched at her ribs. "I've not come all this way to lose you now." Again, she cringed in pain. "You little…"

Craig turned to his mother. "Mum, I have to go with James."

Jean grimaced, then looked at Cimerato. "Could you go with them?"

Cimerato smiled at Jean and the children. "You two," he summoned the remaining Manimal guards. "Come!"

"Son!" Lord Eldane protested. "I should be the one to go."

"Father, it is better that you go back with the Yeltans. We will return soon. The boy's right. Our only chance of survival is to find Mendel."

Craig squeezed his mum's arm and ruffled Helen's hair before setting off after James.

The Manimal fighters followed Craig down the passage and were soon climbing up the ladder behind the boys.

* * *

Cathy Peck rounded on Jean. "Are you just going to let him go like that? It's taken us days to find them and you're just going to let them go? Get a backbone, Jean!"

Jean made an effort to stay calm. "Cathy, you can't control everything. All your shouting and hitting and threats won't make any difference in the long run. I know I'm a bit soft on them sometimes but…"

"A bit soft! You deserve all that's coming to you when that boy grows up, if he grows up. You'll pay the price. They need to know the rules, the boundaries. And by letting your son go, you've just undermined me in front of mine. You deserve…" Cathy began to cough.

Jean knelt down and looked Cathy right in the eye. "James didn't see me letting Craig go after him. He was already gone. When anything goes wrong or something happens that you don't like, you always turn on some poor sod and heap the blame on them. Craig's gone because he wants to help his best friend, because he wants to try and save us. This is like some really bad nightmare, and I don't want them to go either, but they know more about what's going on here than we do, so stop… Just stop it…" Jean stood up. Seeing Helen looking at her with wide eyes she apologised, "I'm sorry you had to see that, dear."

Helen smiled and gave her a little clap. "Well done, Mum!"

The atmosphere in the cave was tense as Cathy tried to pull herself to her feet. She spied Michael, a distraught Ephie still in his arms. "If you were a real gentleman, you would help me up."

Father Michael flushed. "Oh, I beg your pardon, Cathy. Here, take my arm."

"Don't bother!" she snapped.

Cathy's rebuff caused Michael's mouth to drop open. "But I thought…?"

"You thought you would cuddle into Podgy there, and let me struggle with my cracked ribs, here in this…" Cathy faltered. Anxiously, she grabbed the Yeltan leader's arm. "Where are we?"

"We're about four feet below the River Levan, in a Yeltan tunnel that's rarely used and has seen better days." Landris traced the low ceiling with his stubby fingers. "We best get moving, madam."

"Tunnel?" Cathy began to shake. "I can't be in any kind of tunnel…" Her voice shook with fear; her eyes were wide with panic. She pulled Landris close to her. "Get me out of here. I can't…I can't…"

"Garlon!" Landris called the young Yeltan across. Garlon pushed his way through the crowd, fumbling for something in his jacket pocket as he hurried along.

Cathy had gone from being practically dead, to blazing tyrant, to quivering wreck in a matter of minutes.

Helen looked up at her mum. "She's bonkers, isn't she, mum?"

"Not bonkers, Helen, just not very well," corrected Jean.

"Whatever." Helen shrugged her shoulders.

Garlon produced a small, wooden bottle from his belt.

"You have the Lugpus?" Landris asked.

"Indeed, I do," Garlon answered.

"Excellent. I think it should do the trick." Landris took the bottle and knelt down beside Cathy. "Madam? James's mother?"

Half delirious, Cathy squinted up at Landris. "Take this drink. It will make you feel better." Landris offered Cathy an encouraging smile. "Just until we get above ground."

In between sobs, Cathy at first only sipped the yellow liquid. Then, liking the taste, she downed it, soon emptying the bottle of every drop. "Humph!" Cathy sniffed, then began to smile as a look of contentment brightened her face.

When they at last began moving through the tunnel she did not make one complaint or rude remark. She even giggled a little and began to hum a catchy tune.

"Mrs. Peck should drink that stuff all the time, shouldn't she, Mum?" said Helen, her big blue eyes sparkling in the light of the Yeltan torches.

Jean smiled reassuringly. "Just keep moving, Helen. We'll soon be home. I hope…"

* * *

Craig caught up with James, finding him just outside the hatch. James didn't say anything when he saw his friend, but he looked very relieved, which was good enough for Craig.

Both boys called for their magic weapons as Cimerato and the two remaining guards climbed out of the hatch. Together the small group crept to the edge of the tall ferns. Acrid smoke still blew through the trees and little grey flecks of ash floated through the grove like fairies dancing in the breeze.

"It's like a dream," said Craig, blinking in the amber light. Suddenly frowning, he looked up through a break in the canopy at the large orange orb that was Tealfirth. "It's getting bigger," he remarked, twirling his green spear.

James followed his gaze. "Much bigger," he agreed.

"Get down!" said Cimerato. "I can hear voices."

James and Craig quickly crouched low. They could hear the voices too.

Hissing and spitting, several Hedra soldiers moved to within a few feet of their position. They were so close that James could actually smell them—a mixture of damp dog and rotten fish.

A strange voice hissed through the bushes and trees. "Jal, I can still taste them. The Manimals."

The one called Jal's slit nostrils opened wide. "The breeze is pushing the smoke and their scent towards us. We need to move back to the River Levan and onward to Gwendral. They most likely burned on the island along with the Troll."

"It doesn't smell like cooked Manimal," hissed the voice.

Ssslathat moaned in pain, uttering deep resonate wails as he marched along. "Ashthat…oh no…oh no…"

Jal looked up at the wounded Troll, the expression on his flattened, scaly face scornful. "Keep it down, or that Mertol will find us again."

Ssslathat shuddered and creaked as he traced his wounded neck with his long fingers. "I finished it off," he replied. "I made sure it was dead." He eyed the smoked-filled forest suspiciously, as if he didn't quite believe his own words.

As the column of Hedra began to move again, the two Gwendralin guards that had lain beside Cimerato began to inch forward, their swords drawn.

"Stop!" Ssslathat's deep voice shook the branches round the Hedra. He pointed a long sharp finger at the fern grove to his right. Ssslathat jerked his head back to test the air. "Kak, Kak…"

James looked across to Craig who was lying beside Cimerato in the undergrowth. To his left, a Gwendralin guard slowly pushed himself up onto his knees. The guard put his fingers to his lips to signal silence and then, sword in hand, edged forward to where the Troll stood with his back to them. They could see the deep marks on creature's shoulders and neck left by the Mertol. The bushes around them began to rustle as more and more Hedra came back to support the Troll.

"We've walked right into this one," whispered Cimerato. He held his sword at the ready and slowly joined the first guard. "It's always better to strike first," he whispered. He signalled James to go to his left and Craig to his right.

James was terrified, but knew he could trust in his magic sword, Firetongue. Craig's spear, Greenworm, shone like new in his hand and looked no worse for being stuck in the back of Ashthat's throat and then being burned to a crisp under the Eden Tree. Both of the magical weapons glowed and jerked in the boys' hands, ready for the fight.

In front of them, Jal drew his sword. The remaining Hedra slithered and hissed, their grey scales flashing through gaps in the undergrowth as they prowled about. Suddenly, there was a heavy crash, just in front of James. Craning his neck upward, he saw Ssslathat's thirty-foot hulk towering over him. His massive foot had sunk into the leaf litter about three feet from Craig's head. *Just one more step and he'd have been strawberry jam,* thought James.

Thud!

Cimerato's curved sword slammed into the left heel of the Tree Troll.

Thud!

The smaller guard's sword bit deep into the right heel. They'd cut out two huge notches of woody flesh. Shocked by the attack, Ssslathat began to topple backwards.

James and Craig rolled out of the way as Ssslathat smacked down amongst the ferns. He missed the boys, but several of the approaching Hedra were not so lucky.

The bigger Gwendralin guard charged out of cover only to stop dead, skewered to the hilt, on Jal's sword. The Hedra's eyes flashed bright yellow as he pulled his sword back out.

All hell broke loose.

James's sword brought five surprised Hedra down at once, slicing through scales and bone as though they were butter.

Close by, Craig jumped up onto the toppled Ssslathat. Using the Troll's chest as a vantage point, he tried to pick out the Hedra who looked to be in command. When he saw Jal, he let the spear fly. Jal dodged to his left, escaping with a cut that oozed black blood. Instantly, the spear reappeared in Craig's hand. At the same time, Ssslathat moaned and turned, sending Craig flying as the giant hauled himself up onto his elbows.

"Blinders!" Seeing the spear in Craig's hand, the Troll automatically covered his good eye.

Craig stumbled to his feet and loosed the spear once more at four charging Hedra. It passed right through the attackers, leaving them slumped and twitching in the ferns.

Cimerato spun and ducked as he moved forward, slashing at the advancing Hedra while making sure to keep space between himself and the recovering Tree Troll. The remaining Gwendralin guard was less fortunate. He parried several Hedra swords well enough, but in the mêlée the guard failed to see Ssslathat's heavy fist before it was too late. With a sudden rush of air, it flattened him, along with the two Hedra he'd been fighting.

Jal and Cimerato ran at each other, locking swords before pushing away from each other. The Hedra guard was an excellent swordsman and he soon gained the advantage. Once, twice, three times, he parried Cimerato's thrusts and cuts. Then he went on the offensive. With a hiss, he lunged forward, twisting his sword at the last minute so it cut down into Cimerato's shoulder.

"Argh!" Cimerato bit his lip with pain as the black Hedra steel buckled his golden armour and took a chip out of his collarbone. Cimerato kicked himself free, but he was badly hurt.

Jal's tongue flicked with excitement when he saw the Gwendralin Captain stagger backwards. As he fell, however, Cimerato lunged at Jal's legs, catching Jal's shin guard. Jal wavered but quickly regained his stance and raised his sword for the kill.

With a yell of exertion, Cimerato rolled onto his knees and got to his feet. He managed to switch his sword hand and block the blow but blood was pouring down his chest from the cut on his right shoulder. His yellow armour glistened crimson.

Jal ducked down and threw his sword at Cimerato's legs. A blur of steel, it spun forward and smacked against Cimerato's sword, forcing it back between his legs. Cimerato winced.

Moving in for the kill once more, Jal crawled, lizard-style, along the ground. James was too busy fending off his own attackers to help the struggling captain; he could only hope Cimerato could hold on. Just as Jal was about to pounce, the Gwendralin captain yelled and jumped over his opponent.

Jal twisted his head as Cimerato flew over him, his reptilian teeth biting upward.

Cimerato met the bite with a powerful jab of his heel, which caught Jal's nose hole and smashed his mouth shut. Jal hissed in pain as Cimerato sprung off his back and landed, cat-like, behind him. As his Hedra attacker stood up, black blood trickling from his scaly mouth, Cimerato readied himself for the Hedra's next move.

With a roar, Cimerato raised his sword and charged. A nearby Hedra fighter flung his sword to Jal and the leader caught it. Once more, he and Cimerato locked swords. They stood, steel against steel, pitting their weight against each other. As they pushed and skidded in the mud, however, Cimerato's strength began to give. His left shoulder was growing numb; his right arm was useless. In one last furious effort, he smacked his head into Jal's face. Jal merely blinked once then smiled.

"No!" screamed James. Cimerato was beaten.

Jal's black tongue traced Cimerato's face, and the Gwendralin captain turned his head away.

James was also weakening as he cut and parried his way through the Hedra fighters. Almost reaching Cimerato, he heard a roar behind him. Instinctively, he ducked and the air rushed past his neck as Ssslathat's wooden fingernails took a swipe at him. Fortunately for James, the Troll skewered two more Hedra who'd been about to attack him from behind. As he turned round to fight, he saw Ssslathat stagger back on his weakened heels and sit down heavily on the forest floor.

Craig, taken by surprise, barely managed to throw himself clear, but his magic spear now lay trapped under the enormous weight of the Troll. "James, help!" he shouted. But James could do nothing for his friend. He was too busy spinning and cutting his way through the encroaching mass of Hedra. There were just too many of them.

"James!" Craig cried again.

Worried for his friend, James turned back to see Craig edging away from his trapped spear and the Tree Troll. It was only a quick glance, but the distraction was enough for the nearest Hedra soldier to take his chance and move in. As James turned back round, the Hedra brought down a fierce two-handed killing stroke.

With amazing speed, James's right arm shot up and blocked the blow. Swords locked in a spray of sparks and James found himself staring into the hypnotic eyes of his opponent. Unable to blink or break free, his mind grew fuzzy and he felt himself drift away from the fight. Sensing his advantage, the Hedra soldier brought his scaled knee upwards and caught James in the stomach.

"Unghh!" James fell hard. Winded, he lay helpless as another four Hedra notched their bows and took aim. Despair made his gut churn when he realised he had no choice but to surrender.

Cimerato, seeing what had happened to James, shouted out, "Hold your fire! We surrender!"

Halt!" Jal stood over Cimerato and waved his hand, hissing the command once more to his agitated troops. "Lower your weapons!"

Jal glanced down at James's magic sword. "Drop it now, or your friends die!"

Reluctantly, James dropped his sword. The Hedra nearest to James all jumped back in amazement when they saw it dissolve into the forest floor.

"Stay there, all of you!" Jal ordered. "Do not move." One of them kicked Cimerato in the ribs before binding him and retrieving his curved sword.

The deep voice of the Tree Troll, Ssslathat, filled the forest. "Now you will pay, Blinders." Grabbing hold of Craig, Ssslathat lifted the boy high above him. He examined his captured enemy curiously. "Such a little morsel. Hardly worth eating."

Craig, desperate for his magic spear, called out, "Greenworm! Greenworm!" But nothing happened.

"No good calling me names, boy. I won't kill you any quicker." Ssslathat laughed at his own joke, then threw Craig up into the air. He flew a good twenty feet above the forest canopy, spun round in mid-air then tumbled back down, screaming all the way. Ssslathat crouched, catching him with his other hand just before he hit the ground. "Lucky for you I can still manage well enough with the one eye you left me."

James knew it wouldn't be long before their time was up. His mum had been right. They should have stayed below ground with the Yeltans.

"Thirty two, thirty three..." Jal finished counting the dead bodies. "Another thirty three killed by..." Jal looked down at the spot where James's sword had disappeared. "Magic, I presume. However, before I kill you, I should like you to tell me where the other Manimals are hiding. I need to finish this job. King Feldon will be disappointed if I only bring three heads back to our camp."

The rest of the Hedra hissed and gurgled with laughter.

"Then you may as well kill us now, because we will tell you nothing!" Cimerato spat at a Hedra guard who was standing over him.

James wished Cimerato hadn't been quite so unwilling to negotiate. Not that he would talk, but maybe they could at least pretend they would, buy themselves a bit of thinking time. James was, after all, the one who had gotten them into this mess in the first place. Since he'd let them all down, it was up to him to fix things.

"You first!" Jal shouted.

James's stomach twisted. Jal had pointed to him.

"Take him behind that tree." James's heart was pounding as he racked his brains searching for a plan. The Hedra guard did as he was told and escorted the boy behind a broad tree.

"Leave him alone!" James heard Craig scream out from his prison in the Troll's fingers.

Cimerato grimaced and clutched his wounded shoulder.

Jal slipped behind the tree to join James and the Hedra guard. "Time to die, boy!"

There was a sickening thud.

* * *

"Who will be next?" Jal's voice echoed through the forest as he reappeared.

It had all happened so fast. Craig couldn't believe it. "No!" Stunned, he cried out again then dropped down to his knees in despair. Ssslathat whipped Craig over into one hand and thumped his other hand against a nearby tree trunk. Leaves showered down over Craig as Ssslathat's purple eye burned with rage. He addressed Jal. "Why did you kill the other boy? He was mine. He killed my brother!"

"He did not. The Mertol killed your brother with his magic. And besides, I am in charge here, not you!" Jal signalled to his troops and they fixed their aim on Ssslathat.

Ssslathat drew back. "Do not threaten me. I'm killing this one!" He lifted Craig high and opened his hand. Craig looked up to see the Troll's fist above him, ready to drop down in a deadly crushing blow. Just as the Troll's arm tensed for the kill, Craig heard something strange coming from the thickset tree where they'd taken James.

"Woowwwdwwright!"

Ssslathat jerked back. Roots began to sprout from the Troll's toes. They twisted out from his feet and burrowed themselves deeply into the soil. Ssslathat screamed as shins wrinkled and cracked. His skin, Craig realised, was morphing into brown, knotted bark. With every second that passed, a hundred new roots sprung out from the lower half of the Troll's body. Ssslathat tried to twist free, but he was stuck fast.

A loud crack exploded in the quiet woods. "No…!" Ssslathat screamed as his torso became solid wood. "Not tha…!" His voice was cut short as he jerked his head back for the last time. "Ka! Ka! K…." Gnarled woody branches covered his face, cutting off any further protest. He'd become tree, a proper one, indistinguishable from the others that surrounded them in the grove.

* * *

James felt the knock, knock, knocking sensation fade and now dared to look out from behind the broad tree. He saw Ssslathat, or what was left of him, holding a bemused Craig still standing in what had been Ssslathat's outstretched palm.

Tentatively, James whispered the wizard's name, unsure if he'd really said the strange word. "Mendel?"

There was no reply. Just the hisses of the Hedra soldiers. Spooked by what had happened to the Troll, Jal and the others, backed away.

"Hello again, my young friend." James heard the familiar voice and began to laugh with relief and joy.

"Where are you, Mendel?" James shouted as he stepped out from behind the tree.

Hearing James's voice, Craig screeched with delight and began clambering down the Troll. "Thank God you're alive! I could never have faced your mum if..."

The Hedra rounded on their leader. The Hedra warrior nearest Jal gave him a puzzled reptilian stare, his tongue flicking erratically. "Why did you spare the boy, Jal?"

"I was keeping him for the Troll, nothing more." Jal shrugged his shoulders casually, but he looked cagey.

The Hedra warrior tightened his grip on his sword and took a step back, his eyes flicking between the petrified Troll and Jal. "But you said we were going to kill the Troll if we could not find the Mertol, so why try to appease him?"

"He has tricked you all!" accused Cimerato.

James could see the suspicion building amongst the Hedra. All eyes were now on the one they called Jal.

"Get back in line!" Jal shouted.

The Hedra, completely unnerved by the death of Ssslathat, now eyed their leader warily.

"Get back in line, now!" Jal repeated. But the Hedra were already slipping back into the forest. One of them shouted out, "We don't want to be turned into trees or bushes by magic!"

James watched them flee until only Jal remained.

When it was safe, the boys untied Cimerato, and then all three walked over to the Hedra who'd spared James's life.

How quickly the tables have turned, thought James. He had to see Mendel again. "Where are you, Mendel? I can hear you but I..."

Craig stopped and looked up. He caught James's arm. "Look!"

A little blue man, with a shock of white hair, was spinning down from the canopy holding onto a huge strand of moss. "Mendel?"

The blue creature bumped onto the forest floor, took a bow and began to giggle.

"Sorry about the delay, boys," Mendel apologised, his voice filling their heads.

"What happened to you?" James demanded, looking round. "Why did you leave us?" He was still shaking with the shock of battle.

Craig approached the little, blue man. "I think I preferred you as a fish," he remarked after looking the odd creature up and down.

The little, blue man smiled. "Eee...I ees not Mendel. This ees." The creature produced a small bottle from behind his back. Craig and

James, slightly relieved to hear this, peered down into a little jug, which appeared to be made from amber-coloured leaves.

"You're still a fish then?" Craig stated the obvious.

"Yes, and now that the Eden Tree has been destroyed I can't see any easy way of getting back into my own body again." Mendel splashed his tail, spraying the little, blue creature. "This is Eethan, Eethan Magichand."

James nodded, remembering the little, blue figure from the Yeltan tapestry.

Cimerato interrupted the boys' conversation. "Who are you talking to? This is not Mendel." He was staring at Eethan.

Water splashed out of the makeshift jug as Mendel circled round.

"James, tell Cimerato to behave or I will make him recite the periodic table." James realised that Cimerato could not hear Mendel's voice.

With a sigh, he screwed up his face then turned to Cimerato. "Mendel says to behave or he'll make you recite the periodic table." Cimerato's expression changed in a flash. He moved closer and peered into the bottle. Eethan held up for him to see.

Jal remained motionless, apart from his tongue, which darted in and out of his scaled lips.

"Tell the Hedra fighter that he can either run and catch up with his comrades or join us." Mendel's voice once again filled James's head as he issued the command.

"Ask him to join us?" James peered into the flask in disbelief then, on receiving no reply, said, "Em, well, Jal. That's your name, isn't it?" Jal nodded, his tongue still flickering.

"Mendel says that you can either run now and catch up with your lizard men, or join us."

"Join you?" The Hedra's eye slits narrowed and his nostrils flared as he stared back at James.

"There is no way that any Hedra scum is going to come with us." Cimerato's white eyes widened.

Eethan tried to reassure Cimerato. "Ees good scum, ee thinks."

"Don't be stupid, little man. There's no such thing as a good Hedra. The only good Hedra is a dead one."

James shook his head. "Wait a second! If Mendel asked him to join us, that's good enough for me. Besides, he spared my life back there, though I'm not exactly sure why, but he did."

Jal looked as if he was smiling when he pointed to Cimerato and said, "I have spared you twice, great captain."

"What do you mean, twice?" Cimerato lifted the point of his sword until it twitched menacingly under Jal's chin.

"I saw you and your guards slip out of the sewers in your boat. I said nothing." Jal stepped back from the tip of Cimerato's sword.

"But you followed us, with two Tree Trolls! I was there when those Trolls and your Snakemen killed my guards!"

"The Trolls were looking for those two." He pointed to Craig and James. "And anyway, I was not in command at that point, Telan was."

"Telan?" Cimerato questioned.

"I'm afraid your little yellow friends took care of him," said Jal. "Saved me the job."

"Who are you?" Cimerato pressed.

"I am Jal, Royal guard of King Feldon. I was asked to take care of Telan after…"

"After your Snakemen and the Trolls had disposed of us and any other loose ends. Isn't that right?"

"Exactly!" Jal gave Cimerato another snaky grin.

Cimerato moved closer to Jal. "So why should I trust you for one second?"

Undaunted, the serpent guard continued, "Your King Athelstone is an impostor."

"So it seems," replied Cimerato.

"The dark lord, Dendralon, killed your King and now wears his skin."

James could see that Cimerato was unimpressed.

"Feldon, our King, is ready to take Gwendral…"

Cimerato pointed up through canopy at the reddening sky. "If there is time."

Jal moved forward. "I despise Dendralon, and have been treated no better than a slave by Feldon all my life." The Hedra giant looked up at the menacing sky. "Dendralon has said that we only have a matter of days before our world is destroyed."

"Twenty three hours, according to Mendel." James's voice seemed small in the forest, though his words struck fear in them all.

Jal knelt down on one knee and bowed his head. "I will gladly join you, if you will have me."

"Ha! You must be joking!" Cimerato looked round at the boys and Eethan in complete disbelief. "You must be joking... He's a Hedra."

"He spared James's life," said Craig.

"He's just a plant!" moaned Cimerato.

At this, everyone glanced up at the woody remains of Ssslathat.

Craig laughed. "Bad choice of words, mate."

Mendel's voice filled the boys' heads. "Jal is telling the truth. Let this be the end of it. We must go and find the others now."

James glanced up at the smoke-filled canopy of trees. "Mendel says Jal's telling the truth, so let's find that hatch and get back to the others." He placed his hand on Cimerato's arm and looked into his strange white eyes.

James felt Cimerato's eyes burning into his own.

"Fine, fine," hissed Cimerato. "The hatch is back here." He made his way past Jal and without looking at the Hedra directly, warned, "I'll be watching you, Snakeman."

By this time, the wind had picked up and the forest rustled and creaked menacingly. James looked back one more time at the twisted tree that had once been Ssslathat. He felt a pang of sorrow. He also felt a little guilty. They were the 'Blinders' after all. And now the Troll would remain frozen like that forever. James shuddered.

"I suppose you could say he's gone back to his roots," joked Craig, snickering.

James punched Craig's arm. "That's not even funny," he said, trying not to let Craig see him smile. Slipping down the ladder they dropped into the small chamber they'd come from only half an hour earlier.

Above them, Eethan took one last look round the forest, then fastened the little leafy pouch that held Mendel round his skinny waist. A few steps down the ladder, he pulled the hatch shut behind him.

James wondered what kind of creature this Eethan Magichand really was.

Mendel seemed to read his thoughts. "Don't be concerned, James. He is an old friend."

"Eee, very old friendeee. Yes, James, yes," Eethan tittered as they crawled onwards. A faint blue light shone out from Eethan's left hand as they scrambled onwards through the tunnel ahead.

CHAPTER TWENTY-EIGHT

DENDRALON'S PLAN

By now, Dendralon had two of the crystals he needed to open the giant gateway—one from the Salt Troll, Sintor, who had offered it freely, and the second from the Osgrunf leader, Hushna, who was still unaware that he had a forgery. The third was with Feldon, the Hedra King. Dendralon would soon be ready to test the power of all three.

Although there were many smaller crystals that opened doors to other worlds, it had been thousands of years since anyone had opened the giant gateway of Gwendral. Once the city was safely back in the hands of its rightful owners, Dendralon would take it, along with all its powers, to another world, a better world.

So far, his mock invasion of Gwendral was serving its purpose quite well. The ruse had drawn the crystal bearers to the city and had emptied Gwendral of its Manimal parasites. It was time now to follow through on the rest of his plan.

He scratched his left arm and looked down at the pink skin. It was beginning to flake and peel. He pulled his sleeve further down to cover the small patch of grey scales that now glistened in the candle-light.

Dendralon stepped out onto the balcony just as dawn began to spread its fingers over the Denthan landscape for the last time. He was pleased to see that at last there was some movement. The giant Salt Trolls had grouped together, surrounded by their Salteth slaves. Their long whale-tooth spears flashed white as the first rays of Tealfirth caught the polished blades. The Salt Trolls' tactics were well known. They let the vicious Salteths engage first. Then, as the battle intensified, and only when thousands had killed and been killed, the Salteths would part, forming a clear pathway to the enemy. It was then that the

Salt Trolls would rush, like a battering ram, down this gap at their opponents. They would thunder into the breach, splitting any army in two that had the misfortune to stand in their way. Once behind the opposing army, they would turn about and cut down their foes, driving them back onto the blades of the frenzied Salteths.

What the Salt Trolls hadn't counted on, Dendralon mused, was that after such a clash with the fierce Osgrunfs, there would be many losses. When both armies were at their weakest, his Hedra would move in for the kill.

The Osgrunfs only had one tactic when it came to warfare—one huge berserker charge, en-masse and at maximum speed. A solid brigade of steel and muscle, they could trample and defeat most of the foes before the poor fools even knew what had hit them.

"This will be an interesting fight," he murmured to himself, his long black tongue forking through the dead, Manimal King's dry lips.

Looking beyond the campfires to the Forest of Eldane, he sniffed at the air. Smoke still seeped up from the forest near Senegral Island. Feldon's search party must have found the intruders, he decided. The Hedra King should be back soon, bearing the news Dendralon wanted to hear.

"King Athelstone, my Lord." A nervous looking Council Secretary stood behind his King. "The Salt Trolls have begun to group."

Dendralon retracted his flicking black tongue then turned, pulling his sleeve down a little further. "Yes, I know. How many Manima—I mean, how many of our people still remain in the city?"

The Council Secretary blinked. "Only your elite guards at the gates and a few soldiers on the walls, my lord. All the people have now left by the tunnels or have flown north on the Dragons of Hest."

The wizard looked down at the cowering secretary, a Manimal by the name of Elgry, who'd served him well. "Take my dragon, Whindril, for you and your family. She will see you to safety. But before you go, tell the soldiers on the walls to leave by the tunnels. I shall remain here with my elite guards until the end. There is one last spell I may try—a dangerous one. It is our last hope."

Elgry bowed his head respectfully.

Dendralon's hair flicked round his face in the early morning breeze as he listened, impatiently, to the Secretary's mutterings. "Thank you, my King. I will make sure your bravery will be forever told. I will do all that you ask."

Some time later, the secretary emerged from the bottom of the citadel. Whindril, Dendralon's royal, white dragon, was chained to the courtyard wall below. The beast was magnificent. The youngest of the Dragons of Hest, her wings were still intact and her eyes sparkled like diamonds. Gleaming white scales covered her majestic form and soft downy hair hung from her neck like ermine and poked up in little tufts between her powerful talons.

Whindril was once famous for being the dragon that bore Dendralon's enemy, Mendel, in his victory over the Hedra all those years before. The creature had never truly bowed to his will. Her tail flicked as the scampering secretary approached and undid her heavy chain. Dendralon would have no use for Mendel's dragon where he was going, though it was a pity to leave her to die on this doomed world.

"Come, Whindril," Elgry said, far down below. "You are to take my family to safety. You must fly high over the spires, then even higher over the spears and arrows of the Hedra."

Through narrowed eyes, Dendralon watched as Elgry picked up the golden tether and led the dragon down the deserted streets to his waiting family.

* * *

"Oh, Father!" Elgry's little boy, Davado, squealed with delight as they approached the dragon.

As her son marvelled at the animal, however, his wife moved closer and caught his sleeve. "The Hedra have shot down too many of these beasts already," she whispered, not wanting to frighten the boy. "They showed no mercy. It might be safer to go the way we planned, through the tunnels that lead to Nordengate."

"This is Athelstone's own," replied Elgry. "She is the youngest of the Dragons of Hest, and the best. Please..." He looked into his wife's eyes and placed his finger on her reticent smile. "We must stay calm for the sake of Davado."

The little boy tugged on his sleeve. "I want to hold the reins. Can I?"

Elgry's wife sighed when she saw the look of exhilaration on her child's face. Begrudgingly, she nodded her head. "When we are far above the Forest of Eldane, your father will let you hold the reins."

Making haste, they packed what they could and scrambled up onto the large decorated saddle that sat between Whindril's elegant, silky wings. Then, with two huge flaps, Whindril rose up from the cobbled streets. She gained height quickly and they all hung on tight as she veered round and round the main citadel. As they passed the highest balcony, they saw King Athelstone, transfixed and oblivious to all except the amassing armies below. Far above the citadel, they were too high now for the arrows and spears of the Hedra on the ridge.

Below them, the Salteths shrieked and charged the Osgrunfs. This did not suit the Osgrunfs, as they relied on charging first, but they soon rallied and turned back on the Salteths with their cutlasses and claws. The ever-present cloud of black flies lifted as the armies engaged and the stench of death was soon heavy in the air.

"Don't look!" Elgry shielded Davado's eyes and cuddled him in close to protect him from the freezing cold and the carnage below. He peered down at the battle beneath them and shouted across to his wife, "Why are they fighting amongst themselves?"

His wife, holding on tightly to Whindril's seat, pulled her crimson robe around her shoulders. "Take us away from here, Elgry. We might not be high enough." Elgry strained to hear her voice. It was lost in the flapping of Whindril's giant wings.

"Athelstone said that there was one last spell he could perform. Perhaps this is his magic. Our old King may save us yet."

"Just fly high over Eldane, Elgry. Take us to the safety of Hest."

* * *

Dendralon was engrossed in the battle below. He watched as Hushna, the leader of the Osgrunfs, pushed to the fore and smashed into the first line of Salteths. Each swing of his huge cutlass sent five or six Salteths flying back on top of their own kin. It wasn't long before bodies were heaped high all round him. Hushna's ferocity was legendary and he nodded approvingly as the giant cut a bloody swath in the fury of his berserker charge.

Eventually the Osgrunfs and the Salteths made way until it was only the completely stupid, or those off balance, that staggered into Hushna's deadly path. The Osgrunf troops had gained ground and soon the Salteths were struggling against the warriors' greater stature and incredible strength. When the Salteths began to falter, Dendralon heard the trumpet call that signalled them to split into two groups.

Peeling apart from the rear, a channel opened up to form a passageway leading all the way to the front line. Sintor, the King of the Salt Trolls, brandished his white whale-tooth spear as he took in the scene before him. More than three times the height of any Osgrunf, Sintor raised his royal mailed hand high in a fist. "Charge!" he bellowed.

Dendralon sensed the Troll King's anticipation. He tapped the base of his gnarled staff on the floor of the balcony in excitement as almost two hundred giant Trolls thundered toward the Osgrunfs. Hushna was at the front of his troops, standing alone in the circle made for him by his own and the enemy. He was still slashing, carelessly, back and forth when Sintor's spear skewered him.

Hushna wriggled like a worm on a hook, a mixture of surprise and anger on his twisted face as Sintor lifted him into the air. His body jerked several times and then, with a final scream, went limp.

Sintor bellowed and whipped the corpse of Hushna high into the air with a terrible roar. The body of Hushna fell down amongst his own soldiers and a huge cry of fear rose up from the Osgrunf ranks. But they did not run.

Instead, their fear seemed to meld into a burning rage that forced them onwards, like one giant beast, toward the killer of their King. Dendralon smiled. Everything was going beautifully. Even the Centides of Eldane had joined the fight. Several of the bug-like creatures wriggled through the ranks of the raging Osgrunfs and began to climb up the thick legs of the Salt Trolls, nipping and piercing as they went.

Gaining momentum, the main bulk of the Osgrunfs roared as they smashed into the Salt Trolls, cutlasses, pikes and heavy warmaces, all slashing a gory path. When they were close enough, they dug their claws deep into the Trolls' salty hides and climbed up their bodies, tearing at flesh and hacking at bone. They didn't discriminate in their fury, cutting down any Centides or Salteths in their path. No creature was spared.

Through the sheer weight of their numbers, the Osgrunfs soon toppled the giants, who were then finished off by a hundred slashes. Unsatisfied, the Osgrunf mass pushed further into the midst of the Salt Trolls. Always ravenous, the Salteths became crazed by the smell of blood, pouncing on any wounded creature they could, feasting there and then, completely unhindered by the battle around them.

As the dead piled high around him, Sintor, king of the Salt Trolls, scanned the ridge. Seeing the Hedra army, poised but uncommitted, he screamed, "Now, Feldon! Charge now!" The Hedra, however, made no move to help, remaining deaf to the pleas of the Troll King.

Just then, an enormous Tree Troll slammed into Sintor knocking him backwards. Rolling over and over, they crushed countless Salteths until Malkor, the brother of Sintor, forced himself forward and jammed his whale-tooth spear through the Tree Troll's hide. Pinning him to the ground, Malkor stamped down hard until the attacker's backbone cracked and dark green blood spilt thick across the mud. The Salteths swarmed over the felled Tree Troll and finished him off, tearing chunks of bark from the twitching beast.

* * *

High on the ridge, King Feldon looked on, as Dendralon did, with unreserved delight. He'd cheered when he'd seen Hushna's corpse fly high through the air. He bellowed jubilantly when Sintor fell. But when his Hedra troops stepped out of their lines, he checked his own fervour and stood up high on his chariot. "Stay at the ready! Don't you dare move until I say so!"

When they'd settled back into formation, he squinted up at the citadel where the dark figure of Dendralon, still dressed as the Manimal King, stood on his balcony. "The old Hedra wizard's plan is working well," he hissed proudly. "We will soon walk into the city, unopposed."

Dendralon, the last of the true ancient ones, continued to stare down over the battlefield as the amber glow of dawn spread over the growing piles of dead. King Feldon, without once taking his eyes from the battle below, addressed his charioteer. "We Hedra are the only true species. The first to evolve, we will be the last to survive. You are fortunate to be at my side to witness our return to power."

The charioteer hissed excitedly, bowing his head to Feldon before reining in his reptilian steeds. "Hold fasssst," he snapped. "Not much longer!"

* * *

The sounds of war filled the skies as Whindril banked to her left, soaring high over the Hedra. "Look, Father!" Elgry's little boy exclaimed, "The grey Snakemen are making big lines on the ground."

Elgry hugged Davado tightly as he stared down at the sheer size of the Hedra army. Long supply lines, like wriggling grey tentacles, stretched back all the way to the Southern Marshes.

"There must be more than a hundred thousand of them and..." Elgry pulled Whindril round to get a better view of the horde below. "They don't have any siege weapons. As far as I can see, they only have piles of furniture and belongings. King Athelstone told me they had siege weapons."

"They don't look like an army intent on destroying Gwendral," his wife shouted in his ear. "They look as though they intend to move in."

Davado stared up at his father. "But Father, how will the King stop all those Snakemen?"

Elgry gripped his son tightly as a bank of warm air wafted up from the forest below, filling Whindril's massive wings. "Don't worry, Son. We must trust our King." Gripping a tuft of dragon mane, he looked north to the cliffs of Nordengate and beyond them to Hest. "We've dallied long enough. It's time to go." For a brief moment, he glanced across at his beautiful wife, then flicked Whindril's golden reins.

* * *

Dendralon stood transfixed as he watched the Osgrunfs continue to drive the Salt Trolls back towards the Gorton Sea, their sheer animal determination proving to be more than a match for their larger foe. Sintor struggled to stay upright as time after time, Osgrunfs leapt up onto his heavy armour. He kicked at his green-haired assailants and struck out at them with his ivory spear, but he was growing weary. Finally, a particularly determined Osgrunf, leaner than the rest and sporting a particularly long set of hooked nails, managed to find a piece of exposed hide. He plunged his sloth-like claws deep into the Troll King's fleshy hide.

Dendralon watched excitedly as Sintor tried to flick the wretched beast off. But before he could, more Osgrunfs jumped up onto his arms and legs. Within moments, their combined weight caused him to stagger and sway. At the same time, one of the Osgrunfs had reached Sintor's shoulders and was now biting and clawing at his neck. The Troll began to bellow in agony. "Help!" he shrieked. "Help me!"

Hearing his cries of distress, two large Salt Trolls kicked their way through and were soon pulling the vicious Osgrunf attackers from their King's neck. They stamped the writhing assailants into the dirt before guiding Sintor away from the front line. Edging back towards the sea, they supported their King with one arm while swinging their Gnarwhale spears in huge arcs in an effort to keep the oncoming Osgrunfs at bay.

As though sensing the change in the air, the Salteths suddenly ceased fighting and feasting. With a high-pitched wailing, they began to run back towards the sea. They darted between the Salt Trolls' legs, screaming out curses as they ran. Many were trampled in the rush.

Sensing victory, the Osgrunfs ran ahead of the routed Salteths and Salt Trolls, stopping as many of them as they could from reaching the beaches in the distance.

It was not a pretty sight, but Dendralon loved every minute of it. He hissed with glee when a Salt Troll stumbled or toppled over in the mad dash to the sea. These fallen giants were easy prey for the Osgrunfs. Once down, they couldn't right themselves in time to use their deadly spears against an onslaught of swords and pikes.

In the midst of the battle, a small group of Osgrunfs carried the body of their King up high like some gruesome puppet mascot. Over and over again, they chanted his name, proclaiming the battle as "Hushna's victory."

Fools, thought Dendralon. *Entertaining, but fools, nonetheless.*

By retreating, Sintor had surrendered himself to defeat. The King of the Trolls must have known that his only hope of survival was to get back under the waves of the Gorton Sea. Finally at the shore, Sintor turned and looked directly at Dendralon. He met the Troll-King's gaze and heard his voice enter his mind.

"You promised to help us, Dendralon, yet your army holds fast? You have betrayed us!"

Dendralon issued an indifferent sigh. He saw Sintor glance up at the reddening sky one last time before slipping beneath the crimson waves of the Gorton Sea.

Around him, the waters bubbled with Salteths trying to escape. Following their King, several Salt Trolls dived into the red waters, sending huge waves crashing against the shore. Many more Salt Trolls and Salteths fell before they could reach the sea, and still more sunk below the waves, no doubt to die. Across the Plain of Gwendral, millions of flies filled the noxious air, their continuous drone intensifying as they pestered the wounded and hindered the dying.

Feeling triumphant, Dendralon raised his gnarled staff high into the air. "This is the beginning of the end for Denthan. The Hedra will soon have a clear path to the city gates." Dendralon toyed with the heavy gold chain around his neck, revelling in the power of the two blue crystals. Turning toward the Hedra King, Feldon, he gave his signal.

Feldon nodded and relayed the instructions to his captains. Neatly and swiftly, three long lines of Hedra Archers moved forward and knelt in position.

They were ready.

CHAPTER TWENTY-NINE

MENDEL AND THE DRAGON

After an uncomfortable night spent in the tunnels, James could tell by the babbling sound of the Yeltans and the occasional, high-pitched voice of a whining child that they'd almost caught up with the others. James, Craig, Eethan, Cimerato, Jal and, of course, Mendel could at last see daylight as the passage opened out before them. Up ahead, James saw the Yukplug pen and instantly recognised the unmistakable figure of Wee Joe. He was giving his mum a hard time.

"I don't like dat puke! It's not wogurt, it's not!" Wee Joe spat another blob onto the sandy ground.

Jean dipped her finger into the white goo and tasted it. "Look Joe, it's lovely."

"Yuk!" Wee Joe moaned. "Now it's got your germs nin it too. It's agusting! What nelse food is der?"

When James and his group emerged from the tunnel, the babbling stopped instantly as all eyes alighted on the Hedra giant. Hundreds of little swords slid noisily from their scabbards.

Lord Eldane stepped forward, his curved Gwendralin sword at the ready.

"Wait!" James held up his hand and stepped out in front of Jal. "He's here to help us."

Jean held a spoon in one hand and Wee Joe in the other, but the three-year-old slid off her knee, splattering white Yukplug yoghurt all over her mohair cardigan. "Joe!" she bleated. "Be careful!"

Landris moved up to stand beside Lord Eldane.

Tall, even for a Hedra, Jal towered above them all. Flicking his black tongue, he smiled and stooped down to offer a handshake. He quickly pulled his scaled hand away when Landris raised his spear.

The Yeltan leader had seen the dried bloodstains on Cimerato's shoulder, and thinking this was a trap, had made himself ready. He expected to see a Hedra patrol emerge from the gloom at any moment.

The Yeltans' babbling intensified.

When Eethan finally stepped out from the shadow of the tunnel, the noise instantly ceased. He held up a jug made of copper-coloured leaves. To James's surprise, an audible gasp rose from the watching crowd. All eyes were on the little blue man.

"Here, en thees flask, ees Mendel, thee only one who can save ees. Ee has said thees Hedra," Eethan touched Jal's arm, "ees one who can help us." Eethan spoke slowly and waved the bottle in front of him for effect. He turned to Landris and Lord Eldane, smiled, and then gave them an exaggerated bow. This move seemed to appeal to the Yeltans. To James's amazement, they began to clap.

Craig whispered in his ear. "What's going on now?"

James shrugged. "I don't know, but Eethan seems to have struck a chord."

The Yeltans were looking at Eethan in complete awe, their eyes wide with wonder. Some of them even knelt down before the little, blue creature.

Lord Eldane steadied his son, staring at his shattered armour and wounded shoulder. "Who did this to you, Cimerato?" His son had never been beaten.

Cimerato sat down heavily. The Yeltans, seemingly always prepared, surged toward him with packs of cold moss and river mud to put on his wound. He pointed to Jal. "Our guest over there. He's pretty good."

Landris, still wary of the Hedra giant, gave him a wide berth as he walked over to Eethan and took his hand. "He has returned!" he cried exultantly. He lifted Eethan's hand up high.

"You'd think he'd won the bloomin' Olympics," sniggered Craig, nudging James.

Landris continued, "This is Eethan Magichand, friend of Mendel. He is the one depicted on our tapestries."

"He's the nose-picking twit," Cathy cried out, suddenly roused, "who got us into this mess in the first place. And you..." Cathy pointed to James, who tried to look away, "you are grounded!"

James cringed and turned to face her. But to his surprise, by the time he caught her eye, her expression had shifted from rage to complete indifference. She tittered, smiled, and then collapsed back onto a pile of animal skins. His mum had fallen fast asleep.

"Mum?" Concerned and embarrassed at the same time, James didn't know how to react, though he thought he better see if she was alright. As he approached, he felt a renewed twinge of embarrassment when he saw who sat beside her.

"Hello, James."

"Eeh!" James yelped. "I mean, em...eh...hello, Father. I mean, Reverend, I mean..." What the heck were Father Michael and the churchwarden's sister, Ephie Blake, doing here anyway? Could this get any weirder, or more embarrassing? He groaned as he thought back to the swift kick that had felled the Rector. "I hope that your, um, well... I mean, I'm sorry about the church thingy and everything. The gargoyle..." James became tongue-tied.

Michael looked puzzled. "You know who stole the gargoyle from the church tower?"

"Well..." James didn't know what to say. "Not exactly stole..." He stopped again.

Father Michael simply sighed and covered Cathy with a soft, yellow blanket. "She's tired, James. They gave her something called Lugpus. I asked that one over there." Michael was pointing to Garlon. "She began to panic in the tunnel, you see, and..."

"And that must have calmed her down a bit, I suppose," said James.

"Yes, it did." Michael stood up. "You've got a cross to bear there, my son," he mumbled, before moving over to sit down beside Ephie Blake, the village snoop.

Ephie was chewing on some sticky bread. "Mmm, not bad." She offered some to James who was taken aback that she'd even spoken to him. Only weeks before Craig and he had been involved in an apple stealing incident and the last thing she'd said to him was, "Reform School, that's where you two will end up. As sure as fudge!"

James took the sticky bread from her. "Eh, thanks," he said, as politely as he could. He munched on it as he scanned the crowd for Craig, who he spied, sitting with his mum and the kids beside the Yukplug pen. James went over to join them. As he walked along, he spotted the Yeltans slapping some kind of goo on Cimerato's wounded shoulder. Lord Eldane watched the Yeltans bathe his son's arm and neck.

A pang of jealousy gripped James as he passed them. Father tending son; Mrs. Harrison hugging Craig; Helen and Wee Joe laughing.

No one seemed to give a damn about his dad, and his mum was 'out of her tree'. Flippin' heck, even if she were awake, she'd probably be more of a hindrance than a help. No one here seemed to like her much. He could only imagine what kind of commotion she must have made in the tunnels after he'd run off to find Mendel. He really wished she wouldn't get so angry all the time. His life would be so much easier.

James's eyes fell on Jal, standing a few yards to his left. He wasn't the only one who was feeling out of it., he decided. The big Hedra soldier was awkwardly holding a plate of raw meat. James guessed that sticky bread probably wasn't a Hedra's cup of tea.

James sighed and continued walking. As he drew nearer to the Yukplug pen, however, Garlon appeared with Bero. The Golden Retriever was wagging his tail excitedly. James noticed something hanging round his neck. "Craig, look!" said James.

Craig turned from the kids and waved, but then he saw it too. The plastic brandy barrel was back in its rightful place, swinging below Bero's neck. It looked as good as new.

Garlon winked at the boys. "I'm good at fixing things."

Eethan, having escaped from his adoring fans, walked over to join them.

"Garlon's fixed Mendel's barrel," James told him.

"Weeell, it looks a leetle beetter than mine. Eeee…" Eethan examined the flask he'd made from leaves then glanced over at the sleeping Cathy. "Ees your Motheeer?"

"Yes," said James, feeling slightly ashamed.

"Ees a tough ladeee, but shee has a kind heart inside—deeep inside."

"Yes, she can be kind." James racked his brains for an example, but unable to come up with one, he decided to ask Eethan about his dad instead. "I was wondering if you might have seen my dad? He's about five six. He might be wearing a blue fleecy."

Eethan unexpectedly reached out and touched James's temple with his middle finger. It made James jump. "Hees lifeblood and yours are as one. Ee feel theere ees still a connection here." James wasn't sure what that meant.

"I think he's trying to tell you that your dad's okay," Craig explained.

"Ah-hem!" Mendel interrupted. "I think I should like to go back into my barrel, please."

Eethan immediately unscrewed the lid and poured Mendel back into the barrel.

"I suppose I'd better get used to being in here for a while longer," said Mendel, as he splashed about.

He doesn't sound all that thrilled at the prospect, thought James.

Before Eethan screwed the lid back on Craig popped some crumbs into the barrel.

"Snug ees a bug," said Eethan, patting Bero's head.

Craig knelt down beside the barrel. "Mendel, I have to admit that I've missed seeing those googly eyes of yours pressed against this window. Just knowing you're there makes me feel so much better." He grinned and Bero panted and whined with excitement.

"How touching," Mendel replied dryly.

Craig's smile broadened. "It was, wasn't it?"

The wizard flipped his tail. "Good, because we must get into Gwendral today. Are you ready for that?"

"But, Mendel…" said James. He thought back to the hordes of Osgrunfs and Hedra he'd seen from the top of Dunnad.

"Don't worry, James. Jal will get us into the city through the sewers."

James looked over at Jal who appeared to have several irate Yeltans shouting at him. The Hedra giant was pleading his innocence and pointing to his stomach.

Cimerato, now looking much better, walked over. "Your friendly Snakeman has just eaten one of the Yeltans' pet parrots."

"Not one of the little blue parrot things!" Craig yelped. "How did he manage to catch one in the first place?"

"One flick of that black tongue of his and it was gone," said Cimerato.

"Call him over," Mendel instructed.

Eethan scampered over and took Jal's arm. "Come, eets time to prove your loyaltee."

Jal had to stoop under several low branches as he made his way through the disgruntled Yeltans. He gave a large belch as he stopped in front of Bero. His nostrils flared. "What is this creature?"

The hackles rose along Bero's back.

"He's a dog," said Craig, "my dog. And what's more, he's not for eating. Not for breakfast, not for lunch, not for dinner. Not even as a snack. Okay?" Craig scratched the green serpent on his palm preparing to call his spear if need be.

"Whatever you say, little one." Jal eyed Bero curiously. "So, blue man, how can I prove my loyalteee?" He mimicked Eethan's pronunciation, his serpentine mouth grinning widely.

As the others gathered round the Hedra giant, James felt a tingling sensation, which meant Mendel was about to speak. He slowly began to relay the wizard's words to the group. "Mendel says that we don't have much time. Tealfirth has grown in size and reddened." James squinted up at the large, red ball in the morning sky. "In less than twenty hours, it will explode and most probably wipe out all life on Denthan. We have to get inside Gwendral if we are to have any chance of survival."

Michael crossed himself.

Landris spoke up, "What secret lies in the city? I think we should go down to our deepest tunnels. Surely it will be safer there than in Gwendral?"

"Mendel is saying that Denthan will most probably disappear," answered James. "The tunnels won't do you any good."

Mendel splashed in the barrel, his golden tail flashing past the plastic window.

"Can't we just go back the way we came, through that square door?" asked Michael.

"There's no guarantee that will work, and no time to experiment," relayed James. "Mendel says that Gwendral is a giant gateway, capable of transporting itself, and all within its walls, to other parts of the universe."

"I heard Dendralon speak of such a thing," said Jal. All eyes turned on the Hedra giant.

Ephie and Garlon belatedly joined the group as James continued to relay the information as clearly as he could, but he was having a hard time making himself heard over all the muttering. "Mendel says…" James made his voice louder. "Mendel says…!"

The racket stopped.

James swallowed. "Mendel says that Dendralon intends to take his Hedra army back to Drumfintley, to Earth. And that he probably has the three crystals needed to operate the giant gateway."

Everyone, especially the humans, gasped loudly. James was struggling to believe the words coming out of his own mouth. *Dendralon wanted to go to Earth?* Stunned, he could only whisper the last part of Mendel's message. "Our only hope is to get inside Gwendral, find Dendralon, and stop him." His shoulders slumped. It seemed an impossible task.

Landris spoke up. "Our scouts have reported that a battle has begun outside the walls of Gwendral. We should make for Dunnad. It is on our way, and it will give us a vantage point."

"Tell the Yeltans to gather only the most essential of possessions," instructed Mendel. James mechanically repeated what Mendel had said and everybody began moving at once. James remained where he was. He couldn't stop thinking about the Hedra army spilling out over Bruce Moor. Worse, Mendel had said nothing about James's dad. It was as though his dad didn't even exist. Everyone had forgotten about him.

When they were ready to go, the disheartened group, which included a very sluggish Cathy, followed Landris and the Yeltans to the hill known as Dunnad.

As the approached the rocky knoll, James nudged Craig and whispered, "Look, the snakes are still here." As before, a huge gathering of serpents guarded the slopes of Dunnad, hissing and slithering this way and that. James thought about calling his magic sword, but Mendel stopped him. "No, James, I will take care of this," he said. "Wwwswerpwent Swwleewwwp!" James's voice echoed up the rock face. When the sound reached the snakes, their tongues stopped flickering and their heads lowered. Every last one of the serpents had fallen asleep.

Thud!

Startled, they all looked behind them.

There, in an unsightly pile, lay Jal, snoring his head off. He had slumped down beside Cathy, who snorted and twitched as though she was having a nightmare.

"Oops!" said Craig. "Nice one, Mendel."

Cimerato laughed. "Perfect. Let's just leave him."

Many of the Yeltans eagerly nodded their agreement, but James was already moving toward Jal. On instruction from Mendel, he touched the Hedra's scaly temple with his forefinger and watched as Jal began to stir.

"Argh!" Jal opened his yellow slit eyes, then snapped ferocious-ly at James, causing him to jump back in alarm.

"Wow! I was only trying to wake you," exclaimed James, mak-ing a mental note not to do that again.

Muttering what sounded like curses, Jal climbed to his feet, holding his head.

Cathy continued to sleep as the party made their way up through the unconscious serpents to the top of Dunnad, only a short distance away.

"The Osgrunfs have routed the Salt Trolls and their Salteth slaves," Mendel informed them.

"Look at that!" cried Craig. "It's just like a huge, black tidal wave washing over the others."

After glancing back to see that his mother was alright, James joined the others at the top. As his eyes adjusted, he spotted a group of Tree Trolls lumbering toward the sea and shivered. He saw the disgust-ing Centides too. Both groups were joining the fight against the re-treating Salt Trolls.

"Don't look, Helen." Jean covered her daughter's eyes. She couldn't keep Wee Joe back, though. He kept pushing to the front of the group, mesmerised by the sights and sounds. To him, it was as if one of his computer games had come to life.

Lord Eldane looked over to his son. "What's going on, Cime-rato? I don't understand."

Before anyone could respond, James noticed something flying high above them. "Wwwhinwwdril!" he shouted, startling the others. As soon as the words slipped out of his mouth, the white dot banked away from the mountains in the distance and sailed back towards them.

"Mum, look!" Helen pointed. "It's...it's a real live dragon!" Wee Joe and his sister both looked up at the reddening sky. The dra-gon was dropping fast, spinning down through the morning air.

In his head, James heard Mendel say, "Whindril is a Dragon of Hest. Let's see if we can put her to use."

The dragon was close to them now and when she flapped her enormous wings, a huge blast of air slammed into their faces. The en-suing dust cloud blotted out the rout on the plain below.

Finally, the white dragon landed, her razor sharp talons scrap-ing on the rock. Once settled, she folded her silken wings and swished her long tail. Impressive and imperious, Whindril was probably the most beautiful   creature James had ever seen. She looked magnificent, with her snow-white scales, flecked with gold, and her ermine-like tufts of white fur.

"Mum, I'm scared." Helen snuggled into her Mum, but she couldn't take her eyes off the wonderful animal.

In a fit of excitement, Craig rushed over to the dragon but Jal stopped him before he got too close. "Be careful, boy! They bite," he hissed.

Cimerato yanked Craig free from Jal's scaly hands. "They only bite Snakemen like you, Jal," he growled, as he guided Craig forward. Recognising the man on the back of the dragon, Cimerato called up to him. "Elgry!"

Elgry's face lit up. "Cimerato! Lord Eldane! It is good to see you alive and well. We were making our way to Hest when Whindril suddenly turned back round to land here. It is just as well. I can update you on what is happening. Right at this very moment, Athelstone is trying to save the city. Look!"

James tried to see, but there was too much dust still swirling about the knoll.

"I think his magic has caused our enemies to turn on each other," said Elgry.

"He didn't need magic to do that, my friend!" Mendel's thoughts echoed round in James's head. James wondered what the wizard meant.

Elgry continued, "The King said we could take Whindril as he was going to remain behind. He was going to try using his magic to save the city." Elgry glanced down at Whindril. "I haven't stolen her," he added nervously. He seemed a little scared of Cimerato.

Cimerato called the man and his wife and child down. "The thought never occurred to me, Elgry. Come now. You'd all better dismount until Mendel decides what we should do next."

"Mendel?" said Elgry. He looked confused enough, but when he saw Jal, standing unbound behind Cimerato, he tightened his grip on his wife's shoulder. "What is this?" Elgry pointed to Jal.

"Yes, well, I'm not too happy about him, either," said Cimerato. "But you still better come down. Whindril was always Mendel's dragon."

"But why do you speak of Mendel?" Elgry protested. "He is gone."

"Actually, he is here, with us, Elgry. And Athelstone…" Cimerato moved closer to Whindril's heaving breast, her scales shifting as she breathed. "Athelstone perished a long time ago. We have been led astray by Hedra trickery and witchcraft." He sniffed scornfully at Jal then helped a confused looking Elgry down from the dragon.

"Madam," Cimerato addressed Elgry's wife, holding her hand as she dismounted. "If you will please take your boy back there to the crèche." Cimerato pointed towards Jean and the kids, a disgruntled look on his face.

Whindril snorted and yawned, exposing her long, translucent fangs. After shaking out her snowy mane, she began to sniff the air.

"Ssith ta he ttesh, Whindril!" Although James didn't recognise the words coming out of his mouth, he noticed that Mendel had said them in a kind way, as if talking to an old friend.

When Whindril began to waddle towards him, however, he thought of calling for his sword again.

"No, James," said Mendel. "It is alright."

At that moment Bero barked.

The dragon turned her huge head to the side and peered down at the old dog. Her eyes blinked slowly as she studied the strange animal. Bero barked again.

"Ttesh na ta Ssith. Mendel?" The dragon's voice was soft and deep as she addressed Bero.

"Yes, I am before you, Whindril," Mendel laughed. "But I am not the dog. I am the small goldfish trapped inside the barrel that hangs round the dog's neck. Your new master did this to me."

"Arggg Ssssss…Ttishnta nar Athelstone." Whindril exposed her teeth again and flicked her scaly tail twice.

"Quite!" agreed Mendel. "I need you to do something for me, Whindril. You must take the two boys, this dog, and myself back into Gwendral, without being seen."

James could see that Craig, like himself, was almost bursting with excitement at the prospect. He'd been wondering for a while now, if his dad was actually in the city. It seemed probable. He wondered, though, how a forty-foot dragon was going to be able to sneak into the city of Gwendral without being seen by the guards or, for that matter, the fifty thousand screaming creatures that covered the plain below.

By now, Eethan had scampered over to Whindril and was stroking the fine scales nearest to her flattened ears. Flecked with golden ridges, the scales glistened in the strange Denthan light.

"Ttesh na ta Ssith, Eethan," said Whindril, lovingly brushing her head against the little, blue man.

"Eee, thought you ad seen dee last of mee girlee, eh?" Eethan trailed his fingers through the dragon's fine mane and tittered.

While Eethan and Whindril became reacquainted, Mendel asked James to get Jal's attention. James was still wary of the hulking Hedra who'd snapped at him earlier so he kept his distance when he said, "Jal, Mendel would like you to take everyone you can into Gwendral by way of the sewers." James paused to listen to the wizard's next directive. "He says you should hide them under blankets and mats and go in a convoy of boats. Tell your Hedra comrades that you are in charge of supplies for the city."

"It's broad daylight." Jal squinted up at the waxing orb of Tealfirth. "But it might work," he added. "Though if any of my troupe of archers have managed to make it back to the city, Dendralon will be ready for us."

Landris spoke again. "We don't think that any of your brigade survived. Last night they ran into a part of the forest thick with Centides. Many are either dead or, worse still, wrapped up for later."

James thought back to the swinging black Centide pods and shivered.

"Besides," Craig spoke up, "they all ran away before you declared your loyalties, Jal. They're going to think you were either captured or killed."

James looked at his friend in awe, surprised by the way he'd made his point. "Nice one, Craig." Amazingly, he hadn't managed to insult anyone.

"They wouldn't know," Craig went on, "that you simply got scared and bottled out when Mendel killed the Tree Troll," he finished, a toothy smile creasing his freckles.

"Sssss…" Jal hissed at Craig contemptuously.

James sighed deeply.

"I want to go with you this time," said a familiar voice. Cathy, finally awake, had appeared beside them, her green coat wrapped tightly round her. She stepped forward and placed her hand on the dragon's mane. "I would like to go with my son, please." She seemed unusually calm and collected. James didn't like it.

"Mum?" He knew he had to say sorry for disobeying her or he'd be paying for it for the weeks, if not months. "I'm sorry for leaving you like that, but…"

"I've told you a thousand times, James. Never say the words 'sorry' and 'but' in the same sentence. They cancel each other out. Anyway, we can discuss that later." Her words were spoken, not shouted or yelled in her customary way. James braced himself, waiting for a change in tone, but it never came. She turned toward Eethan, who'd busied himself picking his nose again, and asked, "Now, how do we get home?"

Eethan, examining something disgusting on the tip of his thumb said, "Eee es not me who will decide. Ees Mendel." He pointed to the barrel round Bero's neck. His mum glanced down and James's stomach did a somersault.

"My barrel!" She reached down to retrieve it but suddenly stopped herself. "You've filled it with water and there's a bloody goldfish swimming about inside."

"Cathy, language!" warned Jean.

"Bloody, bloody, bloody…" Wee Joe repeated gleefully.

Cathy ignored Jean and Wee Joe.

"James! Your father gave that to me as a gift. How dare you put that stinky fish in there!"

James couldn't help thinking back to the 'flying rings' incident that had followed this particular gift from his dad. She'd has some kind of argument with his dad over him staying an extra night away in Switzerland, and had thrown her wedding rings out of the window in a rage. It had taken his dad two days to find them.

He knelt down beside his mum and toyed nervously with Bero's crooked brown ear. Bero began to pant. "Mum, this fish is the reason why we're all here."

Craig whispered in his ear. "Watch it, numpty! She'll probably tear the barrel from Bero's neck and kick it into next week."

James scowled at Craig. It wasn't the time or the place for one of his stupid remarks. "He's a wizard called Mendel," continued James.

"Ees my friend," Eethan added, rather unhelpfully.

James gave Eethan a quelling look and the blue man shrugged before returning to his nose picking. James continued, "As I was saying, he is a wizard and I can hear him in my head." James looked into his mum's deep brown eyes as he said this, hoping she could see that he wasn't crazy.

"So can I!" Craig interjected.

"Ees can heers him en mee head too," Eethan added, rolling something rubbery between two fingers.

Bero gave a small woof and wagged his tail, as if to let Cathy know he could hear Mendel too.

Cathy looked at them all and nodded. "Fine, I'm standing beside a forty-foot white dragon, looking down on a city surrounded by a million goblins, or whatever they are, and I'm talking to a three-foot high, blue man. Not to mention him." Cathy pointed towards Jal who was standing beside Landris, "or them." She flicked her fingers at the Yeltans. "So, I'm quite prepared to believe that this goldfish, who's swimming in my barrel, is actually a wizard. Okay! Whoever it is I'm talking to, just get me and my boy home because my life is complicated enough as it is. I don't need this." She bent down and peered into the barrel. "Got that, fish? And by the way, where ever James goes, I go from now on. Okay?"

"I think we better take your mother with us too," Mendel sighed.

"Then you better make sure she can hear you," James warned. "I don't want to be the translator all the time."

Mendel sighed again.

While Craig and James strapped themselves onto Whindril, Cimerato and Jal lifted Bero up onto the wide saddle.

"It's a bit like being in a horse-drawn carriage," remarked Craig, grinning widely. He was ecstatic at the prospect of riding on a real live dragon. However, when Whindril arched her snake-like neck and turned to look down at her new passengers, Craig shrieked and drew back.

Last aboard was Cathy, who still looked drowsy after her Lugpus. "Remember to hold on tight," she lectured as she wrapped the golden tether round her wrist and leaned back against the ornate leather back- rest.

Craig whispered into James's ear, "Remember to hold on tight," he mimicked then added, "Or mummy will smack your bottom!"

"Hardee-har-har, numpty!" James was about to turn away when Craig jabbed him in the ribs. "Look, I've still got some."

James saw the top of the small, black bottle that Garlon had given him the day before. "Lugpus?"

"Yeah," whispered Craig. "A drop in her tea every morning and your life is sorted, mate."

"You do talk the biggest heap of dross!" James growled, though a treacherous part of him considered the suggestion seriously.

"What was that?" Cathy demanded.

"I said, I wish Dad could have done this with us," James lied.

"Hmm," said Cathy, nonplussed.

James's eyes widened. "Mum, where did you get that?" He'd just spotted his green rucksack.

"It was on some rocks. Before I was almost crushed to death by a giant moving tree, I made sure to grab it." Cathy looked at her son's dirty face and wiped away a tear from her cheek.

"You okay, Mum?" asked James, suddenly concerned. He felt a tinge of sadness and wondered if maybe she really cared about his dad after all. They'd never really discussed his disappearance properly. Maybe it was less painful for her that way, he decided.

James reached for the rucksack, but Cathy increased her grip and unzipped it. "I suppose you'll be needing this." She produced James's blue inhaler.

"No, Mum. I've been fine here, so far." James grabbed on tightly as Whindril shifted her position. "Mendel says that there's more oxygen here, or something." His mum, however, remained silent. She had always thought that his asthma was a put on, to get out of chores or bunk off school. "About Dad," James broached. "Do you think he's here?"

Cathy looked at him but couldn't speak. She just gave a half-hearted smile and shook her head. "Not really."

When everyone was on board, Whindril unfolded her wings and extended them to their full sixty feet. She tested the air, causing the Yeltans to shield their strange blue eyes from the dust and debris. The dragon placed a knowing eye on Eethan as he jumped up beside the boys. Then she stretched her worm-like neck and shook her white mane before leaping up into the heavy Denthan air. An updraft caught her immense wings, making them tense and fill. After an initial jolt, she soared higher and began to sail effortlessly over the forest.

Cathy was now wide-awake, her lips set in a childlike grin.

Craig held onto Bero's fur and Cathy's green cardigan. "Wow! Yeah!" he shouted.

Far below, James could see Michael and Ephie waving up at them. They looked strangely out of place amongst the little Yeltans. Jean was trying to placate Helen and Wee Joe, who were crying because they didn't get to ride on the dragon. However, they were soon distracted by offers of more Yeltan sticky bread.

Holding on as tightly as he could, James listened to Mendel as the wizard's words formed in his head, "Fly higher, Whindril. Fly high, and away from Gwendral." The dragon obeyed. "Get ready!" Mendel cried as he prepared his spell. The knock, knock, knocking sensation of impending magic began to build in James's head. "Wwwinvisw-wabllwwittwwor!" The words burst awkwardly from his lips and were soon lost in a rush of wind that made them all hold on so tightly that their knuckles turned white.

The weird words were still echoing in his head when all of a sudden, Whindril's snout started to shimmer. Just like heat haze over a hot road, the dragon's head flickered, distorted, and then disappeared. The dragon's neck was next, only wavering momentarily before fading away. James could still hear the sound of her huge wings beating somewhere nearby, but he certainly couldn't see the dragon, or anybody else, for that matter.

"We've disappeared!" Cathy screeched.

James looked down. It was totally disorientating; being invisible while suspended in mid-air.

Mendel gave a second command. "Quickly, Whindril! Take us back towards the city before the spell wears off!"

James hung on as the dragon banked round and flew towards Gwendral. "Look, James!" cried Craig. "Look at the spires. What do they remind you of?"

James looked hard, then said it at the same time as Craig, "The Jesus Rocks!" The positioning of the spires exactly matched the pattern of stones on Bruce Moor. No wonder the city had looked familiar to them up on the knoll.

"Well spotted," said Mendel, chuckling as he explained. "The stones and spires are both set to a certain pattern. The alignment is critical, you see. Hold on!"

As Whindril circled the main citadel, the boys made out a black-cloaked figure standing on a high balcony. Transfixed by the battle beyond the walls, the figure stood motionless, dark and threatening, as he watched the destruction below.

After the slaughter on the seashore the Osgrunfs were now racing back to their positions, though only a third of their original number, perhaps five or six thousand, remained intact. The Salt Trolls and Salteths had taken their toll, but the Osgrunfs were still a sizeable force. The Centides did not follow the Osgrunfs, preferring to stay behind and feed off the dead. The Osgrunfs were on their own.

By this time, the Hedra archers were arranged in three long thin lines and stood ready for the returning Osgrunfs. James realised that the Hedra had stayed well out of the battle between the Trolls and the Osgrunfs.

"I can see the Hedra King, Feldon," Mendel said. "We are in luck! The third crystal still hangs round his neck. And there is Dendralon, wearing his Manimal disguise, watching the battle. The Hedra are about to take advantage of the Osgrunfs. Get ready to head in closer everyone!"

"Who's that talking?" Cathy demanded.

"It's Mendel," James explained, "the talking fish."

For once, Cathy remained silent. James didn't think she liked having a fish speaking to her, especially inside her head.

When everyone was holding on tight, Mendel began to speak to the dragon in her own tongue, which James could actually understand. "Fly over the battlefield, Whindril. Get as close as you can. We need to slow things down a bit—keep that last crystal away from Dendralon for as long as possible."

The dragon snorted and then flapped up and over the city gate. When the unexpected displacement of air caught Dendralon's elite guards on the gate towers they jumped and looked about in terror.

The dark figure on the balcony noticed the confusion at the main gate and scanned the horizon to see what was causing the trouble.

So that's Dendralon, thought James. *He looks different.*

Unaware of what was coming his way, King Feldon lowered his mailed fist and five thousand arrows ripped through the air. When they reached their zenith, they came together to form a black cloud that looked like a swarm of deadly locusts.

"Wwwrongwwflyw!" The power surge from Mendel's magic made James's head feel as though it was splitting and this, combined with the disorientation of being invisible, made him lose his grip on the tether. "Ah!" he yelped, struggling to hang on.

Hearing the cry, Dendralon turned toward their position, narrowing his eyes as though he could see them. Whether he did or not, the "Wrongfly" spell was already doing its work. The needle sharp arrows flew left and right bursting from the black mass in an explosion of sparks, leaving behind five thousand colourful vapour trails hanging in the mid-morning sky. After seeing what had happened, the Osgrunfs gathered into one huge herd and charged, snorting and spitting with anger.

Witnessing the powerful magic that had come to the rescue of the Osgrunfs, the Hedra hissed in fear. They struggled to nock more arrows as the Osgrunfs pounded toward them.

James tried to grab onto a tuft of dragon hair as Whindril lost height. "No!" he cried out as a sudden turn caused his fingers to slip free. Sensing that her son was falling, Cathy snatched out blindly and caught hold of his arm. Panic-stricken, James kicked in mid-air, aware that he was only a few yards above the Hedra below him.

King Feldon shouted up at Dendralon. "What magic is this?" But his words were cut short as a gust of displaced air slammed into his face. The Hedra King ducked down and scanned the skies, confused by the sudden blast.

James felt his mum tug hard on his shirt, yanking him upwards. He managed to grab hold and scramble back onto the dragon seat, dripping with sweat and gripping his mum so tight that he heard her gasp.

"You're soaked through!" she scolded, holding him close to her.

James shook with the nearness of his fall.

Dendralon's head whipped round. He'd picked up Cathy's strident voice, which, James decided, could probably carry over an exploding volcano. He flinched when Dendralon punched an angry fist in their direction.

"I have you now!" The voice sounded in James's head and he recognised it as that of the stranger he'd met in Drumfintley. A second later, a ball of blue fire skimmed the city wall and raced straight for them.

"Turn, Whindril! Turn!" Mendel shouted.

The invisible dragon dipped one wing and dropped to within feet of the Hedra.

Fear shook the reptilian army as they felt another unexplained rush of air knocking into them. They hissed and growled at their invisible tormentor, some of the archers loosing their arrows in panic.

James felt nauseous as the arrows flew past them. "Wwshieldwwbarww!" Mendel's voice roared in his head.

Dendralon's speeding blue ball of fire smashed against Mendel's invisible shield and spread over it like lightning. Flashes and bolts of blue showered down onto the Hedra below and they screamed in agony. The noise was terrifying.

"Dendralon will try again, and my power is waning," said Mendel. "Climb high, Whindril!"

On hearing Mendel's command, the faithful beast beat her wings furiously and climbed up into the morning sky, hoping to escape before Dendralon could let loose another blast of magic.

* * *

Dendralon, however, had been distracted by the renewed screams below. The Osgrunfs had hit the first line of his Hedra archers like a battering ram and, unstoppable, had smashed into the second line just as ferociously.

Dendralon and Feldon, however, had prepared for the unthinkable.

The third row of archers had another defence against the Osgrunf's berserker charge. Twenty feet behind the third line, a thousand light infantry leapt forward and caught hold of their ropes. With a nod, the third line of archers nocked their bows and unleashed a point-blank onslaught. Unfortunately for the first and second lines of Hedra archers, the rain of arrows did not discriminate, slaying Hedra and Osgrunf alike, piercing armour and bone.

Frantic screams filled the morning air and the "Harka!" cry of the Osgrunfs grew louder and more manic. Dendralon was pleased that their thick, matted hair proved useless against the arrows at such close range, but despite this weakness, their relentless charge never faltered.

It was now that the light infantry acted out their well-rehearsed plan. Just at the point when the Osgrunfs were within feet of hitting the third line, they pulled on their ropes, each of which was attached to a long, jagged pike. These black bladed weapons swung up and caught the Osgrunfs as they slammed into the breach. In an instant, hundreds were killed, yet, amazingly, still more crawled and scrambled over the Hedra lines and their own dead.

"No!" exclaimed Dendralon. "Hold fast!" Even from this distance he could tell that Feldon was panicking.

The King summoned his personal guards. "To the ships. Now!" he roared.

* * *

They were still circling above the fight when Craig called out. "Look! Some of those Hedra things are running away!" Hearing this, Mendel, quite uncharacteristically, yelped with excitement and splashed about in his barrel.

The Osgrunfs, now only hundreds in number, continued to cause havoc in the Hedra camp, tearing through tents and routing the Hedra followers.

"This is horrible!" cried Cathy. "Do we have to stay here and watch?" She felt about until she found the barrel round Bero's neck. She rapped the plastic with her knuckles and screamed out, "I don't want my son to see this!" But her words were lost in the wind that rushed by their faces as Whindril flapped her gigantic wings.

"Cathy!" Mendel pleaded. "Please don't knock on the barrel again!" His voice sounded shaky. "Whindril, bank left towards the river. We'll head off Feldon there."

James's was pulled close and he hung on for dear life as they glided for several hundred yards, losing height the whole way. In a short time they were hovering over a long, sleek river galleon, decorated with gold and protected by polished black armour. The deck teamed with grey-scaled Hedra scrambling to untie the mooring ropes. "They know the battle has turned against them. They're making ready to sail," warned Mendel.

Whindril flapped down to the ship and settled on the stern, her polished talons scratching deep into the wooden deck. Her weight almost tipped the boat, lifting the bow clear of the water, causing the Hedra deck-hands to slide backwards. As the vessel splashed back down again, the Hedra fell in a heap, kicking and struggling to right themselves. The helmsman turned round to see what was going on and Whindril's head snapped forward. She caught him in her mouth and gulped him down with two flicks of her head, crunching and hissing as she snacked.

"Yuck!" James thought he was going to throw up.

On deck the Hedra were in a total panic. Seeing one of their own literally disappear in two huge gulps, many of them screamed and jumped overboard. A Hedra sailor dressed in green armour, who looked to be the captain of the boat, froze and began hissing in panic when he heard the sound of Whindril's giant footsteps on the fore-deck. The planking warped beneath the dragon's weight as she moved forward. James prepared to turn away rather than see another Hedra eaten alive.

"Get ready to sail!" It was the Hedra King calling from the river-bank. But the captain continued to stare in horror at the bending floorboards.

Surrounded by a hundred Hedra archers, Feldon screamed out, "I said, get ready to sail!" The Hedra King looked terrifying in his battle dress. His large green plume flickered in the breeze as Whindril's invisible wings began to flap. Feldon stepped back.

"Tetsh Hee!" Mendel's dragon-tongue command sprung from James's own lips.

Soon after the words were spoken, they began to rise high into the air again. They were flying back towards the city.

James heard Craig retch. "I'm feeling sick. I need to get off."

Mendel ignored Craig's pleas. "Whindril, we must go round the citadel and land in the Royal courtyard."

As Whindril climbed higher, James noticed that Dendralon had left his vantage point.

"Where'd he go?" James asked.

"He will have gone to get the gateway ready," replied Mendel. "We've done enough, for now."

"Why deed you not kill Feldon at de reever?" Eethan wanted to know. "Why deed you not take de third creestal?"

Mendel sighed. "That would've been ideal, but Feldon's archers were aiming their arrows right at us. Even though they couldn't see us, they certainly would have hit us. All is not lost, Eethan. I'm quite sure that King Feldon will bring the crystal to the main hall himself. In the meantime, we can get ourselves in place to intercept him."

Just as Mendel stopped talking, there was a loud swishing sound, like the drawing of a huge curtain, and they were all visible again. Whindril landed on the cobbled courtyard with a jolt and James slipped off the ornate saddle. He noticed the look of sheer relief on the faces of his mum and Craig. Only Eethan and Bero seemed remotely saddened to leave Whindril.

The courtyard was deserted and the adjoining streets lay silent. Only the squeaks and chirps of flying reptiles could be heard over the sounds of their footsteps and the scratch of Whindril's dragon claws on the cobbled street.

Feeling exposed, James quickly decided that he might want his sword close by. He whispered the word, "Firetongue," and soon felt the reassuring weight of the crimson sword in his hand.

"Put that away. Now!" his mum yelled, grabbing his wrist and looking him straight in the eye. James's fingers unravelled to reveal part of his crimson tattoo. She saw him glance down and followed his gaze. "What on earth is that?" she screamed.

"But Mum…" he protested, "I had no choice."

"Cathy," said Mendel, "that is the magical mark that connects the James to his sword. We will need all the protection we can get."

"Yeah," added Craig.

Mendel continued to explain, "Dendralon will not be in the best of moods. He knows we are here and is bound to have a few surprises in store for us."

Uncharacteristically, Mendel's words seemed to calm her and she relaxed her grip on James's arm. "Now," he went on, "we need to get to the top of the citadel."

They all craned their necks in an effort to see the top of the main citadel. It stood three hundred feet high and looked impossible to climb or even to enter, being fashioned from the smoothest stone that James had ever seen.

"Bloomin' heck! How are we going to get in there?" Craig asked. He snapped his fingers and Bero shuffled up behind him.

"We use the door, of course," replied Mendel.

"I don't see any doors! Nothing but this stuff." Craig ran his hand over the smooth surface.

"There are two ways into the citadel," Mendel explained. "One is via the main stairs to the Council Chamber, which will no doubt be heavily defended. The other entrance is here."

They all stared at the flawless alabaster surface of the citadel.

"I'm not seeing any door, Mendel," said James.

"Put your hand on the stone," Mendel commanded.

James moved closer and touched the cold, marble-like surface. "Like this?" He looked down at the barrel.

"Yes. Quiet now. I must concentrate," said Mendel.

James grimaced as the knocking sensation began to build in his head.

"James, what's wrong?" asked Cathy. She stepped forward.

In the grip of the magic, James was unable to answer as he braced himself against the smooth wall of the citadel.

It was at that precise moment that they heard the shout.

CHAPTER THIRTY

THE BLACK LAKE

Underground, a long line of Yeltans and Yukplugs made their way down a steep set of slippery steps. The tunnel walls glistened with damp, green algae and the roof dripped continuously. Stalactites stabbed down through the dank air and the taller members of the party—Jal, in particular—had to duck low and weave their way between them.

Father Michael caught up with Landris and asked the obvious question. "There are quite a few of us. How many boats do you have, or are we going to have to make more than one trip?"

"We do not have any boats," said Landris.

"What!" Michael cried. "Then how do you expect to...?"

Lord Eldane cut in. "The Yeltans are very literal. They really do not have any boats. We Manimals, on the other hand, have plenty of boats at the harbour. There were over three hundred the last time I saw the inventory."

"Three hundred and twenty one, to be precise," remarked Elgry. He'd entrusted his family to Jean and Ephie, who were further back with the Yeltans.

"But how..." persisted Michael, "how do you propose to get three hundred boats, full of all these people and animals, into the city unseen and under the very noses of the Hedra?"

Landris placed a yellow finger to his lips, then pointed at the flickering torchlight in the distance. "Please keep your voice down. We are in enemy territory right now."

"Michael?" Ephie's call up the queue to Michael echoed up the tunnel walls.

Cimerato and Jal both stopped and turned to look at her. "Can you keep it down, Madam?" asked Cimerato. "No need to alert the whole world."

Ephie's face flushed scarlet as she reached Michael. He patted her arm sympathetically and she gave him a grateful look.

Without warning, Jal pushed forward and raced ahead until he reached the bend in the tunnel.

"What's he doing?" Cimerato hissed. "I told you he would betray us!" He began to follow after the Hedra but swiftly stopped and flattened himself against the tunnel wall.

In front of him, only yards away, Jal was addressing a Hedra guard. "Anything to report?" he snapped.

The frightened Hedra guard recognized Jal and instantly drew back. Jal's heart quickened. Maybe someone had made it back, after all.

"Sir! I mean, no Sir." The guard had only been startled and promptly slapped his upper arm in a Hedra salute.

"Get back to the surface. Be quick now!" Jal ushered the sentry up the steps he had just come down. "We have to get all of our supplies, some of which are personal items belonging to King Feldon, into the city by way of the sewers. I am putting you in charge of keeping all unnecessary Hedra at bay."

"Yes, Sir," hissed the guard.

"First take your comrades, the ones down there..." He pointed to the flickering torches beside the underground harbour. "Take them up to the surface with you. Things are not going well for us. We are going to need all the troops we can get. I will load the boats with my soldiers," expained Jal, "ones who have been specially chosen by King Feldon."

The Hedra sentry gave another salute and began to shout commands at the guards below.

Soon, the stairs to the river and the harbour were empty and Jal turned back to where the Yeltans were waiting. As he turned round the bend he came face to face with Cimerato.

"Mmm...not bad, Snakeman," whispered Cimerato. "So why are you helping us, again?"

"Why not?" replied Jal. "Not all of us Hedra are deranged killers. Feldon wiped out my family when I was just a child. My father wanted to make peace with the Manimals and paid for the suggestion with his life. Don't forget, Manimal, we built Gwendral when you were still leaping from tree to tree, scratching your backsides."

Cimerato gave Jal a wry smile. Only Mendel had ever dared to remind the Manimals of their true past. "If you don't mind, Snakeman, I think it's time we got to work."

* * *

Cimerato eventually managed to persuade the Yeltans to leave as many of their belongings behind as they could, and soon the long lines of Yeltan families were filing down to the harbour and onto the waiting boats. The Yukplugs were few in number, though they still filled up two of the bigger vessels.

Finally, the Drumfintley contingent lined up on the pier, trying their best to keep the children from falling into the black water. Cimerato helped the young ones onto a boat and untied its ropes. Elgry and his family jumped into the last boat along with Jal, Lord Eldane and Cimerato.

Before long, all three hundred and twenty one boats were under way. In the darkness, they could hear the battle cries in the distance, echoing down through various fissures in the walls. The boats pushed on regardless, eventually passing under a low-ceilinged section of the tunnel that Cimerato knew marked the foundations of the city walls.

Several minutes later the flotilla arrived at the Black Lake. It lay directly beneath the centre of the city. Close by, Cimerato recognised the set of stairs that led down from the cells; the same stinking cells where his father had found him only two days before. Amazingly, there was no sign of any guards or sentries here and Cimerato wondered if his kin still held this part of the city. There could only be a few left now who hadn't already fled the city by dragon or secret passage.

The Yeltans' incessant, high-pitched babbling began to drift over the still surface of the lake, annoying and worrying Cimerato. He wanted to shut them up, but knew that any reproach of his would have to be louder still.

Through the din, Jal's deep hissing voice reached his ears. "Over there!" Jal stood up in the boat beside Elgry, making it wobble in the darkness. "About fifty yards ahead of us... There's a heat trace... It's definitely Manimal. Whoever it is would have to be deaf to miss the commotion made by your kind." He eyed a Yeltan soldier. "He's moving fast. Give me one of your spears, little Root-dweller." He held out his hand in anticipation, but Cimerato reached across the boat with his sword and flicked the Yeltan spear away. "No chance, my friend. Not until we know what we're dealing with."

"Hmmm… Well, there are too many now, anyway!" Jal retorted. A hundred torches flared into life along the underground shore to reveal at least three times as many Manimal archers, their arrows nocked.

Cimerato stood up beside Jal and shouted across the expanse of cold water towards the bank. "Hold your fire!" Several archers had spotted Jal and aimed at him. Alarmed to see a Hedra so close, a few let loose their arrows.

"Get down!" Cimerato pulled Jal down as the first arrow ripped past his scaly neck. "Stop, I say!" Cimerato stood up again and waved his hands, but now even more arrows flew from the shore. He called across to his father. "Father, they think we are Hedra!"

"Stop!" Lord Eldane's rich voice ricocheted off the cavern walls.

The arrows stopped flying.

A voice called out in the darkness, "Lord Eldane, Elgry, Cimerato!"

Cimerato began to row his boat toward the edge of a long, under-ground jetty.

As more Manimals appeared on the quay, Cimerato called out to them, "Help us to unload these people and their belongings."

His fellow Manimals began to gossip and chatter when they saw the Yeltans. "Why bring these creatures here into our city? Don't you know the Salt Trolls have been crushed by the Osgrunfs?"

Cimerato knew the young archer who spoke. His name was Fetrand.

"They all began fighting amongst themselves," Fetrand continued. "Even now, the Osgrunfs are fighting the Hedra archers. Our enemies are falling, but the sentries on the walls say there are still more Hedra on the way. That's why we loosed our arrows. We thought you were…" His voice trailed off as Jal stepped from his boat and gave him a small bow. The Hedra giant then proceeded to lift the three children out of the boat followed by the adults.

When it came to her turn, Ephie shuddered and protested, "It's alright. I can manage!" And she did, though not before almost falling into the water. Michael caught her just in time.

When they were all off the boat, Lord Eldane addressed the young archer. "Why are you not in the tunnels that lead to Nordengate? Where are the others?"

Fetrand replied, "Once we were sure that our old and young were safe, some of us returned to help. We thought we might buy you some time if we held the Hedra a while longer. You should know, though, that some of the people in the tunnels grew impatient and have begun their journey on towards Nordengate."

"I told them to travel for two hours only. They were told to wait!" Lord Eldane's eyes blazed with anger and fear. He beckoned to the Council Secretary, Elgry. "This is your chance to be a hero, Elgry. Take this man with you." He pointed to the young archer, Fetrand. "Run to our people in the tunnels. Go as fast as you can! They must come back into Gwendral now, or there will be no hope for them. As a Council member you have the authority to order them back. Now, go!"

"What of my family?" Elgry hesitated. "What about Athelstone, I mean Dendralon?"

"Mendel is the only one who can challenge Dendralon now," Lord Eldane replied. "We must climb up to the citadel and await his instructions."

Jean looked across at Elgry and smiled reassuringly. "I will stay close to your wife and son." She moved to stand beside Elgry's beautiful wife and took his young son's hand in her own. Wee Joe, who held her other hand, stuck his tongue out at the boy. Davado returned the favour and they both giggled.

Elgry stooped down and kissed his wife, and then his son. "I will see you both soon." He turned away and began running, the young archer at his side, down the jetty and along the ledge that led deeper under the city and to the tunnels of Nordengate.

In the meantime, the Yeltans continued to stream from the boats carrying all they could possibly manage. Before long, the dark, rocky shore was littered with clusters of the babbling creatures. Only a few remaining boats waited for space to dock and unload.

"Don't wike dat!" Wee Joe's voice cut through the din.

Wee Joe seemed to be pointing his little finger straight at Cimerato who wondered what he'd done to upset the little one.

"Not you. Dat!" Joe pointed past Cimerato toward the direction of the lake. Everyone followed his gaze. A large, black boat had slipped round the bend of the river and drifted into the underground lake, its oars muffled. Two more Hedra warships followed, black arrows already flying from their decks into the tangle of boats moored to the long jetty.

"Hedra!" shouted Cimerato.

A tall Manimal archer pulled the children behind a large rock and nocked his longbow. The few Yeltans still floating on the lake began to wail. Amongst the mêlée of arrows, they splashed and scrambled for the safety of the jetty and the rocks behind it. Four of their boats were rammed, smashed to pieces by the full force of the Hedra attack.

Cimerato hauled Jal down beside the women and children. "Be careful, your kin might get lucky."

Next to him, Jean was shaking and Ephie was whimpering. Before Michael could duck down, an arrow caught his left ear. "Arrgghh!" he cried. Blood streamed down his neck.

Behind the first three Hedra boats, the royal battleship barely made it into the larger cavern from the smaller tunnel, creaking and groaning as parts of her rigging snapped and bent on the jagged rocks and stalactites that marked the foundations of the city walls. Several pieces of the main sail crashed down onto the weary crew.

Arrows flew from the jetty now, killing some of the scaled archers, their hisses and screams mixing with those of the stranded Yeltans. The unexpected light in the cavern had confused the Hedra, just as it had Jal, and Cimerato's heart lifted as many Hedra shots fell short or went wide of their mark. Most of the Yeltans were able to make it to the safety off the jetty before the Hedra eyes became accustomed to the light.

Unfortunately, there was no magic to help the Manimals and Yeltans this time and soon their supply of arms was spent. Black arrows splintered behind the crouching children and still more cracked noisily on the rocks in front of them. Blood trickled down from Michael's ear onto his collar and Ephie ripped a piece of cloth from her blue joggers, making a bandage of sorts, which she carefully pinned round his balding head.

Michael beamed at her. "Thanks again, Ephie. You're always coming to my rescue." Ephie simply smiled and flushed a little redder than usual.

Helen began to cry and Wee Joe gave her a big hug. "Never mind, Hewen, I stole some tabwet from her coat when we were in de cage."

As the arrows flew and the eerie screams filled the chamber, Wee Joe carefully unwrapped Galdinie's greaseproof paper and broke a piece of tablet from the bar for his big sister. He kissed her arm and patted her head. Jean pulled them both close. In the middle of the carnage, she smiled. Wee Joe offered a small piece of the tablet to Davado, who took it with a grateful nod. "You're a good boy, Joe," she whispered to him, "such a good boy."

"Back, we need to move back!" Cimerato cried. "They'll soon be at the jetty!" They'd already lost too many of their number to the Hedra arrows and with the tunnels to Nordengate now blocked, they would have to regroup in the city. Cimerato pushed his sword round the rock and saw the Hedra King in the reflection of the blade, a mere twenty feet from the shore. Feldon smiled as the torches revealed the devastation his archers had caused. He summoned his master of arms and pointed to a large decorative door.

"Train all your arrows on that doorway," Feldon ordered. "It's their only escape route. If any of those rats get through it, you will die. Is that clear?"

"Yes, my King." The Hedra archer turned and screamed the order. "All of you aim at the doorway! Shoot anything that moves!"

Cimerato pulled back his sword. "We're trapped! We'll have to wait until they come ashore, then fight hand to hand." Cimerato thumped his fist down on the nearest rock then grimaced as a fork of pain flashed up his arm. He gripped his wounded shoulder. "I keep forgetting about this stupid wound!" He flashed Jal an annoyed look.

The Hedra only shrugged. "It's not my fault that I'm the better swordsman."

Lord Eldane crouched down beside his son. "We don't stand a chance. Those ships can each hold over two hundred Hedra and—"

His words were cut short by a sudden roar of water. Cimerato stuck his sword round the edge of the rock again to see what had happened. He couldn't believe it. The Hedra royal boat had been heaved to one side. It had cracked against the wall of the cavern.

The water around the boat began to boil and lift, falling away to reveal a huge Salt Troll, his neck lined with deep gouges. Two more Trolls burst from the waters of the lake and began to thump their heavy whale-tooth spears down on the Hedra boats.

Feldon screamed and ducked into his cabin. A few arrows glanced off the Salt Trolls' armour as they plucked the screaming Hedra from the ships, smacking them dead on the rocks. With a cold determination, they continued to slam their weapons down on the first boat until it disintegrated, sinking beneath the cold waters along with its crew.

Cimerato grabbed Jean's arm. "Quick, now is our only chance to get through the door." Still unsure what was happening, they staggered to their feet and sprinted for the doorway. The Yeltans followed, their escape masked by the shouts, hisses and roars of the new battle on the Black Lake.

As he urged the others through the doorway, Cimerato kept his eye on the battle. One of the Hedra managed to catch a Salt Troll's throat with a long boat hook. It was a good move, until the giant tumbled forward smashing the boat and the unlucky Hedra under him as he fell.

"Feldon!" the largest Troll bellowed as he began to tip the royal boat. His strength was immense and his black eyes burned with hatred. "Why did you not help us against the Osgrunf horde? Dendralon promised that you would help us!"

Like the slithering reptile he truly was, Feldon slipped free from the shelter of his cabin. "W...why did you attack the Osgrunfs in the first place?"

Cimerato recognised the Salt Troll as Sintor. And he could see that the Troll's focus was now on the blue crystal that swung from Feldon's neck. "You were supposed to help us when we attacked!" Sintor reached down to grab the Hedra King, but Feldon sidestepped his clawed hand. "Dendralon promised us your help in crushing the Osgrunfs." Sintor swiped again and missed.

"I know nothing of this..." Feldon rolled over to his right to avoid another killing blow. "Please, believe me." Feldon's lies fell on deaf ears as he scrambled back into his cabin.

"Liar! You are in league with Dendralon! You still have your crystal!" Sintor smashed the cabin with his spear and found Feldon quivering under a fallen sail.

"I don't know what you mean," Feldon whimpered.

"Dendralon promised us victory and the city. He took my crystal. But I now know that Dendralon, and you, Feldon, only wanted our destruction."

Feldon continued to whimper and hiss his protests.

"Well, I want my crystal back," roared Sintor, "but in the meantime I'll take yours!" Sintor snatched up the Hedra King and held him close to his leathery face.

As Cimerato and Jal slipped through the doorway, they checked to see that they were the last to escape. It was then that Feldon spotted Jal. The Hedra King looked confused and totally broken. "Jal! Hel—" he screamed.

But he never finished his plea. The Troll wrenched the chain from the Hedra King's neck so roughly that his serpentine head flew off and splashed into the water followed, one second later, by his large, decapitated body. Sintor's heavily scarred hand closed round the blue stone, the largest of the three crystals. With a thunderous roar, he signalled to the remaining Troll to return to the depths and they sunk beneath the surface of the Black Lake.

"Sssss!" Jal hissed with delight as the two sprinted up the stairs, then the Hedra stopped at the top to make sure no one was following.

"No Salt Troll will ever squeeze through that door," said Cimerato. He caught his breath beside the great barred doors of the jail where Dendralon had imprisoned him and then followed the rest up the stairs that led to the city of Gwendral.

CHAPTER THIRTY-ONE

THE HAIRY ONE

High up the citadel, in the Council Chamber, Dendralon was setting up the gateway using the precise specifications. In the alcove that housed the ancient scales of Gwendral, he'd placed the two smaller Osgrunf and Salt Troll crystals into the cup on the left. It gripped them perfectly.

In the half-light of the hall, Dendralon now prepared to place the third and final crystal into the right-hand cup. The Hedra crystal, the largest of the three, would balance the other two perfectly. He'd already written the pre-hedran dragon script in the correct places within the alcove and on the walls, and in the correct colours: black and green.

His patience was wearing thin, though, as he waited with growing anger for Feldon and the last crystal. He paced the hall, and eventually ducked behind the curtain that led to the upper balcony to see if he could find out what was going on. Feldon's ship was no longer at the river. *It should be under the city by now*, he decided.

The battle between the surviving Osgrunfs and a new battalion of Hedra infantry was almost over. The Hedra were simply picking off the hundred or so Osgrunfs with their spears. They had even sent two of their large Raptor pets into the fray to speed up the job. The Hedra often used these ancient beasts, descendants of the Saurs, and he wondered why the Hedra King had not used them sooner. In fact, Dendralon wondered how much he should have relied on Feldon to protect the last crystal. The easiest crystal to procure was rapidly becoming the most elusive.

There was no longer any sign of Mendel, nor of any invisible beast. What if the creature had seized Feldon and the crystal while Dendralon had been preparing the scales inside the Chamber? A feeling of paranoia washed over him as he looked once more at the huge, blood red sun, Tealfirth. In the last two hours it had grown rapidly, blistering black and red like an angry wound. The light from the dying sun gave Denthan a red tinge and turned the Gorton Sea a deep crimson. "A sea of blood," he whispered.

Then he saw them—two large Salt Trolls—wading out from the opening to the underground river. They splashed into the River Levan and then slipped under the surface. "No!" Dendralon cried in dismay as he looked at the huge sun, then back at the river.

Knowing something was not right, he muttered strange words and hissed magic prayers until he began to tremble all over. Yellow pus oozed out from between his scales and several more portions of rotting Manimals skin sloughed off. Lifting his gnarled staff, he thrust it forward and watched expectantly as a bolt of silver light circled downward towards the river. The spiralling light hit the surface with a sizzle, and then disappeared.

* * *

Further down the river, a trail of bubbles signalled the Salt Trolls' progress beneath the waters. Sintor felt the stinging sensation immediately. Gripping his throat in pain, his huge frame struggled out of the water, revealing himself all too clearly to the battling Hedra on the riverbank. The other Troll also emerged from the water and stared anxiously at his master and King. "Sintor, we must get back beneath the surface," he pleaded, "They have seen us!"

But the pain of the spell was all-consuming. Sintor twisted and turned in agony, oblivious to the Hedra nearby. "I'm burning!" he screamed out. "Stop the burning!" Sintor dropped to his knees still clutching the gold chain that held the Hedra crystal.

Seeing the Trolls' vulnerability, the Hedra quickly launched hundreds of black arrows at the giants. The deadly fire soon found any patches of exposed flesh and the river began to flow red. The Troll that had stood beside Sintor now staggered back under the onslaught and sank beneath the crimson waters. But the magic silver light that touched Sintor still gripped him and, in the midst of his distress, he pointed to a black figure, high up on the citadel. "Dendralon…" He whispered the wizard's name just as a feathered Raptor leapt from the riverbank and landed squarely on his massive chest. Digging in with its razor-sharp claws, it snapped and bit until it found the golden chain.

* * *

Dendralon watched anxiously as Sintor fell back into the river. He concentrated on the Raptor. "Get the crystal!" he commanded.

The Raptor snatched the crystal and gulped it into its mouth. Sintor's body was now full of arrows and he rolled, face down, onto the surface. At the same time, the last Osgrunf staggered backwards, falling dead into the water beside him. Both bodies bobbed on the bloody waters of the River Levan before they were carried off on the strengthening current toward the Gorton Sea.

After watching Sintor's demise, Dendralon fixed his eyes on the Raptor. He was thrilled to see that it still held the crystal tightly in its mouth. He nodded with satisfaction and it cocked its head to one side as though in response. As the Raptor bounded up the reed-tufted bank, it cried out to its master in the distance. The victorious Hedra on the riverbank cheered and hissed. Ignoring them, the Raptor slipped past the celebrating Hedra and onto the muddy battlefield, picking its way through the corpses and swarms of flies.

Watching the Raptor's progress, Dendralon thanked his own dark god for bringing him onto the balcony in time to see Sintor escaping with the last crystal. A simple beast to control, Dendralon knew the Raptor would bring his crystal to the city. He shouted down to his elite guards on the watchtowers, "Open the gates!"

The gates were some distance away, but his voice was loud and clear. Athelstone's elite guards began to wind the huge mechanism that would swing open the ivory gates to receive his special courier.

* * *

At the base of the citadel, James and the rest of Whindril's passengers heard Dendralon's command echo across the empty city.

"James, place your hand higher on the wall!" Mendel shouted, his voice full of urgency. James hoped the wizard knew what he was doing because so far this was going nowhere. Giving a little shrug, he reached higher.

Shhhooom! This time the wall shifted back at James's touch and a door appeared on the side of the citadel.

"Quick, get inside now! Get..." At that moment, an odd sound interrupted Mendel's command. Everyone in the group turned back and looked up at the huge blistering sun. Tealfirth itself seemed to be the source of the noise. Shielding their eyes, they shuddered as a low moan filled the air. It was a long, endless rumble that sent vibrations through every particle of Denthan, but mostly through their hearts. The sun was almost ready to explode.

* * *

Inside the city, the Yeltans, Yukplugs and Manimals filtered up into the streets from the prisons below. Wee Joe was one of the last to climb up the stairs to the surface.

Cimerato helped the young boy through the last door but as he left the darkness below, a keening noise stopped him in his tracks.

Wee Joe tugged his mother's tattered skirt. "Mum, it's singing!" The little boy pointed up at Tealfirth. It looked like an angry boil, ready to burst at any moment. Joe was right. The sun was singing, a swan song of sorts, that filled the beautiful city with the sound of death. It was the sound of a dying world.

"There's Whindril!" somebody shouted. Cimerato saw the white dragon tethered in the courtyard below the main citadel. He hushed them all. "Quiet!" There was another sound obvious over the steady drone of the dying sun.

"It sounds like chains," said Helen.

"They're opening the gates!" said Cimerato.

The huge fifty-foot ivory gates were beginning to move.

Michael found Ephie's hand. "Do you think we'll make it home, Ephie?"

She held Michael's hand tightly and smiled up at him. "I'm not sure if we'll ever get home, but I need to tell you something—"

"Come on! Get a move on!" Cimerato cried. "We need to get into the citadel and up to the Council Chamber, now!" Cimerato ushered Michael and Ephie across the courtyard. He took Helen under his good arm and signalled Jal to pick up Wee Joe.

Distracted by Cimerato's shouts, Michael glanced down at the beautiful, white dragon. "With any luck, Mendel and the boys will be in the tower already!" he shouted to the others.

Landris nodded. "I hope Michael's right. What do you want us to do now, Cimerato?"

"Get those gates closed," Cimerato ordered. "We need to stop the Hedra from getting inside the city walls. Take your best men. You go with them, Jal." The Hedra giant nodded his agreement. "The rest of us will climb up to the Council Chamber. We may be able to distract Dendralon while Mendel does his magic."

With a salute, Landris began to lead the Yeltans toward the watchtowers. Before getting too far, however, he turned back and shouted, "Good luck to you all!"

Cimerato gave him a wave before striding over to his father.

Lord Eldane stood motionless in the reddening light. Cimerato could see the pain on his face. "Time is running against us, Father. Could you go back down to the tunnels and see if there's any sign of Elgry and the rest of our people?"

"Of course, Son." Lord Eldane turned to go, but not before giving his son a doleful glance, as though he didn't expect to see him again.

The deafening drone intensified.

* * *

James's group were still in the wall of the citadel, struggling up a steep, spiral staircase. The effort was beginning to take its toll on Bero's back legs.

Craig tried to encourage Bero as much as he could, but the old dog's legs had given out. He lay in an immovable heap, spread over three or four stone steps, blocking the way. "Hold on a minute!" pleaded Craig. He stared up at James. "He's never going to make it."

"Ee thinks ee can help." Eethan scampered back until he stood over the old dog. Cupping Bero's head in his small, blue hands, he blew straight into the dog's nostrils. "Whhooo!"

Bero sniffed and snorted, making a half-hearted attempt to snap at Eethan's mischievous face. The old dog's body shuddered, and he issued a small wheeze before flopping back down onto the steps again. He looked quite dead.

"Eethan! What have you done to him?" snapped Craig. He kneeled down beside his dog, his heart beating hard. "Wake up, boy! Please..."

When Bero didn't move, James felt his chest tighten. Eethan's magic had failed. "Bero," he whispered.

Craig stood up briskly, his eyes full of rage.

Eethan cowered.

"Wait!" said James.

Bero's eyes had flicked open. His opaque pupils began to brighten. His feathered tail twitched and then wagged hard. Then something really weird happened, he began to change right before their eyes.

Craig's mouth fell open. "Bero?" He grabbed Eethan's skinny, blue arm. "He's alive! And he's not so fat now; his coat's all shiny! Is it still him? He looks…" Craig could hardly get the words out, "…so young!"

Bero pawed at the ground and wiggled his back end in a fit of excitement.

"Ees about two years old now, ee thinks!" said Eethan. He sprinted up the spiral staircase, followed by Bero who bounded after him, panting and wagging his tail. Mendel's barrel bounced and swayed under the young Bero's blond chin.

James heard Mendel's voice protesting at this rough treatment. "Eethan, what have you done? Slow down, Bero!"

"Slow down," yelled Craig.

"All this bouncing about is making me feel quite ill," moaned Mendel.

Cathy was puffing and panting now too. As Eethan and Bero passed close by, she flicked the little blue man on the arm. "I know we haven't always seen eye to eye, but…you couldn't knock ten or so years off me, could you?"

Eethan grinned and shrugged. "Ees possible."

"Stop!" Mendel's voice instantly filled their heads. "There is a room ahead which would be perfect for a surprise."

Hearing Mendel's words, Cathy fell back against the cold stone wall. She was breathing heavily. As her chest heaved she whispered to James, "You're going to need your puffer for this." She swung the small, green rucksack from her shoulder and rummaged for the blue inhaler.

"No, Mum. I told you, I can breathe here just as well as any other boy…"

"Shush, James!" Mendel scolded. "Someone is near."

They all held what breath they had left and listened. James could hear a shuffling sound, then a click, click, clicking. It sounded as though someone was gently hitting two hollow sticks together, louder and louder until suddenly the sound stopped. For a moment there was silence and then the whole thing started over again.

"Centides?" whispered James.

The sound instantly stopped.

Eethan put a blue finger to his thin lips and winked at them. He scuttled up the wall of the passage until he hung from the roof. The boys hadn't seen this particular trick before, and James marvelled as the blue man scuttled, upside down, into the chamber beyond.

"I don't think it's a Centide," said Mendel, splashing in his barrel and pushing his fishy, gold lips against the little, plastic window. "In fact, I can't say that I've actually ever heard that sound before." This surprised James, as Mendel would usually have given them the creature's Latin name and feeding habits by now.

James edged round the doorway that led into the room to see if he could tell what was going on.

Eethan, still clinging to the ceiling, had just come face to face with a very strange looking creature. They stared at each other suspiciously, their eyes flashing in the eerie light that filtered in from a small arrow slit in the wall.

For a second, both creatures cocked their strange heads, then it pounced.

"Eeeeeeeee!"

"Firetongue!" yelled James, jumping into the room. Looking above him, he saw the thing chasing Eethan round the ceiling. Bigger than a Centide, it looked like a cross between a Praying Mantis and a hairy Sun Spider. James's head thudded with pain as he shouted out, "Wwwspiderwwwart!" But nothing happened. In fact, the spell only seemed to quicken the creature's pace. Eethan was rushing round a central chandelier, ducking and dodging a pair of snapping mandibles.

"Mendel, it hasn't worked!" shouted James.

Craig jumped into the room beside James, followed by Cathy and Bero. He lashed upwards with his spear and cheered when a long, hairy leg thumped to the ground at his feet.

Bero dived in and retrieved the horrible thing, dropping it in front of Cathy.

"Yuck!" she gagged. "Go away, you stupid dog...and take your gift with you." She growled as she kicked the appendage across the cobbled floor. Her eyes widened, however, when the hairy leg jerked twice on the floor, then began sprouting its own limbs along with a mantis-like head. Within seconds, the newly formed creature was stalking Cathy, two bulbous, red eyes fixed on its prey.

James swiftly hacked the smaller creature's head off, but this too began to sprout its own legs and move towards him.

"Stop chopping bits off!" Mendel's voice cut through the confusion.

"We know. We know!" shouted Craig.

Eethan tried his own magic, sending a flash of blue light into the monster's eyes. It stopped for a moment, then dropped off the ceiling right on top of the boys.

"Arghhh!" James and Craig cried out in horror. They shoved the horrible thing off and leapt away, spitting long hairs from their mouths. Once clear, they turned and pierced its hard carapace with their weapons. Viscous, black blood that smelled of rotten entrails began to seep from its sides. Eethan jumped down onto the creature's back and held on tightly as it tried to whip him off. He looked like some weird cowboy, riding the most disgusting bucking bronco ever invented.

The small, decapitated head and the severed leg were now two fully formed replicas of the original, and they'd trapped Cathy and Bero in the corner of the room. The bigger of the two squirted a jet of yellow liquid from its mouth. The sticky stuff covered Cathy's leg and held her fast to the wall.

"Ah! You disgusting…!" Cathy yelped, fumbling inside the little, green rucksack for anything that might serve as a weapon. Eethan was still holding onto his attacker while Craig and James stabbed and prodded at the two others, trying to keep them back from Cathy and Bero.

For his part Bero barked and occasionally bit a hairy leg before yelping in retreat as he ducked from the various searching claws and mandibles. Cathy was still struggling with the rucksack, but then, with a cry of glee, she produced a small rusty, orange can.

Pssssssssssssssssssssssssssss…

She held the tiny, white valve open, releasing the choking vapour into the room. Her finger was shaking as she pushed down on the nozzle, but she held the can straight, spraying and spraying, relentlessly, until it was completely empty.

As the noxious vapour filled the room, they all began to cough and choke. James's eyes stung and he wondered if he'd been blinded. He cringed, waiting for the mandibles to find him…

Panic-stricken, they all rubbed their eyes furiously, trying to focus before a mandible or a hooked leg pierced or slashed their flesh.

Finally, their blurred eyes began to clear and they all assumed defensive positions. They frantically peered about the room. On the floor, they discovered all three giant insects, right where they'd seen them last—all dead.

"Mum? That was fantastic! How did you do that?" asked James.

Craig stepped over the corpse of the biggest insect and took the empty orange can from Cathy. "It's Bero's flea spray! I knew it would come in handy somehow!"

James looked down at the young retriever. "Sure you did."

"To think that Bero's fleas have just saved our lives…" Craig continued, ignoring James's put down.

"I was just about to turn them into stone," said Mendel. "There was no need to panic." The wizard sounded less than convincing.

"No need to what?" Cathy was still shaking as she knelt down beside the barrel and peered inside.

Mendel flicked his fins forward, pushing himself further back into the barrel, away from Cathy. "All the same, that was quite impressive, Mrs. Peck. Quite impressive," he relented.

Craig was just about to throw the empty tin into a corner when Mendel asked, "Um, what does it say on the can?"

"What do you mean? It says 'Flea Spray' of course," said Craig, adding a "Duh!" as he waved the empty can in front of the barrel's little plastic window.

"Yes, but what is the active ingredient?" Mendel splashed anxiously about in his plastic home. "I hope Garlon made this barrel airtight."

Cathy snatched the can back from Craig. "Give it here, dunderhead! It says…" James saw her trying to focus. "It says, 'triazinon'."

"Organophosphate! That's not too bad. Well, I mean, if it had been pyrethrum, the main ingredient in most flea sprays, I would be stone dead. It's quite deadly to fish, you see." Mendel opened his gills again and felt a little rush of oxygen.

"Quite deadly to big hairy spider things too," remarked Craig. "I reckon you're just jealous that Mrs. Peck killed that thing without your help."

Mendel splashed. "Really, Craig, you have quite an imagination."

"Wees needs to geet going," rasped Eethan.

"Quite," Mendel agreed.

"Why didn't your first spell work, Mendel?" James asked as he cut the yellow goo from his mother's clothes, releasing her from the wall.

"Oh, you probably didn't pronounce it correctly. Or..." Mendel paused. "Dendralon put some kind of magical shield round the creature. I suspect it was from the Acranidus family, just in case you're interested."

"We're not," Cathy muttered as she looked up the dark spiral staircase ahead.

"Here, here," agreed Craig. He winked at Cathy, but she was not in the mood to share the moment with him.

Eethan pushed past Cathy and the boys, clicking his fingers at the young Bero behind him. "Eeee, Meee and Beero will go first!"

"When are you going to learn to talk properly, you useless freak?" Cathy demanded.

James cringed at his mum's offensiveness and wondered if the Lugpus was wearing off.

But Eethan only chuckled. "You knows, you likes mee reeely, James's mum. Eee..."

CHAPTER THIRTY-TWO

THE GATES

While the Yeltan crew and Jal raced towards the watchtowers to try and close the city gates, Cimerato herded the remaining Yeltans out of the sun's heat into the city hall nearest to the citadel. Elgry's wife and young son, both of whom wanted to stay close to the tunnels to wait for his return, stayed behind as well.

Once inside, Cimerato squinted through an arrow slit and saw the Hedra army out on the ridge, attempting to pull themselves together and regroup. He thought that they might miss seeing the gates opening, but then one of them shouted something and the rest swung round. Seeing what was happening, the newly formed mass of Hedra broke rank and began what could only be described as a mad race for the opening gates.

Cimerato grimaced and cupped his mouth, shouting down at the Yeltans as they filed into the towers below. "Be quick, the Hedra have begun their charge!" Cimerato felt his heart sink as he stared hopelessly at the mass of creatures roaring down from the ridge like a great, grey river in spate. Hedra chariots carrying the Hedra elite rolled over the fallen on the Plain of Gwendral—they stopped for no one, not even their own.

* * *

The creaking of the giant cogs and chains that operated the gates were loud and grating. Jal hoped the sound would mask their movement and the guards would be unprepared for the Yeltan attack. It was their best chance of success.

While Landris and Jal made their way to the top of the west watchtower, Garlon ran with the other half of the Yeltans up the spiral stairway of the east tower. When everyone was in position, Jal jumped into the guardroom and knocked several terrified guards to the floor. The Yeltans overpowered the rest of the guards and held them fast by their sheer numbers.

Hidden from the group in a shadowy alcove, a Manimal captain leapt out from his nook and slashed his curved sword down at the little Yeltan leader.

"Landris watch that one!" shouted Jal.

Landris rolled over twice, just managing to avoid the razor sharp Gwendralin cutlass. He rolled again, then jumped up onto one of the cogs as it rotated round its giant spindle. The wheel turned slowly as the huge gate opened, taking Landris further away from his attacker. "Drop your sword!" Landris shouted. "We are here to help you. I am unarmed." He held up his empty hands, but the captain did not back down. "Athelstone is dead!" Landris shouted out in desperation as the cog took him round towards the Manimal captain again.

Jal could see that the Manimal captain was unnerved by his presence. "Do not try your trickery on me, Yeltan! You're in league with the Hedra." the nervous man shouted, pointing to Jal.

Landris had to keep stepping backwards as the giant wheel brought him closer and closer to the captain. Three Yeltans ran ahead of Jal and charged the Manimal captain, but the much bigger opponent easily knocked two of them down.

"Hold!" shouted Jal. He'd seen these Manimal guards throw their swords like spears before, and feared that the captain, in his highly threatened state, might use the same technique on the Landris. The remaining Yeltan and Landris tried to reason with the distraught captain, but again he lunged and they both had to jump to avoid his killing strokes.

Jal edged closer, but his foot hit a discarded sword, making a clatter.

The Manimal captain whipped his head round.

Seeing the Manimal's distraction, Landris jumped and landed on a small platform above the main mechanism where he teetered precariously on its edge.

Jal pounced forward to fell the captain, but the captain had already thrown his cutlass at the foundering Yeltan. It spun twice then stopped with a thud. Landris looked down in shock. The blade had pierced him through.

With a roar, Jal cut down the Manimal captain, though it wasn't quick enough to save Landris. The Yeltan leader toppled forward into the gate mechanism.

Garlon and his crew came running through the door just in time to see Landris fall.

"No!" Garlon cried as he fell to his knees in stunned disbelief.

The rest of the Yeltans rushed to Jal's side, but there was nothing that could be done to save their leader. He was gone. Tears rolled down Garlon's face as the word, "Father..." slipped from his lips.

Jal peered down into the deep shaft. He could see Landris's twisted body hanging, lifeless, like some gruesome puppet, far below in the gloom.

Shoulders slumped in grief, Garlon could only stare into nothingness as the low rumble that shook the whole of Denthan continued. Finally, he roused himself and numbly gave the order. "Make sure the gates are closed. I will not have my father die in vain."

Jal hacked at the thick ropes with his sword until they snapped. Slowly, the cogs and chains began to spin in reverse and the gates began to close. However, without the tower guards manning the levers and chains, the progress was laboured and the gap between the two gates was still about twenty yards in width.

Jal peered down at the Hedra army. Joined by thousands more from the south, they were at least ninety thousand strong. Their chariots to the fore, his kin were only five hundred yards away from the tall, ivory gates.

Then something terrible happened. The gates gave a shriek that was momentarily even louder than the dying sun and then shuddered to a stop.

"What is going on, Jal?" Garlon cried, "the Hedra are almost at the gates!" The Yeltan eyed Jal suspiciously. "Was Cimerato right to mistrust you?"

Jal grew angry. "Do not blame me for the gates, Yeltan! There is a second rope beside you. Cut it now!"

The Yeltans nearest to it began to hack at the main support rope that had slowed the progress of the gates; the screams and jeers of the Hedra growing louder as they worked. Dust from the plain billowed upward as over ninety thousand Hedra charged at full speed. They were trained to strike fear into the hearts of their enemies, smacking their shields loudly with their swords and spears as they ran. The first Hedra chariot was now only feet from the gate.

Jal dashed over and began to cut into the thick rope with his own sword. "Cut harder!" To the small Yeltans, the rope felt like steel but they hacked and hacked, again and again until, finally, the cable snapped. There was a loud crack as the thick rope whipped out across the chamber and disappeared. The whiplash felled two more Yeltans, but Jal could hear the heavy gates below slamming shut. He hurried back to the window and peered down. The first chariot had been cut in two, its lizard steeds crushed, its driver thrown against the ivory gates with such force that his body bounced backwards and smashed into the chariot rider behind.

Seeing the gates closing, the screams of the Hedra army became absolutely deafening, the hellish din drowning out Tealfirth's death drone. Thousands were crushed as they were forced against the gates and walls of Gwendral by the ranks behind. To the rear, they began to fight amongst themselves, struggling to escape the deadly wave of bodies.

Jal lowered his head as those at the very back of the charge, mostly younglings and the old, simply dropped their weapons and sat down in the dusty plain. Resigning themselves to their fate, they stared up at the blisters of yellow and crimson that bubbled on the surface of their angry sun.

Only one creature had managed to get through the gates. Almost ten feet in height, it had hopped over the leading chariot into Gwendral. Jal watched it run towards the main citadel. Recognising what it was, he knew he would have to warn Cimerato, immediately...

CHAPTER THIRTY-THREE

STAIRS AND SECRETS

On the main stairway to the Council Chamber, Michael and Cimerato struggled with their charges. Wee Joe kicked against Michael's black, crumpled jacket, whining about days of travelling and no toys, while Helen complained about missing their hamster, Mufty.

"I want down to wook!" said Wee Joe, pointing at the rows of little gargoyles that lined the stairs.

Jean tried to correct his pronunciation. "L... L... Look, Joe. Say it after me."

Cimerato saw the young boy struggling on Michael's shoulders and wondered how long the man in black would keep his patience.

"L... L... Wook!" Wee Joe repeated it back, stressing the 'W' as much as he could.

Unable to keep Wee Joe up on his shoulders any longer, Michael lowered the boy to the floor. Relieved of his burden, he walked on ahead, gasping in wonder every time he caught a glimpse of the city through one of the many stained glass windows. As a particularly spectacular view of the city unfolded, he grabbed Ephie's arm. "You know, Ephie, I've been to every major cathedral in Europe, but I never dreamt that such buildings as these could exist. Just look at this stairwell we're in now," he said enthusiastically. "These arches are incredible!"

Ephie gave him a little smile.

As they climbed, he continued to stare up at the five-point archways above them and marvel at the tall columns that supported the vaulted roof above the massive spiral staircase.

Cimerato couldn't see how anyone could get so excited over bits of stone.

"I can't believe that all this will disappear," Michael went on. "I can't believe all those strange animals and birds, that took millions of years to evolve, will just vanish. There must be some mistake, Ephie, there must be."

Hearing heavy footsteps behind him, Cimerato turned quickly. "It's only Jal. He will be more than happy to remind you that this great city was actually built by the same Hedra that you can hear screaming outside."

Jal was bounding up the stairs two at a time.

"You managed to close the gates, then?" asked Cimerato.

"Yes," panted Jal, plainly out of breath. "But we have an unwanted visitor."

A loud cracking noise up ahead distracted them.

Oddly, the stone around the gargoyles was beginning to crumble. Cimerato cried out, "run!"

The group began to stumble up the stairs as briskly as they could. In front of them, there was yet another large, five-point arch that led into an antechamber. "This is the last arch before the Council Chamber," yelled Cimerato.

Jal tapped Cimerato on the shoulder. "The visitor... It's one of our Rapt—" But Jal's words were cut short yet again by a movement up in front of them. Cimerato made sure that Wee Joe was behind him before drawing his sword.

Fifty yards ahead, the windows were almost shaking out of their frames. The strange little gargoyle-like figures that lined the stairs shuddered and dust belched out from the walls.

"The floor's collapsing!" screeched Ephie, trying her best to stay upright.

"The citadel's not collapsing. It's the figures that are moving!" shouted Michael. He watched in horror as several small figures jumped free from the cloud of dust. They walked steadily towards the trembling group.

Jean pulled Wee Joe and Helen close to her.

The freakish gargoyles crept down the last few stairs that led from the antechamber. Some resembled stunted men with the heads of animals. Others were more like snakes with the heads of men.

"This is dark Hedra magic," said Cimerato, testing his sword.

Jal hissed and lunged forward, slashing down with his black-bladed sword, but the first of the gargoyles spun round with unexpected speed and knocked the sword out of Jal's hand. The Hedra was forced to jump high to avoid the gargoyle's stone mace, but still managed to duck down and retrieve his sword. Again, he slashed downwards, but his blade stopped dead against the stone surface of the gargoyle and the sword ricocheted from his hand a second time. He gripped his throbbing wrist and hissed in pain.

Cimerato raced forward and slammed his heel into the face of a second snake-headed dwarf. The carved statue only slid back a few inches before regaining its forward momentum. The evil-looking creature had fixed its gaze on the children.

Jal turned to Cimerato. "They can't be destroyed by the sword. We will have to try and run round them!" As he sidestepped a third attacker, who had the head of a horse, it slashed at him with a stone flail. He dodged the heavy stick, but ended up tripping over the little fiend. Jal struggled to get to his feet as yet another gargoyle picked up a large stone and threw it down the stairs, narrowly missing Jean and the children.

The stone thudded against something soft and they all glanced round to see what it was.

"Baacckkk!"

Just a few steps below them the large matted outline of the Mertol emerged out of the darkness. His long hair was caked in dried blood and dirt, and his claws hung low at its side. They clicked against the masonry as the beast moved towards them. *They were done for now,* thought Cimerato. Moving swiftly, he tried to shield Jean and the children from the Mertol below.

"Baacckkk!" the Mertol cried again, and they all braced as a black ball shot from one of the leathery pits in his left cheek. The Drumfintley group all ducked at the same time, but when the ball flew past Ephie's face and slammed into the stone attacker with the horse's head, they all gasped with relief.

The gargoyle stopped, mid-swipe, as a thick sooty coating covered it then fell away to reveal wet, green moss. More balls flew from the Mertol, hitting the stone figures one by one. Everyone kept low to avoid the onslaught, pushing themselves flat against the stone stairs.

Beating its massive chest, the Mertol cried out excitedly, "Baacckkk!"

Not one of the gargoyles escaped his attack. Returned to their lifeless existence, each was now covered in a damp, green moss that shimmered in the strange amber light coming from outside.

Lying flat on the floor, Cimerato lifted his head from the stone and whispered to Jal, "It must have followed us here, all the way from the Eden Tree. I remember seeing it attack the Tree Troll, Ssslathat."

Ephie, her eyes wide with fear said in a whimper, "It's come back to eat us."

Jal, his back against the wall, bent down to pick up his Hedra blade. "This thing is flesh and blood. It can still feel the sting of the sword!"

"Stop!" Michael caught Jal's arm. "If it had wanted to kill us, it would have done so by now. I think the Mertol wants to join us."

As though understanding the vicar's words, the Mertol retracted his razor sharp claws and changed his call. He now issued a series of short grunts as he flicked the slits on his face open and shut in intricate patterns. Strangely, the flicking patterns had a mesmerising effect on Jal and Cimerato, so much so that they backed off.

Ephie steadied herself by holding onto Jean. "What's it doing?" she hissed. She hadn't forgotten Eethan's words about the Mertol wanting to eat her.

"I think Michael's right," said Jean, "I think it wants to come with us."

To everyone's complete horror, Wee Joe pulled away from his mum, picked up a stone and threw it straight at the Mertol. His aim was perfect. It hit the beast square in the face.

They all cringed, waiting for a black ball to come flying at them.

The Mertol only grunted, blinked, shook its matted mane, and continued forward.

"Joe, for goodness sake..." whimpered Jean.

Helen caught her brother's arm before he could find another stone. "Don't do that again, okay!"

Wee Joe gave the beast a disrespectful "Hummff!" and stamped his feet. "I'll teach it twoo wock us up in a cage."

"No you won't!," said Helen. "Mum, tell him."

Michael straightened and dusted himself down. "He's pointing to the archway behind us." Michael looked directly at the Mertol and pointed up at the archway too.

The beast grunted twice then pushed past them all, pulling on Michael's black jacket as he went.

Cimerato covered his nose. The stench from the creature was unbearable. Reluctantly, he followed the Mertol through the last archway that led into the antechamber.

Once inside the room, the Cimerato stared out the massive window to their left. The space was completely filled with the image of Tealfirth. "We don't have much time," he stated. The sun had blackened and grown yet again, its surface covered with what looked like rivers of blood. It gave the sun the appearance of an angry, bloodshot eye. The droning noise had become much louder now, and the citadel shook with an endless rumble.

"Mum, its getting really hot," said Helen, as she walked into the antechamber of the Council Chamber. In front of them a large, wooden door, cracked with time and worn by the touch of a million hands.

"I hope Mendel is behind that door," whispered Cimerato.

"Did you see that?" said Ephie. She'd jumped back from the window.

"See what?" demanded Jal, still watching the Mertol closely in case it made any threatening moves.

"She's right. Look outside." Cimerato pointed to the large window to their left.

"I seed it too!" cried Wee Joe.

"What did you see, Joe?" Jean turned Wee Joe to face her.

"Mum," said Wee Joe, it was a Dwinosaur!"

Cimerato squinted out the window, the heat from the sun burning hot on his face. "There's only one creature that could scale the sheer wall of a citadel like this."

"That's what I've been trying to tell you," muttered Jal. "A Hedra Raptor made it through the gates."

"And it's just beat us to the Council Chamber," sighed Cimerato.

* * *

Outside, on his balcony, Dendralon watched as the Raptor made its way up the smooth wall of the citadel. The beast clawed up the flawless alabaster surface, using its talons and sharp elbow hooks. The Raptor still held the crystal in its mouth but had slipped twice already during its climb and had almost dropped the precious cargo on both occasions.

Dendralon leaned over the parapet and reached down towards its feathered jaws. "Come to me, my beauty. Only a few feet more. Bring it to me!" He urged the Raptor upwards, steadfastly ignoring the screams of the Hedra behind the closed gates. He had to focus on the third crystal.

* * *

In the spiral staircase that wound its way upwards, James wondered if they were getting close to the secret door that led to the Council Chamber. His mum was panting heavily, and had just opened her mouth to complain, when they all came to a halt. A smooth, black granite block marked the end of their climb.

"Now what?" moaned Cathy.

James sensed his mum was about to launch into one of her diatribes. "Mum, you're not feeling panicky in here, are you?" he asked, knowing this would distract her for a bit. It was strange that his mum had never once freaked out during her journey up the enclosed spiral staircase.

Cathy stopped mid-sentence and gripped the narrow walls. "Never even thought about that until now. My claustrophobia hasn't really bothered me since those little yellow imps gave me that stuff…"

Mendel splashed loudly. "We have more pressing issues to deal with, people!"

"I think he's trying to remember the spell that opens the hidden door into the Council Chamber," said Craig.

"And to do that, I need a little quiet," grumbled Mendel.

Eethan formed a puckish smile and placed a finger on his thin lips.

"Don't you shoosh me." Cathy gave Eethan a quick slap.

"EEeeeeeH!"

"Please," insisted Mendel, I need some peace to concentrate!" Mendel's googly eye appeared against the tiny plastic window. It glared at them, crossly.

As they stood waiting, trapped in the stairwell, James noticed that the drone of the dying sun was growing louder and louder. Now that they were standing still, he could hear terrible screaming from outside. It sounded as if the Hedra were in trouble. "Have they taken the city?" he asked. But no one answered.

"I remember," Mendel said suddenly. "James, put your hand on the obelisk."

James felt faint as the knock, knock, knocking sensation began to build. He had to fight to keep from passing out...

CHAPTER THIRTY-FOUR

THE FINAL BATTLE

Out on the balcony, Dendralon heard someone trying the door of the Council Chamber. "Come closer, my pet. Be quick!" He almost had the chain in his hands when the Raptor slid back down again, nearly falling off the citadel altogether. It hissed in frustration and sunk its hooks and claws back into the smooth alabaster, determined to heave itself up again.

Mendel is close by, thought Dendralon. He could sense him. He leaned over the balcony to grab for the crystal but he still couldn't reach it. "Keep climbing! I must go back inside and defend the Council Chamber!" He spun round, cursing his dilemma.

* * *

On the other side of the huge door, the Mertol slammed its huge, fifteen-foot bulk against the Council Chamber door.

"Again! All of us!" cried Jal.

As one, they ran at the door as hard as they could, slamming into the ancient wood. The door shook so roughly that several bolts sprung from the hinges and clattered onto the stone floor of the anteroom.

"That includes you two." Jal pointed to Michael and Ephie, who were busy chatting. "It's hardly the time for sweet talk."

Michael flushed crimson, then joined Jal, Cimerato and the Mertol in their effort to break down the massive door.

* * *

Nervously, Dendralon headed toward the throne where the two blue crystals weighed down one side of a pair of giant, ivory scales. Sitting snugly in their predestined slots, their cerulean glow threw long shadows across the seats of the Council Chamber. In front of the throne, a patch of floor spread out in a semicircle from the edge of its ivory base towards the Council members' seats and the door behind.

This strange stone semicircle of reptilian scales was, in fact, a Hedra vision pool. It shimmered now, alternating between dull, grey stone and the vivid, blistering surface of Tealfirth. Angry blood-coloured reds and bile-like yellows oozed between the fissures that lined the sun's blackened surface. Huge flares exploded outward then disappeared back beneath Tealfirth's tortured crust.

As Dendralon checked the crystals, a series of ear splitting screams and hisses echoed out from the vision pool. The sounds cut through the air like the screeches of a million demons.

"The end is only moments away," declared Dendralon. He looked across to the main door of the Chamber. It buckled violently. He could use his magic on it, but didn't want to waste a drop of energy, so close to creating the gateway. He had a feeling he was going to need all his power to operate the magic scales.

"I need that crystal!" He glanced at the door one more time before racing back through the curtain that led to the balcony. Whisking back the black material, he came face to face with the Raptor. It stood on the tiled floor of the balcony tilting its head to the side and snorting in his face.

"It's me. Your master…" Dendralon's words didn't seem to register with the panting beast. It snapped at him, still holding the crystal in its jaws. The dark wizard tried to retrieve the crystal, but it hissed in his face and barged past him, into the Chamber.

"Come back here!" he demanded, before turning to follow.

* * *

"Wwwhedralanwwwa!" James placed his hand on the cold obelisk again and said the word one more time, with all the command he could muster. "Wwwhedralanwwwa!"

With a whoosh, the smooth, black granite slid upwards and the startled group fell into the Council Chamber. A black-cloaked figure turned in surprise.

The stench of King Athelstone's decomposing skin instantly caught James's throat. He barely recognised Dendralon. He tried to imagine the thing standing before them, wearing a pair of sunglasses, back in the village shop, but he just couldn't see any resemblance between this zombie and the stranger he'd met a few days before.

Hackles raised, Bero growled at the gruesome creature. Dendralon clawed a piece of Athelstone's rotting flesh from his scaled face and threw it down at Bero's feet. "There's your great King, Mendel. It's too late for him. And now it's too late for you." Dendralon raised his gnarled staff to cast a spell.

At the same moment something ran out of the shadows behind Dendralon. It was a terrifying beast—half dinosaur, half bird. A few feet from the dark wizard, it hunkered down and screeched to reveal a thick golden chain hanging from its jaws. Distracted, Dendralon turned about to face it. It hissed at him and cried out like a tortured seal. It seemed to be talking to the wizard.

"The last crystal is not yet in his grasp." Mendel's voice sounded louder and more forceful than James had ever heard it before. He felt the knocking sensation build in his head and knew he would have to stand and fight. Mendel needed him to be strong. But before he could push Mendel's spell from his lips, a huge, wooden door exploded inward, showering the crouching Raptor with a cloud of shards and splinters. It yelped in pain.

Through the dust, James saw that a long shard of wood had pierced the Raptor's thigh. Its jagged point dripped black blood onto the cobbled floor.

In less than a heartbeat, Dendralon jerked the shard from the Raptor's thigh and spun round towards the main door. He ducked behind the snarling beast and shouted, "Guard the door!"

In the confusion, Mendel failed to complete his spell. He pushed a googly eye against the plastic window of his barrel and screamed out at James, "Follow the Raptor!"

"The what?" Craig shouted.

"That thing!" said James pointing to the bobbing creature.

It stopped abruptly, its feathers flicking up on end. It had just seen something that it didn't like.

James heard his mum scream out. She was pointing at the hairy ape-like beast that was stepping through the remnants of the shattered door.

"The Mertol!" yelled Cathy.

James stared at the beast standing in front of Cimerato and Jal. Its matted orange hair hanging down from its arms like a badly fitting angora jumper. His eyes were drawn to an array of slits on its leathery face that puffed open and close. It was outside *this* beast's cave that his father's clothes had been found. James's stomach heaved.

"Baacckkk!"

Jumping at least ten rows of seats, the Mertol slammed against the Raptor, slashing down with his claws. The Raptor screamed under the onslaught, but managed to push the heavy Mertol off with a series of violent kicks that cut into the bigger creature's ape-like belly. Falling back, the Mertol cried out and clutched his stomach. Blood seeped through his filthy, orange fingers as he swayed back to avoid the Raptor's snapping jaws. With another leap, the Mertol twisted round in mid-air and kicked off the wall of the Chamber to land on the Raptor's back. Plunging his fangs deep into the Raptor's neck, the Mertol shook his ugly head this way and that.

The Raptor gave a strangled hiss and the heavy golden chain that held the crystal slipped from its mouth to land with a clatter on the cobbled floor.

Seeing the crystal fall, Dendralon raced toward the battling duo. As he ran, the Manimal King's long, black hair slipped from the Hedra wizard's scalp. Sloughed and tattered, it caught on his collar and hung limply like a tattered shawl.

Seeing that Dendralon was distracted, James and Craig slipped under the wooden seats and began to crawl after him, weapons drawn.

As they neared the battling monsters, it was Craig that spied the blue crystal lying on the ground first. As the two beasts continued to knock each other about, he hunkered forward toward the glowing gem, the old timber seats disintegrating in clouds of flying splinters around him.

James followed, a few feet behind his friend, drawing back when one of the Raptor's claws nearly caught his sword arm.

Just as Craig reached out to grab the crystal, the Mertol stepped backward to catch his balance. Craig rolled out of the way of the giant foot, missing his chance.

A second later, James actually had the cool, smooth crystal in his hands but had to drop it when the Raptor pounced, once again just missing him by inches.

"Get the third crystal, James!" Mendel kept shouting at him, not helping in the least.

"What do you think I'm trying to do?" James yelled back, annoyed by Mendel's useless commands. Groping for the crystal, he sensed a dark presence moving toward him. He glanced back to see Dendralon, a hideous ghoul, half Hedra, half corpse, crawling his way. James shuddered. *Had the dark wizard heard Mendel's voice too?*

Bero dashed between the slatted seats, distracting Dendralon, who hissed at the dog, then quickly lunged forward.

James could only watch in horror as Dendralon snatched up the crystal. He had to stop him! But the Mertol and the Raptor were still fighting. He and all the others were trapped where they were as the two beasts snarled and slashed at each other.

The end came suddenly. With a violent twist, the bigger Mertol snapped the Raptor's feathered neck. Giving one last strangled screech, the bird-like corpse fell dead to the floor.

Before Cimerato and Jal could charge forward, the Hedra wizard appeared behind the throne and laughed in triumph. Hearing the chilling sound, everyone stopped where they were.

James steadied himself against a cold stone pillar. The Mertol clutched at his bleeding stomach. Craig had found Bero's collar. Jal hovered back behind Cimerato, who looked ready to attack.

Thinking the worst was over, the rest of the Drumfintley group stepped carefully through the shattered doorway. Michael held Ephie close and stared blankly at the rows of stars and roses that adorned the ceiling. "It looks like a harvest festival carved in stone," he said in wonder.

Unseen by Dendralon, his mum had edged round to join the Drumfintley group. She caught Michael's arm in a vice-like grip. "Michael, shut up!"

He jerked back with a yelp, "Ah!"

Glancing between the monster that was Dendralon and Cathy Peck, Michael gasped in terror, then clamped his mouth shut tight.

Unsure what to do, James began to walk forward, through the debris. As he moved, he raised his magic sword and looked Dendralon straight in the eye.

Ignoring the little 'Manimal,' the wizard peeled the last remnants of Athelstone's skin from his face. It resisted, at first, then gave way with a loud slurping sound. It dropped to the floor with a thunk, revealing the wizard's true features.

"Deceiver!" Cimerato cried, unable to hold back any longer. He rushed across the Chamber towards the Hedra wizard, but stopped in his tracks when he saw that he was holding the third crystal up to the light.

"Marvellous, isn't it?" Dendralon sneered. "Here we are at the end of our world and I have the only thing that can get us out of here in time. So stop where you are!" He stared at Cimerato and then James. "Do not take another step!" Wielding the crystal like a weapon, he began to edge back toward the ivory scales behind the throne.

James could now see the recess where the Hedra crystal would fit perfectly and finally understood what the wizard meant to do with it. At the same moment, James spotted Eethan. The little, blue man had climbed along the roof timbers and now hung above the Hedra wizard's head.

Dendralon must have sensed he was up there, as he swung his staff and ruthlessly knocked Eethan down. There was a loud crack as the stick smashed against Eethan's skull.

As the little blue man's limp body fell to the ground, Dendralon hissed angrily at all of them. "Thanks to you, my Hedra kin will never make it through the gates now." He turned and pointed to the floor in front of the throne. "Look." The image of the dying sun appeared, pulsing like an over-inflated balloon about to pop. "We only have a few moments," he hissed. "I suggest you let me continue with my spell if you want to live."

Dismissing them, he turned to go back behind the throne. With a roar, the Mertol lunged forward, but with a simple flick of his fingers, Dendralon sent the beast flying backwards into what remained of the Chamber door.

Having figured out what Dendralon was up to, James knew what he had to do. With a burst of power, he hurled his magical red sword at Dendralon. As it flew, it seemed to gather speed before sinking deep into the wizard's left arm.

Dendralon spun round and everyone ducked down. "Wooo-denstickalbreath!" Dendralon's angry voice echoed across the Chamber. "There was no need to waste my powers. The boy has just threatened us all."

There was an uneasy silence, then a strange shuffling noise began. They watched in terror as all the wooden shards and splinters strewn over the floor of the Chamber came alive. Twitching at first, they began to move together, forming three separate piles. Quick as a wink, the shards rose up from the floor and formed into three separate monsters.

Jerking awkwardly forward, the twisted wooden skeletons stumbled, at first, towards the onlookers at the door. Two of them then split off and went after Cimerato and Jal. The third cornered James and Cathy, who had rushed over to protect her son. Its splintered fingers began hacking at their faces. James yanked his mum back behind him, unable to do anything else. His sword was still lodged in Dendralon's arm.

Before Jal could lift his sword, one of the deformed puppets lunged forward and thrust behind the Hedra's black and green chestplate. Three long, serrated fingers sunk in deep before Jal managed to push the thing back. He fell hard to the floor.

Cimerato lunged to his left and cut through the wooden shoulder of Jal's attacker and the creature tumbled lifeless at Jal's feet.

With lightning speed, the other wooden man slashed out at Cimerato's neck. He jumped back, then staggered, off balance and exposed. The wooden man hacked down with his knife-like fingers, but Cimerato regained his stance and brought his cutlass down hard, cleaving its wooden head in two.

The third shard man was still focused on James and Cathy. "Get down, Mum!" James cried, bracing himself for the blow. The wooden monster was bringing his jagged fist down to smash in James's head, but his hand froze in mid-air. Craig's magic spear was now poking through the wooden monster's body, shooting out bright green sparks that crackled up through its neck. Mouthing silent curses, it dropped to the floor and promptly fell apart.

With a frustrated frown, Dendralon waved both his hands and chanted something in his Hedra tongue. A strange mist rose up from the floor of the Chamber shifting its shape to form a shimmering curtain.

"It's a force field!" shouted Mendel.

James's temples began to throb as Mendel attempted to destroy the shield forming round the wizard. "Wwwwaywwwwormwfieldw!" As the strange word bubbled from James's lips, a purple flash shot out from Bero and hit the invisible wall like a firebomb.

Bang!

The wall shimmered and split for a second but soon reformed, undamaged.

Dendralon narrowed his eyes and fixed his malevolent gaze on Bero.

James hissed over to Craig, "He thinks that Bero is Mendel."

"He what?" Craig's eyes widened. Both boys ducked down and tried to coax Bero away from the dark wizard, who looked hideous in his rage.

"Your powers are still no match for mine, Mendel," he boomed. "Do you think, for one moment, that I intend to let you live? We, the Hedra, built these walls, dug the wells, carved the foundations of this city from the bedrock beneath us. I will never relinquish this city to your kind. I have only to place this last crystal into the magic scales of Gwendral and we will escape this holocaust. After that, you will all die. As will all those who do not bow to me as their god."

The bitter words made James shudder, but what he saw next was worse. Near to the shattered door, Ephie and Cimerato crouched down beside Jal, trying to make him sit up. But it was no use. The Hedra's head slipped back onto the floor and a gasp spilled from his lips.

Enraged, Cimerato gave a shout and ran at the force field, his sword drawn, but he only slammed into the invisible curtain, falling backwards over the remaining chairs.

"Oh, please. No!" It was Jean. She pointed a quivering finger at something she'd just noticed on Dendralon's side of the force field.

James followed her gaze and to his utter horror saw that Wee Joe standing beside Dendralon. He was alone with the Hedra wizard, trapped on the other side of the shimmering barrier.

"Joe!" Jean cried. "Come over to Mum!" She looked close to collapse.

Dendralon looked down at the little three-year-old boy. "Ha!" he shouted triumphantly. "Thanks for the snack!" With a ruthless grin, he turned again to the ivory scales.

Wee Joe, ignored for the moment, caught at the pretty golden chain that hung over the edge of the throne and pulled hard. The chain slid off the throne and fell, along with the crystal, onto the hard marble floor.

The large blue crystal shattered and the pieces fell into the blistering picture of the sun inside the vision pool.

"Oopsie!" Wee Joe bleated.

James felt his mouth drop open.

Helplessly, Dendralon turned and screamed, "NO!" Unable to reach the crystal or do his magic in time, he reached for Wee Joe's neck, his sharp claws extended.

"Leave him alone!" Cathy demanded, pounding on the force field. Dendralon ignored her, swooping in on the boy. But before he could reach Wee Joe, a bright blue flash of light shone out from nearby, blinding him.

Mendel knew that this would be his last chance. The spell flew from James's lips, "Wwwwaywwwwormwfieldw!"

A solid bolt of green light shot out from the barrel and punched into the force field like a battering ram. Dendralon's protective shield shimmered, wavered and then fell. They all rushed at Dendralon, hoping to save Wee Joe.

Partially blinded by the blue flash, Dendralon still managed to catch hold of Wee Joe's arm. He picked up the three-year-old and lifted him high above his head with his good arm. "We will all die now, thanks to this pathetic, little runt!" Dendralon winced as James's sword seemed to bury itself deeper into his arm, but he did not falter as he held Wee Joe over the blazing vision pool.

The sun, Tealfirth, sang a single, high-pitched note as Dendralon screamed out, "Mendel!" Catching sight of Bero, he dropped Wee Joe at the edge of the vision pool and thrust out his fist at the dog. Light shot from his reptilian fingers and blasted into Bero. The collar round his neck snapped and the barrel fell to the ground as Bero was thrown backwards, yelping in pain.

Seeing their chance, James and Cathy ran forward and snatched Wee Joe from the edge of the vision pool, pulling him over to Jean.

Knowing the little one was safe, Cimerato pounced on Dendralon, his sword flying. But the wizard struck out with his staff, sending the Manimal sprawling beside the vision pool. Bero was back on his feet. He ran forward as best as he could, growling and barking at the wizard. James could see that he was old again, his fur dull, his frail back legs dragging behind him.

Unseen, Eethan stirred behind Dendralon. Cautiously, he crept over to the empty cup meant for the third crystal and climbed in. The fulcrum of the ivory scales pitched downward.

The movement caught Dendralon's eye and he whipped round. As he did, Bero jumped and latched onto the wizard's wounded arm, clamping his teeth down hard. The force of the blow knocked Dendralon towards the vision pool. Stumbling backward, he lost his balance and toppled over Cimerato. Dendralon teetered on the edge of the vision pool, then, as if in slow motion, he fell backwards, his black cloak already ablaze from the intense heat.

Bero managed to grip the side of the vision pool with his front paws but his back legs dangled down into the furnace below. He whined out at Craig and panted as the heat threatened to consume him.

"Bero!" screamed Craig. "Hang on, boy! Please...!"

As Craig shot forward, a scaled claw came from out of no-where and grabbed hold of Bero's tail.

With a grip like a vice, Dendralon jerked the old dog backwards.

"Bero!" Craig wailed.

Bero howled, only once, before Dendralon's tortured voice echoed up from the inferno. "Die, Mendel..."

Craig and James stared at the spot where Bero had been, then watched in stunned disbelief as the vision pool turned as black as night.

Behind them, sitting in the little hollow meant for the third crystal, Eethan was actually glowing a bright iridescent blue. Strangely, his weight matched the two crystals on the ivory scales exactly. For an instant, his whole body shone as bright as any sun. Then, there was a thundering noise and everyone collapsed, their knees buckling as the floor fell away from them.

As Tealfirth exploded in on itself, the room began to spin round and round, ever faster.

James's strong link with Mendel allowed him to see everything that was happening. It was both terrible and awesome...

Outside the city walls, the Hedra looked up at the sun one last time before instant obliteration. All conscious life on the planet had been aware of its imminent demise for a few seconds at most, then, with no time for regret or pain, everything simply stopped. In a heartbeat, Denthan was covered in an all-consuming fire, seas steamed and boiled, mountains were swept clear of trees and earth. The whole planet shuddered and cracked to its very core. For a moment, its mantle expanded like a balloon, then it exploded into a billion pieces. Denthan, along with its five sister planets, simply turned to dust and disappeared sucked into the black hole that had once been Tealfirth.

James shuddered as he watched a trillion zillion tons of stardust pour through the abyss. Tears rolled down his face as an infinity of souls appeared before him, then flew away to a billion preset destinations only they would know.

He hadn't wanted to, but he'd seen and felt everything.

CHAPTER THIRTY-FIVE

HOME

James slowly opened his eyes, blue flashes dancing across his field of vision. Everything still blurred, the most noticeable thing was the complete and utter silence. It was simply amazing after the raging chaos of the moments before and James didn't want it to stop. He didn't feel scared or frightened or upset, he felt comforted, peaceful, calm. The sensation held him, almost cradled him, and he wondered if this was what being dead was like. He felt a tear roll down his cheek.

A small voice interrupted the stillness, "Are we in heaven, Mum?" asked Helen. She yawned and rubbed her eyes.

Jean sat up and touched Helen's arm. "I don't think so, darling."

"We're not dead," said James, quickly wiping his face, "but I'm not sure why," he added. He looked round for the small plastic barrel.

Hearing voices, Michael sat up and slid over toward Ephie and Jean. "God preserve us and keep us." Michael mumbled another small prayer as he gazed round the half-demolished Council Chamber. He looked like a startled hare and James felt himself smile.

Cimerato was still lying on his back close to the vision pool, just a few yards away from Wee Joe.

Craig hadn't moved from the spot where he'd seen Bero disappear. His head was bowed and his body shook with long, deep sobs. "Why did he do that? Why?" Tears covered Craig's freckled face.

The realization of what had just happened came back to James with a jolt. "I'm sorry, Craig." He looked into his friend's bleary eyes and tried to hold back his own emotions. "Bero saved us all. He was very brave." But there was no consoling him. James felt awkward, not really sure whether to hug his best friend or leave him be.

Craig saved him the bother. Edging back from the vision pool, he moved as far as he could away from James and the rest of the group.

Michael had crawled over to where the little plastic barrel sat, about five feet from the vision pool. "Mendel, are you in there?" he asked. "Where are we?"

Close by, Cimerato grimaced in pain as he stretched his arm. He nodded toward James. "You can hear Mendel when others cannot."

"Sometimes." James stepped over to the barrel and picked it up. He peered inside the tiny window. "Mendel, everyone wants to know where we are."

"We are where we should be, of course," replied Mendel, matter-of-factly, as if he'd planned every single moment of their adventure, as if he'd known the outcome all along. "The whole city has been transported, thanks to Eethan and Dendralon, back to Earth, back to Drumfintley, to be specific."

"We're back home?" said James, the words trailing slowly from his lips.

"Drumfintley?" echoed Cathy.

Jean Harrison bristled. "What! We can't possibly bring these, these..." Jean looked away from Cimerato. "Well, this whole thing..." She waved her hand round her head, "back to Drumfintley. I mean..."

Cathy's eyes blazed. "You mean, what would the neighbours think? That's what you mean, isn't that right?"

James flushed with embarrassment. Nothing in the last few days had changed his mum's demeanour. Nothing ever would. She couldn't help it. She was fine for a few hours, even a whole day sometimes, but eventually the anger would erupt. It was always there, smouldering. Nobody ever dared to tell her that her behaviour was unacceptable. Not Mendel, certainly not his dad.

With a resigned sigh, James decided that his mum's anger was a necessary part of her. The power inside her that made her unique and incredibly strong. People found her hard work, mostly because they envied her, he thought. Cathy Peck said all the things they felt, but never dared to say.

As Jean gathered her kids about her, still smarting from Cathy's jibe, James saw something flash in his mum's eyes. He could tell she was thinking about his dad. Her eyes glazed as she looked at him. "Where is he when we need him, eh? Where, James?"

James's mouth fell open, but nothing came out.

Father Michael issued a loud, relieved sigh. "We're finally home! Thank God." He turned to Cathy and beamed. She scowled back at the vicar, and James knew that the moment between his mum and himself had passed.

Michael's smile faded as he looked over at James. "Can I ask him something?"

"You mean Mendel?" said James.

Michael nodded. "Yes, yes, if that's alright."

Sensing a big question coming up, James was relieved when Mendel sent his voice inside Michael's head. "Yes, Father."

Michael flinched. "Um, yes. Um, where did all those creatures go? I mean after the end of Denthan—I'm assuming it's gone."

Mendel audibly sighed and pushed a golden eye against his little window. "They went wherever they believed they would go."

"What do you mean?" asked Michael, lifting the barrel up to his face.

"If you believe something strongly enough," Mendel continued, "it often becomes your own, personal truth."

"The truth! What is the truth?" whispered Michael, his voice wavering.

"The truth is what you believe it is," Mendel replied calmly. "But remember, just because I believe something doesn't make it your truth, or anyone else's for that matter. It's just my truth. For example, you might see true beauty where no one else sees it. That is your truth."

"Ah...I see," said Michael, glancing over at Ephie.

James thought it all sounded very complicated.

Michael stood up and took Ephie's hand. "Well, at least we're all safe now."

"We're not all safe..." Craig interjected, looking forlorn.

As though Craig's words had conjured him up, the Mertol's matted, red back emerged from the debris. As he turned to face them, his cold, black eyes blinked open and shut and his pitted face rippled in strange patterns. The wounded beast faltered, then dropped down onto one knee, clutching his stomach.

"Stay back, and don't threaten it!" Cimerato's hand went to his sword hilt.

James watched in trepidation as the beast issued a muffled "Baacckkk!" before slumping against the wall nearest to the shattered door. The Mertol closed its eyes and Cimerato sheathed his sword.

"I want to go howme!" Wee Joe's voice echoed round the Chamber, cutting through the tension.

"And so you shall, Joe. So you shall," said Mendel.

Judging by the look on everyone's faces, James could tell that Mendel could be heard by all of them. They all began asking questions at once.

"Shhhh!" the wizard scolded. "What I'm about to say is very important." He splashed in his barrel. "First I want you to gather round and look into the vision pool. You see, it's not just a picture, it's a portal."

As the others shuffled toward the pool, Mendel homed in on James's mind alone. "Stay here a moment. I need to tell you something, just you."

James stopped where he was. "Go on," he whispered.

"The pool is how Dendralon managed to steal your father's things."

"You mean the compass and his clothes, but why?" James spoke quietly, though a bit of hope began to burgeon inside him.

"Dendralon knew where Sleven met his death and put two and two together. He probably watched through the vision pool as you confronted Sleven on your roof. As I suspected, he came back to your house and retrieved some of your father's things in order to lead us on a merry dance. He must have read your thoughts and sensed your pain when you held the crystal up to the light in your bedroom."

"You mean the time you shouted at me," James whispered.

"Yes," admitted Mendel, "but I suspect that Craig probably toyed with the crystal even before that. Each time any of you held the crystal up to the light Dendralon would have been able to read your thoughts."

"Really?" said James, a bit louder than he meant to. He actually saw the goldfish give a little nod behind the plastic window of the barrel. "So if that was all a trick, then where's my dad? He isn't here, is he? Don't tell me he's dead!"

There was an uncomfortable silence in James's head as Mendel hesitated. James could see that the others were growing restless at the edge of the vision pool.

"He's not dead, James," Mendel finally replied. James tensed. "How can you be sure?"

"You must join the others now," Mendel directed, refusing to answer.

When James got there, the vision pool was mostly dark, though there were a few points of light flashing across its surface. When he peered closer, he realised that he was seeing the ground below them.

"There's something down there," said Cimerato.

Ephie shuffled in beside the Manimal captain and said, "Torches! I think they're torches!"

"Yes, and look!" James cried, pointing down at the dim landscape below. "It's the Jesus Rocks!"

Cimerato's cat-like pupils dilated suspiciously. "I have never seen torches like those!"

James felt Craig move in beside him. "Look, Craig! Do you see that person down there?"

"I do!" said Michael. "It's...it's..." He peered down at the scene. "It's Archie!"

"Archie MacNulty," whispered Craig.

James was amazed when the small figure below looked straight up at them, though he didn't seem to see them.

"Why is he standing between those two policemen?" James's eye-brows lifted.

Michael gasped and tried to push forward. "He's handcuffed to them!"

"Don't go too close to the edge," said Mendel. "If you fall without my help..."

Everyone took one step back from the edge of the vision pool.

"Don't forget. We've been missing from the village for the best part of a week," Ephie reminded everybody. "They probably think we've all been murdered."

Cathy spoke up. "Let me get this straight. You mean to say that Gwendral, which must cover at least two square miles, is floating above the Jesus Rocks and nobody can see us?" Cathy's voice sounded derisive.

"Three and a half square miles would be more accurate," corrected Mendel. "Don't forget that we have one and a half thousand Yeltans and, I hope and pray, another fifteen thousand Manimals in the city with us, as well."

"Not to mention a forty-foot white dragon," added James.

Craig had been very quiet through all this. James saw Jean move over beside him. "I'm sorry Son, but Bero probably saved us all from that...that thing."

James felt his own tears well up as Craig pushed his wet face into his mum's shabby mohair cardigan and began to sob.

Craig loved Bero like any other part of the family, and now he was never going to see him again, thought James.

With his friend crying beside him, and seeing Bruce Moor again— the last place his dad had been seen alive—James, too, started to weep. He couldn't stop himself. "I'm sorry we took old Bero with us, Craig!" His shoulders shook and his chest heaved. "It's all my fault. I'm sorry!"

Without answering, Craig pulled away from his mum and moved over to the ivory throne.

James watched him for a moment but was distracted by a scuffling sound behind him. He thought—hoped—it might be his own mum come to comfort him.

But when he turned round, he saw a Yeltan standing in the doorway of the Chamber. "Garlon!" James quickly wiped his face on his sleeve and cleared his throat. "Is everybody alright?"

"Most of us are fine, but..." Tears spilled from the young Yeltan's eyes.

"Where's Landris?" James asked, but as he did, he saw the answer in Garlon's deep blue eyes. "Oh no, Garlon. How...?"

"My father died a hero's death." Garlon bowed his head and moved over to the fan of scales on the floor that had become a vision pool.

James looked down at Garlon and whispered, "Bero did too. He saved us all."

Many more footsteps filled the antechamber. Lord Eldane picked his way through the broken seats. "Son!" he cried, clapping Cimerato on the back. The old Manimal was flushed and out of breath, but obviously happy to see his son. "Elgry and the soldiers from the lake met our people walking back to the city. They didn't feel safe in the tunnels with all that shaking and rumbling going on."

"How many made it?" breathed Cimerato. "More than ten thousand."

"What about Mother?" he asked, reluctantly, as though he were afraid of the answer.

"They are safe," his father reassured him.

Mendel cleared his throat, his yellow fins beating against the little window in the barrel. "James, only you can hear me. Listen carefully. I am going to return us all back to Drumfintley. All, that is, except the people and creatures of Denthan. There is another world that will suit them better than yours. Eethan will know what to do. More importantly, I think it would be best for everyone concerned if I relieved them of their memories."

James couldn't believe it. "What?"

"Of Denthan, of this adventure," Mendel continued.

"No!" he blurted. James felt everyone's eyes upon him after his sudden exclamation.

"Shhh!" Mendel's voice was like a whisper floating round inside James's head. "It's for the best. Not you and Craig, of course not. You've both proved yourselves and, well, there may be a chance of returning to my own form on your world, just a small chance. I may yet need your help. The rest of the group, however, will be better off if they return without these memories."

"I need to tell Craig," said James.

"Of course. But be quick about it," said Mendel.

Craig was slumped against Athelstone's throne, wiping his nose with his sleeve.

"Craig, I need to talk to you."

Craig looked up.

"Mendel is going to erase everyone's memory, apart from ours," said James.

"What do you mean? Erase everyone's memory?"

"Basically, they'll forget everything that happened in Denthan, the whole lot. But, you and me, we won't forget a thing," explained James.

"What's the point of that? What about Bero? How do I explain that to my mum?" James looked down at the brandy barrel in his hands. "Mendel?"

"It's for the best, Craig," said Mendel.

James stepped back as Craig let go of Athelstone's throne and pulled himself to his feet. "Mendel, you can't just wipe their memories of Denthan. I don't want them to forget the whole thing. I don't want them to forget what Bero did."

James noticed that Caig's sharply whispered words had reached Father Michael. The Reverend hurried over to the boys.

"Please, Mendel," Michael pleaded, kneeling down in front of the barrel. "I don't want to forget. I'm in love, and so is Ephie, and we might never get a chance like this again. Besides, there are things I believe in now that I never could have before."

Mendel made a little splash. "Sorry, Michael, but..."

"Remember," pressed Michael, "you told me about truth? This, and everything that has happened to me in the last five days, has become my own personal truth."

"Fine, fine," sighed Mendel. "Just get the rest of the villagers ready. You'll all have to jump into the pool when I say so, understood?"

Mendel doesn't sound happy about leaving Father Michael with his memory intact, thought James.

"I mean it, Mendel," said Michael. "I won't have you mess this up!"

Father Michael looked almost angry as he motioned to the others. "Gather round, now. Mendel wants us to stand right here." James stuffed the brown plastic barrel into his battered, green rucksack and closed his eyes. "When Mendel says jump, we all have to jump into the vision pool," he said.

Beside him, Helen held her mother's arm and pulled Wee Joe in close. "But it's a long way down. We'll get hurt," she sniffed.

"You can either trust Mendel or stay here in Gwendral," said James, "It's your choice."

With a mixture of shrugs and scared expressions, they all nodded back at him. They seemed to have resigned themselves to the absurdity of the situation.

Mendel splashed about inside the rucksack. "Please hurry! We have to be quick."

Hearing the urgency in Mendel's voice, James glanced over at the balanced ivory scales where Eethan had transformed himself. He noticed the blue glow falter for a second. "Mendel, just tell us when to jump." James looked round the room. "Goodbye, Cimerato!" he called. "Bye, Garlon." He smiled at Lord Eldane, then his eyes landed on the wounded Mertol. He offered the creature a small nod. "Goodbye, and thanks for taking care of that dinosaur."

"Baacckkk…" the Mertol replied weakly, its cheek holes opening and closing in unison.

"Ssss," a voice hissed from behind him, "Goodbye, boys!"

Every one of the Drumfintley group turned round to look. Jal, the giant Hedra warrior, was trying to sit up. James moved to go to him, but Cathy caught hold of his shirt and heaved him back into position. "We've no time, James."

James blinked anxiously. He saw something that resembled a smile forming on Jal's lips.

"I've had worse, boy," said the Hedra.

James grinned. "Get yourself well, Jal." He felt even better seeing Cimerato move over to Jal and help steady him. He was, after all, the last Hedra left in the universe.

Feeling Mendel's magic, James called out, "Get ready!" The Drumfintley crowd edged closer to the vision pool and looked down. Instinctively, they joined hands.

Predictably, Cathy fidgeted. "For goodness sake, let's get this over with!"

Mendel's voice was loud in everyone's head. "Everyone, jump!"

What They'd all experienced and seen in the last few days was completely beyond imagination, so being told to leap into a pool within a huge alien city, hovering about one hundred feet above Bruce Moor, actually sounded pretty normal.

Without hesitation, they all jumped into the abyss.

CHAPTER THIRTY-SIX

WEE JOE'S SECRET

James shivered in the cold morning mist that tumbled across Bruce moor. But the cold wasn't the worst of it. In front of them, a search party consisting of a bunch of sniffer-dogs, policemen and very wet looking Archie MacNulty were stretched out in a straight line across the moor.

While the others were coming round, James reached into his rucksack and felt for his blue inhaler. His back against the cold stone, he inhaled the fine, white mist and held it in his lungs for as long as he could.

"Got something!" one of the searchers called out, startling James. He coughed out the rest of the mist, and then tentatively peered round the Jesus Rock. Not far from where he crouched, Constable Watt held up a plastic bag that contained something resembling a hardened lump of dog poo. "We might be able to match this with the ones we found in the Harrison's back garden."

"Wather you than me, Sonny," said Archie MacNulty, pulling on his handcuffs, which were attached to Sergeant Carr. The action made the sergeant glare at MacNulty, the hatred between the two men could never have been more obvious.

"Archie?" Michael called out. The line stopped. Michael put his hand on James's shoulder. "Archie, it's me!"

Archie pulled on his chain, almost yanking the sergeant off his feet. "Reverend?"

"Steady on!" said Carr, but when he saw Father Michael appearing out of the mist like a ghost, he juddered to a halt.

Dazed and unsteady on their feet, the rest of the tattered group followed after the vicar. With each person's appearance, the sergeant's eyes widened even further.

Wee Joe and Helen were shivering and Jean pulled them close into her matted cardigan. Cathy gave the policemen a withering stare. "Well don't just stand there gawping, get these kids some coats!"

Five or six policemen jumped to attention, pulling out little silver foil bags from their day-glow rucksacks as they ran toward the dishevelled group.

"Are you alright, Madam?" one of them asked Ephie. She looked a bit worse for wear.

"Absolutely fine, thank you," answered Ephie.

Archie MacNulty stared at her, and then looked over at the vicar. "You war holding hands wif Mrs. Blake, favar."

Father Michael only smiled.

The officer in charge looked James straight in the eye. "Can you tell me where you've been, boy?"

James pointed at Ephie. He was just a kid. There was no reason he should be the one to come up with a quick answer. Ephie looked, in turn, at Father Michael.

"Um, we were walking, officer," answered Father Michael. "We've been walking and um…"

"Yes, that's right," Ephie took over. "We've been walking, just got a bit lost."

"Lost? You've been missing for five days," blurted Sergeant Carr. Oddly enough, he looked disappointed.

"Looks like MacNulty's off the hook, Sarge," said the young constable, sniffing smugly.

Sergeant Carr's eyes blazed as he turned on the constable. "Shut up, Watt. Just shut up!"

"Yes, well…" said Father Michael. "It's certainly not Archie's fault we got lost, is it?"

"Are you all okay, Mrs. Harrison?" a plainclothes police officer from Stendelburgh asked as he approached Craig's mum and the kids.

"Yes, um, we're fine," answered Jean.

She sounds confused, thought James.

Wee Joe was shivering. "Mum, I'm cold."

A smirking Constable Watt unwrapped another foil blanket and put it round Wee Joe's shoulders.

"Mum!" James called out to his mum, but she looked surprised to see him.

She whispered her reply, "James?"

He knew now that she had no idea where she was and, more importantly, she had no idea where she'd been.

"This is Bruce Moor, Mum. Don't you rememb...?"

"I know it's Bruce Moor," she interrupted. "I just don't know how I got here. Is your father here?" James's heart grew heavy. In the chaos of the last few minutes, he'd actually forgotten all about his dad. How could he have? A dark wave of realisation washed over him as he relived the destruction of Denthan. "I hope so, Mum," he answered.

"Have we been looking for him?" His mum didn't seem to notice his distress.

"Kind of..." James felt his chest tighten. "But I don't think we're any the wiser." The cold air was beginning to make him wheeze. Coughing, he stepped back into a strange indentation that reminded him of Sleven's three-toed footprint. He was sure it was the same spot where he'd seen the squashed stoat.

Craig walked up to his mum and his brother and sister. "Come on, guys. Let's go home," he directed, though his voice sounded hollow.

"Why is this man still in handcuffs, Sergeant Carr?" demanded Father Michael.

Archie gave a little tug, and James saw Constable Watt stifle a snigger.

"Well sir, I mean, Father. We thought he might have had something to do with your disappearance, being the last person to see you all, as it were, and..."

"And, nothing! Release him!" snapped Father Michael.

"But sir, there are procedures to go through before we can..."

"What procedures?" pressed Michael, "We're all here, safe and sound."

"That is still to be ascertained sir, and there is the matter of Mr. Peck, who also disappeared, and was last seen here on Bruce Moor."

"Don't be ridiculous, man. Father Michael turned to Archie, "Where's Patch?"

James had forgotten all about Father Michael's little Jack Russell Terrier.

"She's been wif me," answered Archie. "She's safe and sound, too!"

The plainclothes officer shrugged his broad shoulders and gave the order. "Release him for the time being, Sergeant Carr. But don't go disappearing anywhere, MacNulty. Okay!"

"But..." Sergeant Carr protested.

"Scoutff honour, your officership." Archie held three fingers up to his right ear.

* * *

Back in the village of Drumfintley, just before they went their separate ways, a dejected James turned to Craig. "Have you heard anything from Mendel?"

"Not a peep," said Craig, "We'd better check he's alright." Before doing so, though, Craig pulled back his ripped sleeve. "Look," he whispered, "no tattoos."

James glanced at his right hand. His palm was clean and unmarked as well. *What did it mean?* He fumbled for a second, eventually producing the plastic barrel with Wundadoz Chemicals etched on the little glass window. James held it up to the light and peered inside. "Mendel?"

At first there was no movement and James feared Mendel hadn't survived the fall. Then, out of the blue, came the words James had been longing to hear since the whole adventure had begun. "I think I know where your father might be."

James's heart began to pound; he was sure Mendel was going to tell him that his dad had been killed on Denthan when it exploded.

Mendel's voice was laced with excitement. "Sergeant Carr said that your father was last seen on the moor. When, exactly, was he seen there?"

James, totally gobsmacked, stuttered his reply. "Th...th...the first of June."

"Twenty-six days ago, just as I thought," said Mendel, his deep voice sounding smug.

"What does that mean?" James hissed, his hands starting to shake. His mum was already at the front gate of number 45 Willow Terrace.

"Hurry up, James," she moaned.

"Not just yet, Mum!" pleaded James, peering inside the barrel.

Cathy's eyes narrowed. "What did you say?"

"Nothing, nothing. I'm coming, Mum!" said James.

She turned and headed up the path.

Mendel continued his reasoning. "At the end, Dendralon thought I was Bero. But he sent me from Denthan as I am now: a goldfish, Carassius auratus."

"Hurry up, Mendel!" With a thumbs-up, James tried to placate his mum a second time as she glanced back at him, scowling.

"Well, he must have thought that I'd been affected by a phenomenon called thought transference," continued Mendel.

"What the heck is that?" Craig asked bluntly.

"When you use a gateway, or for that matter, if you are close to a gateway when it is being used, it is a very bad idea to think about any other animal or living thing," Mendel explained, "because there is a slight chance you will take on that form. Dendralon obviously thought I had turned myself into a dog, either by mistake or on purpose. Though, I can't think for the life of me why I would choose an old Golden Retriever."

Craig's eyes widened indignantly.

"Right, we get the point," James said hurriedly. "Why didn't you just think of your own form when he sent you through the gateway in the first place?"

"That doesn't work and..."

"Okay," snapped James, "so how does this affect my dad?"

"Your father was on the moor on the same day, possibly at the very same instant that I came through the gateway. There is a slight chance that he was affected by thought transference."

Cathy gesticulated at James from the front door. James waved back at her and smiled, trying his best to calm her. He lifted the barrel up to his face. Mendel's golden fins flashed past the plastic window. "You mean he might have been thinking about some animal just at the point you appeared, and he's been that animal ever since?"

"Exactly!" Mendel cried. "Now you must tell me what animal he may have been thinking about."

Cathy began marching back down the garden path towards James. She looked particularly angry.

James was losing patience with Mendel, and running out of time. "How are we supposed to know that?"

Wee Joe, sent by his mum to fetch Craig, started tugging on his big brother's sleeve. "Hamster!" the little boy suddenly shouted.

James and Craig both looked down at Wee Joe and were about to tell him to shut up when he explained, "James's daddy got me di hamster for mees birfday. I heerd mummy say it. Mr. Peck got it. And now wees got two!"

James looked down at Wee Joe in utter amazement. At the same time James's mum grabbed his arm and yanked him back from the gate. "In! Now!"

As James half tripped, half staggered his way down his garden path, he heard Craig quiz his little brother. "What do you mean we've got two hamsters? We've only got the one...Mufty."

Wee Joe looked up at his big brother as they walked and gave him a little wink. "Mufty's got a pal, and Mum doesn't even knows it!"

As James was packed up to his room, Mendel spoke to him again. "Well, that solves that mystery. I think we must assume that your father was changed into a hamster up on Bruce Moor. After that, he simply waited there, probably in a state of confusion, until that stoat turned up."

"And..." James prompted as he sat down on his yellow duvet. "And it's a good job Sleven came when he did," said Mendel James shook his head as he lowered Mendel into the tin bath.

"You mean Sleven appeared, just as the stoat pounced at dad, and squished it flat?"

"Oh, dear," said Mendel. "That means you killed the very creature that saved your father's life."

James couldn't speak.

Mendel sighed, sending up a trail of bubbles. "Sometimes fate has a very cruel way of unravelling, James. But in this instance," Mendel paused, "I think your dad has been very fortunate. Very fortunate, indeed."

"But what if my dad was thinking of a stoat? What if Sleven stamped on..."

"What are you whittering on about?" snapped Cathy.

James began to wheeze. He reached into the rucksack for his inhaler.

CHAPTER THIRTY-SEVEN

ONE MARRIAGE AND TWO HELLOS

His mum had been up several times during the night pottering about, mumbling to herself. Even so, James was convinced she'd forgotten everything. It was just as Mendel had said it would be. She hadn't once mentioned their adventure in Denthan.

James, himself, had been totally hyper the entire night. He hadn't slept a wink, thinking about the possibility of his dad being squished by a Swamp Troll. He really hoped that Mendel was right. But even then, to be stuck as a hamster, in Wee Joe's cage, behind bars, and with Mufty.

Finally, it was morning. He raised himself up onto his elbows and threw off his duvet. "Mendel? We need to go round to Craig's house and see if my dad's there. I can't stand it any longer."

There was a splash from the tin bath. "Of course, but…"

"But what? There are no buts," said James.

"Well," said Mendel, "I've thought about it long and hard and there is, perhaps, a chance for one of us." Mendel sounded very serious.

"What do you mean by, 'one of us'? Stop talking in riddles all the time."

Mendel darted behind the plastic castle and looked up at James through a window covered in green slime. "First things first. Check your rucksack. Empty everything out."

James picked the well-worn green bag off his bed and turned it upside down. Out fell the empty orange can of flea spray, his inhaler and, to his surprise, a piece of blue crystal. "But how?"

"Wee Joe popped that in there at the last moment. I asked him to. It split off when the Hedra crystal broke on the floor of the Chamber. Of course, the chain and the main portion of the crystal fell into the vision pool, but this fragment…" Mendel poked his golden head above the water. "This one shard may be enough to do the job."

"Do what job, Mendel?" asked James.

"Well, it might be enough to return one of us back to our original form," said Mendel.

"That's if dad's really at Craig's house, and not already eaten or squashed flat," James reminded him. "Tell me more."

Mendel circled the castle. "There's not enough of the crystal here to help us both, but one of us, your father or myself, might be able to change back into their original form."

"Mendel," said James, "My dad wouldn't be a bloomin' hamster, or whatever he is, if it wasn't for you coming here in the first place!"

The water in the tin bath rippled.

"Yes, yes, I know that. And that's why, if your father is indeed in Wee Joe's hamster cage, I will give up my chance and turn him back instead."

"You will?" James instantly regretted his outburst.

"James! What have I told you about shouting!" His mum's voice blasted out from her bedroom.

"Sorry, Mum. Can I go to Craig's for a bit?"

"I want a lie in. Be back by twelve," she said, much to his surprise.

"Okay! Thanks, Mum." James picked up the plastic barrel and placed it in the tin bath for Mendel. "Quick, while she's still in a good mood. They don't last long…"

* * *

Outside the Harrison house, James could hear Mrs. Harrison through the kitchen window. She was frying up some breakfast. "Look, I phoned an advert into the paper. 'Golden Retriever missing, distinctive brown ear. We will be pleased to pay a £25 reward for information leading to a reunion. Please phone Jean on 01389…da, da, da.' How does that sound?"

James heard Craig's reply and felt another pang of sadness. "Look, Mum, he's gone for good. Trust me, he's not coming back."

"I don't like the da, da, da bit," Helen interjected.

Ignoring her daughter Jean continued, "Don't be so negative, Craig. He'll turn up. You'll see. Bero is a boy dog. They go off sometimes. They can't help it."

James decided to put Craig out of his misery. He rang the doorbell.

Craig answered the door and shook his head. "She just keeps going on and on about Bero. It's doing my nut in."

James cut to the chase. "Have you checked the hamster cage?"

Craig sighed. "You know, my great theory about your dad escaping to a better life in France could be a load of tosh after all."

"Just tell me, ye numpty!" hissed James.

Craig nodded. "Wee Joe's right. Mufty's got company."

James pushed his way inside.

Craig followed him up the stairs, talking all the way, "Every time I open the cage, he scampers away from me. But get this, when he does eventually poke his nose out of the shredded paper he holds his right paw up to his ear just like a Scout salute. I can almost hear the Scout pack shouting, 'Dib, dib, dib.'"

James skidded to a halt outside Craig's room. "Hardee-har. Look, you better not be kidding me."

Craig forced a smile. "He's probably just cleaning his ears."

"How come your Mum didn't notice and extra hamster?" asked James.

"Mum only lets that lot have pets on the condition that she doesn't have to clean out their cages," said Craig.

"Speaking of which, where is the cage?" pressed James.

Craig pointed one of the bedroom doors. "In their room, of course."

James eased the door open and stared across at the yellow hamster cage, a sense of trepidation building in his chest.

Craig edged past him and knelt down. "Phew! They stink," he muttered, flicking the water dispenser until the bubbles disappeared.

"No, they don't. It's you who stinks!" Helen and Wee Joe called out, practically in unison.

"How did it get here?" asked James.

Wee Joe gave James a particularly derisive stare and tapped his nose with his forefinger.

"That means, 'he knows, but is never going to tell,'" explained Craig.

"Mendel, what now?" asked James. He began to wheeze as he pulled the barrel out of his green rucksack.

His chest tightened as he moved even closer to the yellow, plastic cage. It contained a blue wheel and a small white house with a red roof. The hamster house was stuffed with pink, shredded paper. James coughed nervously as he pinged open the cage door.

"Mendel, please. Help me." James was frightened at the prospect of finding his dad and also anxious that he might be too late. Mendel's voice filled his head. "Put the crystal down beside the cage and make sure you take the hamster out."

"Wee Joe says that It doesn't like to be picked up," said Craig, tuning into Mendel's voice.

Mendel gave a sigh of exasperation. "James, could you please explain to Craig that it might prove a little painful if your father were to try to stand up in a one-foot high metal cage."

"Ahh…" James scratched a spot on his neck and tried not to imagine his father being sliced and grated.

Craig winced, then took Wee Joe's hand and sat him down beside the hamster cage. "James wants to see the new hamster." He patted Wee Joe on the head, only to receive a brisk kick. "Wee Joe's the only one who can prise the new hamster from the cage, aren't you, you little…" Craig stopped himself in time.

A little piece of white, fluffy hamster bottom appeared at the door of the white, plastic house.

"There he is!" said Craig.

"It's mees secret and it's only me that can holds it! Hmuhh!" Wee Joe sassed smugly, then opened the little door a few inches before plunging his hand into the doorway of the plastic house.

"It's not a lucky dip, Joe. Be gentle," cautioned James, grimacing as he watched Wee Joe pluck the big hamster out from the shredded paper. The creature's little black eyes were nearly popping out of his head.

Helen intervened. "Give him here! You always try to love him too much."

"But I do wove him," said Wee Joe, reluctantly passing the struggling ball of fur to his big sister.

The sunlight filtered in through the net curtain and James immediately recognised something familiar about the hamster's face. He took a deep breath and asked, "Dad, is that you?"

James's words seemed to fall on deaf, fluffy ears.

Seemingly annoyed at the attention shown to the other hamster, Mufty took to her wheel and soon built up to maximum speed. The racket was like a machine gun.

Wee Joe put a finger to his lips. "Wufty, shhh!" "M... M... Mufty! Not Wufty," said Helen.

"M... M... Shut up!" replied Wee Joe sinking his teeth into his sister's outstretched hand.

The hamster dropped onto the floor.

"You animal!" Helen screeched and stamped her foot in anger, nearly stepping on the hamster.

"Watch what you're doing!" yelled James.

Luckily, Mendel stayed calm. "Put the crystal on the carpet beside your father, James."

"Right, okay." James was shaking. He placed the broken piece of crystal beside his 'dad' and stood back.

"Look out the window. Can you see Ben Larvach?" asked Mendel. "No. Wrong window. But you can see it from Mum's window at the front of the house," explained Craig, rubbing his sister's mauled hand.

"Fine," said Mendel. "Point the sharp end of the crystal towards the spot on your wall where you think it is. Imagine you can see Ben Larvach out of your mother's window from here."

"That's easy!" said Helen twisting the crystal round in the direction of their built-in cupboard.

The hamster twitched his little pink nose and looked up at the children. He cleaned his whiskers with tiny a pair of white paws and sniffed across at the cage.

"It's wooking for Mufty." Wee Joe knelt down and tried to pry Mufty from her wheel.

"Not just now, Joe!" hissed Helen.

Craig caught Wee Joe's arm. "Mufty might get hurt. It's safer for her in the cage, just for the moment."

James felt the knock, knock, knocking sensation build inside his head and his lips quivered in unison with Mendel's. The bubbly, fishy sounding words filled the whole room.

"Wwwwretwwwurnwwwwwtoselfwwww!"

Like most little kids, Helen tried to copy the strange words by pinging her lips and speaking at the same time.

The crystal began to glow blue before turning a brilliant white, as bright as any sun. Then it began to make a powerful humming sound.

They all covered their eyes and turned away from the light. Only James still dared to look down at the hamster. The animal stopped cleaning himself and began to shake uncontrollably.

"Stop it! You're hurting him!" shouted James, but it was too late. There was another dazzling flash of light.

"Arghhh!" A loud scream filled the room, but James couldn't see a thing. Blinded, he rubbed his eyes in vain, seeing only white and blue flashes across his field of vision.

"James?" He couldn't see, but James knew the voice at once.

"Dad!" Blindly, James stretched out his arms and gripped onto the soft, familiar texture of his dad's fleecy jacket. "Dad, is it really you?"

"Of course it's me. Why am I covered in sawdust and...?" He put his index finger between his teeth. Confused, his dad poked a finger round in his mouth before producing several sunflower seeds and a half eaten peanut from the inside of his cheek.

"What the..."

Now there was another noise in the room.

Scratch! Scratch!

"Ooww!"

The children jumped onto the bed while a bemused and dishevelled David Peck stared across at the bedroom cupboard. "What have you got in that cupboard, James?"

"Nothing!" James blurted. He was still reeling from the bright lights and the shock of seeing his dad, but his eyes were adjusting now. He saw that his dad didn't look particularly happy.

"Well, there's something in there!" his dad shouted. "I hope you're not being cruel to something."

Mendel spoke up. "Could one of you open the cupboard door?" Craig jumped off the bed and pulled on the brass handle of the cupboard.

"Oohh! It's hot!" he cried, blowing on his fingers. He grabbed one of Helen's dolls. Holding it by the legs, he pushed the handle down with the doll's head.

"Tsssssss!" The face of the plastic doll began to melt and a black, acrid smoke spiralled toward the ceiling. The handle gave and the door sprung open...

"Woof!"

James couldn't believe it. There, sitting on the chipboard floor of the kids' toy cupboard, was a little Golden Retriever puppy, wagging his tail and panting just the way Bero used to do.

James slid off the bed. "He's got the same brown ear!"

His dad's nose twitched as he waved the smoke away from his eyes. "Craig, it's not like you to be cruel to animals. Why did you lock the pup in the cupboard?"

Not listening, Craig crouched down. "Come on, boy. Come on!"

James pulled on his dad's sleeve and gave him a 'don't say another word' stare. Somehow, he knew that the dog in the cupboard was Bero. He was also sure he'd heard Eethan's wispy laugh while the crystal fragment was doing its magic. The little, blue man seemed to possess supernatural abilities that even Mendel couldn't match, or completely understand.

"Bero!" As soon as Craig said the name, the pup bounded out of the cupboard and leapt up into his arms.

Mendel's voice cut into James's thoughts. "Eethan never fails to surprise me."

Helen began to pat the puppy too. "It's a baby Bero!"

Wee Joe beamed up at James's dad. "When dee big Bewo comes back wees will have two doggies!"

"That was a good trick, Mr. Peck!" Helen ran out her bedroom door and shouted down for her mother. "Mum! Mr. Peck's doing a magic show!"

James snapped out of his state of shock and wrapped his arms round his dad. "I love you, Dad."

"I love you too, Son, but…"

Jean Harrison opened the bedroom door. "Craig, Mrs. Peck's on the…" She stood stalk still, fixed to the spot. "…phone," she finished. "David?"

"It's my dad!" James hugged his dad once more.

Looking shocked, Craig's mum handed his dad the mobile phone. "It's Cathy," she whispered.

"Hello. Cathy?" he said.

There was no reply.

James knew this was going to be tricky for his dad to explain. He snatched the receiver from his dad and listened. "Mum?"

"Eh, I think I can see her running down the street," said Craig. "Look."

This is definitely going to be tricky, thought James.

"I'm a bit confused, I have to admit," said David.

"Things are a bit like that just now," said Jean, timidly. "Still, it's nice to see you again, David. I think." Jean paused. "I'd better answer the door."

James heard the Harrison's doorbell dinging. It wasn't a single ring of the bell, it was a continuous racket that signalled trouble.

James was too frightened to move. As soon as his mum appeared at the top of the stairs his worst fears were confirmed.

Her face was ashen grey.

Jean gave his dad a small pat on the back, and whispered, "Cathy's missed you..." He noticed her words trail off, however, as his mum's expression hardened.

James watched as his mum walked up to his dad. Uncharacteristically, a tear traced its way down her cheek and, for a moment, James thought she was going to hug him. But instead, she sighed and slapped him full force across the face.

No one moved or made a sound. In that one moment, the tension seemed to stifle them. It was all too much. The mixture of emotions James was feeling pressed down on him like a trillion tons of rock. He just wanted to run away.

"Um, James," said Craig, breaking the silence and the tension. "Don't forget your rucksack." Glad of the excuse to step back from his parents, James grabbed the bag and popped the barrel inside. To his relief, without saying a word, his mum and dad made their way to the bedroom door. Wee Joe tried to stifle a giggle.

Ah, yes. This was the way he remembered them: at odds, diminished by each other, but a couple again, nonetheless.

Cathy Peck led the way. She stared blankly at some spot in front of her as she walked toward the steps. David, bewildered, his face still bright red, followed.

James smiled and shook his head before waving the Harrisons goodbye. "I think we're off home," he said, "good luck with the new pup, Craig."

"What new pup?" asked Jean, more confused than ever.

Craig lifted the little retriever pup up to his mum. James heard him shout down after them. "Thanks, Mendel!" James twisted round and smiled up at his best friend.

"Thanks to you too, ye numpty," added Craig.

Jean Harrison leaned over to pat the young pup. "It looks like Bero, doesn't it?"

As he stepped onto the bottom landing James saw the young Bero look-a-like licking and nipping her nose in a frenzy of excitement.

Following his parents back to his house James heard Mendel's voice in his head. "Well, all's well that ends well."

"Mendel?" said James.

"Yes, James."

"Shut up."

* * *

Two months later, James sat down to write in his diary:

Michael and Ephie were married today in St. Donan's Church. The whole of Drumfintley was there to see the new, slimmer, Ephie Blake, walk down the aisle with Father Michael. Ephie's weird brother, Kwedgin, gave her away and Archie MacNulty and Patch were Best Man and Best Dog, respectively. I was there with Mum, who's just allowed Dad to move back into our house again. Dad says that he must have fallen and bumped his head, or something, as he can't re-member a thing about his missing time. Mum says 'Yeah, right!' and other stuff that makes me think she doesn't really believe him. My best friend Craig was there too, along with his mum, his sister, Wee Joe and their dad, who, according to Craig, has finally returned from a stint in a submarine under the North Pole. Craig seems to be much happier now that he's got his dad back too.

When he stands on his back legs, Bero is nearly up to my belly button and he continues to get madder by the minute. As I write this, Mendel is splashing about in his tin bath, but I can tell that he is getting more and more restless every day. He's promised to rid me of my asthma when he regains his full powers again but, in the meantime, he helps me to relax and breathe much better than I ever did before. He still drives me and Craig crazy with all his Latin names and stuff when we take him on walks and, only yesterday, he told us that Eethan had managed to get the city of Gwendral to another world but, apparently, not the one he'd planned.

Craig and I often wonder how the Mertol is settling in, and if Jal has re-covered from his wounds. Back here in Drumfintley, the local paper reports that the police have now closed the case on our 'missing time', but the townsfolk will never stop chattering about it. Gauser, the local drunk, says it was a mass hoax, while Mrs. Galdinie tells her customers at the ice-cream shop that we were most likely abducted by aliens. I've got to admit that Mrs. Galdinie's probably closer to the mark.

There's not a day goes by that I don't think or dream about our adventure in Denthan, but the main thing for me is that I have my family back again, warts and all.

James put his pen down and closed the diary. The moon shone brighter than usual above Drumfintley that night and everything was still and quiet. Alone in his little room, he looked out his window at the stars that filled the summer-night sky and wondered if one of the far off specks of light might be Gwendral's new sun. Perhaps Cimerato and Garlon were looking up at their stars too. James stretched and let his diary slip off his bed, too tired to care as it bumped onto the wooden floor. The water rippled in the old, tin bath as his mum's dulcet tones filled the night.

"Who's Mufty?"

James wondered how his mum could possibly be jealous of a female Chinese Orange hamster, but then, as long as his dad continued to mumble Mufty's name in his sleep, and as long as he failed to come up with a plausible explanation, his mum probably had every right to throw a wobbly now and again.

Poor Dad, he thought, smiling to himself as he snuggled into his duvet.

Poor Dad…

ABOUT THE AUTHOR

BORN IN Helensburgh, Scotland, Sam Wilding grew up beside Loch Lomond on the very edge of the Scottish Highlands. He gained an honours degree in Zoology at Glasgow University and always maintained a strong interest in nature and the outdoors. He also became involved in song writing and through the years played rock guitar in the UK, Holland and America. He worked in animal parks for a few years before orientating towards Agriculture, in particular, the sales and marketing sector. He soon moved on from song writing to poetry, short stories and eventually on to his first novel, "The Magic Scales" which he wrote in the early hours of the morning for his oldest son, Ryan. Sam still lives and works in the Scottish Highlands with his wife and four kids, and now has a further two books in the Denthan Series.

Other books in the Denthan Series

Book 2 : The Second Gateway
Book 3 : Return to Denthan

Visit Sam on the web at: www.samwilding.com